Last Reunion

To Chuck
The Best Always

E C Cha

Last Reunion

E.C. Craver

Writer's Showcase
San Jose New York Lincoln Shanghai

Last Reunion

Writer's Showcase
an imprint of iUniverse.com, Inc.

For information address:
iUniverse.com, Inc.
5220 S 16th, Ste. 200
Lincoln, NE 68512
www.iuniverse.com

ISBN: 0-595-19081-2

Printed in the United States of America

ACKNOWLEDGMENTS

My gratitude is never ending to, Frank Lambrith, my editor and mentor. This project might never have happened without his help. And I thank Bill Cross for his critique input and moral support. Also a special thanks to my wife Billie for her understanding when I would let some of my home duties slip to work on the book. And to my faithful Schnauzer dog Ebbie, who steadfastly laid by my side every minute while I typed on the book day or night, a special hug.

CHAPTER I

Slowing the car to a near stop, Amy turned off Main Street into the dark parking area before the abandoned high school. The wind whipped swirls of leaves through the beams of the headlights as she brought the car to a halt. She sat, unmoving for a moment, her gaze scanning the facade of the old building. Lights shone through several windows of the two-story red brick structure's lower floor, but above, on the second floor where there should have been lights, the windows were dark rectangles of nothingness.

Strange. Some of the gang should already be in the home-ec room on the second floor.

Switching off the engine, Amy glanced toward the double doors of the entryway. The light streaming through the glass on the top half of the heavy wooden doors spread a fan of illumination across the wind-swept parking lot and highlighted the leaves, clumps of needles, and bits of paper bounding across its dark surface. Despite the building menace of the approaching storm, Amy smiled. She was seeing the school in the sunshine of yesterday, alive with people, not the night-darkened hulk before her. Her smile broadened, thinking about the reunion, only the second in the fourteen years since she graduated.

Her smile began to fade. Now the town, the school, everything seemed smaller, more insignificant than it had at the last reunion just six years ago. Maybe this was one of the girlhood memories she should forego. Perhaps this should be her last reunion.

Just as the Cadillac's timer switched off its headlights, a clap of thunder, as loud as it was unexpected, made her flinch. Its suddenness brought her back to reality, to an unlit parking lot before a building without enough lights. Her hand reached for the key, ready to leave, to get back on the highway away from this place, but she pulled it away.

Ridiculous! Being spooked by a spring storm. Many a night back in kindergarten days and even after, she had fled her room to seek her mother's arms, cowering against the fury of the spring storms so common in north central Washington. *Just get inside. That's all I need to do. Once I see the gang, their faces lit with big smiles, I'll be okay.*

Gripping the handle of the door, she forced it open and slid out. A sudden furious gust ripped it from her grasp. Fighting the door with all her strength, she got it closed. *Thank God Seattle storms aren't this violent.*

Clutching the collar of her coat about her neck, Amy dashed across the graveled lot into the shelter of the archway that framed the entry. As she paused there, restoring some order to her short dark hair, she glanced back at the Caddy. *My God, my car is the only one in the whole damn lot! I was so worried about arriving on time and getting inside away for the storm I hadn't noticed.*

In that instant the school became a very lonely, too quiet place.

Her mind raced. *Caught in heavy traffic leaving Seattle, I should have been the last to arrive. Sam's diner.*

The small cafe was only a block and a half down Main Street. She could see the lights form the school. *Maybe they have left their cars there and walked down. Perhaps the local kids vandalized cars left in the dark old lot.*

Peering down the street toward the diner, she saw several vehicles parked out front of Sam's in the glow from the neon sign.

She nodded. *That has to be the explanation. Probably met there to have coffee before walking over to the school.* A frown creased her brow. *Why hadn't someone written it in my invitation if they had that planned?*

Turning, somewhat unhappy at their thoughtlessness, Amy tugged open one of the heavy front doors and stepped inside, propelled by a sudden cold blast of air against her back. The door began to close slowly, restrained by its rusty hydrolytic arm, but a second strong gust struck, overwhelming its resistance, and the door slammed with a thud.

Amy stood in the short entry hall which intersected the main hallway that ran the entire width of the school; a stairway to the second floor at either end. The corners where the halls intersected hid the stairs from view. Immediately ahead of her, built into the wall of the main hallway was the school's trophy case, flanked on each side by big double doors that opened into the gymnasium.

Two old-fashioned frosted globe fixtures with their weak light bulbs made the faded yellowish paint on the walls and the age-darkened wood trim seem even more melancholy. Cocking her head, Amy listened for the distant voices that would locate her classmates. As quiet as it was here inside, she should be able to hear them, even on the second floor. But it was void of sounds from human activity. What she heard instead was the ever louder, shrieks of the rising wind.

Darn it! Where are they?

Her nose wrinkled. *That smell! What is it?*

Her memories were of pine oil, disinfectant, furniture polish, and chalk dust. She could never recall her school days, full of laughter and sunshine, without surrounding them with those wonderful aromas. Now the building reeked of stale air and dank, unpleasant odors that suggested long disuse and decay, smells so unpleasant that she thought again of returning to her car.

Without warning, the hall filled with a light so bright it drained the color from the walls. Her gasp was lost in the ear-splitting crash of the gigantic thunder bolt. Amy whirled to stare out the door.

My God, that was close! She bit her bottom lip. Maybe right out front or somewhere on Main Street. *Could it have hit Sam's?* Cautiously she returned to the door to peer out. Nothing. Or at least she could see no signs of fire. *Maybe it struck somewhere behind the building.*

Mesmerized, she continued to stare through the thick glass at the top half of the heavy oak door. In the distance the jagged streaks of lightning were coming every few seconds, causing an almost constant rumble of thunder.

The parking area sprang into focus as a long bolt seemed to reach with its many fingers to play across the sky. In its sudden clarity she saw every detail of the Cadillac. She gasp. *My God! Is that someone crouched behind the car?*

Staring at it so long and hard her eyes began to burn. She blinked, then rubbed them. With the hall light behind her, now she could see nothing more than a dark bulk where the Caddy was parked. *Was it just my imagination? Oh, Lord! I'm scaring myself half to death. Unless I get upstairs and join the others, I just might start screaming.*

Amy licked her lips and took a quivering deep breath, trying to relax. The storm and the old building really had her spooked. At that moment the first raindrops pelted against the door. Soon, she could see nothing but rivulets of rain running down the glass.

Shaking her head, she took another deep breath and turned away. *Just my imagination. I've got to put it out of my mind.*

Amy started in the direction of the trophy case, but as she did, another furious gust slammed into the doors, and she jumped at the sound. "Darn wind!" That was one reason she'd left central Washington.

Amy's gaze settled on the trophy case at the end of the short entrance hall. All of Pine Ridge High's trophies were still in place, left behind when the small school was consolidated with another. The case was dark. The metal on all the awards was tarnished, hidden behind the lacy veils of countless generations of spiders who had found homes within the case. She felt suddenly uneasy and swallowed hard over the constriction in her throat. *This is nothing like the last reunion. Then the case was lighted and clean, trophies shined.*

With an abrupt change in her mood, Amy spoke aloud without intention. "The old building don't look ready for the reunion," her brow knitted. "Could I have gotten the date mixed up?"

She fumbled in her purse, found the invitation and extracted it, reading in the dim light.

Welcome, graduating class of 1980. Let's catch up with what's been happening to out group. Be here early for hors d'oeuvres, punch, and good conversation. We'll meet in the home-ec room.

Checking the date, she nodded. *Tonight in the home-ec room at eight o'clock.* Glancing toward the main hall that led to the stairs, she sighed, relieved. *That's where the gang has to be, upstairs. The big dance isn't until later and they just haven't got around to the trophy case yet. They're all in the home-ec room with the door closed. With that and the storm going on, there's no way I can hear them.*

Shoving the sheet of paper back into her purse, her gaze slid to the linoleum at the base of the trophy case, acutely aware of the age faded pattern under countless layers of yellowing wax. Years ago, it had been clear, sparkling clean, ready for the crowds that came through the building, heading for the gymnasium during basketball season.

The old school had closed after their class graduated. The town of Pine Ridge had started drying up in the 60's. Without jobs, people moved away in droves. Now Sam's Diner was one of a mere handful of businesses left in town, supported mainly by hunters and fishermen, thanks to the many lakes around Pine Ridge. Only the little high-steepled church remained neat and unchanged by the town's hard times.

As Amy walked to the trophy case, the slap of her flat-heeled shoes echoed through the vacant corridors. A slight frown wrinkled her forehead. *With the storm, this reunion feels all wrong. The last one was*

*fun. People everywhere, clowning around, swapping stories. Nothing
like this.*

It was so odd to hear the echo of her footsteps in a place where they
had been drown out by laughter, shouts and the opening and closing of
locker doors.

Staring into the trophy case unleashed a store of memories. Amy
sought and found the Girls' State Basketball Championship Trophy, the
biggest one in the case. A tall girl, standing six feet, one inch, Amy had
been the school's basketball star. She took a deep breath, and uncon-
sciously stood a little straighter. A grin touched her lips as she found her
own name among the six inscribed on the trophy: Amy Housley,
Captain.

Squinting, she eyed the big trophy on the lower shelf, the boys' trophy for winning second place that year. Amy's gaze paused at the top-
most of the seven names inscribed on it; Dain Barlow, Captain. *God, I
had a crush on that guy!*

The broad shoulders, Grecian features, and curly blond hair had
attracted her, all right, but most important, he was the only boy in
school taller than she.

But Amy never had a chance. Dain had eyes for no one but Sheila
Greene. Sheila had a knockout figure even when she was in the eighth
grade. Amy cringed, remembering the trauma of her freshman year,
being a head taller than any of the other girls, and most of the boys,
with a chest as flat as an ironing board. The agonies she had put herself
through to develop a bosom were unbelievable.

One summer she even tried lying on her back, arms out to the side,
lifting small dumbbells. But nothing worked. She remained as shapeless
as a telephone pole. But when it came to playing basketball, the rest of
the girls, breasts and all, were just a supporting cast for Amy.

Musing, Amy bit the inside of her lower lip. So she ended up with all
the trophies and Sheila with all the boys, especially Dain Barlow. But
maybe between the two of them, they did better than the other girls in

the class. On second thought, maybe she had done better than Sheila. She had kept her trophies, but Sheila had lost Dain.

He and Sheila had abruptly broken up and nobody understood why—that is, until Candy told her story. Dain denied the tale, but Sheila ignored both him and the gossip.

Amy hadn't seen Dain since graduation, and realized how anxious she was to see him again. He'd missed the first reunion. Dain had gone to Eastern Washington University and then to Los Angeles where he worked as a homicide detective in the LAPD, Los Angeles Police Department. Still unmarried she'd heard.

He was supposed to be coming tonight. She grimaced. *Terrible! What an awful thing to have happen to his parents.*

Dain was in town for their funeral. His mom and dad had hit some black ice, skidded off the road at Rainbow Lake, and gone down an embankment into the water.

Another tremendous thunder clap shook the windows, joltidng her out of her reverie. At the same instant, from the corner of her eye, she saw movement outside the front doors and whirled. For a moment she saw nothing but the black rectangle of night through the glass, but then the wind came again, and a long drooping branch of an ornamental evergreen shrub beside the archway swept past the window a second time with its wet fingers of green. Amy let out her breath.

Ten seconds passed before she realized she was not breathing. The spell broken, she struggled to get enough air, more panting than breathing. Raising her arm, she pushed up the sleeve to look at her watch. Her eyes tearing—why, she didn't know—she tried to focus on the face of her watch. Finally, the tiny gold hands came out of the mist and she saw it was eight-oh-five.

Why am I standing here, scaring myself to death when the party must have already started upstairs? She had to get to the second floor, open the door, hear the once familiar voices and feel the warm glow of the other

ten graduates of Pine Ridge High as they turned with big grins to greet
her.

Hurrying down the hall, her flats slapped against the hard flooring,
too loud in a dead corridor that had once known laughing voices and
boisterous yells. Nearing the end of the hall where the wide stairway
climbed to the second floor, she caught herself in mid-stride. The fixture suspended over the landing where the stairs reversed themselves to
complete their ascent to the second floor was unlit. *Oh, no! The only
light in the whole damn place with its bulb burnt out!*

Strange how dark the landing was. The corridor lights lit the bottom
flight clearly. It was as if the lights in the upstairs hall were out, too. She
nibbled her bottom lip, remembering the top floor had been unlit and
glanced back over her shoulder. *Maybe I should just wait down here.
Surely someone else will be coming along soon.*

Taking a deep breath, she looked back up the stairs. *Don't be such a
coward. There's nothing wrong. It's not far from the stairs to the home-ec
room. Maybe they've had to rob the lights here and there to have what
lights they have until they get some replaced. Probably have to go to
Crescent Valley to get them.*

Standing there, she became conscious of the open classroom doors
on both sides of her. Amy's skin crawled. They seemed to soak up the
dim light from the corridor, leaving their interiors black, silent, and
hostile. Reminding her of the countless late-night horror movies she
had seen.

Her straining ears caught no sounds of merriment from above. What
she did hear was the wailing of the wind around the building, like soul-
less banshees riding the stormy night. The rain lashing against the loos-
ened panes of the old windows sent a sound like a spectral drumbeat,
rising and falling, rising and falling, loud enough to mask any who
might walk the halls of the old structure.

Amy was mounting the steps, her foot on the fourth tread, when
behind her the front door opened, then closed. With an enormous sense

of relief, she turned, expecting to see one of the gang round into view from the entry hall, looking like a drowned rat. Amy stood and waited, but no one came into view. No classmate, no footsteps, no nothing. Her eager look became one of disappointment. *Just the wind.*

She turned back to mount the stairs. Her next thought froze her in her tracks. *The wind! How coiuld it jerk the door open and then slam it like that?*

She whirled to look back down the hall, her heart pounding. Her breathing labored. For a few minutes she stood still. Taking a deep breath she tried rationalizing. *Or was it the door? Maybe the wind had slammed something against the front doors. A box. A slab of plywood. With this wind anything could have hit the door. That has to be the answer. The door didn't really open.* Breathing heavily, she turned back to the dimly lit stairwell. *Upstairs. I have to get upstairs.*

Nervously licking her lips, Amy climbed the wooden staircase. *God, I have to stop making things worse than they are!*

She was climbing a stairway she had climbed hundreds of times before, her feet sensing the grooves worn in the wooden steps by the thousands of feet that had done the same thing since the school was built in nineteen-twenty-six. *Not one sinister thing has happened in the history of the school, right?*

Just as Amy reached the landing, another enormous flare of lightning showed in the upstairs hall, bleaching the landing with its unearthly light. Amy's sight returned as she made the turn and started climbing the upper flight. A few steps up she stopped. *Oh, Christ! This upstairs corridor is really black. No, not black. The upstairs is dark, but a faint red glow was somewhere in the dimness.*

The longer she stood there, the clearer she could see. A faint red light was burning somewhere in the hall above. The last of Amy's courage deserted her. She turned, ready to dash back down the stairs. Then she heard the sounds from below. Not noise that had anything to do with the storm, not the sound that rats scampering around in a deserted building make, but a faint shuffling sound, like someone trying to walk very quietly.

Without thought, she took a step upward, and the tread creaked loudly. Her heart seemed to skip a beat, then for a moment the memory of it drove the fear from her mind. The step had always made that sound as long back as she could remember.

From below, the sound she had heard before, the odd scuffing, came again, quieter now, a soft sliver of sound that seemed to pierce her very being. Amy, all thoughts of being quiet forgotten, blundered on up the wide stairway into the darkness faintly stained by a blood-red tint, her heart pounding.

As the long length of the second floor corridor came into view, she saw the sources of the red glow, one to the side of the stairway where she stood and the other all the way down at the far end of the long hall where windows opened onto the fire escape. The two exit signs were illuminated. She turned toward the side walls, barely visible in the dim light, searching for a light switch, but there was none. Unlike the lower floor, the classroom doors here were all closed. She glanced down the hall, seeking a strip of light beneath one of the doors. Nothing relieved the darkness.

Another enormous burst of lightning illuminated the dim hall for a split second, and then everything was dark. For a moment she thought she had been struck blind. Then Amy realized what had happened. The lightning had knocked out the power.

Remembering her childhood, with the lights out, it had happened all the time in this little town. *My God! Even if they came back on it would probably happen again. Why did I come up here?* Her heart ran wild. She had to get out of there! But the scuffing downstairs—what in hell had that been?

Then the lights came back on.

Overwhelming relief changed to anger. *The gang has to be here. This is the right night and the right time. They were being quiet in the home-ec* room, teasing her. That's what it was. At the last reunion, a few of the bunch who had never left town had kidded me about being a city girl forgetting how it was to live in God's country. The sick locals with their brand of humor. The storm had given them the idea. That and my being late. They had decided to play, Scare the Hell Out of Amy.

She was surprised that Sheila would go along with it, but she was just one against the pack. Well, if they wanted to play that way, fine. I'll just storm into Mrs. Brown's room, tell them all to go to hell, climb in my car, and head back to Seattle. The reunion be damned!

Amy started toward the home-ec room, her fists clenched, full of fire. Then a monstrous crash of thunder jarred the structure, sending the dozens of windows into a macabre jiggling dance that echoed throughout the building. Nothing happened for several seconds, and then the light from the stairwell vanished into a black void. The dim red glow of the two exit lights leapt out of the darkness as a taunting reminder that there was still power to the school.

She gasp. *Oh, dear God, someone has turned off the downstairs lights.*

The footfalls started again somewhere in the darkness below with no attempt to mask them. Then the sound changed. *Someone was climbing the stairs.*

Amy shouted, her voice taut. "Stop it! You're scaring me." Only the wind screaming past the old school answered her.

Seconds later the wild gust exhausted itself, and the world was quiet for a few seconds.

In the dim hall with its sullen red glow, she heard it. Music. She exhaled audibly. *They must have realized how badly they have frightened me. Maybe now their little game was over.*

Feeling some relief, she mustered the courage to call out again, "Okay, you can stop now. Joke's over."

With her heart thumping, she stood, looking back toward the dark stairwell, waiting nervously for the lights to come on and the few locals to come up the stairs, pleased with their little joke. The seconds stretched. Nothing but the music. *Dammit! Why don't they show themselves? Come out and laugh at me? Anything. Just come out, please.*

The fear returned. Amy hurriedly turned and started down the hall toward the music. Behind her, the loose tread creaked. Whoever was coming up the stairs was near the top. And they were heavy footed, like the heavy logger's boots the locals wore.

"Stop it!" she cried, fleeing down the hall toward the music, toward her classmates. She almost overran Room 206 with its metal numerals affixed to the solid wood door. The music was distinct now—country music, the kind with which she had grown up.

Lunging for the door knob, she broke a fingernail.

Grasping the knob, she flung the door open, plunged inside and stopped. Her hand flew to her mouth to stifle the scream.

The home-ec room was lighted by two candles, one to each side of the small cassette player atop the teachers desk. The wavering light of the candles played over bare walls and empty seats.

Amy was alone in the room!

A gust of wind swept in from the hall of the drafty old building, and the two small candles struggled a brief moment before yielding their light to the darkness. The vanishing light seemed to have taken the warmth with it and she shivered in the sudden chill. As Amy's night vision returned, she saw that the rooms tattered blinds, even though drawn, let in enough light from the flaring storm-torn sky to see the student desks in disarray, like strange creatures hunkered down to rest.

Amy blundered about, whimpering in a mindless litany to terror. No old friends were there. No class reunion was scheduled for tonight. She was alone. No, not alone. Those footfalls continued in the hallway, as slow and measured as if they were part of an approaching processional of doom that would end in Room 206.

Amy dropped down to her knees among the desks, one hand still clamped over her mouth, fingernails digging into her cheeks, trying to muffle the whimpering.

The cassette player continued to play, but to her the country music had become the ghastly songs of a madman. Tears flooded her eyes as she came upright again, bumping hard into a desk. The screeching of its runners against the floor was as loud to her as a power saw. But not so loud that she failed to hear that last footfall and see the shadowy, hulking figure standing in the doorway.

Clasping her hands together against her chest, she pled, "Oh, please, don't hurt me. I beg you, don't hurt me," but she said nothing. Her throat was so constricted she could make no sound beyond that whimper.

When the strange voice came, it was no more than a whisper, "Amy, welcome to your last reunion."

Her Tormentor was almost on her when another burst of lightning brightened the room enough to see the hulking figure. A black sweater covered his torso and a black ski mask hid his features. She had to get past him and out of there! With a desperate effort Amy bolted forward.

CHAPTER 2

Dain Barlow came up on one elbow with the telephone's fifth ring. It hadn't been daylight long. *Who the hell would be calling me this early?*

Just three days had passed since his parents' funeral, but already he had settled into a routine. Each morning he had arisen just before noon and walked down to Sam's Diner. *It couldn't be Mom and Dad's lawyer. The appointment with him was for two o'clock, just like yesterday.*

Grabbing the phone from the bedside table, he mumbled, "Yeah?"

"Dain? Is that you?" A female voice asked.

"That's what they tell me. Who's this?"

A giggle, then, "Someone you haven't seen since high school. Sheila Ste…ah, Greene, Sheila Greene. I just got here late last night. I'm calling from the Starlight Motel in Crescent Valley. Heard about your mom and dad after I arrived. God, I wish I'd known. I would have come for the funeral. I thought the world of them."

"Sorry, Sheila. It was so sudden I wasn't thinking clearly. Forgive me."

"Don't be silly," she said. After a pause she continued. "You want to hear something funny? Can you believe it? I still had your phone number in my address book."

Dain blushed with pleasure. *Jesus, I'm acting like a school kid.* "It's really great to hear your voice, Sheila. It's been forever. What's say we get together and bring each other up to date. Have you had breakfast? I could drive down to Crescent Valley and pick you up."

When she didn't say anything, he added, "Or maybe just a cup of coffee…or just take a ride?"

"How about meeting at Sam's? I haven't been in that place for years. Is it still there?"

Dain threw the covers back, wide awake now, and sat up on the edge of the bed. "Yeah, it's still there. It's a date. How long will it take you to get up here?"

"Great! I can be there in half an hour." Her voice changed. "Oh, by the way, are you married? I mean…if you are, I want your wife to come along so I can meet her."

"Nope, that's something I never got around to. How about you?"

For a moment there was silence, then she said, "I was, but my husband was killed last year, a crop dusting plane crash." He could hear her take a deep breath. "No children, I just have me."

"God, Sheila, sounds like we've both had a run of bad luck. Hey, we'll talk when I see you. Half an hour."

Grinning, he hung up. *Sheila! After all these years.* He laid back and took a deep breath of satisfaction, and was amazed at how excited he was at the thought of seeing her. He wondered whether the years had been kind to her. *What the hell. It hasn't been all that long ago.*

Jumping out of bed, suddenly invigorated, he headed for the bathroom. The only thing that had made him even want to stay around after the funeral was the chance to see Sheila at the reunion.

Twenty minutes later, Dain was humming as he headed toward Sam's on the path through the orchard. He had walked it thousands of times as a boy. The Barlow orchard was one of the largest around town. It had been the family's chief money maker. The property, his property now, ran right up to the Pine Ridge city limits. Beyond the boundary fence stood the abandoned high school and its parking lot. Sam's Diner was on the other side of the road a block and a half beyond the school.

The sun had just cleared the small mountain range into a cloudless morning sky, but still high enough to be shining down onto the ground between the trees. For the first time in days, he had a spring in his step as he walked briskly along the path. Sixty yards ahead, something stretched across the path. *A big tree trunk? Damn, had the wind been that strong last night?*

In a tree off to his left, a convocation of crows became involved in a serious dispute with a lot of cawing and wing flexing. The dispute held Dain's attention until he was within twenty yards of what rested on the path. Then he saw it clearly. Recognition was instantaneous. He was staring at what he had seen far too often the past few years. As an LAPD homicide cop, he'd seen dozens of dead bodies. He shook his head in disbelief. *God, no! Not here in Pine Ridge, and in my orchard!*

The corpse was naked, a woman on her back, a tall woman, but who could it be? Recognition always came hard when there was no head. But he didn't have to search long for it. Averting his gaze from the horror of the neck stump, he saw it immediately. The head was wedged into the crotch of an apple tree, still bare from winter. Its eyes were open, facing the torso as if keeping a vigil over the body. The fine hair lifted and fell in the play of the gentle morning breeze. He blinked, but it failed to alter what he saw, whom he saw.

Dain was looking into the never changing dead stare of one of his old classmates, Amy Housley!

CHAPTER 3

Dain raced down the path to the orchard gate. Glancing down the narrow country road toward the diner, his pulse quickened. He was in luck. Among the three cars parked in front of Sam's was a sheriff's unit. *Maybe Lud was there. The lawyer had said something about him stopping there most days for coffee before heading down the hill to Crescent Valley.*

The sheriff was an old classmate of Dain's. Everybody called him Lud, just the one name. He was a Native American, actually named Luther Light-Under-Deer, but the old gang in school had put the initials together and coined the name Lud for him. The name had stuck.

Lud, a loner, had been a miserable student. He had been the butt of a lot of stupid jokes. Dain, the only real friend he had, wondered how many times he had heard someone yell, *Hey Tonto, where's the Lone Ranger?* Many a time Dain had to come to Lud's aid when one of the school bullies, like Albert Martinson, had been working him over.

But Lud had grown up. Now he was six feet tall, weighing more than two hundred pounds, and had a no-nonsense look. Last Thursday, a sheriff's unit had pulled up in front of Dain's house, and he had gone out on the porch to see what was up. He had been stunned to see Lud climb out of the car in uniform, the sheriff's shield on his chest.

Coming into the lot, Dain veered toward the patrol car, saw it was empty, and ran on toward the diner's entrance. The sound of the door slamming back against its restraint stopped the conversation and brought up the heads of the three men seated at the counter.

The smell of bacon and cigarette smoke hung heavy in the air. No sheriff, just old Ned Parker and two guys he didn't recognize. Ned Parker had been on that same stool for as long as Dain could remember. Turning to scan the booths along the far wall, he spotted Lud in the back one, working on a plate of bacon and eggs.

Hurrying to the booth, Dain leaned forward, hands on the table, close to the surprised Lud. The old timers at the counter, sensing something was wrong, strained to hear. Sam Goller, the owner, came out of the kitchen, saw Dain, and eased out from behind the counter. He was always looking for gossip to hold the coffee drinkers for one more cup.

Looking at Lud, Dain said. "I need to talk to you, old buddy. There's a problem in my orchard."

"Dammit, Dain," Lud said loudly, gesturing toward his plate. "Can't you see I'm eating? Won't be long, sit down and have some coffee."

"Read my lips, Lud. We've got trouble, bad trouble." Without waiting for any further protest, Dain headed for the front door.

Grumbling, to no one in particular, Lud picked up his hat. "Jesus Christ, a man can't even eat his breakfast in peace. These damn fellows go to the city and they get a hair up their butt. Always in a damn hurry."

Outside the diner, he confronted Dain. "What the hell is it you can't tell me in front of Sam and the boys? You know Pine Ridge. Those fellows will know as much as we do within an hour anyway."

Ignoring Lud, Dain climbed into the passenger's side of the sheriff's car and slammed the door. Looking out the window, he said, "Come on, Lud, shake a leg. We've got to get up to my orchard before some kid stumbles in there. I'll tell you about it on the way."

Still grumbling, Lud shot the car into reverse, but by the time they turned through the gate leading to the Barlow house, he was silent, a grim look on his face. Passing the big red barn and the old two-story house, Lud downshifted and turned onto the lane that pickups used to get down into the orchard.

"Stop saying her body, dammit!" Lud said. "You said it was someone we both knew, now who the hell was it?"

"Amy Housley. Christ, Lud, she's been decapitated."

"Amy Housley! What was she doing here. She hasn't got any kin here. They moved to the coast the summer after we graduated. And the reunion don't start until this weekend. You sure it's her?"

Out of the patrol car, Dain pointed to the left. "She's over there about thirty yards. Her head is sitting up in the fork of a tree. Take your own look and see who you think it is."

As they threaded their way through the trees, Lud asked, "You hear any commotion here last night, or this morning? Anything unusual?"

"I was home all night except for going to Sam's for dinner. Of course, after the storm hit, you could have had a massacre out here, and I wouldn't have had a clue. And this morning, I was sleeping like the dead until," He glanced at Lud. "Sorry, bad choice of words. Anyway a call woke me up early and I was on my way to Sam's to meet somebody. That's why I came through the orchard this morning."

"Wonder if anybody saw her in town last night?" Lud asked.

Dain flashed him a smile that had no humor in it. "Somebody did, but I don't think he or she is going to tell us about it."

Lud's face flushed. "I meant whether somebody came to town with her. Better see if anybody made the trip up here with her."

"A man?" Dain nodded. "Yeah, I thought of that, too. You should probably phone her folks right away and break the news. Might ask if she's been keeping company with anyone." Dain paused as he studied the orchard around the corpse. "Odd. Not a stitch of her clothes around. Why take a risk of carrying her in here naked? Or why undress her and take her clothes? Why would the killer want them?"

Lud shook his head. "You got me, buddy boy. The longer I have this job, the more I realize how crazy some people are." Looking down at the body, he said, "Poor Amy. You know, she was prettier than I remember her in school, really good-looking legs. Still flat-chested, though." He glanced slyly at Dain. "Of course, you understand I wouldn't say that to anyone else."

"Christ, no need to apologize, Lud. You don't sound any different from every homicide dick in L.A. when he sees a dead female. Me, too. But this is different. I can't joke about this, not someone I know."

"Sorry, Dain. I shouldn't have said it. But then Amy wasn't one of my favorite people, not the way she used to rag on me."

He knelt by the corpse. After a pause, he continued. "I've got a couple of ideas about this that need checking. The trouble is, I've only got three deputies, and two of them are gone. Bob went to California on a fugitive warrant, then Josh got a ruptured appendix and landed in the hospital. Talked to Bob this morning. Having a hard time with some red tape, said it would most likely be another few days before he gets back."

Pausing, he took off his hat and scratched his head. Glancing sideways at Dain, he said, "Would you be willing to help me on this, Dain?"

"Jesus, Lud. I came up here to bury my family. The estate has a couple of encumbrances on it, so I thought I would spend a few vacation days to get that settled before I go back. Besides, it gives me a chance to go to the reunion. I sure the hell didn't come up here to do what I'm trying to get away from in L.A."

"Okay, Dain, keep your shirt on," Lud said. "like I said, right now I've just got the one deputy to help me cover the county. Even in this sparsely settled place that don't leave me a lot of time to try to catch the son of a bitch who did this. It ain't like the city, Dain, with cops for everything. Up here I'm pretty much the whole show."

Settling his hat back onto his mop of coal black hair, he added, "We don't get many murders here. Mostly cattle rustling or one redneck beating the hell out of another. You have the know-how to go over a crime scene with a fine tooth comb without screwing it up. I don't. I could call in the state boys but they don't have the stake in this we do. I could sure use your help. And this poor woman could, too."

"Can't you find an ex-cop who could help you out."

Lud shook his head. "Budget won't stand nothing like that. And I know and you know, ain't nobody in eastern Washington got your experience. I don't want this," he motioned toward the body, "to go in the files as unsolved, and I don't think you want that either."

Dain sighed. "Okay, you've made your point. But one thing. If I take this on, it's my baby. No interference from you or anyone else if it happens to lead me to some good ole boys. Agreed?"

Lud nodded. "You got a deal." Lud's smile was short lived, and he blushed, not looking at Dain. "One thing, old buddy. I don't really know how to put this, but, well, you remember how it used to be. I mean with me the dumb Indian who didn't know his ass from a hole in the ground. Well, I've worked awfully hard to change that…I mean, people finally give me respect. I can't have them thinking I'm still running around kissing your ass like I did when we were in high school."

He lifted his hand to stifle Dain's protest. "What I'm saying is I want to tell folks you volunteered to help me, not that I begged you to do it. I guess what I'm asking is that you turn over whatever evidence you uncover to me and I can say we uncovered it together."

Dain smiled. "Like you said, Lud, you got a deal. Just that one stipulation is all I want. The rest of it is your case. Any way you want to handle it, we'll be working on it together."

Dain, uncomfortable, turned away to study Amy's body again. "Do you have a tarp or a body bag in your trunk? It isn't right, her lying out here all exposed."

Dain yelled at Lud's back, disappearing among the trees. "Get a call in to your coroner while I scout around here. And tell the ambulance to come in the same way we did. If we get lucky, no one will notice."

Lud came back into sight, a tarp under his arm, yawning. "God, I'm bushed. I was off duty last night, and I slept damn good, considering all that thunder and lightning. Don't remember even getting up to go to the can, can't figure why I'm so tired."

"Damn, Lud, if you'd had some of the strikes at your place we had around here, it'd knocked you out of bed. Couple sounded like they were right outside my door." Dain gave the red eyed sheriff the once over. "Probably just been pushing yourself too hard.

"Lud, I've been thinking about what you said. With no family or close friends in Pine Ridge, why did Amy arrive here four days early?"

Lud dropped the tarp a short distance from the body and turned to stare toward the Barlow house, rising above the sweep of bare tree branches. "Did you know I almost owned this place? My step dad made an offer on it, but then your pop came along and outbid him. I often wonder what would have happened with my mom if we had owned this property. You know, I mean about the accident. She wouldn't have had those long walks along the road when she went for food and supplies."

Dain shot a glance at him, surprised. Lud had never talked about the death of his mother nor let anyone else talk about it.

Lud seemed unaware of him for a moment, his big square face with its high cheekbones taut, intense. Then he grinned, saying, "What the heck? That was a long time ago. Water under the bridge. Right, buddy boy?

"Listen, I've got to get to the office in Crescent valley. Go ahead and nose around. See what you can turn up. I'll check with you every chance I get. And if you find something, give me a ring. I can almost always get loose for an hour or two. Okay?"

Dain followed Lud to the patrol car. "Give me four or five evidence bags and some rubber gloves if you've got them."

He watched Lud back the car out of the orchard before returning to the body.

Having pulled on the plastic gloves, he lifted her right hand, peered at the nails, and then slipped one of the plastic bags over the hand. Maybe the lab would find some skin and blood residue under the nails.

Leaning across her body, he pulled her left hand free from where it was caught under her hip. *My God!* One finger, her ring finger, was missing, hacked off! The memory hit him hard, Amy, and her emerald ring. *She had worn it her senior year in high school. Her grandmother had given it to her as a pre-graduation present, a really big green rock. The thing had to have been worth a couple thousand dollars easy.* Anger jolted him. *The bastard had cut off her finger to steal the ring.*

The arm fell reluctantly when he released it, but rigor mortis was not yet complete. He frowned. *With the air so humid and the unseasonably warm night after the storm, she could have been dead since before midnight. Maybe as early as nine or nine-thirty.*

Glancing past Amy's head to the base of a nearby apple tree, he saw some kind of irregularity in the bare ground. Rising, he saw what it was. A boot track in the soft ground. Walking gingerly across the carpet of damp dead leaves, he squatted to peer at it. *The print had been made after the rain stopped. The edges were far too clean-cut to have been pelted by raindrops.* He closed his eyes in concentration. *What time had the rain stopped? At ten, when he went out on the porch, it had still been coming down in buckets, but by the time he climbed into bed at eleven-thirty, all was quiet. No rain, no thunder.*

The boot, looked to be about a size twelve or damn close. Also, it was new or almost so. The imprint of the maker's logo pressed into the damp ground showed no wear. The boot had sunk well into the ground. *A heavy man.*

He glanced back. The ground around the body showed no sign of a struggle. *She had been brought in here unconscious and naked. Tugging at an unyielding body to get its clothes off would have disturbed the soft ground.*

He crossed back to Amy and knelt, bending forward to peer closely at her pubic hair. Small, hard crystalline bits of material clung to the pubic hair. *Dried semen, no question. She had had sex indoors, at least somewhere out of the rain.* He pulled the flesh inside her thighs up into view and then ran his gaze along the length of the body. *No bruising any-where. The sex had been voluntary or she had been unconscious or dead when it happened.* He stared down at the maimed hand and then across at the severed head. He pressed his lips together. *No way it had been consensual sex.*

Dain bit his lower lip involuntarily. *The son of a bitch! I'll nail the bastard if it's the last thing I do. Raping Amy and then slicing her up like this!*

Rising again with a grunt, he tried to think of what had to be done. *I'll have to get Lud to have someone come out to get a cast of the boot print. And the ring. I have to tell Lud to get a notice out to all the pawn shops in the state about that emerald.*

Rubbing his chin, Dain looked at Amy's poor ruined head, trying to remember back to high school days. *Had she ever had a beau? Albert Martinson. The kid had graduated the year before we did.* Dain nodded. *And he had taken her to his senior prom. I remember how everybody kidded them about neither of them having a date before. And I heard stories of Albert being serious about Amy after that party.*

Dain's memory rambled on. *Just the other morning, when they had sat over coffee, rehashing high school days, Lud had said that Albert Martinson had been out of prison only a year. And that he had been sent up for raping a woman in Crescent Valley.*

The news had blown Dain's mind. It was still hard for him to believe it. Albert was the last guy he'd figured for something like that. *Sure, he was a rough and ready logger type, but I had never heard of him mistreating a woman. He'd been damn rough on Lud, but still...after he graduated I heard he had to be pushed into a fight. Maybe because he was ashamed of his attacks on a small Indian boy. Anyway, I heard the rape was the only really bad mark on his record.* He arched a brow. *All hearsay.*

Leaning over, Dain slipped one of the clear plastic bags over the maimed left hand. As he did, he studied the fingernails. They looked as if they had been cleaned to Dain, like the killer knew what he was doing. He made a wry face, hoping to hell it wasn't Albert. *Still, some of those jokers spent their time in the slammer reading up on criminal investigation procedures. I'll have to find out from Lud where Albert lives. A man could change a lot in a few years behind bars.*

He walked over to the tarpaulin, unfolded it, and slid it across Amy, blotting out the chalky white form, stark in the bright sunlight. He took a last glance around the site before leaving. *The son of a bitch had made one mistake anyway. That might be the mistake that will get him hanged.*

Sheila! Damn, I'd forgotten about her. He broke into a jog, heading for the house. *There would be no leaving here until the ambulance people arrived. I'll have to call her at Sam's and beg off. A hell of a way to get back in the good graces of a girl who still holds more attraction for me than she should. Oh well, I haven't seen her in years. She probably isn't at all like I remember.*

Behind him, in the orchard, the mutilated body of a high school classmate, under the mounded tarpaulin, and the footprint remained, undisturbed.

CHAPTER 4

An hour later, Dain, hurrying along the shoulder of the road, came into view of Sam's. Two cars were in the lot, but he had no idea whether either was Sheila's. Noticing the sign atop the roof of the building, he smiled. Sometime over the past decade, the letter M had parted company from the rest of the sign. Now it read SA 'S DINER and probably would until another of the wood letters fell off. Crossing the unpaved lot, he burst through the front door in almost as dramatic a way as he had earlier.

The crowd sitting at the counter had increased by one. Ned Parker, on the same end stool where he had been earlier, raised a hand in greeting. Sam, fatter than ever, was behind the counter, a towel over one shoulder, his eyes squinting against the smoke, rising from the cigarette that dangled from his thick lips.

Turning toward the row of booths, the seats and backs still covered in the same red vinyl he remembered from high school, he saw Sheila immediately. She was watching him with an uncertain smile, saying nothing. Sheila was dressed in a soft blue cotton summer dress that complemented her light blond hair and added depth to her blue eyes. A warm feeling surged through him, and suddenly it was like back in high school again when he finally got up the nerve to approach her on a personal level and ask her for the first date. His memory served him well. She remained one of the best looking females he had ever seen.

But his fantasy wasn't working out. Sheila was supposed to leap out of the booth, shower him with kisses, and declare her undying love for him. Instead, as he approached she offered her hand, not looking too happy about doing that. Her voice was as soft and sexy as he remembered. Well, maybe not sexy, but sounding like it could be.

"Dain. It's been a long time."

"T-too long," he stuttered and could kick himself for it, then he got control of his tongue. "Sheila, you look like a million dollars. I'd swear you're not a day older than you were when we graduated."

"Dain, you always were full of bull, but it sounds good. I'm glad at least that part hasn't changed." She smiled again.

What was wrong with her? Did I make her wait at the diner too long? She looked as if she was about to bolt for the door any second.

He slid into the booth opposite her, but like an idiot, forgot to let go of her hand, dragging it across the tables surface.

Sam, who had come from behind the counter to stand in the middle of the room, saved him from making a complete jackass of himself. "Dain, what was that business with Lud all about? You really had your feathers ruffled."

Dain took advantage of the interruption to release Sheila's hand. "Might as well tell you, Sam. You and the whole town will know anyway before sunset."

This brought Ned Parker off his stool, turning his head to where the ear with the hearing aid faced Dain.

"I found a body on my property this morning," Dain said. "I was on my way over here, cutting through the orchard, when I stumbled across it."

Sam patted at his face with the towel as if just thinking about a body was enough to work up a sweat. "The heck you say! One of those Mexican fruit pickers? Always a few of them stay around drinking and raising hell during the winter. Knifed to death, I expect."

"Say it was right there in your orchard, eh, Dain?" Ned Parker asked.

"What was his name?" Sam demanded. "Not that I know any of those grease balls."

Dain shrugged. "That's up to Lud. Ask him."

He turned back to Sheila, In the shock of what he had said, her awkwardness had vanished.

"Sam said that you'd gone rushing off with the sheriff. But a body! How awful! You really don't know who it was?"

The diner grew quiet: no banging of cups, no clatter of flatware. Sam and his four counter customers were straining to hear the name that would send them racing through Pine Ridge like the town criers of Colonial days. Dain's answer froze them in their seats. "I'll tell you about it later."

He sought to change the subject, touching her hand with his own. "Thanks for calling. It made my day. I wasn't sure you'd be at the reunion, at least not this far ahead."

Her eyebrows lifted. "Early? What do you mean? My business, I run a boutique, is always a little slow this time of the year, so I thought I would come up in time for tonight."

Dain frowned. "Tonight? What's so special about tonight?" he asked.

"The alumni committee election and welcoming party is tonight. Maybe since you were already here you didn't get a letter."

"I got a letter." He shook his head. "But there was nothing about an election or welcoming party tonight."

"Dain, you never could get anything straight. We are to meet in he home-ec room at eight o'clock for hors d'oeuvres and punch. Good thing I mentioned it."

He nodded. "That's for sure. All my invitation mentioned were reunion activities Friday night and Saturday."

Opening her purse, she pulled out a folded sheet of pink paper. Smoothing it out, she tapped it with one red fingernail. "See right here—May 11th."

Picking up the sheet, he scanned it, frowning. "Mine says the reunion starts the 14th and it's on pale green paper." He handed the sheet to her. "And look. This was done with a typewriter. Mine was done on a dot matrix printer with a ribbon so worn I could hardly read the dim print."

Her reply was lost in the thought that jolted him. *Amy! Could her invitation have read the tenth? He thought back to last night. The lights had been on in the old school when I came out of Sam's after dinner. I figured somebody was at work sprucing the place up. I even thought for a moment about going over and lending a hand, but with all the lightning and rain had decided to haul ass for home.*

Dain gestured with his head toward the group at the counter. "How about getting out of here and taking a ride? I don't want to talk in front of this bunch."

Without answering, she slid out of the booth, and Dain helped her on with her light coat. He looked out the large front windows to hide from her his growing feeling of apprehension.

Nearing the front door, the old high school's parking lot caught his attention. The car he had noticed last night was still there. A Cadillac. His brow knitted. *The Powers were the only people around Pine Ridge who could afford a set of wheels like that. But Mike Powers helping anybody? That was a stretch. Hell would be awfully chilly the day that happened.*

In the flashes of lighting preceding the storm, he had noticed it was a Caddy but had been unable to tell its color. The big sedan was red with white leather upholstery. *Amy's car? Could be. Ned, a friend of her fathers, had said she was doing well in Seattle. If nobody moved it during the day, he would run a registration check on it.*

Outside, at Sheila's invitation, Dain slid behind the wheel of her almost new Audi. Gunning the car out of the parking lot, he turned west onto the narrow two-lane highway which served as the towns main street. The road was a dead-end one, running from Crescent Valley in the flatland below up past Rainbow Lake and through Pine Ridge to a point fourteen miles above, where it ended under the towering crags of the Cascade Mountains. Above town, the road passed a few isolated houses and the ranger station at the boundary of the national forest.

Passing the small green sign on the edge of town, announcing that Pine Ridge had 173 inhabitants, the car began climbing through scattered stands of Douglas firs. Soon the road was winding through a dense forest, broken only by clearings around the occasional house. At intervals, unpaved roads turned off into the woods to service even more remote cabins. Overhead, the sky was an unpolluted blue through which floated the occasional fluffy cloud, looking like gigantic balls of cotton.

Dain looked toward Sheila, who stared out the side window, unaware of his glance. *Was she thinking of how we used to drive up this way in my dad's pickup? That summer between our junior and senior year, we came this way often, just poking along, talking about everything and nothing. God, I had been crazy about her and then had thrown it away because of one miserable afternoon. Was it too late to get her back?*

He pressed his lips together. Turning his attention back to the road, he took a deep breath. *And now this damn thing. What I've got to tell her is sure not going to help rekindle the romance.*

He slammed a hand against the steering wheel, and she looked around, startled. He shook his head, knowing this was going to ruin her day, but she had to know about her dead friend. He blurted out, "Sheila, that body in the orchard...it was Amy Housley."

"Oh, my God!" She gasped. "No! Not Amy!" She burst into tears." Sobbing, she cried, "Oh God! She can't be dead!"

Her tears were contagious. Dain turned to stare out his side window, trying to keep the moisture out of his own eyes. *Some tough guy! But then, those stiffs in L.A. hadn't been sweet kids I'd known growing up.* He debated pulling the car over to the side of the road and gathering Sheila in his arms. *Thank God, it hadn't been her.*

Then he remembered her invitation telling her to come to the school tonight. *Had Amy been killed in the school? Christ, he had to get back to town and check that red Cadillac.*

Sheila's gaze searched his face. "Dain, my invitation. Could—"

"Not a chance. Just a mistake. Listen, I've got to get back to town to check a few things."

As they roared back toward Pine Ridge, Dain was unaware that Sheila still watched him.

CHAPTER 5

Some fifteen minutes after leaving Dain, in his patrol car four miles east of Pine Ridge, Lud cried out and swerved off the road onto the shoulder, gravel crunching under the tires. Clutching at his head, he sent his hat cartwheeling onto the floor. His head was splitting in two. Digging a bottle of pills from his pants pocket with a trembling hand, he crammed two into his mouth, chewing them. Lud had been doing it so often lately he no longer needed water. Closing his eyes, he moaned, then rolled down the window. The light breeze felt good against his sweat-drenched brow."

Ten minutes later, the dope had killed the pain, but he knew from experience that when the first one was this bad, he would have several more skull splitters in the next few hours. The pain was gradually getting worse, just the way the doctor said it would.

He would never forget the morning, with the tests all in, that he had gone back to the office of the doctor in Crescent Valley. The man had come right to the point the way Lud had ask him to. "Have a seat Sheriff." The doctor took his seat behind the desk and looked at Lud a moment. "It's bad news. You've got a brain tumor that is inoperative. Too far along even for effective chemotherapy. You have about three months left, give or take a week or two.

"What I'm going to suggest, Sheriff, is that you go on sick leave, starting right now. That way we will be available for you whenever you need us."

In stunned silence, Lud looked past the doctor's shoulder into an outside world that ceased to have meaning for him with the medic's words. He knew the headaches meant trouble, but not this, not the end of everything. *Probably caused from all the beatings I got as a kid.*

He broke the silence by slamming his fist into his open palm, and the doctor's eyes widened at the violence of the gesture.

"Hell, no!" he cried. "I mean no to the sick leave. I've worked hard as hell to make something of myself, and that's what I want my old class-mates to see, not some sick Indian crawling off to die. I need to keep going until after my class reunion up in Pine Ridge. It's not but three weeks away doctor."

The doctor studied Lud for a moment and then nodded, sliding a prescription pad across the desk in front of him. "I understand, Sheriff, but those headaches are going to get worse. I'll give you a prescription for pain killers, strong ones. I have to tell you, these will lose their effectiveness in time, but, with luck, they'll last you through the reunion." He shook his head. "After that, Sheriff, you're going on sick leave. You're going to need all the help we can give you."

A leaf blew through the window, brushing against Lud's face, interrupting his reverie. His eyes had watered and he sniffed as he picked up his hat. He jammed it down atop his head and leaned back, trying to organize his thoughts.

Thank God, Dain had agreed to find the bastard who had killed Amy Housley. Poor Amy. He hadn't thought about her in years. He had tried not to think of her since that long-ago day when his life had come apart in a split second.

Uneasy with the train of thoughts building in his mind, Lud glanced over his shoulder before starting the engine. The tires spun in the loose gravel, and he came back onto the asphalt in a shower of small pebbles.

He swerved into the first driveway he came to, and reversing directions, headed back toward Pine Ridge. If he was lucky, he would reach home before the next headache struck. As he roared past Sam's, twenty miles over the speed limit, his thoughts returned to Dain and, as quickly, to Sheila Greene. Sometimes he had trouble separating them in his mind.

Lud needed more time before seeing Sheila. He had to face her soon, though, her and the other girls. The prospect of seeing them had kept him away from the last reunion. But a lot of years had past, and now, he had to accept what had happened. And show he could be as forgiving as the next man. *Live and forgive. Hell, if I failed to show up at this reunion, or if I slunk back into a corner, God, I can hear it now. Lud might be the sheriff but that hasn't changed him much.*

Maybe that's how Dain sees me. Damn, I practically begged him to help with Amy. He shook his head in disgust. *No! Christ, that's unfair. Dain had been the only friend I had back in those miserable high school days. And this morning, out in the orchard, Dain treated me as an equal, law man to law man. And goddammit to hell, the rest of the gang is going to see me that way. I swear to God they will.*

Bolts of pain flickered through his skull. He increased his speed, driving as fast as he dared on the increasingly curvy road west of Pine Ridge.

Twenty minutes later, the patrol car, spattered with mud from the rutted lane leading off into the woods, slid to a halt before Lud's isolated four-room log house. The turnaround, like the lane that led into the house, was bare red clay with gravel scattered over it. The wet ground in the grove of tall firs surrounding the house was thick with needles, and shallow puddles of water, two to three feet across, filled the low spots. A dozen cords of wood stood against one side of the house, reaching up to a single window. Weathered boards had been nailed over a second window.

Lud, scrambling out of the patrol car, reeled across the turnaround and mounted the porch, its roof held upright by four peeled log posts.

Entering the house, he fumbled at his gun belt with unsteady hands. Finally freeing it, he hung it over a peg on the wall as his hat dropped, unnoticed, to the floor.

He punched the wall switch, and the room with its pine paneling came into focus. Against the back wall of the unkempt room was a collection of Indian paraphernalia: the head dress of a chief, two war clubs, an old tribal bow, and a quiver holding two ancient arrows.

For one exquisitely agonizing moment, pain flared in his head again. Recovering, he moved to the fireplace, threw in several pieces of kindling and a couple of logs, and watched until the smoldering remnants of the morning fire set fire to the wood.

Moving into the bedroom, Lud sank down onto the edge of the unmade bed. *Thank God, I didn't pass out when the headache hit me out on the highway.*

That had started a couple of weeks back, the passing out. The doc hadn't said anything about that happening. He would be in the throes of the headache, waiting for the pain pills to kick in, and then suddenly, it would be five or ten minutes later with him not knowing what had happened to the time. *Christ! If anyone saw me like that, I would be out on my ass in a New York minute, on sick leave whether I wanted it or not.*

Lud tried to put his mind on something else. *The Barlow house. I haven't been inside the place since before graduation. The Barlow home had been my dream house. I used to fantasize about that place, about mom and I living there. The big home had been called the Doc Tucker place back in those days.*

A slick talking white man, my step dad, the bastard, took mom off the reservation against her peoples wishes, son of a bitch made it so she never wanted to return, the lowlife then screwed that house deal royally.

The bastard disappeared right after that. He had never wanted anything to do with raising a brown-skinned Indian boy anyway. After that, Lud's only family had been his mother, the two of them alone in a white man's world.

A bit of a smile turned up the corner of his lips. *Mom had been a beautiful woman with piercing dark eyes and raven black hair. Her skin was light, not dark like mine. Back in the tribal days, in the mid eighteen hundreds, when the Nez Perce still owned a big chunk of Washington and Oregon, she would have brought twenty horses to her people as a wedding gift. She could have passed for a white woman. But not in Pine Ridge, where they knew what she was and wanted her and her son out of town. None of the townspeople would even give my mother a job.*

Lud had been bitter back then. The land had belonged to his ancestors before the white man stole it. But, after leaving high school, Lud had come to realize that he lived in the white man's world. If he kept fighting them, his fate would be no better than his mother's.

Another bolt of pain ripped through Lud's head, and he fell backward, rolling from side to side, his hands clutching his hair, pulling at it. Frantically he dug at his pants pocket, extracted two more pain pills from the plastic vial, and shoved them into his mouth. Closing his eyes, gasping, he waited for the relief they would bring. At the peak of his agony, he screamed, "Why, why?" and pounded the bed with his fists.

Later, in the euphoria produced by the narcotic, he lay, thinking of the class reunion. *Could I make it till then?* Suddenly, unbidden, unwelcome, the four girls whom, even though he tried, he could not forget or forgive floated into focus. The court record, still vivid in Lud's mind.

That day, those long years ago, the four of them, barely sixteen years old, had taken Amy's parents' car and gone for a joyride. The idea for taking the car out had come after they had shared a quart of Mogen David wine from Amy's parents' liquor cabinet.

Lud bit down hard, jaw muscles flexing. *Mom had been on her way home, walking along the road's shoulder, her arms loaded with groceries, so clumsy with the weight of them she was heavy-footed.*

The girls had been having a high old time, racing back and forth through town, no one willing to report them and cause their families trouble. Mom had been a mile and a half beyond Sam's Diner, crossing the road, ready to leave the highway, when they came flashing around the curve at high speed and struck her. The girls had been so terrified, they kept on going. Lud clutched his head with both hands and groaned. *Just a few more feet and mom would have been off the roadway.*

The inquiry had ruled it an unavoidable accident with no responsibility assigned. The young Lud had jumped up, screaming at the judge, until the bailiff dragged him out of the courtroom.

The accident left his mother paralyzed from the waist down and blind in one eye. Her face was horribly mutilated from being dragged along the pavement until her foot came free of the bumper where it was caught. The beautiful mother he had known was gone, and he could hardly stand to look at her. She required his care, day and night.

His mother had removed all the mirrors in the house. A year later to the very day, she put an end to whatever little life she had left. Lud came home after school and found her. Entering the house, he discovered her in the middle of the living room, lying in a sea of blood, next to the overturned wheelchair. She had cut her wrists. Lud had wanted to die, too.

Placing her body back in her wheelchair, he sank onto the floor next to her, sitting in the drying blood. He would do as she told him the Nez Perce did in the old days. He would sing the death chant and sit there until he died.

For two days Lud sat there in the reeking presence of death without food or water. From time to time, he would sing aloud the tribal death chant she had taught him, and strangely, that one thing had saved his life.

A passing forest ranger, Charlie Young, hearing the faint sound, found the young boy, badly dehydrated, still seated by his mother. Thereafter, the youthful Lud accepted the ranger as one of the few outsiders who deserved to live among his people.

Trying to shake off the train of bad memories, Lud rose from the bed, swaying, his uniform blouse damp with sweat. The pain was gone from his head, but he still felt unsteady on his feet. He thought again of his mother with her smooth, unscarred face, the beautiful face.

Lud felt the need to see her picture, the one they had had taken in Crescent Valley three years before her death. The photograph was one of the few luxuries they had allowed themselves. Years later, Lud had had a Seattle artist create a portrait from the photo and had hung it on the wall of what had been her bedroom.

In his anxiety, he reeled across the room, still shaky, and gripped the knob of her bedroom door. The door stuck, refusing to open. He tugged at the doorknob, then realized it was locked. A strange feeling, one somewhere between shock and bewilderment, surged through him. Lud stepped back, gazing at the door, puzzled.

What the hell! I never locked this door. His brow knitted. *The key has lain on the dresser in her room for years, undisturbed. This door is never locked, not even when mom was alive.*

He stared at the door, bewildered. *Christ! Has somebody been in the cabin?* He spun around, his gaze probing the room. *Nothing seems to be missing, not even disturbed. At least not that I can tell right off.* He frowned. *Why would anyone enter my place, not touch anything and lock the door?* He turned back and looked at the door. *They wouldn't. One of my damn blackouts? But why?*

Slowly he backed away from the door, step by step, toward the middle of the living room.

CHAPTER 6

Sheila's sobs subsided. Her voice was so soft Dain could barely hear it above the road noise. "Amy was a dear friend to me. After David, my husband, died in the plane crash, I was a nervous wreck. Amy took a week's vacation, came to Wenatchee, and took charge of my life. I don't know what I would have done without her." Tears filled her eyes again.

Dain, reaching for her hand, missed it, and his fingers settled on her thigh. He jerked back his hand. "Sorry," he mumbled. Then in a stronger voice, he said, "Yeah, she was quite a gal. I remember how she used to kid me about how her scoring average in basketball was higher than mine."

He knew she wanted him to go on talking about Amy, but he couldn't. The more he thought about the invitation Sheila received, the more he decided someone wanted to meet her at the high school, alone, tonight. *If I could just find Amy's invitation! The car. In the school parking lot, maybe it's there.*

Sheila must have thought his silence was embarrassment at having touched her leg. Straightening, she flashed him a weak smile and pulled down the sun visor with its vanity mirror on the back. Changing the angle of the mirror, she cried, "Oh, my goodness, I can't be seen like this."

Glancing over, Dain said, "You look plenty okay to me, lady."

After touching up her makeup, Sheila lowered her gaze, peering intently out the windshield. "Dain, didn't Lud used to live out this way somewhere?"

Dain nodded. "Yeah, still does…about a mile ahead. A poor excuse for a gravel road leads through the woods to his place. I don't know why he doesn't move to Crescent Valley and avoid the commute. Guess maybe these woods hold too many memories. You never have been to his place have you? Why don't we take a run by there?"

He wanted to get back to town and check out that Cadillac, but maybe this would help keep her from thinking of Amy.

As he turned onto the narrow lane leading back to Lud's, Sheila said, "I was amazed when I learned Lud is the sheriff. I mean, back in high school, he never showed any interest in activities. He was a real loner. Of course, everybody teased him…but you. I remember the way he used to stare at all of us with those black eyes. Sometimes I thought he hated us, especially us girls."

Dain frowned, thinking. "I doubt that. Leastwise, he never said anything to me. He was different, that tended to make him shy, and people like that always feel more awkward with the opposite sex. Personally, I was proud of Lud, the way he used to take care of his mom, and stand up to Albert Martinson even though he knew it meant another butt kicking."

Dain devoted himself to avoiding the deeper ruts of the lane for several seconds, then added, "What I didn't like was the way some of the guys in class were always picking on him, and laughing at him, just because he *was* different. He deserves a lot of credit for coming through all of that and having made something out of himself."

"I know what you mean, Dain. Maybe I'm acting Like a bigot."

Glancing at Sheila, he said, "Yeah, Lud may not have had a lot of people skills in those days, but even at seventeen, he was a hell of a woodsman. He could track a cougar across as rocky a patch of hillside as you'll find in the Cascades. And shooting, he's unbelievable, he didn't need a rifle. He is deadlier with a bow and arrow than most of us are with a thirty-thirty rifle."

The car slowed and turned off the gravel lane onto mere tracks leading into a heavy stand of timber. Sheila stared into the dark forest, and got quiet. Dain leaned forward, gripping the wheel, as the tires bounced along the rough trail. The car dipped as it crossed a rivulet cutting across the road, then threw a shower of pebbles against the underside of the vehicle as the tires lost traction and then regained it. Dain muttered, "What a road."

"Good gosh, he really lives out in the boonies, doesn't he?" Sheila said, glancing about at the towering firs that hemmed in the soggy track. The forest floor was choked with the decaying trunks of fallen forest giants. The ground between them was overrun with a profusion of ferns and low bushes bearing huge leaves. Little of the bright sunlight reached the ground, and the moist air was rank with the fusty smell of decay.

Dain smiled. "We're almost there. Just a couple hundred yards more."

The branch of a small pine slapped against the side of the car, and Sheila yelped. "My God, I'm jumpy. I like the woods, but not like this, not so wet and gloomy. I wish—" She screamed.

Dain came perilously close to swerving head-on into a tree, slamming on the brakes at the last moment. "Jesus Christ! Are you trying to wreck us? What in the name of—" When he saw how white her face was, he choked off his words.

Turning toward him, she grabbed his arm. "My nightmare! It's my nightmare!"

He tried to pull his arm free to slide it around her shoulder, but she held onto it with extraordinary strength.

"I don't understand," Dain said.

"This spot. I started dreaming about this place about a month ago. This exact spot! See that big stump—the one with all the mushrooms growing in the crack on the side of it? I'm always standing by it, lost, scared, and then something comes out of the woods behind me. That's always when I wake up. I never find out what happens, but if it continues I just know whatever it is…it's going to kill me. Dain, I've had that dream a dozen times in the last few weeks.

"Let's get out of here. Let's go back to town. We can see Lud some other time."

Breaking free of her grip, he drew her close. "Hey, calm down, little lady. It's okay. Lud's house is right beyond that screen of trees. Nothing's going to get you. I promise. Besides, I think since he's the sheriff now you need to know where he lives. You know, just in case."

Slipping the transmission back into drive, he drove the last few yards and came out into the clearing where Lud's hunter green and white patrol car was parked. He examined the front of the house for a moment before pointing at the chimney. A thin gray thread of smoke climbed toward the open sky. "Looks like we're in luck."

Sheila, still shaken, showed little sign of agreeing with the lucky part. In a voice so soft that she might have thought Lud was lurking near the car, she protested, "Dain, I don't feel much like visiting. You know…with Amy dead and everything. Maybe this isn't such a good idea. Besides, he surely heard the car. If he wanted to see us, he'd be out on the porch. Maybe he's asleep."

Dain nodded. "Maybe, but if he is, I'm going to wake him up. We won't be long. I want to see his invitation for the reunion. Somebody has made a big mistake. Does it start Friday night, like mine says, or tonight, as yours indicates?" He had to watch himself. He had almost said the wrong thing. He wasn't going to have Sheila scared to death unless he was sure something funny was going on.

Sliding out of the car, Dain mounted the porch steps and advanced on the door. He raised his hand to knock, then hesitated. Bringing his ear near the door, he listened. The house was quiet, but he could hear something. A faint sound, like radio static, then the woman's loud voice came through the door at him, and he jumped. "Unit 2, I have a domestic violence report at fourteen-sixty Meadow Lane."

The county radio! No way Lud could sleep through that.

Dain drove his fist hard against the door several times. The banging brought no response. The silence inside was eerie. His concern mounted. *All cops have enemies, one never knows.*

Sheila lowered the window and stuck her head out. "Come on, Dain, let's go. Please."

Damn, he was being thoughtless. Sheila was upset. Maybe Lud was sleeping, and he was so used to the radio it wouldn't wake him…then again, suppose some lowlife had been waiting here for him. He took a step back, then gave the door a hard kick in his frustration. The noise inside, the sound of footsteps, came immediately. Looking over his shoulder, he called to Sheila, "That woke him up."

She bit her lower lip, seeming less than elated by the news.

The door swung open behind him, revealing Lud, his eyes red, their lids puffy. He frowned. "Dain? What are you doing out here? I, is that Sheila with you? I'll swear, it's like old times seeing you two together. Come on in and have a cup of coffee."

Dain shook his head. "Better not, Lud. I don't want to take up too much of your off-duty time. I've just got a question. Something odd that's come up."

"Hell, Dain, I'm not doing anything." He leaned out the door and yelled, "Sheila! Come in and let me take a look at you. Been a long time since I laid eyes on you."

Dain looked at Sheila and shrugged. "Come on, Sheila. We'll just be a minute."

Looking unhappy, Sheila slid out of the car. Gingerly crossing the strip of gravel, she mounted the steps and edged past Lud into the house.

Closing the door behind them, Lud said, "I'll just be a minute," and disappeared into the kitchen.

Pulling at Dain's arm, she whispered, "Let's not stay long, please."

Dain nodded and answered in a sotto voice as he scanned the room, "Okay, just a few minutes. I promise."

The room was unchanged since the last time he visited this house. The Indian paraphernalia affixed to the walls was the same. Glancing toward the glass case, which had housed Lud's mother's collection of trinkets, he saw that he was wrong. The case was empty except for a modern compound bow and a quiver of at least twenty modern arrows. He recognized the model of bow, not that he knew anything about archery. A buddy on the force in L.A. had one just like it.

The bow was a *PSE Mach 4* with an *M-1* over draw and sixty percent let off with a four-arrow holder attached. The arrows in the holder were vicious four-bladed hunting arrows which looked to be a match to the arrows in the quiver. The thing had the penetration power of a high powered rifle. An elaborate Indian ceremonial outfit hung at the back of the case, probably a Nez Perce chief's rig like the one Lud's great great grandfather must have worn.

Lud's heartiness seemed to have disappeared with his return. They drank the coffee in near silence, interrupted only by Dain's few questions about the season's hunting.

Returning his empty cup to the table, Dain fished for another conversational gambit. With Sheila listening, he wanted to slip in his question about the reunion invitation as casually as possible. "I noticed you boarded up the window in your mom's old room."

"Yeah, I don't use it, and a lot of heat escapes that way, so I thought, what the heck."

"Oh, Lud," Sheila said. I still feel so terrible about what happened to your mother, even after all these years. She was so attractive."

Seeing Lud's change of expression, Dain flinched, knowing she had made a blunder.

*   *   *

Lud glared at Sheila, stunned by her remark coming out of the blue that way. He struggled with a wild desire to seize her by the hair, yank her upright, and slap her as hard as he could. *My God, to kill a woman and then say that to her son, she was so attractive. Sheila was the one driving the car. Hit my mother, then dragged her down the street till she didn't look human anymore. Yeah, she was a beautiful woman until you took it away from her. And you feel terrible? How do you think I've felt all these years?*

Lud figured enough time had passed to dull the pain of his loss, thought he would be able to begin forgiving the four girls who had taken his mother from him. *But it was going to be damn hard if they kept talking about it, saying things like, she was so attractive.*

He struggled to control himself, knowing he must be staring at her, saying nothing, the hatred showing in his eyes. Lud managed to shrug, saying, "Thank you, Sheila. I know she would appreciate hearing that as much as I do."

He caught Dain eyeing him. *Barlow was no fool. He's sensed the depth of my feelings. Knows the anger is still there just under the surface. Dammit! I don't want to hurt Sheila's feelings concerning this, none of the girls. I know they have gone through a lot as well. It's water over the dam. I've got to toughen my hide to this before the reunion gets here. Maybe Sheila being here three days early was a God send. Seeing her from time to time might be just what I need.*

Lud changed the subject, willing them to forget the moment of unpleasantness. "Refill, anyone?" he asked. "No? Then what's on your mind, Dain? How can I help you?"

Dain leaned forward, elbows on his knees. "What date was on your invitation for the first reunion get-together?"

Lud frowned, hesitated, then said, "Friday. Why?"

"We have a discrepancy here. "Sheila's has tonight's date on it."

"I'll be damned," Lud said. "Somebody must have screwed up...or could be a typo. What's the big deal?" He turned to Sheila. "That explains why you're here. I wondered why you had come early. Though maybe you just wanted to get here to see your old boy friend. Kind of mend the fences so to speak."

Sheila was silent.

Lud studied Dain's face. "Are you saying you think it was deliberate? If that's true," he shot a furtive glance at Sheila, "then Amy may have gotten a bogus one, too. That could explain why she was in Pine Ridge last night."

"Another thing is bothering me, Lud. There's a red Cadillac in the parking lot at the school. The Caddy was there last night just as the storm struck. It's still there this morning. I wonder if it could be Amy's. If it is hers, then I think we have to figure her invitation bore the wrong date. And that, Lud, sounds like we have something very nasty going on here."

Sheila, who had been watching him and Dain, eyes growing wider, blurted out, "Oh, My God! You're suggesting Amy was sent an invitation with the wrong date just to lure her to town. Then what about me? Does he intend to kill me, too?"

Don't you worry your head," Lud said. "This guy may be after you, but now that we know what's going on—"

Dain, out of Sheila's line of sight, was glaring at him, shaking his head vigorously. Lud rose to his feet to cover his sudden pause. "Tell you what. I'm going to have the patrol tonight and I'll check your lodgings every half hour. Where are you staying?"

"I'm at the Starlight Motel in Crescent Valley, room twenty."

Dain had taken advantage of Lud's rising to come to his feet and was helping Sheila up. "Listen, buddy, we've got to get back to town."

"This killer—" After Dain's quick slight shake of his head, Lud amended his remark to, "I don't really mean killer. Heck, we're just getting excited over a fouled-up invitation. We don't know that's what brought Amy to town. Probably just a typo, like I said."

Sheila gave him a wan smile, and Dain hurried her to the door, muttering to Lud as he passed, "I'll get in touch when I find out about the Caddy."

Lud called after him. "And I'll pick up Albert Martinson this afternoon and have a little talk with him."

From the porch, Lud watched the car disappear around the clump of firs, remaining there until its engine noise faded in the heavy air of the wet woods.

Back inside, he slumped against the closed door, drained, thinking about the sudden anger Sheila's thoughtless remark had brought. He thought of Amy Housley. *I have to find the guy who killed her. Avenging her would show them that I retained no malice toward them. Jesus, the worst crime in my tenure as sheriff, and the goddamn crazy bastard had to strike when I was short handed. Well, thank God for Dain.*

CHAPTER 7

Sheila glanced back at Lud's cabin just before they rounded the stand of saplings that shielded the cabin. Her last sight was of Lud on the porch, watching them.

She shivered. "Thank God, that's over." Turning to face Dain, she said, "I sure blew it, didn't I? I mean, saying that about his mother. I understand why he hated us, why he still dislikes us, but why can't he talk about it? Why can't he bring it out in the open? He needs to know how we feel. He should listen to what we have to say, how it still haunts us after all these years. I would do anything to bring her back, but I can't." Sheila shook her head. "God, I realized in there how much it still hurts Lud."

Dain said nothing until he had eased through one of the larger pools of water across the track. "Don't feel bad about it, Sheila. I've had no better luck when I've tried to talk with him about it. But I don't think he hates you girls. He knows what happened that afternoon, that you four were sneaking a little wine out of Amy's house. The accident was a once in a lifetime thing. He knows you wouldn't have hurt her for the world, that you four girls weren't wild."

Looking at Sheila and knowing he hadn't consoled her much, he slowly shook his head. "I think you're wrong about him hating any of you. It's just that every time Lud thinks about it, even now, it starts him to grieving about her. He's not going to get over it either, not as long as he lives there by himself without a woman. But Lud's a fine man, and I'd be willing to have him stand with me in a fight anytime."

Sheila said nothing more, staring out the window until they reentered Pine Ridge.

Slowing as they reached the high school, he turned into the parking lot. Easing in next to the Cadillac, he said, "I'll just be a minute."

He climbed out of the car and, crossing to the Cadillac, tried its driver's side door. "Locked," he muttered. Walking back to the rear of the car, he jotted its license number onto a pad he pulled from his pocket. *I'll have Lud's people run a check on it.*

Sliding back into Sheila's Audi, he asked, "Want to drop by the house a minute before we head for Crescent Valley?"

Sheila brightened for the first time since they turned down the lane into Lud's. "Great idea. My eye teeth are about to float."

A few minutes later, Dain turned into the driveway leading to the Barlow place. The two-story structure, on rising ground, loomed over the orderly rows of apple trees, beginning to show signs of white blossoms.

"I've always loved this old place," Sheila exclaimed. "I wonder if it will still seem as impressive to me as it did when I was in school."

She was out of the car, scampering toward the house, before the Audi came to a full stop. Dain, called, "Wait up! You can't get in the door's locked, an L.A. habit."

Sheila waited impatiently until he unlocked the back door, the one the family always used because of its closeness to the big barn which housed the cars, and almost every other piece of equipment on the orchard. They entered a small room with a row of pegs on the wall, where work coats and muddy shoes could be left before entering the kitchen. Inside the kitchen, Dain gestured toward the doorway in the far wall. "Be my guest," he said.

Dain followed her as she entered the parlor. Sheila circled the large room, trailing her hand over the polished surfaces of the beautifully preserved antique pieces. Pausing, she gazed at the gorgeous Persian rug covering most of the floor. Glancing up at Dain, she blushed. *Was she thinking of the last afternoon of vacation before their senior year started? When we were alone in the house and began to wrestle. Off balance, we had tumbled onto the rug, continued to struggle, and then came danger-ously close to consummating our romance.*

Dain, uncomfortable with his memories, made a sweeping motion with his arm. "You know where the bathrooms are, Princess. Take your time. Look till your heart's content. I'll be in the kitchen."

The minutes dragged by, and Dain, his fingers tapping the surface of the breakfast table, yelled, "Sheila. Where the hell are you? My stomach is growling."

She answered, her voice distant. "I'll be right there."

Moments later, Sheila erupted into the kitchen, wearing a huge floppy hat. Pirouetting, she sent her skirt twirling high around her thighs. Laughing, the dark mood from Amy's death gone, clamping the hat down atop her head, she cried, "Just what I needed. A new ensemble."

Dain's gaze was on the shapely legs revealed by the high flying skirt, not the hat. He felt the all too familiar heat surge through him and averted his eyes. *Christ, here she was, looking like the school girl she had been those long years back, and all he could think about was how it would be to have those legs and all the rest of her in bed. Women were right. Men were a bunch of assholes at times.*

Removing the hat, she turned to stare back into the parlor. "Just the sort of bachelor pad you need, Dain. Eighteen rooms, by my count. Why in the name of God did anyone in Pine Ridge build a house this big? Especially Doc Tucker, he didn't even have any kids."

"Dad told me Doc intended to make it the town hospital," Dain said, "hoping the town might grow into it. But about halfway through its construction he faced up to the fact that Pine Ridge would never be big enough to support it, so he decided to convert it into his home. What else could he do?"

"Are you going to keep it?"

He shrugged. "I haven't decided. I need more time." He smiled. "This house is full of good memories."

Dain stopped himself before he almost added, "a few bad ones, too."

It had been a few hard months after Sheila dumped him, because of that one afternoon in the barn, the one that had cost him Sheila's love. And would he ever forget finding Amy in the orchard, even if he lived here a lifetime.

Jumping to his feet, he said, "Hey, young lady, if I don't get something to eat soon, I'm going to turn into a cannibal, and you're the only food in sight."

CHAPTER 8

After picking up his car at Sam's, Dain followed Sheila to Crescent Valley. They lunched at a new restaurant with lots of glass and chrome called Kenn's.

The meal was a disaster. Foremost among all the people he didn't want to see, especially with Sheila in tow, was Candy Burns. She was waiting tables at Kenn's. Dain had paid no attention when the menu settled on the table next to his forearm, but the mocking tone of the voice saying, "I'll be back in a moment to take your order, Mr. Barlow," had brought his gaze up. Candy stood there, looking as if she were going to burst out laughing any second. His gaze followed her back to the kitchen before he risked a glance at Sheila. She was not smiling.

He gave her a big grin, trying to make a joke of a bad situation. "Looks like we made Candy's day, eh?"

Sheila's voice was as icy as an arctic wind. "I would say so."

They ate in a chilly near silence while Candy's grin grew larger each time she passed their table. At two-thirty, he dropped a grim Sheila off at the Starlight Motel. The goodbye had frost on it. Her words almost lost in the rumble of the car's engine, she said, "Thank you for lunch, Dain. It was good to see you again."

Turning left onto the highway, he drove the half mile to the sheriff's office.

The large woman at the dispatcher's desk behind the heavy mesh screen, which ran from the counter top to the ceiling, glanced up as he entered. So did the thin, gangling deputy seated at one of two cheap pine desks flanking the door to the sheriff's private office.

"May I help you?," the dispatcher asked.

"Is Lud in?"

The deputy called across the room. "The sheriff's not here, but maybe I can help."

"I'm Dain Barlow. I guess the sheriff told you about me. Lud was going to talk with Albert Martinson this morning. Do you know how it came out?"

"Not too good, at least for Albert. The sheriff questioned him for a while, then locked him up. Albert is still in the back." Swinging his legs off his desk, he clambered to his feet. "Lud mentioned you were giving him a hand on the Housley case. He said we're to assist you any way we can."

Dain was in no mood for chit-chat, not after what had happened at Kenn's. Digging in his pocket, he pulled out a slip of paper. "I would like you folks to run this license number for me. While I'm waiting, I'll slip back and have a chat with Albert, if it's okay."

"Be my guest," said the deputy. "Come on in and I'll take you back."

The dispatcher buzzed Dain through the locked counter gate, and he followed the deputy into a long corridor at the rear of the room. The air was heavy with the odor of pine oil disinfectant.

The cell block's lone occupant, Albert Martinson, was stretched out on a bunk. The lockup was a far cry from L.A.'s holding tanks with prisoners packed in like bees in a hive.

With a wink at Dain, the deputy ran his night stick along the bars, yelling, "Get up, Albert. You got company." The young cop, all arms and legs, turned to Dain. "I'll leave you with him. Better get back up front. I'm the whole show till Lud gets back."

Dain turned to find the black-bearded, burly Albert, resting on his back, with his hands behind his head, staring at the underside of the bunk above him, the feet of the big man dangling over the foot of the cot. "Whatcha you want to know, Frank?" Albert asked without moving.

Dain stared at Albert's feet. They were about the right size to have made the print by Amy's body, but the boots were a long way from new. "I'm not Frank, whoever he is. I'm Dain Barlow."

Albert reared up as if he'd been goosed with a cattle prod, his big head swinging around. "Jesus H. Christ! Dain Barlow! What are you doing here? Sorry about your mom and dad. Two better people never lived."

"Thanks, Albert. Look, I've got—"

"Jesus, am I glad to see you!" Albert cut in. "I could sure use a little—"

"Wait just a minute, Albert. I've got a few questions to ask you about Amy Housley."

Albert swung his legs over the side of the bunk. "You, too? You can't be serious, Dain. You remember me. I was crazy about Amy. I would have done anything to have had her. But I was from the wrong side of the tracks. Lud knows how I felt."

Dain scowled. He had heard similar stories a thousand times. Innocent as hell. Some cop picking on him or some jealous bastard lying about him. They all told the same story.

His gaze returned to Albert's footwear. "Those boots look like they're about shot, Albert. Isn't it about time for a new pair? Or maybe you have some new ones you're saving for a special occasion, eh?"

The bearded man gaped at him. "Has everybody gone loco?"

"Lud calls me a damn murderer, saying I killed a woman I haven't seen in years, and you're standing there ragging me about my frigging boots. Hell, do you think if I could afford a new pair of Red Wings I'd be wearing these pieces of shit?"

Clambering from the cot, Albert walked over to the bars. "I don't know why you're here, Dain, but thank God you are. You were always a square shooter. You've gotta talk to the sheriff. He won't listen to me. Hell, I keep telling him. I didn't even know Amy was in town."

Tugging at the snarls in his shoulder-length black hair, Albert said, "I gotta get out of here, man, before the boss at the mill decides I'm not coming back and hires somebody else. You know what Lud did? He came out to the mill and hauled my ass off, right in front of the whole damn crew, too. I just hope I can convince the boss it was all a mistake. That was the first halfway decent job I've had since I got out of stir. It was damn hard coming by, too. Had to damn near kiss his ass. Nobody wants to hire an ex-con."

"You're breaking my heart." Dain said. "Let's get down to business. Where were you last night, Albert?"

"Jesus Christ! Lud asked me that a half dozen times already. I was home, H-O-M-E. And no, I ain't got anybody to vouch for that. What the hell do you think I do—run a rooming house? Tonight I would have had an alibi, and damn near any other night, I would have been at Brown's Tavern, but with that storm last night, I stayed home."

Dain stared at him, letting the seconds pass, before he asked, "What were you in the joint for?"

Albert slammed his open palms against the bars. "Shit, you know the answer to that." He shook his head. "I shoulda known. Dain, you're just like every other cop I've ever known. I was screwed, but you're not going to believe that." He stopped suddenly, took a deep breath, and said, "Sorry, man. It's just that I served my time. What is it they say? Paid my goddamn debt to society? Yet they won't leave me along. They keep bringing it up. Gives them a chance to show they got balls, I guess. How the hell is a fellow supposed to work his way back into this goddamn society?"

Dain started to say something, but Albert cut him off. "I ain't no Easter bunny, but I sure the hell didn't rape any woman. I picked up a gal here in Crescent Valley and bought her a few drinks. Hell, she acted hot to trot, so I invited her to come up to the house. I damn sure didn't have to do any arm twisting. She was a big girl, old enough to say no, but she agreed to come."

"You contend she went with you of her own free will?" Dain asked.

"Hell, ain't I speaking English or you having a problem with your hearing? You're damn right, she did! We got liqueured up and started wrestling around the bed. Sure, it was a little rough, but that's what she wanted. That gal had screwed half the guys in the county. I figured it was my turn.

"Finally, I tore her panties off, and that really set her on fire. She almost screwed my pecker off. Then, along about three in the morning, she cooled down and asked me to drive her back to Crescent Valley. After that bout with her, I was pooped. Told her I'd run her down there before work. The bitch didn't argue, just snuggled up and went to sleep. But when I woke up the next morning, she was gone."

Telling his story seemed to have exhausted Albert. He walked back over to his bunk and sank down onto its edge before continuing. "Turned out she got a ride with old man Powers." He glanced up at Dain. "Be surprise if the old fart hasn't had her a time or two himself, the son of a bitch. Anyway, the lying slut told him I made her go home with me, raped her, and left her to find her way back to Crescent Valley on her own.

"To this day, Dain, I don't know why she made up that story. Unless she was trying to get the old bastard's sympathy, or she had a sweetie she was supposed to meet that night. Anyway, when the cops came, they found the bottles and glasses, the messed up bed, and the torn panties lying on the floor. Hell, she'd yanked my shirt open, tore half the buttons off it helping me to get undressed, but they ignored that. Said that could have happened when she was trying to fight me off."

Albert's look took on a stern appearance. "I put in some hard time there, hard time I didn't deserve. Meanwhile that little bitch was having the time of her life, banging any guy who would buy her a drink. Goddamn, slut. If I was gonna kill somebody, it would be her, not Amy."

The door to the cell block opened, and the deputy, sticking his head in, yelled, "Lud, just called in, Mr. Barlow. When I told him you were here, he said for me to pull the rap sheets on known sex offenders for you. I've got them ready for you. Lud said he should be here soon. He wants you to wait for him."

Dain turned back to the man in the cell. "I'll get back to you, Albert. Count on it."

When he came out of the cell block, the deputy pointed to the folders, "Why don't you sit at the other desk. There's more room."

Seating himself opposite the deputy, Dain shuffled through the folders, counting five. He smiled. *If it had been L.A., the stack would have reached the ceiling.* He flipped open the first one. The file was about an Indian from the reservation and contained little information, and what there was was carefully worded. *That wasn't surprising. The reservation covered damn near half the county, and its inhabitants had political clout. Their votes, no doubt, had been what put Lud in office.*

The next folder, Albert William Martinson's, was the one he really wanted to see. Settling back in the chair, he scanned the rap sheet.

The logger had had several scrapes with the law, but none recently.

Public drunkenness, disturbing the peace, brawling, destruction of property, and the like. Nothing that involved women, not until the rape charge.

Glancing toward the deputy, Dain asked, "How long you been on the job?"

The young officer stammered, "Ah—It'll be two years next month, sir."

"Why don't you call me Dain? I'm just an old country boy who grew up in Pine Ridge."

The deputy nodded. "Sure, thing, Dain. I'm Ralph, by the way."

Dain said, "I notice that most of Albert's scrapes with the law go back quite a way. Has he given you guys much trouble since he got out of prison?"

"Nope, wouldn't know he was even in the country, he's been quiet as a church mouse. Matter of fact, I find it hard to believe he killed this Housley lady." He grimaced. "But maybe Lud knows something I don't."

Closing the folder, Dain leaned back, lacing his fingers across his chest. *Albert Martinson didn't meet the standard profile of rapists who killed their victims. And decapitation…the only people who did that were psychopaths or some mob hit man trying to conceal his victim's identity. Still, there was a first time for everything.*

His train of thought was interrupted by Lud charging through the front door. As he was buzzed through the counter gate, Lud called, "Find anything interesting in the creep sheets? Can't find anybody in Pine Ridge, or Crescent Valley, who will say they saw Albert last night. Nothing more I can do now. Until I can find something against him, I can't hold him. I'm gonna have to kick him loose for now."

Lud settled his rear end on the corner of Ralph's desk. Pulling off his hat, he wiped the sweat off his brow with the back of his hand. "You were right about the Caddy. Its plates were issued to Amy." Toying with the emblem on the front of his hat, he added, "In my book, that places her at the high school last night."

Shoving his chair back from the desk, Dain rose. "That means I'd better hightail it back to Pine Ridge. I want to interview everyone who lives within sight of the school. Must be three or four houses near enough to see it. Maybe we'll get lucky. If she was killed there, the bastard had to have walked out of there carrying her in his arms. Course the way the storm was raging, he might have got away unseen. Can I get into the school tomorrow? I want to nose around in there."

"You betcha. I'll get the key from Vern and drop it off at your place first thing in the morning."

As they moved toward the front door, Lud said, "It ain't none of my business, but I can't help wondering, how come you never married, old buddy? You've got looks, a great personality and a good job. What more could a woman want. I figured you'd be hitched and have a couple of kids by now."

Dain made a face. "Never found the right woman, I guess. Or maybe I never got over Sheila. I sure the hell tried, but I suppose I measure the ladies I go out with against her and find them wanting."

His face hardened. "My senior year went down the drain after she dumped me. After graduation, I got out of town as fast as I could and promised myself I'd never come back. I swore I would forget her, but when I saw her this morning, my knees turned to jelly." He frowned. "Lud, you'd better damn well keep this to yourself."

"You may be selling yourself short," Lud said. "I thought I saw a bit of the jelly in Sheila's cute little knees, too. I got the impression she was still stuck on you."

Dain frowned. "Well, I sure as hell didn't help my cause much today. Guess who our waitress was at lunch. Candy Burns. How's that for piss-poor luck? Sheila took one look at her and closed up like a clam. When we got back to her motel, she said thanks for lunch, Dain, then said goodbye like I was some door-to-door salesman she wanted nothing to do with."

"Jesus, Dain, you don't want to get her so upset she cuts out and goes back home before the reunion. Don't screw up a second shot at her if you feel the way about her you say you do. If you'll take ole Lud's advice, you'll go back over to that motel, hat in hand, and try to sweet talk her into staying."

"I don't think there's much danger of her taking off," Dain said. "I think she's really looking forward to seeing her old girlfriends. She won't let anything keep her from meeting them." He stopped, his hand on the door handle. "You can do me a big favor, Lud, keep a really close watch on that motel tonight.

"Those screwed-up invitations bother me. I have a hunch that there's a nut out there using the reunion as a means of getting people together for his pleasure, and he plans to do more killing than just Amy." Stepping out onto the sidewalk, Dain turned back. "I'll tell you, Lud, all hell may break loose if we don't find this guy."

CHAPTER 9

Closing the door, Lud turned back into the office, glancing at his watch as he did. *I better catch a nap before dark. My shift starts at eight P.M. And this is one night I gotta be on my toes. No goddamn dozing off tonight. But first, I'm going to have to release Albert. The frigging legal system makes me sick sometimes. I have to charge him or release him. What a crock! The guy could have killed Amy Housley, and I'm letting him out with another potential victim just a half mile away.*

Charging through the gate in the counter, he yelled, "Ralph, toss me the cell block keys. I couldn't dig up anything to hold Albert on, found a couple people who saw Amy's car coming into town and swear she was alone, and Albert didn't hit any of his usual haunts in Crescent Valley last night. I'm going to release him."

Handing the ring of keys across the desk, Ralph smiled. "It, doesn't surprise me, Sheriff. Ole Albert's got a lot of rough edges, but I can't see him going off the deep end like that."

Lud glared at him. "Any time I want your opinion, Deputy, I'll sure the hell ask for it. Albert can be one mean bastard, believe me. I've got another woman who may be in jeopardy, and I'm trying to cover all the bases." With that, he disappeared into the cell block.

Albert, sprawled on the bunk, raised up on one elbow to stare when Lud came into view. "Well, Sheriff, you couldn't find anybody who saw me last night could you?"

Lud plastered a smile onto his face. "Good news, Albert. You're right. We're gonna have to let you go. There wasn't a damn soul who could dispute your statement about being home last night. No hard feelings, eh? A man has to do his job, disagreeable as it may be sometimes."

Unlocking the cell door, he swung it open. "I heard you saw Dain. He's giving me a hand on the Amy Housley case. Come on in the office, and I'll treat you to a cup of coffee before you go. Least I can do after all I've put you through."

Albert wasn't buying. Unsmiling, he asked, "Are you saying I'm free, no charges?"

"Hell, yes, man. What have I got to do? Paint you a picture? I—" Pain flared in Lud's head, quick, needle sharp. *Christ, not another headache! Not now.* He dropped the key ring to cover his hesitation, then leaned over and retrieved it. "I don't guess you have a ride since I picked you up at work. Come on, I'll take you home."

Albert still looked unhappy. "Naw, you don't need to do that. I expect I'll be able to get a ride, hitch-hiking."

Lud's smile faded. "Dammit, Albert, I think I'd better. You see everybody in Pine Ridge knows about Amy's murder, and some folks are talking tough. You know, what with that rape conviction and everything. They'll all know I picked you up by now. I got to make sure you get home and let them know you're not a suspect. My mistake. Besides, I want to drop by the mill and see your boss, make things right with him. You shouldn't be blamed for what wasn't your fault."

Albert gave in. "Well, thanks Sheriff. That's real nice of you. That job means a lot to me right now. Jobs don't grow on trees, not for ex-cons."

Lud busied himself with paperwork at his desk until Albert had finished his coffee. Rising, the sheriff said, "We'd better get going. It's getting late. Don't guess I have to tell you not to leave town till this is all cleared up."

Albert nodded. "You don't have to worry about that, Sheriff. You can always find me at home, at work, or at Brown's Tavern."

After returning Albert's personal belongings, Lud hustled him out to the patrol car. Albert looked as if he were having second thoughts as Lud climbed into the car. The logger had been avoiding him ever since Lud had been elected sheriff, and he knew why.

He had hated Albert when they were in school, especially in the lower grades. Lud saw that Albert was going to get in the back seat. "No, buddy," Lud said. "Get up here in the passenger seat with me, this is just a social ride."

Albert climbed in. It was all Lud could do to be social to him. *The bastard used to lay for me on my way home, cornering me once every week or two and beating the hell out of me. The son of a bitch had always made a point of tearing my few clothes, knowing there would be a fresh patch later to point out to the other guys for a good laugh.*

Five minutes after passing through Pine Ridge, Lud abruptly slowed the patrol car and turned off into a narrow lane, more dirt than gravel, that plunged into a thick stand of timber. "Shortcut," he explained, glancing at Albert. "I found it one day when I got lost out here. It runs up to Peddler's Point and then cuts straight across toward your place."

Albert seemed apprehensive. "Don't go to any extra trouble for me. I ain't got nothing I have to do."

"No trouble. Besides, I want to catch your boss before he leaves work."

The neglected road snaked through a quiet world of filtered green light. Albert swallowed hard and turned to look out the window, but said nothing.

The car bumped along the old logging road until they reached a second one that appeared a twin of the first, splitting off to the right. Lud maneuvered onto this second right-of-way and within five minutes had turned twice more. He nodded toward the track stretching ahead of them. "I figure we save damn near eight miles coming this way."

"May be shorter, Sheriff, but are you sure it's any faster? I've lived here all my life and I ain't never been on these roads."

Lud had no answer for that. The maze of neglected byways were all that remained of a long ago logging operation. With the passing years, the forest was slowly erasing the scars with a small pine tree occasionally gaining a foothold in the tracks. Soon the labyrinth of logging roads would be obliterated.

Lud was slowing to traverse a series of deep corrugations in the lane's surface when his world came apart. Color drained out of the green woods around him as if someone had pulled a plug, leaving his surroundings a shimmering mass of gray vague shapes. Pain lanced through his skull, and he cried out in anguish.

Albert whirled toward him. "What is it? What the hell's wrong, Sheriff?"

The pain slowly receded, and color flooded back into the world as quickly as it had disappeared. Lud, avoiding his gaze, muttered, "Nothing. Something flew into my eye, that's all. It must have blown in the window."

Lud's jaw tightened. *Thank God I didn't pass out. At first, that was all my spells had been, the incredible pain in my head and then the vision misting over. Not like the other thing that was happening now, the losing time. It's like I'm unconscious and don't realize it. The very first time, I had lost about two minutes. So minuscule I wasn't even sure. But over the last two weeks or so of the black outs, I'm having periods of up to two hours that I can't account for.*

He glanced covertly at Albert. *What would have happened just now if I had blacked out? Would I have piled into a tree? Dammit! My spells have never happened before with anyone around. I have to hurry and get the logger home before the next one comes on. If the bastard sees me while I'm out on my feet, he will tell everybody in Pine Ridge.*

Suddenly everything seemed clear, and the panic ebbed. He relaxed. He exhaled slowly. *Everything's okay.* Lud risked another glance at Albert. He was slumped back in the seat. *Better get him thinking about something else.*

Lud grinned. "Hey, buddy-boy, you ought to come to the reunion this weekend. As I remember it, when we were in high school several of the gals used to have a twinkle in their eyes when you were around. I wanted to ask you what your secret was, but I figured you might beat the hell out of me again."

Seeing Albert's eyes narrow, he knew he had made a mistake. Winking, he said, "Hell, it's a joke, man, I was just kidding. I mean, about the beatings you gave me. You turned out to be a pretty nice guy by the time I graduated. Matter of—"

Someway Lud's vision shifted, and Albert became a vague gray figure. He shook his head, trying futilely to clear his vision. "Watch out! You're gonna hit that goddamn tree!" Albert cried.

Lud's vision cleared just in time to swerve back onto the track through a cluster of two-foot high pine seedlings.

"Jesus, Lud, what's wrong with you?" Albert shouted.

Lud, avoiding his eyes, muttered, "Sleepy, I guess. Haven't been resting very good. With two deputies off, been pulling double shifts."

Why in the name of God did I offer to give Albert a ride home? I've got a bad spell coming on sure as hell.

They were coming out of the grove of trees into the small cleared area that marked Peddler's Point. Albert, leaning out the car window and peering downward into the gorge, bare yards from the edge on the track, said, "Jesus, Lud, it's a long way down there. Looks more like a thousand feet than five hundred. Those damn trees alongside Deer Creek seem like match sticks from up here.

"You feel okay? If you ain't, I'll sure drive. Hell, if we went over the edge, they might never find the car, tall and thick as that brush is alongside the creek."

"Think I'll stop for a minute," Lud muttered, "Get a breath of air."

Relieved that he had reached a place he could stop for a few minutes, Lud turned to look into the emptiness above the gorge. The next instant, the pain exploded in his head. In a last moment of consciousness, he slammed on the brakes.

Albert, unprepared, pitched forward, striking his head on the edge of the windshield frame. He cried out, holding his forehead with both hands. "Jesus, what in the—"

CHAPTER 10

Chief Looking Glass blinked several times, trying to sort through his confusion. The magic was about him again, possessing him. He was wearing the garments of the white man. The clothes were becoming familiar to him now. The stirring next to him sent a thrill of alarm through him. His hand, clawing at his hip, found the leather holster with the white man's gun.

His vision clearing, he saw that he shared the ponyless coach with a bearded man. Looking Glass brought the gun up just as the man looked up at him, his eyes widening.

Looking Glass said, "Get out, you son of a snake! Prepare to sing your song." His mind fuzzy, an uncertainty gripped him. The magic was still clouding his mind.

Albert, white-faced, fumbling for the door handle, cried, "Song? What the hell are you talking about, Lud? What are you doing, pointing that goddamn gun at me?"

His tone harsher, Looking Glass ordered, "Get out!"

Albert, his voice rising in pitch, cried, "Hell no, I ain't getting out. Not till I know what you intend to do."

Looking Glass spat into his face. "Are you a woman? Stand under the sky and die as a warrior." He brought the revolver up to where its sight was centered between Albert's eyes. "Make your choice."

Crying, "Don't shoot, for God's sake!," Albert pushed open the door. But in his haste to get out, his foot caught on the underpinnings of the seat, and he sprawled out onto the damp ground. In one continuing motion, he thrust his arms under him, and pushed himself upright, scrambling to his feet. The motion of his eyes, quick and darting, examined the tree-lined perimeter of the clearing.

Looking Glass motioned with the gun. "Move around to the front of the coach, rest your hands on the hood, and then take two steps backwards." *Hood? The strange word is from another place. It just came to my mouth.* His mind reeled.

When Albert hesitated, Looking Glass shouted, "Now, son of the snake!" Looking Glass was sweating so profusely that the drops ran down his face like rain. "Do as I tell you or you'll die without time for your song."

Sliding out of the car, Looking Glass stooped and ran his hand under the seat. His fingers closed on the handle of the long knife, a ceremonial blade used by Nez Perce chiefs in the days when they owned the land. He shoved the knife in under the belt of his pants at his back and walked around to where he stood behind the pale-faced Albert, the gun still in his hand, pointed at the logger's midriff.

Albert looked back over his shoulder, his words hard to understand now because of his rapid breathing. "Listen, Lud, don't do this. Sure, I used to pick on you, beat your ass every chance I got. Okay. It was wrong. It ain't worth killing me for." He swallowed noisily. "Okay. Pistol whip me. Knock some teeth out. I won't tell nobody. I'll say I had an accident. But for God's sake, don't kill me! That's crazy, Lud, just crazy."

Looking Glass gave a shrill cry of derision. The words of a squaw. He spat onto the ground. "Where is your heart? Be a warrior. Go to the dark land beyond with the blood of the brave in your heart. Dishonor your father no more with your words."

Albert turned to say something more, but Looking Glass, seizing his neck, slammed him down against the hood.

"Goddamn you, Lud!" Albert cried. "You put that gun away, and I'll show you who's a frigging woman. I Always could whip that ass of yours, and I can still do it. Give me a chance, and I'll beat the shit out of you, You're a—"

Looking Glass drove the long-bladed knife into Albert's heart from the back. The logger gave a sharp gasp and fell apart at the joints, collapsing into a heap beneath the car's front bumper. Looking Glass had rolled up the sleeves of the white man's garment so the blood of the coward would only splatter where he could wash it off.

For one long moment, Looking Glass stared in silent contemplation at the fallen man from whose back protruded the handle of the ceremonial knife. Then he stepped back, tilting his face skyward, his arms raised above his head. Chanting, he asked the Great Spirit to witness his triumphs and the defeat of his enemies to note one more fallen foe.

His prayers completed, he returned to the fallen Albert. Placing his foot on the dead man's back, he seized the dagger's grip with both hands. Grunting with the effort, he drew it clear of the body and wiped it on the sparse grass.

Sliding his hands under Albert's arms, he backed toward the cliff, dragging the body. He worked at the corpse until it teetered on the edge of the rocks, and then, with a hard shove, sent it over the edge. The canyon wall at Peddler's Point was so sheer that the body hit but twice on the way down. With a second impact, it bounded far enough out from the wall to crash through the heavy brush beside the stream, no longer in sight.

Moving swiftly, Looking Glass cut a small branch from one of the pines and used it to sweep needles and dirt across the dark pool of blood beneath the bumper and the straggling trail of it that led to the canyon's edge. The branch vanished as the body had over the sheer drop. Hurrying back to the car, he slipped the knife under the seat. He then bent to a clump of dried grass to vigorously rid hand and arm of the traces of the cowards blood.

Sliding into the car, he started the motor.

An hour later, the patrol car slid to a stop in front of the house. Looking Glass bounded up the porch steps and into the cabin, sweat pouring from his face again. Once inside, he ripped off the sweat soaked shirt and tossed it to the floor. Crossing to the bathroom he washed the remaining stains of blood from his hands. Quickly moving to the cabinet containing the compound bow, he extracted an old fashioned iron key from behind the quiver.

Unlocking the door to Lud's mother's bedroom, he stepped inside. One corner was filled by the woman's unmade bed, subdued now with the dust that had settled onto it since that day, years ago, when she had left it to commit suicide. At the center of the room, facing Looking Glass, was the old dresser, a three by four oil painting, done by a Seattle artist from the photograph of Running Fawn, Lud's mother, was leaning up against the high backed mirror. On the bureau top, flanking the portrait, were two candlesticks holding long white tapers.

Looking Glass crossed the room with a measured stride, lit the candles, and sank onto a pad of folded Indian blankets facing the portrait. Beside the dresser lay the expensive but stained clothing that had been Amy Housley's. Her black purse sat beside the garments.

Looking Glass's fierce black eyes stared at the woman in the portrait. His voice was low. "Walk proud, Princess Running Fawn. The one whose blood flowed in your veins, Looking Glass, has counted the first coup. The first of the bitches who took your life has gone to the world of darkness, her body shamed with the seed of her enemy, her head offered for the face she took from you. The warrior in whose footsteps you followed will take no rest until the other three join her. Both sun and moon will light the untiring hand that will strike down your foes."

Bowing his head, he began to chant, a dirge that lasted several minutes. Finally rising, he lifted his hands, palms upward, above his head. Turning, he quickly left the room, locking the door behind him. Crossing to the cabinet he replaced the key.

The pain struck with the force of a buffalo lance driven into his head. Crying out, he reeled across the room and collapsed onto the bed. Pawing at his pocket, he pulled out the vial of pain pills and shoved two into his mouth. Looking Glass slumped back, flat on the bed. A momentary panic gripped him as the room faded from view.

Lud bolted upright. *What the hell? Where am I? The car…I'm not in the car!* The last of the gray mist drifted away, and he knew. *What the hell am I doing on my bed? Jesus, I blacked out again!* His confused mind wavered, and he tried to remember. *I was at…* He blinked and tried to focus. *Peddler's Point with…* He closed his eyes and sank back on the bed. *Oh, Christ, I was taking Martinson home.*

In his agitation, Lud swung his legs off the bed and stared at his image in the mirror across the room. *Jesus, now what? Where is my damn shirt, my uniform blouse?* His gaze swept the room. He spoke aloud. "The goddamn blouse isn't here."

Clambering off the bed, he lumbered back into the living room, still shaky. There it was in the middle of the floor. "What the hell! I'm tired, yeah, but to take off a fifty-dollar shirt and just throw it on the floor." *Christ, am I losing my mind is that part of this damn brain thing.*

The patrol car! Did I drive it home? Grabbing the shirt, he rushed to the front window and peered out. The unit was there, where he always parked it. But the woods were full of shadows. *What the hell time is it?* He glanced at his watch. *My God, I've been out cold for better than two hours.*

"Albert! I have to see the bastard." *Christ, where the hell would he be? What did the damn guy do after I passed out? I have to get to him, put the squeeze on him before Albert starts shooting off his mouth around town.*

Glancing at his watch again, he said, "Shit!" *Ralph is going to have to do a little more overtime, like it or not.* Dashing out the door, he put on the blouse and climbed into the car.

The patrol car sped down the track, flinging sprays of mud and water against the nearby trees. Lud's mind raced. *Where is Albert? Could he have driven me home, carried me inside, and put me on the bed? If that is what happened, where did he go after that? Hitchhiked home? That sure don't sound like something he would do. Use the radio and call the office?* Lud shook his head. *Man, if he done that, my damn sheriffing is over.*

Once on the highway, he thumbed the mike to the radio. "Unit one to base." Ralph's voice burst through the fine fuzz of static. "Yeah, Sheriff, what's up?"

Ralph sounds like everything's normal. Lud spoke into the mike, "Ralph, give Albert Martinson a call on the land line. See if he's still home. Something I forgot to ask him."

The deputy seemed cheerful enough, despite my being late for his relief. "Sure thing, Sheriff. Get right back to you. Out."

When he came back on the air five minutes later, he said, "Nope, not there, Sheriff. I let it ring fifteen times."

Lud sighed. *Christ! I can't let it go at that. Albert might be outside with that milk cow of his. I'm going to have to check his place.*

Thumbing the mike again, Lud said, "Ralph, I'm gonna be a little later. I noticed a strange car parked down below the Ludlow place. I won't be happy unless I check it out."

The last of the daylight was almost gone when he climbed out of the car in front of Albert's house. The place was dark. *Son of a bitch, gone to the tavern already. I'll stop by there on my way to relieve Ralph. And hope to hell, I can catch the bastard before he has the story of my passing out, from one end of Pine Ridge to the other...*

CHAPTER 11

The knock at the door drew Sheila's attention away from the Crescent Valley newspaper she was reading. "Yes?" she called.

A female voice, muffled by the solid door, answered, "I'm a Playboy Magazine representative. We want to do a spread on Pine Ridge High School prom queens. You think this little jerkwater town can stand that kind of publicity?"

Letting the newspaper fall, Sheila shrieked, "Pat! Pat Cromwell!" and rushed to the door. She yanked open the door, and a short, auburn-haired woman seized her in an embrace that left Sheila gasping for breath.

Releasing her, Pat stepped back, laughing, her green eyes dancing. "Sheila! My God, you look great. Better than ever."

Grabbing her hand, Sheila pulled Pat into her room. "You should talk. I swear, Pat, I wouldn't have recognized you. That hairdo, I'd like to take your hairdresser home with me."

Pulling free, Pat sank into a chair and said, "What a day! I had car trouble before I had gone ten miles. Lost one of the fan belts."

Jumping up, she slipped her arm around Sheila's waist. "I couldn't believe it when the manager said you were in room twenty. I came up early because I wanted to visit my grandfather. You remember Gramps.

"What's the word, kid? Why did you arrive early?" Her hand flew to her mouth and she giggled. "Oh, my God, that's right. Dain's still here from his parent's funeral. Maybe I'd better go. Wouldn't want to throw a monkey wrench into a little pre-reunion hanky-panky."

Sheila realized that Pat had not heard about Amy. She motioned toward the sofa. "I think you'd better sit down. Something bad has happened."

Pat's usually ebullient face altered as Sheila told her what little they knew about Amy's death. As she continued her story, mentioning the invitation she had received with the incorrect date and the probability that another bogus invitation had drawn Amy to town early, Pat's now solemn face showed signs of strain. "Oh, my God, Sheila. What night were we supposed to be here?"

When Sheila told her, Pat's voice was little more than a whisper. "My invitation is for tomorrow night." Shuddering she hugged herself. "What are you telling me, Sheila? Are you saying someone intended to get us up here early to kill us?"

Sheila sank down on the sofa next to Pat and seized one cold hand between hers. "It's horrible, I know. But it's okay. Dain and Lud, did you know he's the sheriff now? Anyway they are watching out for us. They're going to keep an eye on the motel all night."

Pat seemed startled. "Lud? He's the sheriff here?" She shook her head. "I'm not sure knowing that makes me feel any better."

Sheila squeezed her hand. "I know. I thought the same thing when I heard. But Dain says he's changed. He says Lud is a good lawman. People around here really respect him."

"Have you seen him, Sheila?" Pat asked. "You think he's forgiven us…for what happened?"

Releasing Pat's hand, Sheila sat back and closed her eyes. After a moment she said, "Who knows. With my guilty conscience, I can't judge what he thinks. After all these years, I still see the expression on that poor woman's face when she realized we were going to hit her. Why didn't I make Amy get in the back seat? I knew the three of you were too tipsy to be out in that car, especially with so little driving experience." Her eyelids flew open. "Oh, jeez, let's talk about something else, for goodness sake. I can't stand to think about it."

Pat straightened up, a big smile illuminating her face. This was the Pat she remembered, changing moods like a strobe light. "What was that Dain you let casually slip? Have you seen our handsome Mr. Barlow? How does he look after all these years? I can't see him losing his hair or getting a pot belly like the slobs who come on to me. Tell me he's not like that."

Sheila giggled. "God, Pat, the way you talk! But, yes, I have seen our Mr. Barlow, and no, he hasn't gone to pot. He looks just as good as he ever did, maybe even better with a little mileage added. He can still make the pulse rate go up when he smiles at you, or at least mine. It was great seeing him again, but," she frowned, biting her lip a moment before adding, "but then we went to Kenn's for lunch, it's a new place since I was here last. Guess who was there?"

She didn't pause for an answer. "Candy Burns. She's working there as a waitress, that little…slut. She really had a ball, all smiles, but smirking at me at the same time." Her temper began to show. "Dear little Candy had a great time, laughing in my face."

Pat protested, "Wait a minute, Sheila. There's something you don't know. I started to write you, but with you being married and all, I thought better of it. When I was here three years ago, right after my grandmother died, I had a talk with Candy's used to be best girlfriend. You remember Betty Schuller? She told me what happened that day between Candy, Dain, and her."

Sheila came off the sofa and turned to Pat. "I don't want to hear it. I mean, it's still a sore point."

"Dammit, just listen. Betty and Candy have been on the outs the last five years. She—"

Sheila interrupted, "How can you believe anything that piece of trash says? She was in on it, too."

Pat glared at her. "Sheila, shut up! You're going to listen. What Betty told me doesn't make her look like any fairy princess, and I believe her. You've been too hard on Dain. He wasn't responsible for what happened. Candy and Betty caught him unloading hay in the barn when his folks were gone. The poor boy didn't even know they were there."

Sheila settled onto the edge of the bed, watching impatiently as Pat paused, slipped off her shoes, tucked her feet under her, and leaned back in the curve of the sofa. *Vintage Pat. She had always loved to keep people on tenterhooks once she had their attention.*

Pat continued, "Betty said Candy found out that he was there alone. It was her idea that they go and give him a hard time. Candy was the ring leader. Betty just trailed around after her, a sort of a go-fer. You remember that."

Sheila still wanted to stop her but couldn't, she might as well let Pat say what she had to say.

"After they entered the orchard, Candy removed her panties and left them on a tree branch. She was wearing a miniskirt. You remember, that's all she ever wore. Every guy in town would give her the eye, even the ones on Social Security. It was so embarrassing, watching her strut around wearing those tight T-shirts. She looked like a teenage Dolly Parton in heat."

Sheila's anger threatened to bubble up again. "Dain didn't have to look. I always thought he had more character than that."

Pat exploded into laughter, and Sheila bridled. "Stop that, Pat. He said he loved me. He should have told her to get out, that he wanted nothing to do with trash like her."

Pat shook her head. "Sheila, Sheila, Sheila. The guy was just seventeen. Heck, Candy had been fooling around with grown men since she was fourteen. Poor Dain was just a babe in arms. Betty swore she wanted to split when she saw what Candy had in mind, but it was too late."

Sheila protested, "But can't you understand how it was with me? How humiliating it was? Everyone knew. They were all watching me out of the corner of their eyes. I was so embarrassed I never wanted to see him again. I cried all night after I found out."

"She sprang off the bed. "I don't care what you say, Pat. The thought of it still makes me mad. He could have walked away. I know it."

"Sheila, grow up! That all happened fourteen years ago. You were both kids. Give the guy a break, for goodness sake. He must still have the hots for you. He's never married, and I've gotta believe a lot of gals have tried to hook him."

Sheila bit her lip. "You think so?"

Pat nodded with a smile. "You bet—"

They jumped at the noise.

Somewhere outside the motel room's second door, the one that opened onto the alley running behind the building, what sounded like an empty tin can had struck the paving with a metallic clatter and rolled a few feet.

The talk of Dain forgotten, silent, they stared first at the door and then their gazes moved upward to the glass panes of the transom over the door. The small drape that shielded the transom had been pulled back, exposing three squares of night sky.

"My God, what was that?" Sheila whispered.

Pat put a finger to her lips as she slid her feet into her shoes. Reaching for her purse, she slipped her hand in and extracted a small Lady Smith and Wesson revolver.

Sheila, wide-eyed, whispered, "A gun? My gosh, Pat. Be careful. It might go off."

Pat smirked. "It's every girl's best friend when you live in San Francisco. Come on. We need to check this out."

Sheila remained where she was. "It was probably just a dog, rummaging in the garbage."

"Yeah. A dog or a peeping tom or the bastard who killed Amy. You can stay here, but I'm going to find out what's out there." She tiptoed across the room to the door, unlocked it, and flung it open.

Sheila, realizing she was about to be left alone, charged after her.

Light spilled out from the room to reveal a diet cola can on the asphalt paving about two feet away. Cautiously stepping outside, they glanced up and down the alley. The paved passageway, which ran the full length of the motel's rear, was bordered on its far side by a head-high concrete block wall. A large trash bin stood across the alley next to the fence, but the alleyway was deserted.

Pat shrugged. "Nothing but a pop can. I guess our nerves are on edge."

Shepherding Sheila ahead of her, she stepped back into the motel room and locked the door.

Slipping the revolver back into her purse, she said, "Probably a rat or even a raccoon burrowing around in the trash. Lots of those in this country."

Muttering an apology, Sheila brushed past her and drew the narrow drape over the transom windows. "I guess I'm being silly, but this business with Amy and those invitations, I'm getting scared, and I don't mind admitting it. Would you think I'm acting like a baby if I ask you to stay in my room tonight and maybe till the reunion's over? I mean, perhaps they can move another bed in here. I don't think I can stand to be alone."

Pat nodded, smiling ruefully. "Sounds like a great idea. I wasn't too happy about being alone either, not after hearing about Amy."

Seated on the sofa again, they soon relaxed, rehashing, as old classmates will do, their shared good times in growing up.

Something heavy struck the wall immediately behind the sofa. Sheila frowned. "Just what we need. Noisy neighbors next—"

Seeing the look on Pat's face, the words stuck in her throat. "What's wrong?" she blurted out.

"No noisy neighbors." Pat's voice dropped to a whisper. "That's my room. There shouldn't be anyone in there."

CHAPTER 12

Sheila and Pat stared at each other, eyes wide.

Sheila, her voice low, strained, asked, "Could your suitcase have fallen against the wall?"

Pat shook her head, "I set it down by the bed. Then I checked the alley door to see if it was locked, went potty, and hurried on over here to see if you were in." Rising, she stared at the wall. "Lot of these motel's walls are pretty thin. Maybe there's a water pipe in the wall, knocking. You've heard them do that."

"You think so?"

Pat frowned. "Just one way to find out." She started for the door.

A scraping against the far side of the wall and Sheila's tiny squeal stopped her in her tracks.

In two quick steps, Sheila had Pat by the arm, dragging her backwards. "Don't go out there, for gosh sake. I'll call the manager. Let him find out what's going on."

Pat resisted the pressure for a moment, then relaxed. "You're right. And tell him to hurry. "We'll—, oh, my God, the door!" She lunged toward it, and it took the terrified Sheila a moment to realize that she was throwing the dead bolt. Pat rested her back against the door, puffed out her cheeks, and said, "It's going to stay that way until that manager knocks on the door and identifies himself."

A rattled Sheila seized the phone. Her fingers trembling, she had to try twice before being connected with the office. When a male voice answered, Sheila demanded, "Are you the manager? I, we're in Room 20. There's a prowler. Come quick!"

She slammed down the phone, cutting off the request for more information.

Sheila said nothing to Pat, who had moved away from the door, staring silently at it, listening.

The two or three minutes seemed to last forever before they heard shuffling footsteps approaching on the concrete walk. The cry of alarm lasted but a split second, followed by a heavy blow against the exterior wall of the motel that rattled the front window of Sheila's room. The silence that followed was absolute except for the sound of traffic on the street in front of the motel.

Sheila's hands balled into fists, her nails digging into her palms as the silence dragged on.

"What the hell is going on?" Pat cried. Grabbing her purse, she lunged for the door, threw back the dead bolt, and opened it.

Sheila grabbed for her arm and missed. "Wait! Don't go out there!"

Ignoring her, Pat vanished through the doorway. Sheila, rushing after her, crashed into her friend, who stood, unmoving, on the sidewalk, gaping at a motionless form some ten feet away. Sheila saw immediately what was wrong.

The elderly motel manager was sprawled on the sidewalk, a long cut on his forehead bleeding.

They started toward the fallen man, but Sheila grabbed Pat's arm again, pointing to the adjacent doorway. "Look! Isn't that your room? The door's open."

The unconscious manager forgotten for the moment, Pat started toward her room, then flattened herself against the wall next to the door.

"What's wrong?" Sheila demanded.

"The lights are out. I could swear I left them on."

Sheila eyed the darkness beyond the partly open door, vaguely aware that Pat was reaching into her purse. She had no time to protest as Pat, gun in hand, kicked open the door. Reaching inside, she flipped on the light switch.

No one was in the room, but a cool breeze wafted through the back door, which stood wide open, revealing a night-filled alley.

Rushing past the bed, she paused in the doorway, leaning out to scan the alley in both directions. "Nothing out there." Slamming the door shut, she locked it and crossed to the bathroom. Flipping the light switch, she peered inside before declaring, "All clear."

Turning, she surveyed her surroundings. "My suitcase has been moved. That's what we heard hit the wall."

Sheila's hand flew up to her cheek. "Oh, my gosh! That poor man! I forgot. He may be dead." Whirling, she disappeared out the door.

In the dim light from the fixtures outside each motel room door, she saw a man kneeling beside the prostrate manager. Sheila screamed.

A moment later Pat smashed into her, knocking her off the sidewalk onto the paving of the parking lot. The gun hit the concrete with a solid metallic clank. Pat's snarling, "Dammit to hell!" was overridden by a loud male voice, shouting, "Hey, it's me!"

A thoroughly shaken Sheila regained control of her senses. The man crouching by the body, rising now, was Dain Barlow. Pat, still confused, was scrambling for the gun.

"Goddammit, Pat, leave that gun alone!" Dain shouted. "What in the name of hell's going on here?"

Pat slumped against the wall. "God, I just lost ten years off my life. We heard someone in my room, and—"

Sheila was trying to talk at the same time.

Dain held up his hands, and roared, "Hold it! One at a time. Please. You tell it, Pat."

"I'd gone into Sheila's room to visit, and we heard a—"

"Can't we do that later?' Sheila cried. "This poor guy looks like he's hurt bad."

Calling attention to him seemed to rouse the fallen manager. Groaning, his eyes opened and he raised his head. Dain was back on his knees beside him in an instant. "Easy, old-timer. Don't move. I'm a cop." He glanced over his shoulder at Pat. "Those room phones probably go to a switchboard that he operates, so they would be useless. Run in the office and use their phone. Call an ambulance and then notify the sheriff's office."

Pat hurried toward the office.

Despite Dain's admonition, the motel manager pushed himself into an upright position. Wiping at the bloody cut in his forehead, he mumbled, "Boy, am I dizzy. I feel like I've been kicked in the head by a horse. Stomach's a little queasy, too."

Dain, putting his hand on his shoulder, said, "Take it easy, friend. The ambulance is on its way. Just sit there till it comes."

The gray-faced man, licking his dry lips, looked up at Dain. "I'm okay, I think." He blinked his eyes. "Just woozy as hell. What happened?"

"I was hoping you could tell me," Dain said.

He slowly shook his head. "A dark figure plunged out of the shadows, then nothing."

Sheila tapped his shoulder. "I think I hear the siren. That was quick."

"Should be," the manager muttered. "The hospital's just four blocks away."

Minutes later, while the medics were loading Harry Blackwell, the manager, into the back of the ambulance with him protesting every step of the way, Sheila told Dain about the noises from the alley and from Pat's room.

He stopped one of the medics as the man was closing the ambulance door. Leaning in, he asked the manager, "Sir, where do you keep the extra room keys? Apparently, somebody entered one lady's room."

The old-timer, feeling better by the moment, glared at him, "Probably the same guy who ran me down, but he couldn't have had a key, unless he got one of the ladies keys. Every guest gets two keys to their room, whether they are alone or not." As he talked, he was struggling to extract something from his jacket pocket. Bringing a ring of keys into view, he said, "Here's the set we keep in the office, in the desk drawer. I grabbed them when those ladies called me. See, here are their room keys, twenty and twenty-one."

He fumbled with the keys, separating the bunch of them in the middle. Frowning, he glanced at the space between the separated keys. Bringing them closer to his eyes, the manager slipped the keys around the ring, one by one, studying the number inscribed on each.

"What's the matter?" Dain asked.

"I…Damnedest thing! Those keys are missing. Twenty and twenty-one are not on the ring. Some son of a bitch—" He stopped abruptly. Lowering his voice, he said, "Officer, I don't want to scare those little ladies, but somebody stole those two keys. I'd better notify the owner."

He struggled to rise, but the medic pushed him back flat.

"Don't worry," Dain said. "I'll take care of everything." Backing away, he slammed the ambulance door before Blackwell became further upset.

Pat, who had been talking to another of the motel's patrons, joined them as the ambulance glided out of the parking lot and onto the street. Turning, they started back toward Sheila's room. Pat stopped abruptly.

Looking at sheila, she said, "I didn't think you closed the door when you left your room." Her voice was so shrill that Sheila wouldn't have recognized it had she heard it on the phone.

Staring at her friend, then the closed door, Sheila reached for Dain's arm. "I…I didn't. I'm sure I didn't. And look. There's no light around the edge of the drapes. It's dark in there. I left the lights on. Oh, God! Dain, quick, let's get out of here."

Pulling free of her grip on his shirt, he said, "Don't be silly. You girls get back." Drawing his snub-nose thirty-eight from the waist holster concealed under his jacket, he said, "Give me your key, Sheila."

Her face fell. "Oh, no, it's in my purse. I left it in the room."

Dain's "Shit!" was said so softly Sheila wasn't sure that was what he said.

Crouching, he tiptoed to the door and gently settled his hand onto the knob. He looked surprised when it yielded under his touch.

Dain exploded into action. Slamming the door back against the wall, the light came on to reveal him on one knee, the gun held straight before him. From where Sheila stood, the room looked unoccupied. He clambered to his feet and plunged into the bathroom.

A couple of seconds later, he was back out into the room, still crouched low, moving toward the now wide open door at the back of the unit. Dain paused a moment at the doorway and then burst out into the alley. A long half-minute passed with Sheila and Pat huddled together, still on the walk out front. Dain came back into view, his hands empty now. He slammed the rear door shut and locked it before calling, "Come on in, ladies, and close the door."

Sheila felt a flutter of relief and then saw her purse. The bag lay open on the sofa, its contents; lipstick, cosmetics, key ring, billfold, pen and all the other junk she had accumulated since the last time she cleaned it out, scattered over the cushion.

Blushing, she moved toward the sofa, embarrassed somehow for Dain to see all the junk. While, behind her, Dain was checking Pat's gun for damage, she worked at sweeping the mess back into her purse. She was glancing back over her shoulder at them when her fingers encountered an object that felt strange. The sudden sensation of something long, cold, and slender caught her attention. *The thing felt like a—*

Sheila screamed.

The room spun, and she sank to the floor on nerveless legs. Her hand released the object, which bounced on the cushion, rolling free of the purse's other contents. She could not take her gaze from it.

The unflawed red of the fingernail contrasted with the bluish tinge of the puffy flesh. Tiny glints of green fire from the emerald ring touched her eyes with their sharp caress.

Dain cried, "Pat, don't look," but he was too late.

Pat said, "That's Amy's ring. Sheila has—" She shrieked. "God! God! That's a finger! It's Amy's finger."

Sheila became aware of the scuffle behind her.

Pat, gasping, cried, "Let me go! Let me go! Goddamn you! How did Sheila—"

"Listen to me!" Dain shouted. "Her finger was missing when we found her. Whoever killed her cut it off."

Pat suddenly calmer, asked, "You mean he killed her for the ring?"

Her question broke the fascination the dreadful bit of flesh held for Sheila, She managed to scramble to her feet, crying, "No. Don't you see? He's insane. He left the finger here so we'd know who it was. He was telling us he could get to us anytime he wanted. The killer was here in our rooms!"

In the silence of her pronouncement, they heard cans clinking together out back.

Dain raced for the door, shouting, "I'll get the son of a bitch!"

In the out fall of light from the room, Sheila saw him careen to a stop, pawing at his belt holster.

CHAPTER 13

Lud stared open-mouthed at the man who had popped out of the motel. *Jesus Christ! Dain!* He noticed his extended arm. *A gun!*

Lud shouted, "It's me, Lud! Careful with that gun!"

Lowering his arm, Dain peered into the darkness. "Lud? What the hell are you doing here? Christ, am I glad to see you!" He hurried down the alley.

"You sure have a funny way of showing it," Lud said. "What the hell are you doing out here waving that gun around? Thought you were going back up to Pine Ridge."

Gripping Lud's arm, Dain walked him back down to the mouth of the alley. Lud teetered on the edge of panic as Dain explained what had happened in the motel room.

Frowning Lud thought, *Christ, I can't go on like this, however, the reunion is but three days away. I have to make it just three more days. Things are getting worse though, another goddamn blackout.*

Lud had found himself in the alley, not knowing how the hell he had gotten here. Staring at Dain, hearing little of what he was saying, he tried to remember. *I stopped at one of the local hamburger joints for a bite to eat and…yeah, I remember getting back into the car. I started to check the motel.* The frown deepened. *Then what, goddammit? Christ, it looks as if I keep on functioning while I'm blacked out. How the hell else could I be here now, checking on Sheila Greene?*

Dain had quit talking and was staring at him.

"Sorry," Lud muttered. "Let's go talk with the gals."

Grinning, Dain said, "That would have made a hell of a story, wouldn't it? Two cops blowing each other away in an alley." The smile disappearing, he added, "It's my fault. I shouldn't be here, but I got antsy. I didn't have anything to do, so I thought, what the hell, I'll drive back down to Crescent Valley and see if Sheila is still upset with me."

They entered the motel room to discover Sheila perched on the edge of the desk chair and Pat sitting on the bed, facing the door, her purse in her lap. Once they had greeted Lud, they both started to talk at once, frantic with the need to let him know what had happened in the motel. The smile with which Lud had greeted them faded as the jumble of words continued with the two women's voices rising as they tried to out talk each other.

Finally, he raised his arm, yelling, "Okay ladies, I think I get the picture."

He frowned. "Should have started the damn checks when I first came on duty, the son of a bitch is everywhere."

Lud, to hide his frustration, made a great show of peering out into the alley. Then he locked the back door and straightened the curtain over the transom before apologizing for not having started his surveillance earlier. Watching Pat's face, Lud sensed that nothing he was going to say or do would make her happy. *Can't blame her, not much of a welcome back home for the ladies.*

He motioned with his head toward Pat's purse. "Be careful with that gun you're carrying. With the doors locked, and the telephone by your bed, and Dain and I outside on guard I don't think you'll have any need for it. But if you do, make damn sure you know what you're shooting at."

Before Pat could remonstrate, he said, "Come on, buddy. Let's let these ladies get some sleep." Seizing Dain's arm, he hustled him out the door onto the sidewalk. Behind them, he knew the door was locked, but it was rendered useless by the two missing room keys.

*   *   *

A cover of high clouds concealed the near full moon from view, but yielded enough light that the car in the pasture was visible in every detail, even the black and gold stenciling that identified it as a sheriff's unit. The same night light revealed where the car had torn out a section of the barbed wire fence as it swerved off the highway and plowed into the field. The vehicle had been there long enough that the staccato pops of the cooling engine had died away some time ago.

Hard to see in the car's dim interior, the driver was slumped forward against the steering wheel as if asleep. But the eyes staring through the windshield were wide open, unmoving, catching the outside light in such a way that they glittered with a startling brightness.

The driver stirred. His black eyes blinked, then he moved slow and saw the car was stopped. He looked around. *The ponyless coach had darted off the path. Not like a Nez Perce war pony that could stay the course even when a warrior looked away.*

Shifting his head, he glanced down at the car's floor. The ceremonial knife, barely visible in the dimness, had slid from under the seat and lay at his feet. The sight of it sent a surge of anger through him.

He scowled. *The rich bitch, Sheila. The steel would carve her flesh before the moon had gone to rest as it had that of Amy, the tall one. Amy had owned the ponyless coach that had destroyed Running Fawn, so she died first. The slut Sheila had driven it, she must go to the dark world second. Only then would the knife's sharp edge open the throats of the other two. They had taken the life of Running Fawn. They had dared to kill a women of the Nez Perce in whose body flowed the blood of chiefs. The four would serve her as slaves in the spirit world.*

With the witches dead, the magic that holds my blood brother Dain enthralled will disappear. His eyes will be clear again, and he will join his brother on the path of warriors.

Looking Glass glanced at the sky. The night was fleeing quickly now, chased by the father sun. *Sheila! I must find her now, kill her, bring honor to Running Fawn and her people. I will humiliate the bitch, strip her and use her as I would a common slut. She shall die filled with the seed of her enemy.*

Looking Glass's loins stirred with the thought. *Thus humiliated, I will take her head and cast it away. Like Amy, she will wander the spirit world forever without sight, without hearing, in a land twice dark for her.*

Slipping the knife back under the seat, he glanced again toward the night sky. But all he saw was the vast dark cloud sweeping down on him, blotting out the world.

Lud shot upright in the seat, striking his head on the roof. The squawking of the police radio shattered the quiet of the darkened car's interior. "Unit one, unit one. Come in, unit one."

"Unit one. Whatcha got?"

"Just wondered if something's up. You're over an hour past the time you usually check in to eat. You sound like you've been asleep."

Lud looked at his watch, astonished. Three-oh-five A.M. He glanced about him, puzzled. *My God! I'm parked out in the middle of nowhere! The field looks like Ferguson's front pasture.*

He lowered his head against the cool rim of the steering wheel. *Jesus Christ! Another Blackout! Hell, that's three, or is it four today? Damn, I've been unconscious, or whatever the hell it is, this time for over an hour and a half.*

He shook his head, concern for his precarious situation. *Well, at least it's the middle of the night and nobody has noticed what's happened.*

Lud tried to think. *Where have I been? Damn, trying to trace where I've been and what I've been doing is becoming more trouble than sheriffing. Gotta hang in though. Just three more days. I remember leaving Dain outside the motel. Then what? Albert! I decided to check on Albert, make sure he was still around. I drove up to Pine Ridge and checked Sam's and Brown's Taverns without finding him. No one has seen him. Two phone calls, no results. I then headed back toward Crescent Valley and…nothing. That had to be when it happened.*

The radio came to life. "Lud?"

Thumbing the mike, he said, "Sorry. Dropped my hat. I just wasn't hungry. I had a couple of burgers earlier, and I'm still enjoying them every time I belch."

"Okay, Sheriff. Just checking up, after not hearing from you for a while, like you said. See you later."

He started to get out of the car to take a leak, and then he remembered. *Sheila and Pat! Nobody would have checked on them since me and Dain left the motel.*

Climbing back into the car, he forgot his need to relieve himself. Bringing the engine to life, Lud flipped on the lights. In their beams he saw the strands of barbed wire stretched across the grill of the patrol unit.

"What the hell?" he said, climbing out of the car again. He had assumed he had felt the blackout coming on and entered the pasture through the gate. Glancing around he saw where the fence had been torn down. *Christ, I swerved off the highway still going fifteen miles per hour. The wonder is that nobody has seen me just this short way off the highway and come to investigate.*

Once free of the wire, he backed the car out onto the highway, the tires throwing clods of turf against the underside of the vehicle. Slamming the transmission into drive, he roared off in the direction of Crescent Valley.

The neon glow of the Starlight Motel sign came into view in the same instant it began to fade, as though being enveloped in fog. Lud shook his head, trying to clear his vision. A moment later the bolt of pain split his skull asunder.

Looking Glass leaned across the seat of the idling patrol car to stare at the long low building. The motel sign itself, blocked by tall trees, did little to illuminate the front of the structure. What light there was came from the low wattage fixtures beside each door.

He pulled away from the curb, slowly past the front of the motel, and turned onto the side street running beside the building. Breaking next to where the rear alley joined the street, he turned off the motor and doused the headlights.

Slipping out of the vehicle, Looking Glass walked back to the trunk and raised the lid. His gaze lingered on the black ski mask and sweater for a moment, then he shook his head. "Not need now." His voice was low. "Put behind extra wheel. Place only Looking Glass know."

Extracting a pair of rubber gloves from the box in the trunk, he slipped them on. He opened a small plastic shaving kit, removing a hypo syringe and a small vial of liquid, clear in the dim light. Lowering the trunk lid, Looking Glass moved past the car and into the alley. He proceeded slowly, pausing every few steps to listen before moving on. His heart hammered with the fierce pleasure of the stalk.

A few yards into the alley, Looking Glass stifled a smile. The can he had dropped, to see which of the back doors without numbers attached the women would come out of to check the noise, still glistened in the dim light. *Only a short distance now from the door to room twenty, where the enemy slut would be sleeping soundly.*

Extracting from his pocket the stolen room key marked twenty, Looking Glass quietly slipped it into the lock. *It worked!* His hands shaking in the excitement of the moment, he slid the syringe out of its plastic sheathe and pierced the rubber nipple of the vial. After filling the syringe with liquid, Looking Glass slid the vial back into his pocket and slipped inside the room, easing the door shut behind him.

He paused to let his eyes adjust to the dimness. The air was strong with the scent of the bitch's perfume, quickening his senses. Knowing she was at his mercy, a thrill coursed through his loins. With the thought, his breathing grew harsher and sweat beaded on his brow, despite the coolness of the night.

Looking Glass moved through the darkness toward the pale rectangle of the bed. The slut lay there, defenseless, open to him. His heart was pounding and his temples throbbed. Another of Running Fawn's foes gone!

His leg touched the bed, and he lunged, ready to cover her mouth while he plunged the needle into the creamy flesh in one swift thrust.

CHAPTER 14

Dain sat in the breakfast alcove of the Barlow house, thinking about the last couple of days. *This business with Amy makes no sense. Everyone liked her, and besides it's been years since she's been here. How could she have made an enemy? Seattle maybe? But why follow her over here when he could do it in the big city? It has to be a random killing by some sickie. But if he had her in the high school, why take off her clothes and carry her naked to my orchard? Damn risky. Why not do his thing in the school?*

Dain frowned, and slowly exhaled. *A lot of sick people rape, then kill to keep the victim quiet. But why cut off her head, and, stranger yet, why put it in the tree fork that way. And if it was random, how did the son of a bitch see well enough to be able to find his way around in my orchard on a dark cloudy night?*

He shook his head. *I can't buy any of this. Just a rape and murder, yeah. But this act has all the ear marks of some sort of a ritual. The bad news, this type of killer can look like a saint on the street.*

Albert Martinson the killer? Well, Lud knows the locals better than I do after all this time away. But back in high school days, everybody knew Albert was sweet on Amy. And even if Lud was right about Albert wanting to avenge himself on women, why didn't he go after the gal who put him in jail or some sex pot like Candy?

As Dain mused, a thought crept into his mind. *Albert had admitted having no alibi for the night of Amy's death. But he told me he had a sure-fire alibi the night after Amy's death.*

The thought struck him. *If Albert had someone who could vouch for his whereabouts last evening, he would be in the clear. He couldn't have been at the Starlight Motel, leaving that finger in Sheila's room.*

Dammit! I have to talk to Albert. Dain glanced at his watch. *If I hurry, I can catch him before he leaves for the mill.*

Rising, Dain walked out through the parlor and climbed halfway up the stairs, listening. The bedroom where Sheila and Pat slept remained quiet. *The girls are sleeping better than I did. Remarkable, considering the shock of finding Amy's finger.*

Turning to descend the stairs Dain suddenly stopped as he thought of Lud. *Man, I hate to think what Lud is going to say, having guarded empty motel rooms all night.*

Last night Dain had no more than reached the city limits of Crescent Valley, heading toward Pine Ridge, when the thought hit him. *Why take a chance by leaving the girls in that darn motel? I have plenty of room for them in my house, and they would be a hell of a lot safer.*

He had made a sudden U-turn, much to the displeasure of a carload of teenagers, who zoomed past, showing him a forest of upthrust fingers. He followed them back through town as far as the turnoff to the Starlight Motel.

He had expected an argument, especially since they were probably getting ready for bed, but they had jumped at the chance to escape the motel with its unpleasant association. They had redressed and repacked in record time and were on their way to Pine Ridge within thirty minutes.

Dain hustled back down the stairs. *Lud will probably be at the house by eight-thirty with the key to the high school, so there's no time to waste.*

Slipping into his jacket, Dain grabbed a writing pad. He scribbled a note for Sheila and Pat and left it in the middle of the breakfast table. On his way to the car, he mumbled, "Route 2, box twenty-seven...sounds like the old Fisher place."

Twenty-five minutes later, Dain turned off the blacktop west of town onto a gravel road leading into the woods. The thickening forest masked the roadway in shadows. A small mountain creek, a brook really, ran alongside the rapidly climbing road, its roar audible even over the engine sound. The cool morning air was heavy with the smell of pine.

He had come about two miles when the road entered an area that had been logged in the distant past. Ahead of him, a house nestled in the one remaining clump of mature trees in the cleared area. Alongside the road stood a silver mailbox with Martinson hand-painted on it in black.

Turning off immediately beyond the mailbox, he inched across a culvert onto a dirt track and came to a stop before Albert's house. He eyed the small house, disappointed. What passed for a carport was empty, and no smoke rose from the chimney.

Dammit to hell! Albert's already gone. I'll have to track him down at work. Reaching for the ignition key, he hesitated. *After being hauled off work yesterday he's not going to like another cop showing up there. Aw hell, I might as well give the place the once over. A search without a warrant is illegal, but then, so am I. Lud didn't swear me in as a deputy. I'm just a guy looking for an old friend.*

Slipping out of the car, Dain immediately slapped at the back of his neck. *Jesus, I forgot how the mosquitoes swarm in these woods in the early morning. The damn things will suck a man's body dry of blood in an hour.* Approaching the house, he watched the windows for signs of life. Nothing.

Apparently Albert wasn't much of a hand for taking care of his property. The steps and flooring of the small porch looked spongy with decay, and the roof over it, held up by two narrow posts, both out of plumb, appeared ready to collapse with the next hard wind.

Glancing toward the front door, Dain's eyes widened. *What the hell!* The door was ajar. *Strange. Albert might leave it unlocked, but he would damn sure make certain it was closed.*

Gingerly climbing the steps onto the porch, Dain eased the door slightly open, and called, "Albert, you here? It's Dain Barlow." Only the squeak of the hinges disturbed the silence as he eased the door on open. *If Albert was home, he was taking the Fifth Amendment.*

Dain stepped inside. He could see through the tiny hall to the kitchen where a typewriter sat on the table. A fat calico cat sat on the kitchen floor next to two empty plastic food dishes. The feline studied Dain with slitted-eye suspicion.

Dain called again. "Albert, you home?"

The house was cold, as chilly as the air outside. Crossing to the wood stove, he opened the door and stirred the acrid smelling ashes with a poker. *The remains of the fire is at least twenty-four hours old, maybe more.*

Dain frowned, rubbing his jaw. *When I checked the orchard's frost warning system this morning, it showed an overnight low of thirty-six degrees, two degrees short of sounding the alarm. Here at Albert's place, seven or eight hundred feet higher in elevation, the temperature had to be colder.*

Dain scanned the room, his gaze pausing to examine a checker board, its pieces in place, atop the coffee table, one of whose legs, broken, had been bound back in place with tightly laced baling twine. Two chairs, one on either side, had been drawn up to the coffee table.

He had the damnedest feeling that the players were there somewhere, watching, just waiting for him to leave to start the game. A beat up old pair of house slippers were neatly placed on the clean floor next to the repaired broken leg.

In contrast to its exterior appearance, the house was clean inside, and nothing slovenly placed anywhere. Leaning over, he checked the surface of the table. He looked at his fingers. *No dust. Albert couldn't have been away from the house long.*

He turned to glance at the wood stove again. The absence of a fire bothered him. That and the unfed cat. Dain was getting bad vibes, though he had no concrete reason for it. He didn't know Albert that well. *Dammit! I've got to check this place out.*

What he found in the bathroom heightened his concern. The logger's shaving brush and soap were both bone dry and so was his toothbrush. The single towel, hanging on the hook by the wash basin, held no hint of dampness. *Having a full beard, Albert might not have used the shaving brush, but why didn't he wash up and brush his teeth before leaving for work? He was neat or the house wouldn't be this clean.*

Dain shook his head. *God, I don't want to believe it, but the answer is as plain as the nose on my face. Albert's running. Guilty as hell. Lud will brag about having had Albert figured right.*

But somehow Martinson hadn't struck Dain as the kind of guy who would abandon his pet cat. *He'd ask a friend to take it. Wouldn't he? The guy always had a soft spot for animals, especially cats. And why hadn't he taken his razor and his toothbrush?*

When Dain returned to the kitchen, the cat had apparently decided he wasn't going to lose anything by acting friendly. Dain glanced down at the cat, rubbing against his leg, purring. "Hungry, kitty? Where's your master? Too bad you can't talk." He turned toward the refrigerator. "Let's see what we can find for you."

Three magnets were on its white metal door. Two held handwritten notes, one reading:

Call the Starlight Motel Friday to see if Amy has checked in.

The other read:

Monday, Wednesday, and Friday, my days to drive this week.

The third a surprise for Dain. Two photos that didn't seem to belong together, one of Amy, the other of Candy Burns, pictures at least ten years old.

Candy was wearing the miniskirt and tight T-shirt that had been her uniform in those long-ago days. He thought of her as she had looked yesterday at the restaurant. *Candy was going to seed. The spectacular curves of her high school days were lost in hills and dells of fat.*

He looked at the picture a second time. *She had really been something back then, though. And she had come near to ruining my life, or at the very least, she had made one hell of a change in it. Candy probably was still unaware of what she had done. For her, it had been an afternoon's amusement, making a fool out of a naive seventeen year old boy.*

As he looked at the picture, the sad memory of that afternoon, that had been seared in his mind, unfolded as clearly as if it had happened only yesterday.

That long-ago Saturday afternoon in September, I was listening to a portable radio while unloading hay from our flat-bed truck, backed into our barn. I was sweaty and tired, trying my utmost to finish the afternoon's work. Looking forward to the date I had with Sheila that night. A malted-milk and a good movie in Crescent Valley.

Dain stared mesmerized at the picture as the unpleasant memories flooded forth. He even remembered what he had for lunch that day. *A peanut butter sandwich and two hard boiled eggs. Not long after I had finished my lunch I heard laughter from the orchard. Maybe Sheila was coming by. Standing atop the truck bed, tossing the bales of hay off had made me ready for a break. Leaving the hay fork driven into one of the bales, I walked down the flat bed's length about ready to jump off when I glanced out through the barn door into the orchard.*

I was instantly worried. About fifty yards away, Candy and her sidekick Betty, scantily clad as usual, were in the driveway, coming toward the barn. Panicking, I ducked back out of sight, hoping they hadn't spotted me. Maybe they were just taking a shortcut to town, but I knew enough about Candy Burns to know she was trouble.

I was more afraid right then than I had been in a very long time. I actually thought about jumping off the truck and running out the back door to escape them, but as quickly decided that the town slut wasn't going to make me run.

In school, I steered clear of her, trying to pretend I didn't hear Candy's suggestive remarks, even though my blushing betrayed me. From everything I'd heard, she was little better than a whore. Everybody in Pine Ridge knew that. Even my mom and dad had talked about the way she behaved.

Dain's gaze dropped to the floor and he arched his brows as he took a deep breath. *I had dreamed about her a couple of times and hated myself for it. I have never told a soul.*

He looked back at the picture. *God, how I hoped they wouldn't stop. But my hopes that they were just passing by vanished with Candy's, Dain, Dain, sweetie, you've got company. She had to know I was alone, that my mom and dad had gone to Wenatchee that day. I could only stare at the girls as they came into the barn, stopping alongside the truck. Candy, leering at my body, clad only in cut-offs, said, Lookee here, Betty. Ain't he just the yummiest thing you've ever seen? Just looking at that sweaty body makes me horny as hell.*

Still staring at the picture on the refrigerator door, the sad memory brought a slow shake of his head. The two girls were a contrasting pair. Betty was a short, petite, dark haired, well built girl, while Candy was a tall blond Amazon with broad shoulders. Though still a teenager, Candy had the body of a voluptuous twenty-five-year-old. Both wore miniskirts, tight T-shirts and, as the nipples poking against the fabric on the T-shirts attested, no bras.

Dain sighed. *God, I remember trying so hard not to look at them, focusing instead on the brown sack in Betty's hand. Then Candy made me more nervous when she climbed onto the bed of the truck, and suddenly, she cried, Party time.*

The memory brought a baleful look. *In one swift motion she pulled her T-shirt over her head and threw it to Betty. A moment later, the miniskirt fell about her ankles. She wore no panties. Candy launched herself at me, and I tripped, falling onto my back in the hay with her atop me.*

A burst of bright light enveloped us, then another. Looking past Candy's shoulder, I could see Betty beside the truck, aiming a Polaroid at us, ready for a third shot.

In one fluid motion, Candy lifted herself off me, grabbed her skirt, and jumped gracefully off the truck. I scrambled to my feet, spitting loose straw out of my mouth, and yelled, "Are you crazy, Candy? Get the hell out of here." Then I remembered the explosions of light. Pointing at the camera, I shouted, And give me those pictures.

Grabbing the camera from Betty, Candy cried, The hell, you say! Okay, Betty, get up there. Let's see lover boy in action.

I backed against the bales of hay as Betty hoisted herself onto the flat bed. She looked at me seductively, then begin slowly coming toward me, she writhed in rhythm to the tune coming from my radio, stopping within arm's length of me. I was trapped by the bales stacked to either side of me. Giggling, her face red, she pulled off her T-shirt in an abrupt movement. Then reaching for the waist band of her skirt she hesitated, looking toward Candy.

"Do it, Betty! Don't be chicken shit," Candy yelled.

Betty pulled her skirt down over her rounded hips and stepped out of it. Like Candy, she wore no panties. No matter how hard I tried to fight it, that old familiar hot feeling of sexual stimulation enveloped me, blush crept into my face. I looked away, struggling to find an answer to my dilemma. No way out except through her. I didn't dare hit her. God knows what they would say about me then.

Dain bit his lip. *My resolve was too weak and I looked back at the attractive female body. Betty cupped her breasts, her thumbs worrying the swelling light brown nipples, an uncertain smile on her face.*

My body, caught up in my ravenous attraction to her body, brazenly betrayed me. Nothing I could do would disguise my ragged breathing and the bulge in the front of my cut-offs. Candy, leveling a finger at me, cried, "Look at that boner, Bets. Lover boy is getting the hots for you."

God, I didn't want them to see it. I pushed against the bulge in my shorts, but it did no good, I couldn't hide it, she was the first real live female I had ever seen naked. And the touch of my hand only made me more aroused.

The thoughts went on. *Candy's face was flushed, and she yelled. "Go on, Betty! You've got him where you want him. He can't stop himself now." I was in the throes of lust and knew I was sunk, but I made one last try. With my voice cracking, I cried, "Stop it! Get away from me. I don't want anything to do with you sluts. I won't—"*

Candy's voice, shrill with excitement cut through my words. "Won't, hell! Get those pants off him Bets. He's dying for it."

I was ready to sweep Betty aside and escape off the side of the truck, and yelled, "Screw you," when Candy brought the Polaroid photos into view.

"Screw me, hell! If I show these pictures around town, little Dain's goody-goody image will be shot. And how about Sheila? You want her to see them? Now take those shorts off, let us see what you got. I'll tear up these pictures after we've had our fun."

With me distracted, Betty lunged at me, jerked down the cut-offs, and grabbed my erection. I made a few paltry attempts to make her stop, but it felt so good, they were short lived. Candy quickly joined us on the bed of the truck.

I suppose I convinced myself I couldn't fight them for fear of hurting them, and they pinned me beneath them in the hay. They both took turns, the first two times my erection touched moist flesh, I ejaculated a surge of shameful pleasure. I didn't struggle any longer. Finally after Candy took me all the way, she, and, a Betty looking somehow relieved ceased their efforts.

Only Candy had truly enjoyed the afternoon. Humiliated by the scorn Candy heaped on me, I lay as if exhausted. Ashamed of what had taken place, hoping they would finally leave me alone.

Only Candy's arrogance saved the day. Thinking they had left me so weak I couldn't move, she had come too close, waving the pictures in my face, telling me she was going to hand deliver the photos to Sheila. I snatched them from her, but my relief was short-lived.

Candy spent the next day spreading the word around Pine Ridge, authenticating it with a description of the small birthmark at the base of my penis. Every guy in the Pine Ridge High locker room had seen that birthmark.

Dain closed his eyes at the painful memory. *Had I secretly wanted to feel the sexuality of a woman's body, know the pleasure it could bring? Had I given in too easily? Was it partly my fault I lost the precious love of my high school sweetheart?*

He shook his head in disgust. *The story reached Sheila's ears before the week's end. I tried several times to phone her and explain, but upon hearing my voice, she would hang up. The romance that was supposed to last all our lives died in that one short afternoon.*

He came out of his reverie with a start. The phone was ringing.

CHAPTER 15

Dain, lifting the receiver, said, "Yeah?"

"What's wrong Al? You got a cold? You don't sound like yourself. Are you going to work or not?"

"This is Dain Barlow. I'm a friend. Al's not here. Who's this?"

"Don Murphy. I work with Al. Where the hell is he? Al was supposed to give me a ride to work this morning. He left me up a creek without a paddle, sure as hell. Shit! The wife is gonna be raisin' six kinds of hell, what with me havin' to take the car again today." His voice changed abruptly. "Say, what are you doing there anyway?"

Dain replied. "I was trying to catch him before he left for the—"

Murphy cut him off. "Goddamn sheriff's probably still got him locked up. Lud picked him up at work yesterday. I heard he wanted to question him about the Amy Housley killing. Hell, ain't no way Al'd hurt her. If you got any clout, buddy, you oughtta hightail it into town and get him out of that jail. He sure as hell don't belong there."

"What are you talking about?" Dain protested. "He was released from jail yesterday afternoon. Maybe he skipped town."

"Bullshit! Al don't run from nobody. I, Jesus! I gotta get my butt in gear or I'm gonna be late!" The line went dead.

Setting the phone in its cradle, Dain filled the cat's dishes with water and food pellets. Straightening, he glanced around the room again, pausing at the checker board with its pieces in position. Call it a cop's intuition or whatever, he couldn't escape the growing feeling that something was wrong.

Dain toyed with the idea of bolting out the door and heading back to town. But the cop in him wouldn't let him walk away from the place without thoroughly looking it over.

Barlow headed for Albert's bedroom to start a methodical search. He struck pay dirt the first place he looked, in the closet. On the floor rested a pair of cowboy boots, well worn, and beside them a spanking new pair of Red Wing boots. To Dain's practiced eye, they were the same size as the boots that had made the print in the orchard.

He lifted the pair of Red Wings, puzzled. *Why was Albert wearing a beat-up pair in the jail when he owned these?* Then he remembered. *Albert claimed he had no new boots. He was going to have to do a hell of a lot of talking to explain these. Maybe Lud was right! Dried mud was caked between the corrugations on the composition soles. The Boot's tread pattern was the same as the one form the orchard, sure as hell.*

Dain glanced down at the floor. *Odd. Martinson must have taken them off outside. No mud marred the floor, inside or outside the closet.* Dain frowned. *If the guy took them off outside, why didn't he clean the mud off them. This way it was going to be all over the bedroom floor when he put them back on.*

Tucking the boots under his arm, he returned to the kitchen. *The typewriter. I need to take along as well to check it against Sheila's bogus invitation.* Cradling the heavy machine under his other arm, he left the house.

Dain was loading his two finds into the car's trunk when he heard a vehicle approaching. Looking up, he saw a Bronco through the fringe of the trees, coming fast, kicking up a trail of dust. As it turned into the driveway, he recognized the man behind the wheel.

Dain smiled. *Old Charlie young. God, he's been the ranger in the forest service as far back as I can remember. He was white headed even back*

*then. Charlie's the one who found the young Lud maintaining his lonely
vigil beside his mother's body two days after she killed herself.*

As the Bronco eased to a stop, Dain closed the trunk lid and walked
over to greet the old ranger. "Charlie Young, how the hell are you? I figured you'd be retired by now."

He waited while the old man, a puzzled look on his face, worked it
out. Then Charlie's weathered features exploding in a wide smile, "Dain
Barlow! I'll be damned! It's been a long time, ten years at least. You've
filled out some. I believe you're bigger now than your daddy was. I hear
you're working down in *L.A.* A cop, right?"

"Yeah, I'm a sergeant in *LAPD*, a detective working homicide."

"A detective! How about that. I've never been down to sunny
California. Maybe when I hang 'em up, I'll take a little trip down that
way for a while. That sun would probably feel good to these old bones."

Abruptly, Charlie's smile disappeared. "Say, what are you doing out
here? I never knew you and Albert hung out together."

"I guess you heard about Amy Housley," Dain said. "Well, I'm giving
Lud a hand with the investigation. That's why I'm here. I wanted to chat
with Albert. The trouble is, it doesn't appear he's been home since he
got out of jail."

A blue jay's sudden shrill chatter shattered the morning silence, and
Charlie, distracted, turned toward the house. "Never made it home,
huh?"

Dain shrugged. "Don't look like it."

Charlie shook his head. "I'm getting worried. Matter of fact, that's
why I drove up here this morning. Hoped maybe he came in late last
night. You see, Al and I started playing checkers two or three nights a
week since my wife died. She's been gone eight months now. Some
nights he even cooks me a meal. Albert's been a saving grace for me, trying to brighten my spirits. It takes a while to adjust without a wife after
forty-six years of being together. You just don't know what to do with
your free time."

Dain's gaze sharpened. "You never saw him at all last night?"

"No, dammit, that's what I'm trying to tell you. Last night was our Tuesday night checker game. I got here about five, went in and set up the board. That's the way we do it, first one here sets up the board. If something comes up that we can't play, we call. Way it's been for months. We got two nights regular, Tuesday and Thursday, once in a while we'll throw in another. He was due home by 5:30. I shoulda known right then something was wrong. I got concerned, and I called Don Murphy about 6:30. He was the one who told me that Lud had picked up Al at work."

Charlie grinned, a smile that had no humor in it. "I waited till about seven, then gave it up. Knowing Albert, I figured maybe he got out of jail too late to call and headed for the tavern. He does that sometimes when he gets upset. Sits there and drinks himself into a near stupor. But he never drives when he's that way. Sleeps it off till dawn, then drives home."

"Well, I can guarantee you he didn't come home this time," Dain said. "Listen, Charlie," he pointed toward the trunk of his car. "I've got a typewriter and a new pair of Red Wing boots in there, took 'em out of the house. Know anything about them? You know, when he got them…anything like that?"

"New boots? Typewriter? What the hell are you talking about, Dain?"

"I found the pair of boots in the bedroom closet, and the typewriter was sitting on the kitchen table. I wouldn't have figured Albert had much use for a typewriter."

Charlie shook his head. "Type? With those big clumsy fingers of his and the way he spells, Albert couldn't type a line in a week. Hell, you'll be telling me next you found a computer in there."

The old ranger appeared to be growing indignant, sputtering. "And as for the new boots. Last Sunday we went fishing. He sure didn't have any new boots then. You don't know Al. When he buys something, he wears it out of the store, never has it wrapped. And I'll tell you something else. Last night there was no typewriter on the kitchen table."

Pausing, he eyed Dain. "Let me guess. These two items, they could be damaging evidence against Al. Right?"

Dain nodded.

"Dammit, some son of a bitch is trying to set him up, sure as hell."

He glanced toward the house. "Wait a minute! Where the hell is his Jeep? It was here last night when I came by. Don said he picked Al up yesterday morning, that it was his day to drive. They take turns. Dammit, he must have come home later last night and picked up the jeep. No other explanation for it."

Dain grimaced. "Charlie, you sure aren't helping his case. That sounds like he decided to clear out, make a run for it."

Charlie's face reddened, and his faded blue eyes developed a sparkle of anger. "Goddammit, Dain, you don't know that boy like I do. You've been away too long. The dumb bastard has had a secret crush on Amy Housley ever since high school days. Sometimes in the shank of the evening, after we've had a few beers, he'd tell me that some day he's going to the city and ask her to marry him. Can you imaging that?"

He shook his head. "Silly bastard. Actually, he was just blowing smoke, and I think he knew it. Albert would have been happy just to be a big wooly dog curled up at her feet, somebody she'd notice and pat on the head every once in a while. Kill Amy? No goddamn way."

Dain studied him before asking, "But what if he bumped into her the other night, after he'd had a few beers and had the courage to ask her to marry him? How would he handle the situation if Amy had laughed and rejected him? I mean, she's a successful career woman now, she may have humiliated him."

Charlie was having none of his arguments. "Ever yell or take a kick at an old dog you've had a long time, Dain? What happens next time he sees you? He comes running up, wagging his tail like nothing ever happened. Right? Well, that's Al, the proverbial, good ole hound dog."

Dain hesitated a moment before telling the old ranger what had happened at the motel the night before. "Hell, nothing adds up," he added. "If Albert was trying to get away, why would he have pulled that stunt at the motel? And if you're not mistaken about the boots and typewriter."

Barlow. paused and nibbled at his bottom lip. "And if he's not on the run, where the hell is his Jeep?" He turned his gaze back to Charlie. "If there's one thing I've learned as a cop, it's that leopards don't change their spots. Once a rapist—"

"Goddammit, he's no rapist!" Charlie looked as if he was about to have apoplexy. "There wasn't any rape. The little slut who fingered him would be too busy getting the pants off a man to yell rape. I know for a fact they had two witnesses that could've blown that case right out of the water."

"Why didn't they?"

"It was like this, Dain. A couple of weeks after the so-called rape, the bitch got drunk and told two gals what really happened. But because of some technicality they weren't allowed to testify.

"Then there was the judge…a woman. Some of the boys say she was out to get him, out to get any man. The way I heard it, her own daughter, the girl was in school over in Seattle, had been raped and beat all to hell about a year before that. They never found who did it. That damn woman was ready to take it out on any poor bastard she got her sights on. Al's lawyer tried to get her tossed off the case, but they ruled against him.

"I went to as much of the trial as I could. That she-devil overruled every objection Albert's lawyer made." He sighed. "Poor Al never had a chance. That was the biggest miscarriage of justice this county's ever seen."

"Could've appealed. Sounds like he had grounds."

"Goddammit, Dain. You know what that would cost? Albert didn't have a damn dime. One of those people the system can tie up and just roll over."

Dain stepped back from the Bronco, glancing down the road. "That's all the more reason for Albert to be here willing to answer questions. Whatever the reason, it doesn't look good, disappearing this way."

"Okay, Dain. I'll drive by and see if he showed up at work. Always a possibility he stayed someplace else last night. Although I can't think of where it could've been. If he's not there, I'm going to see Lud."

"Good idea Charlie. If you find out anything give me a call at home. Better make it tonight, I might not be there till late."

"I'll do that, Dain."

Charlie cranked the engine and backed around to where he faced down the driveway. He had gone perhaps twenty feet when he braked, stuck his head out the window, peered back at Dain, and shouted, "Goddammit, Al didn't do a damn thing to Amy, and I know it." With that, the Bronco shot down the driveway in a cloud of red clay dust and, turning onto the county road, vanished in the direction of town.

Dain turned back to study the front of the house again, uneasy with Charlie's words. If the old man was right, then Albert's disappearance might have a more sinister explanation.

CHAPTER 16

The rays of the early morning sun, barely above the horizon, knifed through the venetian blinds covering the windows of the sheriff's office, bathing the figure slumped at the desk in an orange-red light. He stirred, moaning, then pushed himself upright.

The sunlight played over Lud's sharp features and high cheekbones as he threw his hand up to shield his eyes. Blinking, he scanned the room, his eyes moving frantically. *My God! The office! And the sun! It's day light. But the motel!* He groaned. *Jesus Christ! I just hurried back to the motel after finding myself in the middle of that pasture.*

He slammed his fist against the desk in frustration. *Goddammit! It seems I'm having more black outs now than conscious time.* He frowned. *But not a damn soul's said anything about me acting strangely. If anyone does, I'm back to that doctor, pronto. But with only a couple more days to the reunion…maybe I'll make it.*

The sound of the door to his office opening exploded through his head like a gunshot, and he lunged to his feet, almost tumbling forward across the desk, dizzy, catching himself with one hand.

"Lud, are you okay?" Alice, one of the department dispatchers, was standing just inside, eyeing him with a look of concern on her plump, moon-shaped face.

110

Lud managed to grin. "Yeah. Sure. It's just that you startled the hell out of me. I was daydreaming."

She came farther into the office, still looking unhappy, and he tried again. "Oh, hell, confession is good for the soul. You caught me snoozing. I was on the go all night, what with that stake-out at the Starlight Motel. Didn't get my usual catnaps."

As he said the word Starlight, he remembered Sheila and Pat. *Oh Christ, are they all right? What the hell have I done while I was blacked out? Did I stay there on guard, or did I come back here and sleep at my desk all night? Maybe Alice will have part of the answer.*

"I was damn beat when I came in this morning, maybe you noticed."

"Musta been. You didn't say a word when you came in about a half hour ago. When I asked how the night went you just stormed past into your office."

"Sorry, Alice, I got a lot on my mind."

"Hey, I'm not complaining. I understand."

Well, at least she hasn't noticed anything wrong with me. But in my black out state, will I recognize it if the women are in danger and do something about it? I gotta check on them.

Automatically, Lud reached for the telephone, then remembered what he had just said to alice about being staked out at the place all night. Jesus, unless he watched himself, he was going to give away his mental lapses.

Lud moved around the desk. He had to get away from Alice so he could think. "Hey, I'm heading home for bed. Ralph should be here any minute." Not waiting to hear any comments Alice had about how he usually stayed until Ralph arrived, he brushed past the open-mouthed Alice. He charged through the gate that screened the office's working space and out the door without as much as a goodbye.

He crossed the lot to the patrol car, knowing Alice would be at the door, watching him. Glancing back over his shoulder, he gave her a wave and a smile, and went on to the car. *Have to keep her thinking everything is normal. She is a sweet lady, but she is also the kind of women who looks after me like a mother hen. If she suspects something is wrong, she'd sic the doctor on me without letting me know.*

A few minutes later, on the highway to Pine Ridge, Lud tried to relax. The drive, with the road passing through stands of timber with the occasional distant view of the snow-capped mountains, usually did the trick, but not this morning. His hands gripped the wheel so hard they ached, and the sound of the tires against the pavement, which usually lulled him with their sibilance, was like a cloud of insects around his head.

Oh, Christ! The first thing Dain's gonna do is ask me how the girls are. I gotta contact the motel.

Grabbing the radio mike, he said, "Unit one to base. Alice, patch me through to the Starlight Motel office."

"Roger, Lud."

A raspy female voice escaped the speaker. "Starlight Motel. Thelma speaking."

"Thelma, this is the sheriff. How's your husband?"

"Fine, Lud. His head is just a little sore."

"I wanted to let you know that things were quiet all night, but we'll be keeping an eye on the place till the two ladies check out. I don't suppose you've seen them this morning, have you?"

"No, Sheriff. I expect they're still asleep. The way I heard it, they must have had a real scare."

After a few more words, Lud escaped from the manager's wife, who seemed ready for a full morning's conversation.

Slipping the radio mike back onto its hook, Lud rolled down the car's window, letting in the spring air with its hint of the coming summer heat. He glanced toward the distant peaks, with their already shrinking snowpack.

The snow melt is increasing fast now. This winter's snows were heavy enough that the thaw will flood the road at Rainbow Lake. That happens every three or four years, but the state is too damn cheap to correct the problem.

Five minutes later, he swung left around a sharp curve, and the lake sprang into view.

Jesus, the water is less than three feet below the road. This is as high as I've seen it this early in the season since the big flood of nineteen seventy-nine. I'll have to stop by Sam's and tell him to spread the word. A thin smile cut his face. *He'll have it all over town by noon.* He pursed his lips. *At the rate the lake is rising, the road will be closed within forty-eight hours. Gonna play hell with the reunion.*

Coming up on the second, sharper curve, he slowed. Despite the warning signs, five cars had gone off into the lake here in the past ten years. The number included Dain's parents. The curve had no guard rail, not that it would do much good for a car going too fast. As he came out of the curve, he passed a state survey crew, who looked up apprehensively as he whizzed by.

Damn guys should have flagmen out.

Looks like what I heard in Wenatchee must be true. The state has finally decided to do some blasting to make the curve a more gentle one. Maybe the Barlow deaths had put a rocket up their butts. When prominent people die, things get done.

A few years back, two cars, driven by Indians, had gone off at that point. One had held a family of five. Nothing had been done then. He sighed. *At times it's hard not to get pissed off at the big shots who don't seem to give a damn about people like me.*

With the lake receding in his rear view mirror, his thoughts returned to the Barlows and the day they had died. Lud remembered it clearly because that was the first time he had blacked out.

How ironic that it was me, Dain's friend, who discovered the accident. I was headed toward the lake, checking on road ice for the highway department. One moment I was on the road, still about two miles from the lake, reporting icy patches on the radio as I encountered them. The next thing I knew, I was standing in the curve, staring at tire tracks that came off the highway across the narrow shoulder and down the rock facing into the lake, vividly etched in the light snow. As I watched, the water just off shore turned frothy with exploding air bubbles, and I saw the first rainbow glints of oil on the surface.

Without thinking, I leaned over, ready to pull off my boots and dive into the lake. But the curve was on a rocky point that plunged into deep water. The vehicle would be at least fifty feet down, maybe more. And without the proper equipment a person could last only minutes in the cold water.

I became aware of an idling motor and, turning, saw a car, mostly on the road because of the narrow shoulder some thirty yards away. I was confused, for a moment I failed to appreciate that what I was looking at was my own patrol car.

Back in the unit, I radioed for help. The thing that had scared me, still scares me, was that I almost said, "The Barlow car has gone off into Rainbow Lake." But how the hell did I know? Had I seen the car, recognized it, and watched it skid off the icy pavement into the lake?

Lud slapped his open hand into the steering wheel. *Damn it, I gotta quit thinking about things for which I have no answer.*

A strange feeling slowly enveloped him. *Dain didn't come to the first reunion. I had just talked to his mom, not too long before the accident, and she told me he couldn't get any vacation time to come to this one because of a big case he was working on. The deaths of his parents was the only thing that could bring him back to Pine Ridge. Now they were dead, and Dain was here.*

As Lud neared Pine Ridge, he continued to think about the tragedy. *Goddamnit, I was exhilarated when I found out Dain was coming for the funeral. Being the best friend I ever had, I should have been saddened, his parents were the only family Dain had.*

What was wrong with me? Maybe because it gave me one last time to see my old buddy before the tumor takes me out? Could be, but Christ, I had even felt excited when I found out the four girls, Sheila and her friends, were going to be here. Why? I damn sure had no desire to see them again.

They had paid no attention to me back in high school days. Every one of them looked right through me as if I wasn't there. By rights, I should hate them. Those four caused the accident that destroyed my mother.

He slowly shook his head. *Jesus, I'm fucked up.*

Sam's Diner came into view on the road ahead, and he felt a sense of relief. *Too much thinking. This reunion is going to be tough enough, going through all the heart ache it'll bring up about my mother's death. I shouldn't be looking forward to any part of this.*

CHAPTER 17

Dain pulled out onto the blacktop, leaving Albert's, picking up speed. Out from under the trees, the sun warmed the car's interior quickly.

A mile down the road, he saw a Jeep parked on the shoulder. His pulse quickened. *Albert's? Charlie said he had a Jeep.*

He slowed, pulling over to the side of the road. As he coasted onto the shoulder behind the Jeep, a tall, thin man slid out of the vehicle and started back toward Dain's car.

Recognizing him, Dain grimaced. Mike Powers had been a member of Dain's senior class, the only one whose family had real money. He had always treated the rest of the student body like animated door mats.

Dain sighed. *I should have passed the vehicle to see who was in it before I stopped.*

Rolling down the window, he stuck his head out and called, "What's the trouble, Mike?"

Ignoring him, Powers walked around to the passenger side door, opened it, and climbed in. His lower lip bulged with a wad of snuff. Dain recalled he had been using it even in high school.

Without bothering to look at Dain, Mike asked, "What the hell are you doing out this way?" Not waiting for an answer, he continued, "I'll just ride into Pine Ridge with you. I called Brown's station on my cell phone, but the piece of shit said he wouldn't have anybody available to come out and get me before ten o'clock. Wait until my daddy hears how he let me set on the side of the road."

Same old Mike. Dain thought. *The world was put here to serve him. And Powers still looked exactly like a vulture; stooped shoulders, long neck, an adam's apple that could cut glass, and a nose like a bird's beak.*

As he pulled back onto the road, Dain spotted the Jeep's trouble, a flat front tire. He grinned at Mike. "Just like the old days, eh? You never did carry a spare in your car, for some damn reason."

Powers shrugged. "Hell, no. I'm not changing any flat tires. I didn't change them in the old days, and now that I've got a cell phone, I'm sure as shit not going to start. With the money my old man pays Tom, I expect him to drag is ass out to help me, day or night."

He chuckled. "I got the old bastard up one morning at three o'clock. When I say jump, he makes like a bull frog. If he pisses me off, I'll tell Dad to take his business elsewhere, and the old bastard knows it."

Powers belched and added, "Besides, the Jeep don't look good with a spare hanging on the back."

Leaning back, he pulled his badly soiled cowboy hat down over his forehead, and put his knee on the dash to get more comfortable. Rolling his head sideways to look at Dain, he said, "You never did tell me what you're doing out in my neck of the woods."

"I went out to see Albert Martinson this morning," Dain said. "Thought maybe I'd catch him before he went to work. He wasn't home, though."

Dain grimaced as a piece of horse dung fell off Mike's boot onto the auto's carpet. Before he could protest, Mike said, "Goddammit, I must have stepped into some horse shit out in the feedlot. Shoulda told Dad to feed the horses his ownself this morning."

As if the mess on the carpet was forgotten, Mike chuckled. "So you figured ole Albert porked that big tall piece of ass and then killed her,"

Suddenly turning his head, Powers spat a long, brown stream of juice out the open window. Through the road sounds, Dain heard it splat against the side of the car.

Looking back toward Dain, he winked. "Of course, I gotta admit, I wouldn't have minded having a piece of that long-legged bitch myself."

A sudden rage, hot, exhilarating, swept over Dain. He swerved off the road, fighting to control himself.

Powers' eyes narrowed. "What the hell are we stopping for?"

So angry he could hardly talk, Dain said, "You're going to get out and clean that tobacco juice off the side of my car. Then you're going to get that horse shit off my carpet."

When Mike made no move, just stared at him, Dain opened his door and started to get out. "Well, I see we have to do this the hard way."

With that, Mike scrambled awkwardly from the car. "Now, hold it, boy. Don't go getting your bowels in an uproar. I didn't mean to get your frigging car dirty."

Dain eyed Powers across the car's roof until he had scooped the fragments of manure on a piece of cardboard that he found alongside the road and wiped the side of the car with his handkerchief. Once he finished and restored the soiled handkerchief to his jeans pocket, Dain pointed at him. "Now, if you want to ride on into town, you're going to spit out that snuff and you're going to talk about Amy Housley in a respectful way."

Mike stared at him in disbelief. "Jesus, I didn't know you had gotten so damn uppity since you left Pine Ridge. I don't know if the trip to town with you is worth it or not."

Dain settled himself in the car again and said, "Make up your mind. I'm leaving."

Mike hesitated a moment before muttering, "Shit," and spat out a thick brown wad of tobacco. Then he climbed into the car, settled back as though nothing had happened, and commanded, "Get this show on the damn road."

They rode a couple of minutes in silence. Then Mike said, "So you think Al's the guy who killed Amy, huh?"

Dain shook his head. "I didn't say that. I don't know. That's why we're investigating. What do you think, Mike? I mean, being a hard-working cowboy and man about town like you are, you must hear things."

Powers obviously didn't understand sarcasm. The ugly bastard was preening as if he had just been proclaimed the stud of the western world. Flashing Dain a tobacco stained toothy grin, he snickered. "Sounds like people have been talking about me. But I don't know anything about ole Albert. He don't run in the high class crowd I do. Oh, yeah, I see him every once in a while in the tavern, but the women I know pay no attention to him. Hell, all they want to talk about is me." He winked again. "To tell you the truth, when I'm around women don't pay much attention to anyone else, I have to beat them off with a stick. Daddy says no swollen-bellied woman had better show up at his place claiming I gave her a baby. As a matter of—

"Hey, wait a minute! I saw Albert yesterday. Yeah, yesterday afternoon late."

He had Dain's full attention. "What the hell are you saying, Powers?"

"Son of a bitch was with Lud in the sheriff's car, heading up an old logging road, one of the ones they put in to log that acreage up near Peddler's Point. Nobody uses them much anymore. Hell, another two or three years, and you will need a four-wheel-drive to get back in there."

"Where exactly is this road you're talking about?" Dain asked. "That land was logged after I left here."

Powers thought for a minute. "You remember the way out to the O'Neil place?"

Dain nodded and he continued, "About a half mile west of their house, this logging road takes off toward the canyon. You need to know what you're doing, or you could get lost in that maze of trails back there. Anyway, I saw the sheriff's car out there. He had Albert with him, no question about that."

"What time was that?"

"Hell, man, what is this, twenty questions? I don't know what time it was. Christ, I didn't punch no clock. Wait a minute. I'd been visiting O'Neil. He told me I better get a move on if I was gonna make it to Sam's by five." He smirked. "I was supposed to meet this broad from Crescent Valley there, she'd heard about me, just had to meet me, a sure-fire piece of tail. From what some of the hands on the ranch say, she fills out a dress like she was poured in it."

"Then it was after four when you saw them?" Dain asked.

"Four-thirty, at least. I'll guarantee that."

Dain was silent. More puzzles. *Lud took him home, but what the hell happened then? If Albert went into the house at all, he wasn't there long enough to feed cat. Did he get out of Lud's car, go over and get into his jeep and drive away without ever going inside? Only Lud could answer that.*

Some quarter of a mile ahead of them, a small band of bikers crested the low hill and roared toward them. The six bikers were a cruddy-look-ing lot, all except one riding bikes that showed evidence of too many miles and too little care. The one biker sported a Harley-Davidson that looked as if it had just come off the showroom floor.

As they passed, giving Dain the hard, challenging stare that all outlaw bikers exhibit, Mike Powers thrust his arm out the window, moving it in an up and down motion, his middle finger extended. Leaning his head out the window, he shouted, "Biker pussies!"

In a moment the band was past, leaving only the thunder of their exhaust to tear up the calm of the early morning.

Dain glared at him. "What the hell are you doing? Are you completely crazy, you son of bitch? They'll turn around and be on us like maggots of meat."

"What the fuck, you scared of the assholes?" Powers, looking out through the rear view window, continued, "Oh, Christ! You're right. Those bastards are turning around."

"No, shit, Sherlock!"

"Dain, you'd better put that pedal to the floor."

Dain glanced at the rear view mirror. Two or three of the bikers had completed their turns and were coming after them. He shouted at Powers, "What the hell's wrong with you? Why did you do that?"

"Hell, I was just screwing around. I didn't think they would come after us."

Dain glanced at the rear view mirror again, they were gaining fast. "Hell, I can't outrun them on a curvy road like this. Here goes nothing." He took his foot off the gas, and the car slowed quickly. Braking, he pulled off onto the shoulder.

Mike's eyes widened in disbelief. "God, man, what the hell you stopping for? That's Logan back there! He carries a hunting knife a damn foot long, and don't give a rat's ass who he uses it on. That motherfucker could kill us all by hisself, and the other five are just like him."

Dain cut off the engine and slid out of the car. "The best way to handle this is to nip it in the bud. If we run, it'll be like dogs after a car. That bunch will keep after us till they corner us, so why not get it over with? The longer we wait, the meaner they'll get."

Cowering down in the seat, Powers opened his mouth to protest, but Dain glowered at him. "What the hell did you expect? Are you just naturally stupid or did you have to work at it?"

The bikers halted some twenty yards behind the car and uncoiled from their bikes. They advanced with that stiff-legged strut that all bad guys seem to think they need.

Powers's voice lost some of its down home quality. You got a gun with you, right?"

Dain, never taking his gaze from the advancing

bikers, muttered, "Yeah, I've got a gun. But what the hell do you suggest I do? Shoot them because they didn't like you flipping them the bird?"

Dain recognized the group's leader. The biker already had a reputation as a hard guy back when Dain graduated.

At six-six and more than two hundred and fifty pounds, Ray Logan was a mountain of a man with a scar across that part of his cheek that was not hidden by his full beard. His sun-bleached brown hair. greasy and unkempt in the sunlight, hung down onto his shoulders. He was clad in a black leather jacket with fringes, dirty jeans, and worn logger's boots. A scabbard encased knife, belted around his waist, completed his outfit. To Dain it looked the size of a Samurai sword.

With a negligible motion of one arm, Logan brought his followers to a halt. He continued on several steps, stopping two yards from Dain. The biker leader used his two-inch height advantage to stare down at him.

"Ray Logan, right?" Dain said. "I remember you from the old days, riding around on that beat-up Kawasaki." He glanced past the towering man at his motorcycle. "Things must be looking up. You and the boys out getting a little sun and air."

The big biker frowned, staring, and then recognition came into his eyes. "I'll be Damned!" Ray's voice had more of a rumble than the transmission of an eighteen-wheeler on an upgrade. "I remember you. You're Dain Barlow. As I recall, you were a tough little shit, starred in every sport in the high school."

He shifted his gaze toward Mike Powers. "Looks like you've taken to running with bad company, though. What are you doing with this miserable motherfucker?"

Dain shook his head. "No company of mine. Just giving him a ride to town. He had a flat and no spare. Powers doesn't have any more sense than he ever had, couldn't understand why you might be a little upset. That's why we stopped…so he can apologize."

Logan looked surprised. Whatever he had expected, it obviously wasn't this. He studied Dain for a moment before turning his attention back to Powers. "I'm not sure me and the boys are interested in any of the little pissant's fucking apologies. That skinny son of a bitch needs to have his ass kicked. That's what he needs."

Dain took a covert glance at Powers cowering against the passenger door. *I wish to hell I could tell the scruffy bunch before me that I agreed. As a matter of fact, I wouldn't mind taking the first shot. But the way things stand I'm probably going to get he hell beat out of me, too, for taking up for the asshole.*

Dain scuffed the dirt of the shoulder with his foot, making a great show of thinking about it. He tried a grin on the big man, hoping he would unwind a little. "I'll admit the idea has merit, but not today, Logan. Trouble with you is the last thing I want—"

The biker guffawed, and the rest of his bunch followed on cue. After a moment, Logan cut off their mirth with the same quick arm gesture Dain had seen before. "Oh, hell, no, you're not looking for trouble. He just gives everybody you pass the finger."

He twisted around to face his five buddies. "What do you think, boys? We're just supposed to wave back when that little peckerwood gives us the finger. It's just Mike Powers' way of saying howdy. Maybe he'd like for all of us to get down and kiss his ass, too."

Dain gave up on the grin. These bikers didn't understand the word friendly. "Okay, Logan, you've had your fun. Just let Mike apologize and we can all be on our way. No one wants to spend a nice day like this in the hospital or jail when this can be settled real easy."

The big man's hand slid down to grip the handle of the huge knife, Dain, taking a step backwards, shook his head. "Don't get any ideas, Logan. I'm packing.

"Look, man, the poor bastard hasn't got enough common sense to know when he is pissing people off. Why not let him off the hook with an apology today?"

The biker stared at Dain, saying nothing, as the long seconds dragged on. Behind him, the other five men had quieted, watchful now. Finally, Logan nodded in the direction of Powers, and said, "Ain't heard him say nothing."

Dain kept his gaze on the hand against the knife handle. "Apologize, Powers!" he ordered.

"Goddammit, he's got his hand on that pig sticker," Mike screeched. "Blow his fucking head off! Your gun's the only thing that's holdin' him off our ass right now."

Dain whirled to look at Powers, still cowering on the far side of the front seat, the threat of the knife forgotten in his anger. "Apologize, you skinny son of a bitch, or so help me, I'll kick your ass out of that car and they can do whatever the hell they want with you."

After what seemed like an eternity, Mike mumbled, "I'm sorry."

Logan's face relaxed to a slow grin. Turning to Dain, he said, "You got balls, man. I would have given the bastard up. The pissant ain't worth no kind of aggravation."

The issue resolved, Logan grew chatty. "What the hell you doin' out on this road this time of day? Little early for a ride in the country, ain't it?"

"I went out to see Albert Martinson, but he wasn't home."

The fattest of the bikers, clad in a worn leather vest and jeans that looked as if they were about ready to pop at the seams, chuckled. "You're not likely to see him, either. Not unless a dead man can crawl out of a canyon. Go out to Peddler's Point and—"

Logan spun, shouting at the man. "Shut your fucking mouth, Gordy!" He turned back to Dain, showing him a smile that looked as artificial as hell. His voice had lost its rumble, when he said, "Don't pay him any mind. He can't tell the difference between when he's dreaming and when he's awake."

When Dain continued to stare thoughtfully at the plump biker, Logan leaned over and stuck a meaty fist in the car window and pointed one grimy finger at Mike Powers. "Don't think you're getting off. I'm not forgetting you, you pissant. I owe you an ass kicking."

With that, he wheeled around, hurried back to his bike, and brought it to life. Above its roar, he shouted, "Come on, boys, let's go to camp."

The other bike engines exploded to life, and in a maelstrom of noise and flying dust, they sped off down the road.

Dain stood, unmoving, watching them disappear around a curve. He had the impression that the need to get Gordy away from Dain had been the reason for the gang's abrupt departure.

Opening the car door and sliding into the seat, he glanced over at Mike, who was straightening up in the seat now that Logan had gone. Dain sighed and slowly shook his head. "Boy, you're something else."

Mike reared back. "Least, I didn't kiss his ass. By God, haven't you got any cojones at all? Licking Logan's ass like that when you've got a pistol with you? Man! My daddy's gonna hear about this. When I tell him the way Logan talked to me today, he'll run his ass clear out of the country. And you, with a gun, just letting it happen, he's gonna complain to Lud about that, tell him what a chicken-shit your are."

Dain, in the act of pulling back out onto the asphalt surface, braked hard. "Okay, that's it! Get your skinny ass out of the car or I'll throw you out! I've had all the crap from you today I'm going to take."

Powers stared at him incredulously. "Who do you think you are? Talkin' to me like that. Ain't nobody leaving me out beside the road. Can't treat me like no bag of trash."

"You want to bet?" Dain opened his door and started to climb out of the car.

Hastily, Powers opened the passenger side door and scrambled out. "Okay, goddammit, keep your shirt on. But I'm warning you. My daddy's gonna fix your ass."

Lowering himself onto the car seat again, Dain muttered, "God, I'm just scared to death."

As he pulled out onto the pavement, he heard Powers' high voice behind him shout, "Motherfucker!"

A few miles down the road, Powers forgotten, he began to think about Albert again. *Charlie was right, something stinks to high heaven. Finding those boots and typewriter at Albert's was too damn easy. Left where a first week cub scout could find them. And what the hell did that fat biker mean, that Gordy?*

As he rolled into town, he glanced along the two blocks of the so-called business district, which had more vacant lots than buildings. Main Street had five businesses: a small post office, a market with a deli, the service station, Brown's Tavern, and Sam's Diner. The only other buildings standing were the abandoned school and a small steepled church.

He pursed his lips and pushed his tongue to the inside of his cheek. *In L.A., there were days when I have picked up a homicide report in the morning and have the guy in cuffs by the middle of the afternoon. Here in this little pimple on the world's hide, I'm working into my second day and I don't have a clue. Some detective! I have to admit this big city cop isn't doing so well.*

As he slowed to turn into his driveway, he wondered whether his guests were awake yet. Rounding the corner that put the house in view, he saw the sheriff's car parked before it.

Oh, my God! Sheila and Pat! For a moment he couldn't breathe.

CHAPTER 18

The white Cadillac limousine's engine purred to life in the crowded high school parking lot. Sheila and Dain were seated in the back, their first time to be in such luxurious surroundings. An extra pleasure furnished by Dain's father for his senior prom. The slow music for the last dance of the evening wafted, subdued from the lighted school house.

Dain's arm was around Sheila. Her anxiety over what the next few minutes might bring, caused her breathing to quicken as the limousine started to slowly make its way through the crowded parked cars. She had had a wonderful feeling of elation all evening. Now the dancing was over, the time of intimacy with Dain at hand.

The warm night air, scented with the spring apple blossoms from the Barlow orchard next to the school parking lot, was intoxicating as it drifted in through the one open window. Leaning back, Sheila took a deep breath, trying to quell the butterflies that had her feeling light headed and antsy, as they pulled out of the lot.

Glancing at his handsome face, the feeling changed to giddiness as he drew her near for a passionate kiss. She was nervous about where it might lead, but was unable to fight it and responded eagerly, as he kissed her long and urgently. His one hand moved slowly to her knee, then searched for the hem of her dress. The hand felt warm and wonderful as it slid under the gown, and rested on her smooth nylon covered leg. Their breathing became more labored as their passion grew.

Through the back window, the few lights of Pine Ridge faded in the distance as the car whisked them away. Closing her eyes, she swallowed nervously, they had come close before, but she had always been able to resist.

Tonight, prom night, with the insouciant way she felt and the love she had for him, she knew she was in danger of letting Dain go all the way. Sheila knew it wasn't right, she should save herself, but he was the only man she would ever love, she knew that for sure, and if he really tried to seduce her....

Sheila didn't hear the patrol car turn into the Barlow driveway. She even failed to hear her evening's roommate until Pat, smelling of soap, pushed against her shoulder and yelled, "Get up, sleepy head. The shower's all yours."

Groaning, Sheila turned her back to Pat, trying to burrow her head under the covers. *What a time to have a dream interrupted.* She tried to will herself back to sleep, but Pat wouldn't shut up.

"I've been up for an hour. Dain's car engine woke me, and I couldn't get back to sleep. I'm going to go find the coffee pot."

Sheila clawed at the pillow, trying to pull it over her head. It was snatched from her hand. She made a futile try to retain the covers, but they went the way of the pillow. Rolling onto her back, Sheila opened her eyes to find the grinning Pat staring down at her.

"Up and at 'em, girlie," Pat commanded. "I'm not going to rattle around in this big old house all morning while you sleep."

Sheila raised up on one elbow. "Darn you, Pat. You ruined one of the best dreams I've ever had. Dain and I were at the senior prom, the one by the way, I never got to go to. Actually, we were riding around in the back seat of a limousine, making out like crazy. Now I'll never know whether I got laid or not."

Pat laughed. "You should thank God you have a friend like me. You know how those dreams end. I helped you keep your virtue intact. By the way, Dain left a note on the kitchen table."

Sheila swung her legs over the edge of the bed. "Dain? Isn't he here?"

"No, the note said he had to see somebody before they went to work. It also said the refrigerator is packed and to make ourselves at home. Go ahead and grab a shower and I'll toss together something for breakfast."

"Okay, but I think I'll take a bubble bath this morning, so not too fast with breakfast."

She was about to step into the tub of frothy white mounds of bubbles when she saw her image in the full length mirror on the closed bathroom door. Standing straight, Sheila drew her shoulders back. She cupped her hands under her big breasts and pushed up slightly, still firm. The sight brought a smile. *I could look more provocative in a T-shirt than Candy ever did if I dared.*

Turning, she moved to the tub and stepped into the warm water. "Oh, how wonderful." she murmured as she lowered herself into the bath. Leaning back, she closed her eyes and the dream she was having with Dain sprang to mind.

A thrill had gone through her the day before when he said he had never married. *He had been such a good boy friend. Kind. Considerate. Understanding. Oh, why had I been so immature that I couldn't look beyond that one afternoon with Candy. I was such a fool. But I'm here now and Dain's here.*

A serene smile slowly formed as she relaxed in the tub, and came to her decision. *I'm going to find out if there is a future for a mature Dain Barlow and a mature Sheila Greene.*

*　　　　　　*　　　　　　*

Lud would have driven past the driveway, but the pain had become intolerable. He had to get off the road. The full force of it had hit him without warning, like always, just as he climbed back into the patrol car, the school key in his pocket. With the world dimming and brightening around him, he decided to by pass Dain's and find one of the deserted logging roads a few miles beyond. He would be safe there, unobserved, until the attack passed.

But this time an intense nausea had followed the onset of pain, like nothing he had experienced before. Lud's trembling arms felt so weak that he could barely turn the steering wheel. He was going to fly off the road if he didn't stop immediately, so he took the only option he had, turning left into the Barlow driveway.

Ahead, the drive among the flowering apple trees dimmed, and he wheeled to the side and slammed on the brakes—

＊   ＊   ＊

Lights flashed in Lud's head, and the buzzing inside the car was as loud as a buzz saw in his pounding head. Lud slowly moved the tingling fingers of his right hand. Flies buzzed around him, and two flew off his parted lips as he stirred. He felt the drool they had been feeding on, making its way down from his mouth.

His numb hand moved awkwardly, like a lifeless appendage as he tried to wipe his chin. The movement caused his head to slide sideways against something hard, evoking a groan as he opened his eyes. *The steering wheel, he was still in the car.*

Grimacing at the tremendous pain throbbing in his head like a cue ball bouncing off the side rails of a pool table. His body convulsed. Lud struggled to shove his hand into his pants pocket where he had the vial of pain pills. The cloth clung to his sweaty hand, and he cried out in frustration.

Finally, freeing the plastic container, he dumped three of the big yellow pills into his hand. His strong teeth crunched them into a bitter-tasting gritty mass, the dryness gagging him as he struggled to swallow the larger dosage. For the next few minutes, he shifted violently about in the seat, his hands spasmodically opening and closing into fists until the narcotic took effect.

God, the pain was getting worse. I thought it couldn't get any worse. The doc warned me about taking three pills at once, but two just ain't doing the job anymore. I know I should call the doctor and get something stronger, but I know what I would hear. Get in here right away.

But until the reunion is over, I'm not going to do it. Why? Why is that goddamn reunion so important to me? I don't owe anything to a bunch of assholes who used to stick their noses in the air every time I walked by. But I've been going through misery, more every damn day for the last month, to make it to the damn thing. So, by God, with only three more days I'm going to make it, even if I walk in the front door of the high school and collapse on the spot.

Lud glanced at his watch. *Almost eight-thirty. I've only been out fifteen minutes, at least that's a plus. What time did I tell Dain I would be here? Somewhere around now? Yeah, I think that's about right.* Pulling out his handkerchief, Lud toweled the sweat off his face and neck.

He frowned. *Martinson! Damn, I wish the hell I had told Dain I would leave the key on the porch earlier. This way, I can't get hold of Albert again until after work. I don't want to go out to the mill again. Not that Albert had any pull, but his boss could sure raise hell about him being harassed.*

Lud grimaced. *Shoulda been out at Albert's place in time to kick the bastard out of bed. Once a bully, always a bully. Put pressure on a guy like that, show him you're not going to back away, and he'll crack, sooner or later. It would sure be a big coup if I could wrap this Amy case up before the reunion.*

Lud knew his town. *Pine Ridge had its hard cases, but Albert was the only rapist in the lot. I'll break the son of a bitch and that's a promise.*

The sudden thought chilled him. *Had Albert sensed anything wrong? No calls or rumors about it has reached the office, but then, it had only happened yesterday. One thing was sure. If that goofus realized I had head problems, the whole damn town would know it soon.*

He took another peek at his watch. *Eight forty. Dain would be getting tired of waiting. Better get on up to the house. I don't want to be caught parked here in the edge of the orchard without an explanation.*

Reaching for the door to climb out of the car, his hand slipped off the handle. *Damn! What's wrong with my arm? My hand, whole arm for that matter, still feels sort of numb. I've got enough strength in it, but I can't really feel what I'm touching. Well, I'll let the Doc worry about that in a few days.*

Once outside the car, Lud stretched. *Still feel weak in the knees, but I'll pass muster. I've got to get the key to Dain, grab a little breakfast, run back into Crescent Valley to see Pat and Sheila, and straighten up the trunk.*

The trunk? What the hell made me think of the trunk? Have I been in the trunk while I'm blacked out? Goddamn, I'd better check.

Dammit! The key almost slipped from the numbed fingers of my hand as I fitted it into the trunk lock. God, at this rate I'll be an invalid by the weekend.

Lud lifted the trunk lid, and the bright sunlight revealed its contents. *Jesus H. Christ! Why did I put my travel kit—*

Lud jumped. A vehicle had pulled into the driveway behind him. Dain. He closed the lid so fast that it struck the brim of his hat, pushing it down over his eyes. Panicking, he pulled at it with both hands, yanking it off his head.

Dain, climbing out of his car, laughed. "Jesus, Lud, you act like I caught you with a pile of girlie magazines."

Lud, spun around to face Dain. *I must look like a frigging fool, standing here with my hat in my hand.* "I, ah, I'm jumpy as hell. Didn't even get a cat-nap last night. Just wanted to check and make sure the emergency kit was in the trunk. Ralph is so damn forgetful about things like that."

Dain shook his head, a huge grin on his face. "Come on, Lud. You can do better than that. Open the trunk and let an old buddy see what you've got stashed in there."

"Goddammit, leave me alone!"

Dain took a step backwards, staring at him.

Seeing the hurt look on his friends face, Lud mumbled, "Hell, I'm sorry, man. It's just that I need sleep. And this business with Amy has upset me. You know, having somebody you really knew well get mutilated that way, and the county fathers want you to find out who did it, in just one or two days, it puts you under a lot of pressure."

Relaxing, Dain said, "Hell, that's okay, buddy. I thought maybe you were pissed about Sheila and Pat."

"Sheila and Pat?"

"Yeah, they're here, up in the house. You didn't know? I left a message at the sheriff's office."

As Lud listened to Dain's explanation of why he had gone back to the motel and collected Sheila and Pat, he felt a surge of anger. *What the hell! They are supposed to be under my protection. I ask Dain to help with Amy's murder not take over my damn job. Who did Dain think he was, deciding what's best for the women without even talking it over with me?*

About to chew on Dain for not making sure dispatch got him the message, Lud thought back to last night and suddenly remembered. *My damn black out lasted most of the night. Maybe Alice did try to get hold of me, maybe she told me during my black out state.*

Dain may even have told her to make sure and get on the radio right away and tell Lud, don't want him to be tied up at the motel watching empty rooms. And maybe I gave her a roger. Christ, this thing's got me so mixed up I don't know whether I'm coming or going.

CHAPTER 19

Dain slapped him on the back, and said, "Come on up to the house. The gals must have a pot of coffee going by now."

Lud, back in the patrol car, followed Dain on up to where the drive opened up into a circle of gravel in front of the big double door barn.

Pat's head popped into view through the kitchen window as they made their way to the back door. As they climbed the steps, Lud said, "I'm worried about Rainbow Lake."

"Yeah, it's getting pretty high."

"Pretty high? The lake level is really climbing, worst I've seen in years. Pine Ridge could be isolated for several days. They're predicting the snow melt will keep Rainbow Creek over flood stage for at least another week.

Once the crest is past, the lake level will drop damn fast. But still, we could have a flood to equal seventy-nine. Remember the hell that caused?"

"Yeah, no one in or out of Pine Ridge for a week."

The smell of bacon and coffee greeted them as they opened the door, and by the time they entered the kitchen, Sheila was there, too. Lud saw her light up as if someone had flipped a switch, and he knew who had flipped that switch, Dain. *Christ, If Dain can't read those signs he has to be blind. Why can't I find a woman who looked at me that way?*

Boy, she was a looker back in high school days. But now, her figure more mature, She has turned into a real stunner.

Embarrassed by the way Sheila was staring at Dain, ignoring him, Lud turned toward Pat. *Christ, she's staring at Dain, too. Just like high school days, women never could keep their eyes off him.*

Lud fought against the urge to yell, *Hey, I'm here, too, and then storm out of the kitchen. But what the hell. They always treated me this way. Why expect two big city gals to treat me any different just because I had become the sheriff of a little back-woods county?*

If Lud had any hopes that the girls were going to settle around the breakfast table and let him be part of their conversation, he was quickly disappointed.

Clapping her hands together, Sheila cried, "You men help yourselves to the coffee. Pat and I need to finish putting on our war paint. We have a couple of errands to run, and we don't want the locals to think we've turned into bag ladies."

As Sheila followed Pat out of the room, she turned and said, "Dain, I know you left the house without eating anything, would you like me to fix you some breakfast before we go?"

Lud frowned. *Dain! Goddammit, what the hell does she think, that Indians don't eat breakfast? Or maybe she thinks the noble red man likes to eat over the tepee fire.*

After Dain laughingly declined Sheila's offer, he glanced at Lud. "What's wrong with you? You look mad enough to chew nails."

Lud stalled for a moment, picking at a hangnail, before he dared speak. "Nothing. Don't pay any attention to me. Like I told you, I'm on the edge."

When Dain came back to the table with two cups of coffee, Lud said, "And the worst part is, when things happen they come in bunches. I'm gonna be tied up part of today testifying at a DUI trial and serving some legal papers. And I need to get hold of Albert again, but that will have to wait till after he leaves work this afternoon.

Dain, about to take a sip, lowered his cup to the saucer. He told Lud about the morning visit to Albert's and about his chance encounter with Charlie.

Then Dain said, "By the way, I ran into Mike Powers. He's still the most useless bastard I've ever known." Lud listened as he related what Powers had done as they were passing the biker gang.

Lud grinned. "Still got the old Barlow Luck, eh? Ray Logan's not a man who usually walks away from something like that."

"He probably heard I was working with you."

Lud shook his head. "That don't mean shit to him. Logan's not as dumb as most people think. He knows enough about cops to know you wouldn't just flat-out shoot him, and if you weren't gonna do that, he'd have his fun with you in front of his men. Pestering you. He likes that. He'll push you right to the damn limit. But what the hell, you got no worse out of it than wasting a little time."

Dain finished the last of his coffee before saying, "I might have come away with something useful. You know one of his bikers, a fat guy named Gordy?"

Lud shrugged. "Not by name. A fat guy, you say."

"Damn near busting the seams of his britches."

"Yeah, I have seen him hanging around the last couple of months. Why do you ask?"

"He was about to tell me something about Peddler's Point, and I thought…say, you were out that way yesterday, right?"

Lud jerked upright, his hand striking the spoon protruding from the saucer, sending it spinning across the table. "What the hell do you mean?"

Dain wore that same look he had when Lud raised his voice out in the orchard. "Mike Powers said he saw you out there yesterday," Dain said, "turning down one of the logging roads. The way he told it, you had Albert Martinson with you."

Lud relaxed. Thank God. Powers had seen him while he was still conscious, apparently just after he had turned onto the logging road he was using as a shortcut to Albert's. Christ, what if it had been while he was blacked out?

Then Dain brought that nightmare into reality, asking, "What happened on the way out there? Did he say anything about meeting someone, being away for the night?"

Lud, back on surer ground, said, "No. You know better than that, Dain. I gave him the usual caution about staying close so we could reach him. What did you think he was gonna do? Say, 'Hell, no, Sheriff, I can't do that. I'm going on the run tonight. You'll never see me again.'"

Dain's next question cut the ground out from under his feet again. "But when you let him out at his house, what did he do? Did he say anything then?"

Lud looked doubtful. *God, how should I answer? How can I explain? When Dain got hold of Albert, he might say something different. And Christ, for all I know, one of the logger's buddies might have been sitting in the house, waiting for him. Goddammit, what should I say?*

The seconds were dragging by, and Dain was watching him the way a king snake watches a mouse. "Er...hell, I don't know," Lud said. "He didn't say much, one way or the other. I mean he wasn't exactly feeling happy with me. He just got out of the car. I sure the hell wasn't going to act all friendly with him."

"How about his Jeep? Was it parked beside the house?"

Oh, damn, Lud thought. *How the hell would I know?* Lud made a great show of thinking. "Well, ah...yeah, sure. I mean, he went to work with somebody else yesterday. That's why I was driving him home." *He saw Dain's eyes narrow. Oh, God, I guessed wrong.*

"Wait a minute. On second thought, I don't think it was there. What I mean is...hell, I can't be sure. I wasn't thinking about his damn Jeep."

The appearance of Sheila and Pat in the doorway saved him from further interrogation.

"Dain, do you mind if Pat and I use your car to go down to Crescent Valley?" Sheila asked.

"It's okay by me. I can use Dad's Blazer. As a matter of fact, it should be run, good for the battery. Take the car. It has about three-quarters of a tank of gas."

"We need to pick up some toiletries. Pat is as bad as me about packing. You know, ten pairs of shoes and no toothbrush. Besides, we want to be at the motel when Bev arrives. She has a room reserved at the Starlight. We figured we would all stay there and do everything together.

"Listen, Dain, would you mind if we brought her back up here…you know, to stay? I mean if anyone's interested in getting the women as they come for the reunion, Bev's among that group, too. Right? And I want to see her invitation. Do you realize she's coming a day earlier than necessary? We need to know why."

"Sure. I think it's a damn good idea. I'll rest a lot easier. What do you say, Lud?"

Damn Dain! He's assembling a harem, asking me my opinion as an afterthought. Well, I am going to drop a little rain on his parade.

Lud frowned. "The problem is we don't know how crazy this guy is." He glanced at Pat and Sheila. "Hell, what if he sneaked in here…with a machete or something like that? Dain won't be here every minute. The guy would have all three of you in the same place."

"But the motel…I just shudder at the idea of going back there," Sheila protested.

"That may be, but we know what keys this guy stole. You could move into other rooms. Sure he's been there—"

Dain interrupted, "Good God, Lud, you're going to scare the hell out of them."

"Well, with constant patrols, and them in different rooms, I feel they would be safer."

"Why don't we let them decide where they want to stay? After all, they are the ones in danger."

Sheila and Pat said in unison, "We'll stay here."

Then Sheila added, "Don't get worried if we're not back before late afternoon."

"When's Beverly coming in?" Lud asked.

"Early afternoon," Pat answered. She grabbed Sheila by the arm. "Hey, let's make tracks. We can't stand here all day gabbing."

Dain opened the door for them, dropped the key into Sheila's outstretched hand, and watched as they descended the porch steps, laughing at heaven knows what.

Dain took Lud's cup and filled it, along with his, before returning to the table.

"I was thinking about those bikers," he said. "You know, those guys really stick together. You can't get them to rat on one another. It must be true, you know, that stuff about the secret initiation ceremonies they have, the way they swear, one for all and all for one."

Lud gestured with his head toward his wrist, exposed by the pushed-up shirt sleeve. A small white scar ran part way across the inside of his wrist. "It's no different from us, being blood brothers."

Dain shot a glance at his own wrist and laughed. "That's right. I had forgotten. How old were we then? Ten or eleven? I saved your ass that day. You were a goner. Rainbow Lake was too cold for you to try to stay in that long." He rubbed at his wrist. "I thought you never would quit shivering. And then we cut our wrists with your hunting knife and held the cuts together. Christ, I cut mine so bad I was bleeding like a stuck pig. Just kid stuff, but either one of us could have ended up dead."

Lud frowned. "Not kid stuff, Dain. Don't tell me it never played a part when you'd drag those bullies off my ass at school. Blood brothers are bonded for life, regardless of when their pact is made."

Dain nodded. "I know. If your grandfather told me that once he told me a dozen times. It was that same summer, about six weeks after I pulled you out of Rainbow Lake, that my folks let me go with you and your mother to visit the reservation. I met all your people that summer.

Who was that guy your granddad told us about, the one who was a famous Nez Perce warrior? He was and ancestor of your mom's. Yours, too, I guess. Right?"

Lud hesitated a moment before answering. "Yeah. You've got a good memory, Dain. He was the first of the great Nez Perce chiefs…fought against the whites and against other Indians, too."

He laughed. "Remember? I used to pretend I was him when we played games in the woods. Chief Looking Glass must have killed all the white kids in Pine Ridge about five times over the next few summers."

Lud scowled. *Dammit, what the hell am I babbling about? If I keep it up, I will call Dain's attention to how I preserve my ancestor's memory in my cabin. How I still have the walls cluttered with paintings and drawings of Looking Glass, and the shelf over my desk is stacked with books and magazines about Looking Glass and the Nez Perce. Dain will think I'm obsessed with it.*

But what the hell is wrong with that? I have a right to be proud of my ancestors. I could never tell Dain that for a few years after my mother's death I daydreamed about being Looking Glass, avenging the wrongs against the Nez Perce and against my mother.

Suddenly uncomfortable, Lud rose from the table.

"Listen, old buddy, I've got business. We can reminisce later."

As Dain followed Lud onto the porch, he asked, "Say, buddy, did you get the plaster cast of that boot print in the orchard?"

"Yeah, it's in the evidence room at the station," Lud said. "Why do you ask? We have nothing to match it with…or have we?"

Dain explained about finding the boots and typewriter at Albert's.

"Hell, Dain, what I hear you saying is we have him dead to rights," Lud said. "You admit the boots probably match that cast in the office. Right? I'll call in for an all points bulletin on him."

Dain touched his arm. "Hold off on it a while, Lud. I'm beginning to agree with Charlie. Something is wrong here. All this evidence is just too damn convenient."

Lud sighed. *God, Dain could be irritating. Why in the hell couldn't he accept that we have a cut-and-dried case? Well, I'll humor him, but in the end, Albert Martinson will get his neck stretched.*

Lud tried to smile. "Jesus, Dain. Most people in this county would never hurt Amy, much less kill her. And you think someone put those things in Albert's house. But who?"

"What do you think of that biker, Logan, as a candidate?"

"Well, if Albert is innocent, then maybe…yeah, maybe it was Ray Logan. That damn knife he carries around could cut somebody's head off in a couple of swipes."

"Do you know anything about Logan?" Dain asked. "Is he a nut case? Have you heard anything like that about him?"

Lud held up his hand. "Whoa. I'm not saying Ray Logan is a psycho. I'm just thinking he might be mean enough to cut a woman's head off after having sex with her."

Dain shook his head. "No, this crime wasn't committed by someone just mean, too ritualistic. How about Albert? Ever hear he had mental problems?"

"No, I haven't heard—"

"Do you think we could get access to their histories, you know, military and local, without having charged either of them?"

"That's pretty sensitive stuff. They start talking about court orders, and most judges would rather offer you a weekend with their wives than issue a writ without having something dead bang.

"Oh, before I forget it, here's the key for the school."

Dain trailed down the steps after Lud. "But aren't you going over to the school with me to check it out? I mean, four eyes are better than two."

Lud glanced at his watch. "Christ, Dain. I've got lots to do today, and I've got to be in court at two. But what the hell. I'll run by there with you for a few minutes."

When they reached the patrol car, Dain said, "I'd better follow you in the Blazer. By the way, nobody saw anything around the high school night before last, at least not the ones I found at home. I looked all over for Joe Woods. Sam said he did most of the planning for the reunion. More important, he said Joe had a computer, and a typewriter. We need a sample from his typewriter."

"Come to think of it," Lud said, "I haven't seen Joe around for a while. But he's been working his ass off to put this thing together for the last two months. He'll be back by Friday."

"Must be out of town. He wasn't at my parent's funeral and that's not like Joe. He thought a lot of them." Dain shook his head. "I'll tell you what, Lud. Lot of people seem to just be disappearing."

Lud's jaw tightened. *What was that, a slam on my lawmanship. Christ, I don't have everyone check in and out when they come and go in my county.* Lud sat on the edge of the car seat, staring at Dain's back as he headed for the Blazer.

CHAPTER 20

Lud, waiting in the patrol car, watched the side mirror until the Blazer came into view, crossing the parking lot to stop behind him. Climbing out of the car, he hurried back to open the Blazer's door.

As Dain climbed out, he said, "Man, the wind is picking up, all of a sudden. I wonder if we have another thunder storm coming in?"

"I don't know. I—Jesus!"

Lud just managed to grab his hat as a gust of wind threatened to lift it off his head.

A dust devil careened across the parking lot toward them, scattering leaves and bits of paper as it came. They barely had time to close their eyes and avert their faces before a fine spray of grit peppered them. The whirlwind was gone as fast as it had appeared, leaving rearranged drifts of leaves and paper.

Lud opened his eyes, blinking, to find Dain staring down at a brown button on the parking lot a few inches from his shoe. Picking up the button, Dain turned it over and scratched at a dried brownish coating on it's back.

"Look, Lud. I think this is blood. This button couldn't have been here before that hard rain the night Amy was killed. The stain is still thickish, and the button's shiny." Pulling an evidence envelope from his pocket, he slipped the button inside.

"You don't miss a thing, do you, buddy?" Lud said. "Think it might be Amy's?"

Dain shrugged. "Your guess is as good as mine. Might not have anything to do with it. But it's sure worth the lab boys taking a look."

Lud motioned toward the front door. "Listen we better get a move on. I've got that court appearance this afternoon. And this judge is, Hard Ass Hanna. If I'm a minute late she'll have my buns on a plate."

He waited impatiently while Dain scuffed with his foot at the drift of leaves and papers, blown against the front door, before unlocking it. They stepped into the chilly interior.

Dain, pausing by the trophy case, said, "Jeez, it seems lonely in here. Remember when it was a madhouse all the time."

"Well, those days are gone forever," Lud said. "The only reason it's still standing is because the 4-H group, the Grange, clubs like that, need a place to meet. The county pays Vern a few bucks a month to take care of it, but the roof will be gone in another ten years. They'll tear it down when that happens. Last winter—Jesus!"

Dain looked up. "What's wrong?"

"Frigging headache." Without thinking, Lud pulled the bottle of pain pills out of his pants pocket and extracted two.

Dain, staring at the big yellow pills, asked, "That's strong stuff you're taking, Lud. I recognize those babies. I took those for a couple of days when I was at Central Receiving Hospital, after being shot. What did you say you're taking those for?"

"Headaches."

"Headaches! God, what kind of headaches?"

"Migraines, goddammit!" Lud exploded. "You're not my fucking doctor. Get off my damn back!"

"Hey," Dain said, raising his hands in a placating gesture. "I didn't mean anything. Just worried about you. You don't mind an old buddy being concerned do you?"

Lud slowly shook his head. "No, course not. Sorry."

"Well now, let's get busy and see what we can turn up here," Dain said, moving up the hall.

As they neared the stairway at the end of the corridor, Lud said, "Hey, aren't we gonna look around here?"

"The flier Sheila received said the first meeting would be in the home-ec room. That was on the second floor. It must have been pretty unpleasant down here that night, what with the wind and the lightning and the lights flickering on and off. If Amy was by herself, I don't think she would have lingered down here before she went upstairs. Doesn't take much imagination to know what it must have been like, especially if the lights had gone out."

Pausing at the top of the stairs, Dain asked, "What time did you get Albert home yesterday?"

Lud was annoyed. *Jesus Christ! Not on that again. Dain acts like he has a schedule of my black outs. I got no memory of any of the things he keeps asking about. Should have waited until after the reunion to enlist his help.*

Struggling to find a safe answer, he said, "We left the office not long after you did. Went straight there. Hell, your guess is as good as mine."

The answer seemed to satisfy Dain for the moment. He started down the hall with Lud following.

Halfway down the corridor, Dain stopped. "Vern hasn't been in here cleaning up since the night Amy was killed, has he?"

Lud shook his head. "I didn't know where the investigation would take us, so I ask him not to go into the school until he got the word from you or me."

"Look here," Dain said, pointing at the floor. "A boot print, several of them, in this spot of dust sediment. Unless I miss my guess, they'll match the one in the orchard. Looks like we guessed right. Our killer was here."

He took a few more steps down the hall before turning back to look at Lud. "About Albert. When you took him home, you didn't stop any-where on the way, did you?"

Lud sighed. *Goddammit! Is Dain going to ask me where the hell I was at the time Amy was killed?*

Fighting to stay calm, Lud demanded, "What the hell are you getting at? What's the bottom line? You act like I drove Albert to the airport and bought him a ticket out of the country. Goddammit, man, I just gave him a ride home. I didn't write down the times. I didn't check for his Jeep. I just put the son of a bitch out and drove off."

"Sorry, Lud. I'm just trying to figure out how much time there was between you leaving him there and Charlie finding him gone. The house was neat as a pin, nothing disturbed. Are we supposed to believe, as soon as you left, he jumped in his Jeep, took off and left that type-writer and those boots for us to find? Had to be in a hell of a hurry. I need to contact those bikers again."

"Bikers? What the hell have they got to do with anything?" Lud asked.

But Lud's question went unanswered. Dain had reached the open door of the home-ec room. His voice low, he said, "Uh-oh."

Lud, behind him, glanced past his shoulder. The dusty floor immediately before the door bore three sets of footprints. Two of them were large treaded boots. one set entering the room and the other coming out. The third set, going in, was smaller, the sort of print that would have been made by a woman's footwear.

Dain, standing at the open door, pointed toward the teacher's desk at the front of the room. "What's that on the floor next to the desk?"

Lud squinted. "Hard to tell, the way it's busted up, but it looks like one of those little cassette players. It must have gotten knocked off the desk, then stepped on to be smashed like that."

Lud bent forward to peer under the desk. "What's that under the table, that small white cylindrical thing? And, look, there's another one."

"Candles, sure as hell. Let's move inside, Lud, but step over those prints. We don't want to contaminate them."

They stopped next to the desk.

"Something must have slammed into this desk. See those scuff marks the legs made? It got pushed back against the wall. That must be what knocked the cassette player and candles off," Lud said. He scratched at a pool of hardened wax on the floor. "Still not brittle. This wax has been here less than two days I'd say."

Dain, removing a handkerchief and an evidence envelope from his pocket, reached past Lud to retrieve a small plastic object wedged between the desk leg and the wall.

Lud motioned toward the evidence envelope. "What do you have there?"

"I'm not sure, but I think it's one of those little thingamajigs they put over hypo needles to avoid accidents. Who knows. We might get a partial print off it."

Lud, rising, nodded towards the disarray in what had been orderly rows of student chairs. Several had been knocked over onto their sides and others shoved together to leave a cleared space in the middle of the room. Here the dust on the floor was badly scuffed, without detectable footprints. "That must be where he caught her, Dain. Looks like she put up a pretty good struggle."

When Dain said nothing, Lud glanced back at him.

Dain was bent over the desk, his face only inches from its surface.

Lud felt the anger rising in him again. Dain had turned into a goddamn bloodhound, sniffing at everything in sight. Ignoring his impute. He tried to curb his annoyance. After all, he had asked his old friend to help him because he was a trained homicide detective.

Straightening, Dain said, "I'm not going to touch that desk top. I want the state lab boys to take a look at it."

"Why? What makes you think that's necessary?"

"I think it's dried semen. Christ, this is bad."

"What do you mean?" Lud asked.

"If she was laid out on top of this desk and raped, she must have been unconscious. And why put her on the desk top? It would have been far more natural for him to rape her on the floor where they had struggled. Laying her out on top of the desk, using these lighted candles and that cassette player. Looks like we called this right from the start. This whole damn thing was some kind of ritual.

"And look there on the floor. Four pools of wax. This means those candles were knocked off the desk, then relit, and later knocked off a second time."

"This is really spooky stuff," Lud muttered. His voice strengthened. "Dain, there's blood over here. This chair has blood spots on it, and there's a big stain on the floor. You better get a sample. Maybe it's the killer's. This would give us a DNA base."

Dain shook his head. "No. As long as we're going to bring the state guys in here anyway, they can check it. We'll just close the door and put a police tape across it. You should notify them today."

Forty minutes later they exited the front door, having checked every other room in the building without results. Lud paused to look back through the front door as Dain locked it. "Well, we found where the bastard killed her, anyway."

Dain shook his head. "Not necessarily. That footprint isn't worth a damn until we locate her shoes. Unless that blood proves to be hers, or the lab boys can find her prints in there, we have no evidence she was in that room. Even if we can get a DNA reading from the blood or semen and find a match, it means nothing unless we can put both Amy and her killer in that room."

He handed the key to Lud. "Let's just hope with the semen for his DNA the blood is Amy's.

"Listen, you tell Vern to stay out of the building and to allow no one else inside, not till the lab boys have checked that room."

The rising wind that had greeted them when they reached the school had brought with it a building canopy of dark clouds. Lud, eyeing the sky, said, "Jesus, I hope we don't get a heavy rain out of this. Rainbow Lake is going to be bad enough without more water."

CHAPTER 21

As Lud's patrol car disappeared in the direction of Crescent Valley, Dain glanced upward at the white frame house perched on the hillside across the road. He had better check on the old coot again. Fred Griffith had given up his job as county building inspector years ago and moved into the house across the way.

According to the townspeople, his only hobby was watching what went on below his house. The school and all of Main Street was in clear view. If anybody had been watching the school two nights ago, it had to have been Fred. He wouldn't have been using his binoculars as he did during the day, but still, with the lightning flashes, he might have seen something.

A few minutes later the Blazer rocked to a stop in front of the weathered house, badly in need of paint. Crossing the road on foot, Dain climbed the path that wound up the hillside to the home. As Dain came out into the clearing before the house, the front door creaked opened.

Good ole Fred, still on the job. The old man was more stooped than Dain remembered, and now, he supported his frail frame with a crooked stick cane, but his bright blue eyes still had their color. His sparse gray hair was askew, and whether he recognized Dain or not, he was wearing a broad toothless smile.

His pointed nose and chin seemed they would touch if not for the open mouthed grin. Fred wore a faded plaid shirt and sweat pants too large for him. He had them pulled up to where they encircled his lower ribs. His voice revealed his age with a slight tremor but was still strong.

"Dain Barlow, by God!" Fred exclaimed with a wet lisp. "Didn't think I'd remember, did you? I spotted you and Lud coming out of the school, and then saw you coming up the path. It's about poor Amy Housley, right?"

Dain mounted the porch steps and shook his hand. "Mr. Griffith, you're right about that. I'm helping Lud with the investigation into Amy's death."

"Mr. Griffith, Hell! I'm plain ole Fred, boy. Don't be giving me any airs.

"I heard about what happened to that girl and figured Lud would be around to see me. But when Vern was carrying me down to Crescent Valley yesterday, he told me you were helping the sheriff."

"I wasn't sure you'd remember me."

The old man laughed, a high-pitched cackle. "I'm getting feeble, and have lost all my teeth, but I haven't quite lost my mind yet, Dain. Come on in and sit. I can't stand for long. Legs aren't worth a damn anymore, and it takes a passel of pills just to keep me breathing, that's why I went to the city yesterday, to load up on the damn things again. Guess I shouldn't complain though. Least I'm still here."

Inside the house, the sharp odor of a cat litter box in need of cleaning mingled with the pungent smell of tobacco and mildew. Right away, Dain spotted Fred Griffith's observation post. A well worn brown easy chair, its cushion patched with duct tape in a couple places, faced the big window. A large pair of binoculars were suspended by a strap over the wing of the chair. On the floor next to it stood a brass spittoon. A big black cat, surely as old as Fred in its own way, was curled up on a pad on the wide window sill.

With a groan, Fred settled himself by degrees into the chair, then leaned the cane against the armrest. He waved in the direction of the sofa. "Grab a seat, boy."

Dain eyed the ruin of a sofa. Cotton poked through the covering on each arm rest, and a couple of springs protruded from one of its three cushions. The surface was flocked with several years' supply of cat hair.

"That's okay, Fred. I'll stand. I won't be here long."

Fred, for all his slowness of movement, got down to business right away. "I suppose you want to know what I saw, er…night before last, wasn't it? Over at the school, I mean."

Dain nodded, but Fred seemed to feel the need to think on it awhile. Closing his eyes, he leaned his head back. He stayed that way so long that Dain was beginning to think he had gone to sleep. Then the old man's eyes opened, and he turned to eye Dain. "The school was all lit up, figured Vern was getting it ready for the reunion.

"The storm came up sudden like. The evening started out quiet, and then that wind came out of nowhere, blowing like hell, with lightning all over the place. I knew right then we were in for one of them hell raisers. Just before the rain started, a car pulled into the parking lot. The wind was blowing so hard by then that the driver had a hell of a time closing the door."

Fred blinked several time. "Now, Dain, I can't swear it was a woman. My eyes aren't as good as they were once, and those things," he glanced at the binoculars, "aren't worth much at night. It was the lower legs, what I'm saying is they looked too slender to be wearing pants. Know what I mean?"

Dain, nodding, said, "Notice anyone else around the school that night? You know, before the car arrived. Or afterwards, while the storm was going on?"

"Saw Vern go inside in the middle of the afternoon, but I never saw him come out. But of course, one of my pills makes me go to the bathroom a lot, water pills they call 'em. I was away from the window a couple of times before dark. Maybe that's when Vern left."

Fred fumbled in his pockets and drew out a folding knife and a plug of chewing tobacco. Opening the stained blade with bony dark veined fingers, he laboriously worked it until he separated a bite size sliver.

Bringing the piece up to his mouth with the jackknife, he nibbled it off the cutting edge, folded the blade, and dropped it and the tobacco back in his pocket. He glanced up at Dain again. "Amy, or whoever it was, was damn lucky she got inside before the rain started. It was a regular cloudburst." He gestured toward the window. "Water was pouring down the glass so damn fast I couldn't see a darn thing."

"Damn pills." He grabbed his cane, and with a prodigious grunt, he heaved himself to his feet, tottering dangerously close to pitching forward through the window before steadying himself.

Dain, leaning against the wall, pushed himself upright. "Thanks, Mr. er, Fred, you've been a big help."

Fred, forgetting his urgent need to relieve himself, followed Dain toward the door on shaky legs, and said, "Sorry I can't help more, but the last thing I saw was that man coming around the building."

Dain's, "What?" was so loud that the cat came awake and leapt from the sill in a single motion.

The startled Fred said, "Christ, boy, I'm not deaf."

"Man? What man are you talking about, Fred?"

Fred's voice held a touch of indignation, "Well, I saw a man come around from behind the school a few minutes after the woman went in. But don't know where he went. It was getting hard to see. Coulda been a big kid, they're down around that old school all the time, just thought it was one of them making for home."

"Couldn't tell if it was a man or a boy?"

"Nope. The rain streaks on the window made everything waver. This guy would look thin one second and bulky the next. To tell you the

truth, it was the way he walked. The first one, the woman, kinda wiggled, you know

what I mean. But men don't walk like that. He was male, coulda been
a kid though. I tell you this. I saw this guy under the light. He was a blur,
but I guarantee you he was dressed all in black. Now don't hold me to
this, Dain, cause I'm not sure, but it even looked like he had something
black pulled over his head.

"Not long after that the lights went out. I waited, but when they did-
n't come right back on, I went to bed. Almost broke my fool neck, too. I
walked right into the open closet door."

As Dain opened the door, the old man said, "Oh, I forgot. About an
hour after I went to bed, the damn thunder kept me awake, I heard an
engine. Sounded like a motorcycle."

"You mean coming along the highway?" Dain asked.

"Nope, that's just it. The noise just started all at once, like someone
had just cranked it. At the time I thought it was that Ray Logan leaving
Brown's Tavern. He does that a lot."

His words stirred Dain's own memory. He had heard a motorcycle
during the night, racing by his house.

As he started onto the porch, Fred tugged at his sleeve. "You don't
suppose that coulda been Ray Logan. Watching that guy come from
around the school, I thought, damn big kid, thought he looked pretty
tall, too. But then, depending on what the raindrops did, sometimes he
looked shorter and bulkier, like Lud. You don't suppose Ray Logan
coulda killed her, do you? God knows he's surly enough to. Folks say he
got a discharge from the army for being unhinged, say he's crazy as a
loon. And that whole bunch is as mean as a diamond back snake."

He tugged harder at Dain's sleeve. "Listen, Dain, I can heat up some
coffee," the old man said. "Maybe if we go back in, I'll remember something else after a while."

Dain gently detached Fred's fingers from his sleeve, smiling at the
lonely little guy. Backing across the porch, he said, "Tell you what, Fred.

How about I make you my deputy in charge of surveillance. Keep your eyes open for anything suspicious. No matter what. I'll check back with you in a couple of days."

Dain was at the bottom of the steps, turning away toward the path, when he heard Fred, Griffith's last words, apparently addressed more to himself than Dain. "Of course, Albert Martinson rents a bike in Crescent Valley sometimes and rides it around for a few days. Hell, I've even seen Lud on one when his patrol car was in the shop. Too damn many people riding cycles."

Dain paused to catch his breath, where the path, winding down the hill from Fred's, met the highway. The scramble up and down the hill had winded him. He glanced up and down the road, trying to decide whom he should see next. The market, a block down the road, caught his eye. *Joe woods. He worked there. He wasn't at home the other night but he should be working today. Might as well find out what Joe has to say about those invitations.*

Dain pulled up in front of the market. Both the parking lot and store were empty. As he stepped inside the store, only the sound of a TV betrayed the possible presence of someone.

Dain yelled, "Hey, anybody here?"

He heard a protest, made up of equal parts of leather and wood, and the TV went silent.

Puffing noisily, Chet Becker appeared in the doorway leading from the back, where he lived. Chet was the fattest man by far in Pine Ridge. His eyes, barely visible among the folds of flesh, peered at Dain. Waddling out into the grocery, Chet wheezed, "Dain! I wondered when you were going to come in to buy a few things. Of course, I guess with all the food brought to your house by the good people of Pine Ridge while you were arranging the funeral for your parents, God rest their souls, got you fixed up for a while. Damn, I was sorry to hear about your folks."

Dain held up his hand. "I'm not here to buy food. I've got more food there, Chet, than I could eat in a month. Actually, what I came in for was to see Joe Woods." He went through the useless charade of glancing about the small store.

Becker, having reached the counter with the cash register on it, sank atop a stool with a loud groan. "Funny you asked, Dain. I was about to call Lud. Joe hasn't been in to work since before the weekend. I must have tried phoning him a dozen times.

"I figured maybe an emergency came up. His mother's been in a bad way the last year or so, lives in Yakima. He could have gotten a call during the middle of the night and just took off, but when I didn't hear anything yesterday, I decided to contact her. Didn't know her name, but Joe's neighbors did."

He leaned forward to stare at Dain, his huge, pulpy arms resting on the counter. "She hasn't heard hide nor hair of him, so I sent my boy over to the house. He could see into every room from the outside. He said nothing looked disturbed, but Joe wasn't there."

With his mouth hanging open, Chet took in a big labored breath. Wheezing he continued. "I heard you was working for, Lud. What's wrong? Has Joe been up to something?"

Dain grimaced. *Joe Woods! I hadn't thought of Joe Woods. The guy seemed as meek as a church mouse. No real interest in women. A loner. What the hell, more than one ax murderer has gone to church every Sunday.*

Disturbed, he blurted out his reason for wanting to see Joe before he could check himself. "It's the invitations for the reunion, Chet. Some of them were bogus. I don't suppose you know anything about it."

Chet grinned. "I sure the heck do. Joe used the computer I have in the back room, conned me into getting it, said he could hook it up some way to the one he has at home and work on things from either place, said it'd make inventory a lot easier, too."

The folds of skin on his neck waved as he shook his head. "Can you imagine that, one computer knowing what the other one's doing a block away. Anyway he typed one day after work while I was restocking shelves. Didn't take him long. Them computers are a whiz."

"Did he do them all, that night, do you know?" Dain asked.

"Yeah, he did. I was about through, taking boxes back to the store room. He said he was gonna take them over to the post office and put them in the night box, but he came back inside while I was still in the store room."

Dain's interest quickened. "Oh, he didn't mail them, then."

"Well, yes and no. Said he ran into somebody who was going by the post office, so he asked whoever it was to mail them for him."

With a mental crossing of his fingers, Dain asked, "Did he say who it was?"

Chet lifted his eye brows. "Heck, he might have. I don't know. By that time, I was in the middle of counting the days take in the cash register, and I wasn't paying a whole lot of attention to him, concentrating on what I was doing. I wasn't much interested in the reunion. Don't mean nothing to me."

Five minutes later, Chet Becker still had no answers, and Dain was back in the Blazer. *Joe Woods. Dammit! Was he on the run?* His brow furrowed. *Or was he dead because of those invitations?*

Dain had swung the Blazer around in the store's parking lot, ready to drive back out onto the highway when his cell phone, lying on the front seat beside him, began an insistent bleating. Halting the Blazer, he punched the phone's *SEND* button and drew it to his ear. "Dain Barlow here."

The voice sounded far away, knifing through a hailstorm of static. "Dain, this is Sheila. I can hardly hear you."

"What's up, Sheila?"

"Thank God, I remembered your cell phone number. We're stranded out here on the highway. We ran over some junk, little bits and pieces of rusted metal, scattered all over the pavement. I couldn't help it, Dain. There was no way to avoid the stuff. Both front tires are blown out and one of the rear ones." She sounded on the verge of tears.

"Jesus H—It's okay, Sheila. It's not your fault. Just hold on. I'll be there in about twenty…wait a minute. You've got a cell phone. Call Staley's down in Crescent Valley. My dad had an account there. Tell them what happened. I'm afraid it's going to take about two hours out of your afternoon, though, but it can't be helped. Listen, I'll—"

"Dain, Pat says it's the phone's battery. She forgot to charge it, and she didn't pack the recharger. I'd better call Staley's before it goes flat."

The phone clicked off before he could ask about Beverly.

CHAPTER 22

Beverly Taylor glanced first at her watch and then at the speedometer. Seventy-five. She slowed. One thing she didn't need, especially while driving her husband's Porsche, was a speeding ticket. The building crest of the Cascades, a ragged frieze of smokey blue, stretching from horizon to horizon, under the light gray of the overcast sky lay like a distant barrier across the arrow-straight road.

She licked her lips. *I should be in Crescent Valley by one o'clock, even if I slow to fifty-five.*

Beverly chuckled as she recalled the hectic night before. *I stumbled into the house at six, dead on my feet, and Derek yelled, Hey, you missed your phone call. I normally love it when he acts like a big, happy sheep dog.*

But that night he was treading on dangerous ground. I was in no mood for his antics.

I just dropped my purse on the easy chair and stood glaring. What call, I demanded. The day had been pure hell. My biggest sale ever didn't go through. I was running late at the office, unable to break away from a client who seemed more interested in talking than buying.

Hey, go easy, honey. Derek walked up and kissed me. It was about your reunion. Some guy called me at work. Said he'd lost your phone number but remembered my name. His name was, oh, what the hell...er, Joe Woods, or something like that.

My spirits lifted immediately. Oh, yeah, Joe Woods is in charge this year, he sent the invitations. What did he want?

He said to tell you several of the folks were coming in early, about noon, so they decided to have a picnic out at the Pine Creek Campground, whatever the devil that is.

I felt bad, I had thought, no chance. I wish I had known earlier. No way I could possibly get ready in time. Then I gave him my cute smile, and laid it on thick. Especially, I said, if I have to take the time to get you and the twins in condition to survive without me for four days. That smile did it, he melted like hot butter.

Oh, yeah? Well, I'll tell you what, woman. Derek was bound to show me he could get along without me. Grab your shower, and I'll order take-out. Chinese okay? Oh, you know what I like, I cooed, getting sexy. This was going to be a night to hold us both over for the four days, and then some.

Then before I could leave the room, he told me that to make sure I get to the reunion on time, he would keep the Camry and have me take the Porsche. His last word on the subject was you don't mind taking the Porsche do you love? My God, no I didn't mind. I love this car. She slowly caressed the leather covered steering wheel.

Flashing past the sign reading, Crescent Valley, 10 miles, Bev smiled, wanting to hug herself. *The other three members of our quartet of high school friends, Amy, Sheila, and Pat, have all done well, I've heard, but none of them has a Derek Taylor, and none of them have two adorable little look-alikes who acted almost human this morning, running into the kitchen all smiles and giggles.*

Beverly passed the city limits sign with the Porsche's motor purring contentedly after its two hundred and fifty-mile romp. A new motel, all of its landscaping still not in, stood just inside the city limits. *I wonder why the girls didn't choose to stay there? The place looks a lot nicer than the Starlight. But, of course, they probably didn't know about that one, I've been here since they have.*

Crescent Valley was growing in this direction, and she passed several new buildings before she saw the starlight Motel sign rearing into the overcast sky ahead. Like the motel, the sign had seen better days, and like the motel, it was better seen after dark.

Turning into one of the angled parking spaces before the motel's office, she cut off the Porsche's throaty ruminations. Somehow, the car and the starlight Motel didn't seem to go together. She hoped the others had arrived. For whatever reason, the excitement of the reunion had paled on her during the long drive.

She arched her brows. *Maybe Derek and the twins were too sweet, after all. But, then again, maybe when I see the others the excitement will return.*

Once out of the car, Beverly paused to check herself in the reflections of the motel's glass front door. She was much shorter than her old classmates. Her raven black hair was straight and long, hanging down to her shoulder blades. Bev had a truly lovely creamy complexion that made her warm brown eyes seem extraordinary. Her petite figure was clad in navy blue slacks and a bulky white sweater. Satisfied, she charged the door, pushing her way into the small office.

No one was behind the desk. She frowned. *Good old Crescent Valley, nothing has changed, as if business, though necessary, is secondary to their mundane existence.*

She went from fingers drumming on the counter to pacing back and forth within a minute. Finally stopping, she yelled, "Hey, isn't anybody here?"

From somewhere back in the bowels of the motel she heard an indistinct voice but had no idea what it said. By the time a portly gray-haired woman came in from the back, her hands patting her hair, Beverly was pacing again. The woman looked flustered.

"Sorry. I was changing clothes."

Bev caught herself before she said something ungracious. *What's wrong with me? I've really got the willies. As much as I want to see Amy,*

Pat, and Sheila, I'm about to decide this hurry up trip, just to be here in time for the picnic, was a bad idea.

Working a smile onto her face, she said, "Hi, I'm Beverly Taylor. I think you have a reservation for me."

Recognition was like a light bulb coming on in the woman's face. "Oh, yes. You're one of the young women coming up for the reunion in Pine Ridge."

Bev glanced back over her shoulder, down the long line of motel rooms, before asking, "Yeah, I'm one of the old Pine Ridgers. Are my friends in?"

The woman shrugged. "Well, I haven't noticed them going out. But then, my husband's been on the desk most of the day."

Seeing the woman was about to launch into an explanation of motel operations, Beverly cut her off. "I'll get checked in, and then I'll call them. What rooms are they in?"

The question proved to be a stunner for the woman. She pulled open the file of registration cards, shuffled back and forth through them several times, scratched her head, then had a second try at it before saying, "That's Steele and Cromwell, right? They're in rooms twenty and twenty-one."

"How about me? Room Nineteen or twenty-two?"

She wished she hadn't asked. Finding the answer required another search, first through a second small metal file and then through a folder of correspondence. With a quizzical look she glanced up. "My husband usually does this, I'm really sorry."

Finally, the woman, with a visible start, cried, "Oh, that's right. The gentleman running the reunion, what was his name, Wells, Woods? She waved her hand in frustration. Something like that, he wanted some of the rooms switched around. Listen, let me go get my husband. He was the one who talked to him. He's in the back, repairing a lamp. Just a minute." The woman vanished before Beverly could assure her that any room was okay.

Derek could have told the woman that Beverly was a bit impatient at times. But before the petite brunette could get past the finger-drumming stage, a man popped out through the door, moving much faster than the woman had, despite the sizable bandage on his head. Sixtyish, he was clad in paint-spattered fatigue pants, and a faded plaid work shirt. The thinnish thatch of what must once have been bright red hair had a couple paint smudges as well.

"Mrs. Taylor? I'm the manager, Harry Blackwell. Your reunion director, Joe Woods, called this morning about the room change. We had to scramble a bit, but we talked one of our guests into transferring to another room."

Beverly was puzzled. "Room change? Why on earth change the rooms?"

Mr. Woods asked if we had adjacent rooms with connecting doors. I told him we had two sets, so he made a reservation for one of them. He said to put you in the other one. Okay?"

She shrugged. *One of the gals must have told Joe to do it. That way, they could go back and forth between rooms.*

She grinned into Harry Blackwell's anxious face. "Hey, that's a great idea."

Filling out the registration card, she shoved it back across the counter. As the manager turned to extract the keys from one of the pigeon holes on the wall behind the counter, Beverly asked, "You know if any of the other ladies are in their rooms?"

"Nope. But their cars are here." He waved his hand toward the scattering of cars parked in front of the motel units. "Give me time to get my shoes on, and I'll take your bags to your room for you."

She shook her head. "Never mind. They're not heavy. Besides, I need the exercise."

Harry pointed through the plate glass window. "It's the unit—"

"I can find it," she interrupted. "You go back to what you were doing."

As she turned to leave, hc gaze fell on a copy of the weekly Crescent Valley Courier, its front page lying face up. A bold headline read: **PINE RIDGE VICTIM IDENTIFIED.** "Goodness," she cried. "What's that all about?"

Harry Blackwell shrugged. "Some woman was murdered up there in Pine Ridge. Had her head cut off."

"Who was it?"

He shrugged again. "Don't know. Didn't read it. The wife and I don't pay much attention to stuff like that. Seems like there's something about killing or fighting in the paper all the time. The world's going to hell in a hurry, if you want to know what I think."

Beverly toyed with the idea of dropping onto the sofa and reading the story, but if the picnic was to start at two, she had to shower before then. *Probably Amy will know something about it. In the old days, she knew everything that went on in Pine Ridge.*

Leaving the office, Bev considered the Porsche. *Should I leave it by the office where it will be parked under bright light? Derek will kill me if anything happens to that car.* The two heavy suitcases tipped the scales in favor of pulling up in front of her room.

She circled the flower bed that made a loop of the drive and spotted rooms twenty and twenty-one. Completing the loop, she eased into the parking space next to one of the cars and shut down the power plant.

Sliding out of the car, she glanced at the number on the room key tab, blinked, and looked a second time. *Fourteen! The motel guy must have made a mistake. No, Sheila and Pat had twenty and twenty-one probably connecting. The manager said they just had two sets of connecting rooms. No doubt she and Amy would have the other two. Good, she and Amy had always been good friends.*

Bev started to climb back into the Porsche but thought better of it. *Number fourteen is only five doors away.*

She staggered down the walk with the two big bags, unlocked the door, and reeled into the room's dim interior. Tossing the two keys onto the bed, Beverly sank down next to them. She eyed the alley door's lock. *In a minute I'll make sure it's locked, but for now, just let me stretch out and get the kinks out. God, this feels good after the long trip.*

She glanced at the connecting door. All was quiet in the next room. *The woman at the desk said Sheila and Pat were here, but she said nothing about Amy. Probably hasn't arrived yet, she has a pretty lengthy drive ahead of her, too.*

Bev glanced at her watch again. *Just time to check in with Pat and Sheila before a quick shower.*

She dialed room twenty, counted eight rings, and then hung up. Maybe they were in the other room. The phone rang eight times in room twenty-one, and again there was no answer. "Well, so much for that, no welcoming committee." She mumbled. *Darn it! Could they have gone on without me? Well, why not? No one knew exactly when I was going to arrive. I left a message at the motel desk that I was going to be in early this afternoon but they may not even have gotten the message. But their car's are still here, probably in town, main street's only two blocks away.*

Beverly had one suitcase open on the bed and was extracting a pair of jeans and white walking shoes when she heard the knock. Whirling, she had a big smile as she started for the front door, then realized that the raps had come from the connecting door. *Good, Amy's here after all.*

Stepping over to the connecting door, she called, "Amy, I was thinking you hadn't made it here, yet. Come in and let me look at you."

A few seconds passed, and the knocks came again.

"Darn it, quit fooling around. I need a shower before we can go. Oh, my God, I forgot. The door must be locked from my side. Just a minute."

Fitting the key into the lock, she swung it open.

The eyes! She had only a few minutes to consider the hate that blazed from them.

Chief Looking Glass came into the room far to quickly for Bev to Scream.

CHAPTER 23

Scrambling out of the Blazer, Dain raced through the falling rain for the back porch. He'd been in L.A. so long that he'd forgotten what spring weather was like in Washington. Forty minutes earlier, the sky had been cloudless. Now the overcast promised rain that could last into the evening hours. Unlocking the door, he stepped into the small mud entry which led into the kitchen, dim now in the gray light coming in from outside.

Entering his bedroom, his gaze was drawn to the answering machine with its insistent red LED. The digital display told him he had two messages. *Sheila again, sure as hell. Staley's must have found something besides flat tires to repair.*

He punched the playback button. A cool female voice declared, "This is John Finestein's office, Mr. Barlow. John needs to see you as soon as possible." Finestein's secretary gave him a number to call and a curt goodbye.

He frowned. *Lawyers! In the movies, one always sat down, usually in the midst of scowling distant relatives, heard the attorney read the will, and then gather up the deeds, bank passbooks and safe deposit keys, and walk out. Not so, at least with the Barlow estate. I must have signed twenty documents already.*

He punched in Finestein's number and waited through seven rings before a female voice came onto the line, younger this time, more cheerful, telling him that Mr. Finestein would be with him in a moment. *This was different from L.A. shysters. There they were always in a meeting.*

Finestein hadn't changed much over the years, still tall and thin, hair a little whiter. But the thing he remembered most about him was his fetish. Everything was gray; hair, suits, car, office carpets and drapes. The man even had a gray pallor to his face.

His speech was disconcerting. With each fact he pronounced, the man hesitated. Dain didn't know what he was supposed to do, marvel, applaud, shake his head in disbelief, or trade dead silences with him.

John Finestein's soft sibilant voice came on the line. "Dain, thanks for returning my call. I thought I'd better get in touch."

Dain sighed. *Jesus. The lawyer is going to throw a monkey wrench into the proceedings. Why can't things go easy, just once.* "What's the trouble, Mr. Finestein?"

"John," the lawyer corrected. "No problem. Were you expecting any?" He paused. "I need three more signatures from you. After that, everything's on automatic pilot. What do you say to that?" He paused. "What I need for you to do is run in sometime this afternoon and sign these documents. You don't want this to drag on, don't want to come back up and appear in court." He paused. "Do you?"

Dain glanced at his watch. *The trip down to Crescent Valley and back would probably take an hour and a half, at least. Still, if I leave now, I could be back before the ladies arrived home.* "I sure don't. I don't have a lot of vacation time left. Tell you what, I'll see you in about forty—"

"Five P.M."

"Five? It has to be earlier, Mr., ah, John. I have to be back up here by five o'clock. Listen, I'll be in Crescent Valley tomorrow. Why don't I—"

The relaxed voice changed, became insistent. "Really, Dain, things are a little tight. I'm leaving town after dinner this evening. I'll be in Seattle seconding a civil case. The trial will probably last ten to twelve days. In fact, what I was proposing you do is that you meet me at the Tender Hereford restaurant. You are batching it, aren't you? And certainly you're no longer short of funds." His laugh had the warmth of a glissando on a Xylophone. My secretary will be with us, and she can take the documents back to the office."

"But I—"

"Oh, well, maybe in four or five weeks, when we can find a weekend that I'm available and you can fly up. I have to go, Dain—"

"Okay, okay," Dain interrupted. "I'll be at the Tender Hereford at five." He broke the connection, not wanting to hear Finestein's final sly note of triumph.

Dain punched the playback button on the answering machine again. He waited impatiently through the voice of Finestein's secretary. She and her boss sounded like the perfectly matched pair.

The second caller was Lud, wanting Dain to phone him as soon as he got in. To his surprise, he found the sheriff at his office.

Lud's voice exploded through the phone's earpiece. "Dammit, Dain, I thought you were gonna get in touch with me."

Dain winced. Laughing, he said, "Calm down, big guy. You just about blew my ear off."

"Sorry, but I'm worried. Oh, hold on a minute, buddy," Lud said.

For the next couple of minutes Dain heard nothing but the distant sound of people talking. Then Lud came back on the line, his voice sharper and surrounded by static. "Okay, Alice, hang up. I've got it." Dain heard a click on the line, and then Lud said, "I'm out in the car. I'm so spooked by this business, Dain, I don't know who to trust."

"What happened?"

"Nothing I can put my finger on. But I think from this point on, we'd better keep this between the two of us. Dain, the gals aren't back yet, are they?"

"No. I think Sheila said something about late afternoon. Why do you ask?"

"I just wanted to make sure that somebody was with them all the time. After what happened to Amy and that thing with the finger last night, I'm on edge. Maybe the three of them together would be safe, but we can't take the chance."

"Yeah, I know. I was going to call you. Something's come up."

"Come up? What the hell's wrong?"

"Keep your shirt on," Dain said. "I have to run down to Crescent Valley at five to see my lawyer."

"Your lawyer? Are you in some kind of trouble?"

Dain laughed. "Oh, hell, Lud. What a question! Seems like I've had nothing but trouble since I came home. I have more papers to sign. If I don't do it now, I'll have to fly back up here in several weeks. I'm having dinner with him, so it will be eight by the time I'm home, well after dark. Could you or Ralph swing by here a couple of times to check on them? I hate to ask."

Lud's voice grew in volume. "Hate to ask, hell! I'm as worried about those little gals as you are. It's my damn county this shit's been happening in. Listen, the house has good locks, doesn't it?"

"Sure. Dad must have changed them a couple of years back. The only easy way into this place is…but I don't think anybody knows about that."

A moment of silence, then Lud said, "Knows what, Dain?"

"About the outside cellar door. I don't think the folks used it much. It's on the back side of the house. The ivy growing on the foundation has covered it completely."

"Does it have a dead bolt?" Lud asked.

Dain laughed. "Christ, Lud. That lock, actually an old padlock, is as old as the house. The thing is so badly rusted it's ready to disintegrate." He thought for a moment. "I'd better stop by a hardware store in Crescent Valley tonight, pick up a good lock to put on that door."

His voice rising, Lud said, "Jesus, that rain's really coming down. Hey, don't worry about tonight. The ladies will be okay. But I would take care of that cellar door. Better safe than sorry. I've gotta get going. I want to run up to the house and grab a few things before I relieve Ralph."

"Lud, better not mention that lock to—" He was talking to a dead phone.

*   *   *

Charlie Young brought the four-wheel-drive utility vehicle to a halt. He was back in the maze of logging roads that formed a triangle between Peddler's Point, the O'Neill place, and Albert's house. He had been wandering about in the labyrinth of lanes that were more tracks than roads since ten that morning. The rain was responsible for Charlie noticing the tracks leading off toward a copse of young pines some thirty yards away. The rain water, caught in the tracks, was what made them noticeable.

Slipping out of the vehicle, he struggled into his poncho. Clamping his campaign hat down atop his head to thwart the rising wind, he rounded the front of the Bronco. The tracks disappeared immediately into knee-high grass.

Still, it was easy to see where they led, once he noticed them. Puzzled, Charlie walked several yards down the muddy road, studying the grass between him and the stand of trees. What he saw brought a tiny chill to the back of his neck.

The twin furrows led directly to the copse, but they didn't come back out. More importantly, there was no vehicle where the tires' indentations ended.

As he returned to the four-wheel-drive, he looked up at the sky, dumping a rivulet of water from his hat brim down the back of the poncho. The clouds, very dark for mid afternoon, the isolation, and most importantly, the tracks that went nowhere brought him a sense of unease. *I wish to hell the radio transmitter in the Bronco wasn't on the blink.*

He was staring at the woods when the next gust of wind hit. *What the hell? One of the head-high shrubs seemed rise right out of the ground and then settle back down.*

With a grimace, he stepped out onto the narrow strip of wet weeds. By the time he reached the edge of the thicket, his pants legs were wet and coated to the knees with seeds and burrs. He had lost sight of the acrobatic bush and was ready to return to the car. *Goddammit, I better come back tomorrow after the rain stops, and bring somebody with me.*

An appreciation of what he was looking at brought such thoughts to an end. He saw a first, a second, and then a third branch stub where they had been cut off just above the ground.

Seizing one of the shrubs, he pulled at it, and it dragged free, bringing a second with it. The needles were still flexible and tight, the cut bushes hadn't been there long. His pulse quickened. *Somebody has driven a car back in among the trees and concealed it.*

Charlie took two quick strides, pulled another shrub free, and saw it. Brush had been piled around a canvas-topped Jeep to hide it.

Charlie backed away a couple of steps, ready to run. What he was looking at was Albert's Jeep. *By God, Albert didn't run, I knew he didn't. I'll head for town, get help.* He hesitated. *What if Albert was in the jeep, hurt, or maybe just knocked out and tied up? Goddamn, I'm getting too old for this shit.*

Reluctantly, he walked over to the abandoned vehicle. He found himself grabbing at the branches, pulling them free and hurling them aside, his breath coming in great gasps. When he had the Jeep's rear cleared, he peered through the age-yellowed plastic of the back window. He could see nothing. Stumbling around to the front side of the Jeep, he pulled aside two cut bushes leaning against it, sure he would see Albert's body.

The interior was unoccupied.

He felt his knees weaken in relief. But the feeling was temporary. *Albert would never leave his jeep like this if he had a choice. He loved that beat-up old green vehicle.*

Crawling inside the Jeep, he reached for the registration in the glove compartment, knowing how stupid it was to hope that, somehow, the four-wheel-drive was registered to someone other than Albert. In the dim light he could just make it out: *Albert Martinson.*

The fear had been building in Charlie since he first noticed how the tracks had seemed to disappear. Now it exploded in him. He clambered out of the Jeep, desperate to get away. The canvas top caught his hat brim, spinning it off his head onto the water-soaked ground.

As he swooped it up with one pitch-stained hand, he saw the brush, piled in a heap, some fifteen yards beyond the Jeep. Through the heavy rain, he saw what appeared to be a shoe-clad foot protruding from beneath it. And for the first time, even with the wind coming from behind his back, his nose caught the sent of decaying flesh.

What Charlie did in the next few seconds was a blur in his mind until he found himself clawing at the heap, tossing the wet pine limbs aside. The enormity of what he was doing, the utter vulnerability of his isolation, slammed home as he pulled the last thickly needled branch away and stared down into the waxy, dead face of Joe Woods.

Terror overwhelmed the old man. He lumbered back through the copse out into the weedy strip separating it from the road. By the time he reached the Bronco, his vision was dimming with each pounding beat of his heart.

Seeing his footprints on the road, deep imprints in the mud. He knew the road would soon be an impassable quagmire, even for a four-wheel-drive vehicle.

He paused. *What should I do? The cops need to know what I've found. Which of the damn miserable logging roads should I take? Albert's place is no more than a mile and a half away, but, there is a hill the Bronco will never be able to climb in this mud. I could keep going the way I'm headed. It will take me back to Pine Ridge.*

Wait a minute. The turn-off up ahead comes out onto the highway near Lud's That's the place to go. The sheriff can radio Crescent Valley from his house. And if he isn't home, I can damn sure do it, even if I have to break in. Lud will understand.

He climbed into the four-wheel-drive vehicle, his boots so thick with mud he could barely feel the pedals. Charlie had gone less than one hundred yards when he realized he was in for the drive of his life. The long series of hard rains had turned the road into a bottomless muck. Between rains, the top three or four inches of the roadway would dry, enticing vehicles into the maze of roads. But with an hour of rain like this, it bordered on impassable.

The Bronco skittered back and forth across the soupy surface of dirt and gravel, moving forward only when one of the tires slid to where it found roots or heavier stones to grip. The defroster ran full-blast to counter the old ranger's rapid moist exhalations, misting the windshield. Fatigue and arthritis made Charlie's desperate grip on the steering wheel agonizing.

He lost an old friend near the halfway point of his trek. Charlie, leaning his head out the window, studied a washout gnawing against the side of the road. A sudden gust of wind whipped his Stetson, a companion of fifteen years, from his head, sending it tumbling down the muddy lane. The old man was beyond caring.

When Charlie saw the pavement ahead, it took a moment for him to appreciate what he was looking at. Stopping, he eased himself out of the four-wheel-drive vehicle and pulled the poncho over his head. Tossing it into the back seat, he worked at getting the pad of mud off his boots, kicking them against each other, but the brown muck clung to the leather as if it had glue in it. Charlie, so tired he was trembling, gave up and climbed back in.

A mile down the road, he slowed and turned onto the lane leading through the woods to Lud's. The sheriff had had it covered with crushed rock, thank God. Charlie, plunging into the darkness of the stand of tall timber, was near the end of his tether.

Within a hundred yards of Lud's cabin, Charlie brought the Bronco to a halt. The small pool of water covering the track immediately ahead of him had been churned into a mud hole. Apparently Lud, in the two-wheel-drive patrol car, had come perilously close to getting stuck.

Charlie shook his head. If I make it any worse, Lud sure won't be able to get through it today in his two-wheel rig.

He turned the Bronco around to where it was headed back toward the county road and climbed out. Reaching for the wet poncho, he paused, then waved it off with a tired hand. *To hell with. My pants legs are already a sodden mess, the next hundred yards wouldn't matter. The rain has slowed to a fine mist, and whether Lud's there or not, I'll be able to dry out.*

By the time he rounded the thick grouping of saplings that concealed the front of the cabin, he was regretting his decision to leave the four-wheel-drive vehicle behind. Already wet and exhausted, Charlie was so cold now his teeth were chattering. But he forgot his discomfort when he saw the sheriff's unit parked before the cabin. *Thank God, Lud's home.*

Hurrying across the open area, sidestepping the puddles, he mounted the porch steps. His eyes widened when he saw the front door. It was ajar, no, not exactly ajar but not shut enough for the latch to have caught.

Charlie paused, uncertain of what to do. The old ranger gave the door a tentative knock. The tap was enough to swing it open to where he could see inside. He called quietly, with hesitation. "Lud? Lud, are you home?"

Charlie heard nothing but the rain against the porch roof and in the drains. Pushing the door open, he leaned inside. The warm air from inside washed against his face, and sent a comforting shiver through his body. The room was almost dark. Only the crackle from the wood in the stove broke the silence of the darkened interior.

"Lud?"

His low voice, with everything so quiet, seemed almost to echo off the walls. An odd feeling crept over him. God, this didn't set right with him. He felt like a thief in someone else's house. What should he do? *Lud has to be home. Asleep. Maybe I should head for town.* He shook his head. *No, hell, I need Lud's radio. My discovery is damn sure worth waking the sheriff.*

Stepping into the room, the old ranger closed the door behind him. Flickering light from the stove danced around the room as the fire ate the fresh wood. In the dim glimmer from the leaping flames, he saw the reflection of water on the floor and beyond it Lud's yellow slicker in a heap. Lying next to the front legs of a straight chair, Lud's hat, brim down, was half concealed beneath his balled-up shirt, upon which Lud's sheriff's badge was a pale glint, reflecting the dancing light.

He frowned. *What the hell? This don't make any sense. Lud liked to look neat. I can't believe he would treat a good shirt that way. He's the kind of a man who wants to look better than his Indian brothers. Something he's felt since he first ran for office.*

Suddenly he felt he had intruded. *Whatever was going on, Lud wouldn't want him sneaking around his house. I'll quick get back outside and knock on the door loud enough to wake Lud.*

Charlie was tiptoeing toward the door, eager to escape, when he heard a voice behind him. He spun around. Someone was chanting behind the closed door of the room on the left. With his eyes adjusted to the darkness of the room, he could see a faint strip of flickering light coming from beneath the door.

The chanting stopped abruptly, and Charlie thought he had been discovered. But the voice, louder now, started again.

Charlie frowned. *Lud's? The tone's deeper, and the words, I can understand them but they make no sense.*

The old ranger's curiosity got the best of him, and he eased across the room to where he could rest his ear against the wood of the door. *I was mistaken. Part of it I can understand and part is in some other language, maybe one of the Indian tongues.*

He strained to understand, but the voice, muffled behind the door and masked by the popping of the wood, yielded only an occasional word or phrase.

"…Running Fawn…Looking Glass…sacred oath…dark world…the second of them…revenge…and soon all…so I swear."

He took a deep shuddering breath. *The voice was a lot like Lud's! But, Christ, he sounds spooky!*

Charlie was afraid again, scared shitless, just as he had been after he found the Jeep and Joe Woods. Whatever was going on behind that door was weird, really weird.

Suddenly he knew he wanted no part of seeing Lud. The thing to do was haul ass, get in the Bronco, and head for town, fast. No. Dain Barlow's. Dain would know what to do. He could get the ball rolling as well as Lud could. Besides, Dain needed to know what was going on here.

The sudden loud cry from behind the door so startled Charlie that his fatigued legs gave way, and he sagged sideways against the door. The freshly oiled hinges swung it wide open as Charlie struggled to regain his balance.

He saw everything at once: Lud on his knees, atop some folded Indian blankets, in front of the antique dresser with the painting of a woman in Indian dress leaning against the bureau's tall mirror, flanked by burning candles. Even as he saw Lud beginning to rise from the floor, his head turning, he saw what was on the floor beside the dresser.

Just to its right was a neatly folded pile of women's clothing, garments marred with rusty stains. Next to it a black purse. Atop the clothing was a framed picture of, he squinted. *My, God! Amy Housley!*

He glanced toward the other side of the dresser. This stack of women's apparel was much more heavily discolored with the rusty stains.

Charlie, feeling as though someone had pulled a plug on his guts, gazed at the framed picture atop this pile. A laughing, long-haired pretty lady stared back at him.

The ranger's cold body began to shiver. *God in heaven! What have I blundered into?*

He backed away a step, and a second step, not consciously trying to run, just attempting to get a distance between him and the man, clad in some strange-looking shirt, who had risen to confront him.

His throat dry, his tongue and lips so stiff he could barely move them, Charlie mumbled, "Excuse me, Lud I—" His constricted throat barely let his words escape, and his eyes grew wide.

The candlelight reflected off the man's face as he turned and lifted the knife from the dresser where it had lay beneath the portrait. The long steel blade was crusty with blood.

This was no Lud Charlie had known. The face was rigid, the mouth a hard line, the eyes boring into him. Charlie had looked into a lot of hostile eyes over the years, but had never felt the raw terror the dark eyes left him with. This man was an alien, something out of a horror movie, as if something had managed to take over an old friend.

Charlie struggled to force more words out. *Maybe if I talked, said something, anything, maybe I can break through.* "Lud, I'm sorry. I didn't know if you were here. I—I just got here. I—I knocked but I guess you didn't hear me. I'm sorry," he repeated.

As he stammered, he backed through the doorway, the friend who had become a stranger following, the arm with the knife coming up from his side.

Charlie's voice rose as he blurted out, "Lud, I'm a white man who is your friend. I'm the one who helped you when you were a boy, remember? I can help you again. Lud, listen to me! I didn't see anything. Honest," Charlie croaked. "I—oh, God, save me."

The dark figure, silhouetted against the lighted doorway, grew enormous, gathering Charlie into his shadow.

CHAPTER 24

Sheila, staring out through the street side window of the telephone booth, watched as the lube bay doors at Staley's directly across the street closed for the night. She and Pat had barely made it back in time to reclaim Dain's car. The Barlow phone had rung ten times, and she was ready to give up when a breathless Dain came on the line. "Dain Barlow here."

"Dain, this is Sheila. We just picked up the car."

"It took that long?" he said.

She laughed. "Oh, no, We walked down town, did a little shopping. We just did get back here in time to pick up the car before Staley's closed. I could swear they said they stayed open till six."

"I'm glad you called. I was just leaving for Crescent Valley. This saves me writing a note. Finestein, you know, the attorney, wants to see me. We're having dinner together. Are you and Pat ready to head back to Pine Ridge?"

Sheila turned away to avoid the gaze of the guy from Staley's who had worked on the car. She figured him for the type who would try to hit on her if she gave him the chance. "Gosh, no. We have to run out to the Starlight Motel and pick up Bev. She's checked in, but I've called twice and didn't get an answer. It will probably be dark before we get back to

Pine Ridge. Oh! You...you won't be home by then, will you? Will it be okay, I mean...you're locking up right?"

Dain paused before answering. "Yeah. I tell you what. I'll leave a light on, and Lud said he would check by. He figured you'd be late. Listen, Sheila, I've been thinking. We need to talk."

She laughed. "Don't you worry about that. With three women in the house, you'll get all the talk you want."

Dain hesitated again. "I...well, I didn't mean that. What I mean is I want to talk to...well, just you."

Her heart skipped a beat. Was he saying what she thought he was saying? She tried to hit a light note. Laughing again, she said, "Well, I should hope so! I mean it isn't every gal who borrows your car and shreds your tires. You should thank—"

"Sheila, listen to me. I...I want to talk to you alone, talk to you about...well, us, dammit."

Sheila suddenly felt all gooey warm, but she tried to conceal it from Dain. "Oh, my, this sounds serious. Am I going to like what you have—"

"Sheila, what in—"

"Oh, hush, Dain. I'm just teasing. I'll see you later tonight. Have a good dinner."

She more floated than walked back into the cafe.

Pat looked up from her latte, frowning. "Well, that took long enough. You and Dain reminiscing over old times?"

Sheila dropped into the seat opposite her. "You know, Pat. That's exactly what my mother said when I told her I was coming back to the reunion."

Pat grinned. "That's what you need more of, a little motherly direction. Say, do you suppose Bev's back by now? Want to try her room again?"

Sheila glanced toward the wall clock. Four-thirty-five. "Why don't we just drive on out there? We'll have to do that anyway. She's probably out looking for us. After all, we were supposed to have met her over two hours ago."

Shoving her cup aside, Pat said, "Yeah, and I'll feel better when we get her away from the Starlight." Her voice lowered. "That motel gives me the willies. And that guy's probably still here in Crescent Valley."

Ten minutes later, they pulled into the motel's parking lot, passing a magnificent Red Porsche, parked beside their cars as they circled the lot. Sheila then nosed the car into a parking place directly in front of the Starlight's office.

The rain had become a typical Washington storm, neither light nor heavy, just steady. Reaching around the bucket seat to lift an umbrella from the back seat floor, Sheila declared, "You know, it's only been two days since I pulled into this motel on Monday afternoon." Looking toward the office door, she continued, "But with all that's happened since, it seems more like a week. I was really excited about visiting with my old classmates and…seeing Dain." She made a face. "But then, my God, Pat!"

She shook her head, and exhaled, as she opened her door. "I know," Pat answered. "It still hasn't sunk in that Amy's dead."

Jostling each other as they tried to stay under the shelter of the umbrella, they lumbered toward the office. The rain had brought cool air with it, and goose bumps stood out on both girl's bare arms as they lurched through the office door with Sheila struggling to close the umbrella.

Pat, hugging herself, said, "Feels good in here. The temperature must have dropped twenty degrees since noon."

The noise of their entrance caused Harry Blackwell to look up from his book. He was perched behind the counter on a high stool, a pair of reading glasses resting on his long nose.

"Man, it's cold out there," Pat said. "I should have had a jacket with me."

The motel manager nodded solemnly. "You know what they say about the weather here in the spring. If you don't like the weather—"

"Just wait ten minutes and it'll change," Sheila and Pat shouted in unison, then dissolved into laughter.

"Do you know if Beverly Taylor is in her room?" Sheila asked. "We phoned a couple of times earlier and got no answer."

"Should be," Harry said, nodding toward the door. "That's her little car out there, the red one."

Pat whistled. "Oh, my, a Porsche! That explains why Derek won our little Beverly's affections with a three months' courtship."

Sheila's murmured, "Don't be catty," was overridden by Harry's inquiry. "Want me to ring her room?" he said, getting up. "She checked in quite a while ago. Haven't seen her come out of her room. Doesn't seem likely she's gone anywhere, not out walking in this weather. It's four blocks to the main part of downtown."

After glancing at Sheila, Pat said, "Never mind. She was probably in the shower or something when we called earlier. We need to talk about checking—"

Sheila, her elbow catching Pat in the ribs, finished the sentence for her. "Checking on her room number."

Harry Blackwell blinked. "What? Oh, that's right you wouldn't know her room number. It's fourteen."

Pushing Pat ahead of her, Sheila hurried out of the office. She opened the umbrella with Pat glaring at her.

"Why did you dig me in the ribs?" Pat asked. "I thought we were going to tell him to check us out. We are staying with Dain. Right?"

Sheila glanced back into the office to where Mr. Blackwell had retired to his stool again. "We need to talk with Bev before we give up our rooms. Come on. It's getting late."

They stepped out into the rain, walking awkwardly again with both of them trying to stay under the umbrella's protection. Reaching room fourteen, Pat tapped her knuckles against the door. They waited several seconds, shivering in the ever-cooler wind. Pat rapped at the door again, harder this time.

Sheila, leaning against the door to listen, said, "She must be asleep." She pounded the door hard, yelling, "Bev!" conscious that she might be attracting the attention of other motel guests.

Still no answer.

She became aware that Pat was staring not at the door but at her. Her voice rising, Sheila said, "What?"

"You don't suppose…I mean…you know, what happened last night. He couldn't have, well, gotten into Bev's room? Do you think?"

"God, don't say that," Sheila said, blanching. "To get here when she did, she must have gotten up before dawn. She's probably sound asleep. Besides, he wouldn't be running around in broad daylight," She nibbled her lower lip. "would he?"

Turning, Sheila pounded on the door again, hurting her fist with the force of her blows. Loud now, she yelled, "Bev, wake up! Bev!…Bev!"

Sheila leaned forward to press her ear against the door. But the next instant she jumped back, suddenly not wanting to touch it.

Pat, watching her, understood. She cried, "Oh, God! I'm going to get the manager. He'll open the door."

Sheila reached for her, desperate to keep her there, but Pat broke free. She ran across the parking lot through the rain, heedless of the puddles of water on the asphalt.

Sheila's gaze stopped on the red Porsche, and she dropped the umbrella. Looking back, her heart pounding, she backed, step by step, along the walk, retreating until she was two doors away from room fourteen. The door held her attention, unmoving, holding God knows what behind its smooth wood surface. Time seemed to stop, encapsulating her, the cold needles of rain, and the silent door in a void.

Pat's excited voice carried across the parking area, slicing through the susurrus of falling rain, jarring Sheila from her shocked state. Realizing she was beginning to be soaked to the skin, she retrieved the umbrella.

Pat, her blouse darkened now by the steady rain, charged into view, followed by Harry Blackwell, his olive drab parka unzipped and flapping in the rising wind. The bandage on his forehead was a startling white in the watery gloom of late afternoon.

When they reached Sheila, Harry, his voice querulous, demanded, "What's going on? I can't make heads or tails out of what she's saying. With my head busted, and pounding, I don't feel good, dammit."

With a shock, Sheila realized that he was frightened. She fought against her own panic, striving for rationality.

"We can't rouse her," Sheila said. "We thought maybe, well you know."

Turning his back on her, muttering, Harry charged the door. He struck it hard several times with the balled side of his fist. "Mrs. Taylor, it's the manager. Are you all right?"

After several seconds, he pounded on the door again. "Mrs. Taylor, open the door!" Without waiting for an answer, he whirled toward Sheila and Pat, putting a tentative hand to the bandage. "She could be in the shower. If she don't want to get out and answer the door what do you expect me to do. Our guests are entitled to their privacy. You ladies will just have to try again later."

As he stepped off the curb onto the pavement, Pat cried. "Wait a minute! You're supposed to check on your guests when things don't seem right, too. And I say something's damn sure not right. Beverly came here to see us, if she heard us she'd come to the door naked if she had to."

Harry Blackwell stopped, brushing the hood back off his head, despite the rain. "Listen, missy. You people from Pine Ridge are causing me a lot of grief. I'm not—"

"You've got your keys," Pat said, changing her attitude. "Just open the goddamn door, look in, see if she's there." Her voice softened. "Please."

The red-faced Harry turned his back on them and marched across the parking lot with what dignity he could muster. Calling over his shoulder, he said, "I'm calling the sheriff. Things like this are his job. Especially after that business last night."

Crestfallen, Sheila and Pat watched as he disappeared under the shelter of the drive-through before the office.

Pat, tears in her eyes, looked at Sheila. "What can we do now? Something's wrong. I just know it is."

"Come on," Sheila said. "We'll make sure he called the sheriff."

But as they approached the office, Harry reappeared. Still looking unhappy, he said, "Ralph's on his way over. He said for me to go ahead and unlock the door, but we were not to go in until he got here."

They followed him back across the parking lot, saying nothing. Sheila was conscious of her clothes, thoroughly soaked now from the waist down, and Pat, who had made the trip to the office without the umbrella, was in even worse shape. Shivering violently, they watched Harry, who was making a great show of locating his master key for room fourteen. He did not fool Sheila. Harry Blackwell was stalling, giving the deputy time to arrive.

Watching him, Pat pointed to the key ring. "It's the one with fourteen on it. You've passed over it twice."

With a muttered phrase that sounded suspiciously like, "Bitch," the manager slipped the key into the lock and, turning it, pushed open the door two feet or so. The room was dark.

Poking his head in through the opening, Harry called, "Mrs. Taylor? Are you okay? Jesus Christ!" He yanked back his head and pulled the door closed, gagging as he did.

The warm air escaping the room reached Sheila. Her nose wrinkled at the odor. My God, it smelled awful, as if the sewer had backed up in the room. No wonder Bev had gotten out of there.

Pat, who apparently had not caught the stench, eyed the manager. "What's wrong with you? The deputy won't mind. Let's go in."

Harry had recovered somewhat as she tried to step past him, and he threw out his arm to bar her way, his hand accidentally cupping her breast. Pat, blushing, started to voice her outrage when she saw Harry Blackwell's face.

"Goddammit, we're not doing anything till Ralph gets here," he yelled.

The next moment a sheriff's car swerved into the Starlight Motel parking lot, the blue light atop its roof flashing. The vehicle halted behind the red Porsche. Ralph, scrambling out of his car, broke into a run.

The white-faced motel manager, pushing himself upright, said, "Thank God you got here so quick, Ralph. Inside…the smell. I didn't turn the light on, but I think it's bad."

Ralph turned toward Sheila and Pat. "Stay back, ladies, till we see what we've got here." His hand closed on his revolver and began to pull it free of its holster. Then, obviously realizing he was being watched, he released it, but his hand remained near the holstered gun.

Opening the door a foot or two, he reached his long bony arm through, found the light switch, and flipped it on. Leaning in farther, he tried a second switch, and the room sprang into view.

The deputy called, "This is the police. Is anyone in there?"

Glancing back at the trio, he said, "Stay back till I go in and check the place out." Ralph disappeared into the room, shutting the door behind him.

In the moment it remained open, Sheila heard an odd rhythmic sound, like metal rubbing hard against metal.

The door was closed no more than thirty seconds. It opened with such force that it slammed against the wall and almost closed again on the rebound.

Ralph, charging through the opening, his hand over his mouth, struck Harry Blackwell a glancing blow that sent him reeling. The gangly lawman ran towards his patrol car but he never made it. He stopped, bent over, and vomited with great retching sobs onto the pavement.

Sheila had felt a thrill of terror as the tall, thin officer charged out of the room. Now she felt strange, not like fainting but as if she were in a dream, as if Pat, her knuckles pushed against her lips, her eyes wide with shock, were a creation of Sheila's dream. Harry Blackwell was a mere mannequin, foolish looking, with bulging eyes and gaping mouth. *And Bev? Is she a part of this, the beginning of a another nightmare to haunt me more?*

She glanced at the deputy, still bent over in the parking lot, hands on knees, staring into the pool of vomit at his feet. *A policeman has seen everything. What could be so hideous in that room to make him react like that.*

Sheila, still in her dream-like state, desperately trying to hang on to a modicum rationality, yelled, "Stop it. What is it?" Why did her voice sound so odd, so hollow? No one answered her. She had to see.

Starting toward the door, barely aware of fingers plucking at her blouse, Pat's fingers, she pulled free and stepped inside.

The odd, rhythmic screeching was louder with her in the tiny hall-way. *God, my legs feel like jelly. Got to sit down.*

Sheila took another slow step and could see the whole room. The sound of tortured metal and the movement drew her gaze to the slow-moving blades of the ceiling fan. The fan was askew, pulled off-balance by what was secured to one of its paddles.

Beverly's long dark hair had been brought up in two plaits and tied around the blade. As the fan turned, it brought first her face, the eyes wide open, and then the back of her head into view. Dangling cords of tendon and muscle and a pinkish spur of bone trailed below the neck where it had been severed, like gaudy red streamers.

Below the fan, on the bed, the nude, headless corpse lay, its shoulders resting in a great bloom of dark red, made startling by the white of the rest of the sheet. In the kaleidoscope of colors, of motion, of smells, Sheila could see one thing with a terrible clarity. Bev's hands had been arranged neatly atop her stomach, but not too neatly. The ring finger of her left hand was missing.

Sheila's throat closed on a scream that came only as a gasp, her stom-ach churned and she became nauseous. The dream world that had enveloped her vanished as quickly as a soap bubble bursting. *I got to get out of here!* She couldn't breath, couldn't scream.

She banged into the door and fought it, seeking the doorknob. The door came open, and she reeled out, reaching for Pat. The world tilted, and Sheila fell into a well that had no bottom.

Chapter 25

When Sheila came to her senses, she was lying on a gurney in the ambulance. She struggled to an upright position, then paused to let the world steady. The ambulance wasn't moving, and the back doors were open. Swinging her legs over the edge of the gurney, she sat up. One of the medics, seeing her, rushed over, motioning for her to lie back flat. The way he started to protest, she wondered if he was employed on a piecework basis.

The sidewalk in front of unit fourteen was swarming with men in both uniform and civilian clothes. Pat was nowhere in sight. Climbing out of the ambulance, Sheila spotted her standing under the drive-through next to the office, observing the scene around room fourteen.

The medic must have scurried into the room to complain that Sheila was fleeing the scene. Before she had taken a half dozen steps in the direction of the office, someone called her name.

"Mrs. Steele. I'd like a moment of your time."

A portly man in his mid-fifties, wearing a wrinkled gray suit with a vest, introduced himself as a state police detective. "We were waiting for you to get over the shock you had," he said. "Must have been horrible, you knowing her and everything."

But he was not there to commiserate with her. Having already questioned Harry Blackwell, he wanted to interrogate Pat and her. After herding Sheila over to join Pat, he led them through their stories twice before releasing them.

With the heavily overcast sky, the day was fading quickly by the time they drove out of Crescent Valley. Their plan to separate, with Sheila driving Dain's car and Pat her own, had been discarded. Both felt a need to talk, to reassure each other. Pat, after a look at Sheila's still pale face, declared she would drive.

Within ten minutes of leaving town, she switched on the headlights and was squinting at the rain-darkened pavement, soaking up their bright beams. Glancing at Sheila, Pat said, "Feel like talking?"

"Sure. I'm okay now. You know, that's the first time I've ever fainted." Sheila took a deep, shuddering breath. "God, why did I go in there? That scene will haunt me the rest of my life. Now I'll have another nightmare to contend with. I should have known it would be terrible...you know, with the way the deputy acted, heaving his guts out." She smiled, a weak smile. "At least I didn't toss my cookies like he did."

Pat laughed, but it held as little humor as Sheila's smile had. "Do you...you get the feeling that he's after us?"

"Us?"

Pat shook her head. "You know what I mean. The four of us. You, me, Bev, and Amy."

Sheila shrugged. "I don't know what to think, Pat. All I know is there is a psycho out there somewhere whose killing young women."

"I think he's after us, the four of us. Amy was killed in Pine Ridge, and Bev in Crescent Valley. There's some psycho out there all right, but he's got us in his sights. I'm heading for the big city in the morning where I'll be safe." She laughed, a brittle artificial sound. "That sounds like a contradiction, doesn't it? The big city and safety. I'll tell you this. Nobody there is sending out phony invitations, luring me and my friends to our deaths. Jesus Christ, Sheila. I'm scared shitless."

"I know how you feel, Pat. I want to get in my car and leave too, but—"

Pat managed a smile and cut in. "But what, princess?"

"It's Dain. I might as well admit it. I've been so lonely the last year. It's as if I've been counting the months, hoping he would be here. I…God, I hate to admit this, but when I got to Crescent Valley and heard his folks died…oh, forget it! It's terrible."

"I know what you mean, Sheila. And it's perfectly natural, nothing to be ashamed of. You heard his parents had been killed. Don't let your conscience get the best of you. It wasn't that you were glad they died. You knew Dain would be here, and you were just excited over the opportunity to see him again. They just died when they did. That's the breaks in life."

"I know," Sheila said, her voice soft, "but I still feel guilty."

As they rounded a curve, Rainbow Lake came into view, looking huge, somber, and gray in the dusk.

Pat whistled. "Holy cow, look at that! The water must be up another foot since we came down this morning. If we're going to get out of Pine Ridge tomorrow, we'd better leave early."

They passed the sharp curve where the Barlows had been killed and came out onto the level stretch that was closest to the rising water. Pat nodded toward the lake. "Look at that, will you? Another foot, and it will be up to the road."

Sheila's voice was quiet. "If the killer gets back up here, and the road gets flooded with us in Pine Ridge…we'll be trapped with, that psycho."

As they toped the last hill before going down into a little valley and entering Pine Ridge, lights blazed in the town's handful of business establishments. As the lights disappeared behind the trees of Dain's orchard, Sheila cried, "Watch out! You're passing the driveway."

Pat hit the brakes hard, and Sheila had to throw her hands out to avoid being flung into the windshield.

"Sorry," Pat said, turning into the driveway.

The headlights picked up the front of the barn. One of its doors was closed, but with the other wide open, they could see into its interior. The space where the Blazer had been was vacant.

"Oh, I was afraid of that," Sheila said. "Dain's not back yet."

"I hope that steak dinner gives him indigestion," Pat said. "Keeping him away long enough that we have to come home to an empty house."

With hardly a pause, as she braked to a near stop, Her voice quiet, she continued, "Sheila, I wonder why that door is open. Dain must have secured the barn before he left."

"Stop that talk, Pat. It's bad enough coming here, and Dain not home, without you getting both of us spooked. My nerves are on edge enough. It just must have been as windy here as it was in Crescent Valley. The door probably blew open. Now let's quit acting like little girls telling ghost stories…please."

Sarcasm is her voice, Pat said, "Yes, ma'am," and stared at the back door of the house. She nodded toward the darkened building. "I thought Dain was supposed to leave the house lights on. The only light I see is on the back porch. Sheila, I don't like—"

Sheila exploded. "I don't like it either. But I'm not going to allow myself to be terrified all the time. Let's don't talk like that anymore." She took a deep breath and hoped Pat wouldn't take her up on her next statement. "Now you can let me out and go back to Crescent Valley if you think you're safer there, or you can come on into the house with me."

At that instant, the two floodlights mounted along the roof line of the back porch came on, triggered by their motion sensors.

"That's better…some better, anyway," Pat said. "Now, if you're through dumping on me, let's get inside and fix something to eat."

Sheila opened the car door, then closed it again. "You want to go to Sam's, get something to eat there?"

Pat shook her head. "Nope. I'm a mess, and you're right, we're just making a big thing of nothing. We have to go in sooner or later anyway. So let's just get it over with."

"Well, we could stay at Sam's until we were sure he was back." Sheila bit her lower lip as she looked at the darkened house. "I'm still a little shaken. We could call here every few minutes till he answered."

Pat shook her head. "Dammit, Sheila, if he didn't get back until nine or nine-thirty and then drove in here and found no one home? He'd come unglued. The phone would be so busy, we couldn't get through. He would be calling every cop in this part of the state to be on the outlook for us. Besides, look at us, we both look like we been drug through a cow pasture. I know you don't want everyone in Sam's see you like that. Now, come on. Let's get inside. After all, he left the place locked up."

Sheila exhaled noisily to show her reluctance before muttering, "Okay, you win."

Pushing open the door, she climbed out of the car. Before they reached the steps, their bare arms were covered with goose bumps. For the moment, the rain had diminished to a fine mist, but with their damp clothing and the brisk breeze from the northwest that had brought in the storm, they begin to shiver.

Sheila rubbed her arms and her body shook visibly. "I'm about to freeze to death." Then she paused at the foot of the steps to glance at her watch in the light from the porch fixture. Seven-forty-five.

Pat, studying the dark windows above them, grumbled. "The least he could have done was to leave some lights on inside. A dark house with a porch light on is just saying, 'Hey, ain't nobody home here.'"

Starting up the steps, Sheila said, "Stop your complaining. Let's just get inside and warm up, I don't want to get a cold a day before the reunion."

Unlocking the door, Sheila reached inside and flipped on the dim light on the mud porch, then scurried to the kitchen and switched on the bright fluorescence.

"That's better," Pat said as she came into the room.

Turning toward her, Sheila grinned. "You know, you're right. I'm going to turn on every light in this house. If Dain doesn't like it, then we'll take up a collection to pay his electric bill. But I want to be able to see into every nook and cranny."

She started toward the door to the parlor, and Pat cried, "Wait for me! I'm not standing here in front of these windows all by myself."

They completed their circuit of the downstairs, but Sheila, her foot on the first tread of the steps leading upstairs, hesitated. The stairway above her disappeared into darkness. Glancing back at Pat, she said, "Do you have your...you know, with you?"

Pat made a show of hefting her purse. "You bet your booties, I have. I wouldn't be within fifty miles of this house right now if I didn't."

"Do...do you really know how to use that thing?"

The smile Pat gave her was exaggerated. "Is the Pope Catholic? I spent six hours on the range with this thing, as you call it. Not only that, but I've got a permit to carry it. Now, lead off, girl. You've got Dirty Harriet riding shotgun."

Pat's bravado lasted until they returned to the kitchen and seated themselves at the table. Glancing up to the top of the window frame, she demanded, "Why in the hell didn't they ever buy shades for this window?"

Sheila laughed. "What happened to the Annie Oakley routine? That's Dain's window to see clearly into the orchard during the day. Says the house sits far enough off the highway no one can see in, anyway."

"Yeah, well, I don't like sitting before windows at night with the lights on, not even at home. It gives me the willies."

As if to give emphasis to her remarks, a sudden gust of wind struck the side of house, rattling the windows, building in a long plaintive howl as it curled in under the eaves.

Sheila shuddered. "Oh, rats! I thought the storm was over. Sounds like it's starting in again."

She jumped to her feet. "I'm going to make a fresh pot of coffee. Dain will want some, for sure, after making that drive through the storm."

"How about me fixing us something to eat?" Pat asked. "Maybe some sausage, eggs and biscuits? There are some canned biscuits in the refrigerator."

Sheila looked up from where she was dumping ground coffee into the basket of the coffee maker. "I'll bet we could find a casserole in the freezer, if you're hungry enough. Dain said folks brought over a whole freezer full of food before the funeral."

Pat blinked. "Freezer full? I didn't notice anything like that in the fridge."

Sheila shook her head. "No, no. In the big freezer in the cellar." She pointed toward the door in the wall opposite the outside entry. "That door goes to the basement."

"What's it like down there?"

"Just the usual cellar…cobwebs, everything dusty, piles of boxes, and one dim little light."

Pat eyed the white painted door for a moment in silent contemplation before asking, "You want sausage or bacon with your eggs?"

CHAPTER 26

Looking Glass reached for the radio mike, then, remembering, pulled back his hand. *Alice will be home, and Ralph is off duty. Calls for the sheriff's office will be coming through the Crescent Valley Police dispatcher.* They contracted with the local *PD* to furnish night service. Very seldom did he or his deputies have to do more than acknowledge the dispatcher's calls.

The roadside brush along this stretch of pavement was so thick that he slowed, sure he would drive right past the gate without seeing it. But he did recognize it in time, although he had passed the spot only once during the last month. The gate consisted of a long and heavy length of steel pipe painted silver and suspended between two larger, upright pipes anchored in concrete. The long length of pipe was hinged to one post and attached to the other with a length of chain and a padlock.

Sliding out of the car, Looking Glass unlocked the padlock, caught in the beams of the headlights. Swinging it open, he drove through the gateway, and then locked it behind him.

The road had been abandoned for almost four years and showed it. Branches littered its surface, and enough weeds sprouted through the hard-packed gravel to make it difficult to see in the headlight beams. Despite its neglect, it remained in good shape, having been used by

heavy trucks on their way to the old Pine Ridge dump. New state
ground water regulations had closed the place down.

The abandoned road ran along the heavily wooded slope that rose
abruptly to the rear of the Barlow orchard. The distance was less than
three-eighths of a mile, but the steep grade made a hike from the
Barlow place to that road a difficult one.

Five minutes after turning onto the old road, Looking Glass doused
the headlights. After that, the vehicle moved no faster than a walking
man would have, but he had to find a spot where he could turn around.
Ten more precious minutes passed before he found a spot where the
trees thinned enough that he could turn the vehicle around.

Shutting down the engine, he climbed out and hurried around to the
trunk. Unbuckling his gun belt and removing his hat, he chucked them
into the trunk before donning the black sweater and ski mask. Looking
Glass slipped the heavy hunting knife in its ornamental sheath onto his
pants' belt and lifted the wire cutters from the trunk before slamming
the lid. The sound was lost in the building wind. The rain remained a
drizzle, but a stinging one at times with the gusts driving it into his face.

Looking Glass started down the wooded slope, but before he had
gone ten strides, he knew he had made a mistake, wearing white man's
shoes. Their hard leather soles and heels gave little traction on the wet
forest floor. Halfway down, glimpsing the Barlow place at the bottom of
the slope, he frowned. *The house was not the pale white bulk he expected
but was ablaze with lights.* For a moment he hesitated, uncertain. He
could tell nothing from this distance.

Near the bottom of the slope, he came out unexpectedly into a
freshly cleared area. Barlow must have cleared it shortly before his
death. Looking about him, trying to find a reason for the devastation,
Looking Glass did not see the slick strip of mud just ahead of him. His
slick-soled shoes flew out from under him, and he crashed onto his side
in the near-liquid mud. The muck had a glue like consistency, and by

the time he reached firm ground, his shoes were soaking clumps of thick, clinging mud.

For the second time, Looking Glass paused, uncertain. *I might never have this good of an opportunity again. The two bitches are there in the house, alone, with no one to hear their screams. The revenge of Running Fawn will be complete before daylight. The two of them, just waiting for me, all white and soft, waiting for my seed, waiting for their deaths.*

Conscious of the swelling in his loins, he rushed the rest of the way down the slope as fast as he dared. He came out from the trees to be confronted by the ten-foot high fence that barred deer from the Barlow orchard.

Kneeling, he cut an opening through the heavy wire, eased through the gap, and moved quickly across the orchard. When Looking Glass reached the spot behind the barn where a pickup lane turned off into the orchard, he ducked in behind one of the oaks screening the orchard from the house. Beyond this point, there was no cover, only ninety feet of open lawn.

Looking Glass caught himself within a split second of making a terrible mistake. Anxious to assure himself that the Blazer had not returned, he almost stepped out in front of one of the floodlights mounted above the porch roof. The motion sensor would have turned on the light, leaving him exposed on the open lawn.

Quickly Looking Glass moved down the line of oaks to the back of the house where he could see the ivy concealing the cellar door. Taking a deep breath, he launched himself across the lawn and fell flat, face first, onto the wet grass.

He scowled. *White man shoes, no good, slick like spear head! Looking Glass, not like walking in white man's shoes, bottom hard like tree branch.*

Pushing himself upright, aware he was visible in the out fall of the light from the house, he inched across the soggy lawn, each step an uncertain adventure. By the time Looking Glass reached the cellar door, he was in a towering rage. *Enough of white man's shoes!*

He pulled the sodden clumps of leather and mud from his feet and scoured them against the grass to no avail. He would have to enter the house barefoot.

With the back wall of the lower floor windowless except for those in a bathroom and pantry, Looking Glass risked tearing away long streamers of ivy. Balling them into his hands, he cleared the blobs of mud from his sweater and trousers.

Returning to the cellar door, he paused a moment, listening, to see if the women had picked up any sound while he pulled the ivy away from the house. He could hear only faint talking. No hysterics. *Everything good.*

One quick yank, and the women would be his.

He would lay them out, side by side, nude, and then he would take them, the blond one first. He was trembling in his lust as he steeled himself to snap the lock.

       *   *   *

"What was that?" Pat asked, glancing toward the rear wall of the kitchen.

Sheila stopped talking in mid-sentence. "What was what?"

Pat was silent for a moment, then shook her head. "Nothing, I guess. Thought I heard something in back of the house. Probably just the wind." She made a face. "This is one night I'm going to be as glad to see Dain as you are."

"Nights like this remind me of when we were kids," Sheila said. "We'd be playing outside after dark, and somebody would think she heard something. She would take off running with the rest of us at her heels, scared to death without knowing why. Fear is contagious."

Rising, Sheila picked up her cup and saucer. "The wind is making us antsy. It's blowing harder again, and I think the rain has picked up, too. The last straw would be for the lights to go out."

Pat, who had been leaning forward with her elbows on the table, sat back so quickly that her hand, striking her cup handle, sloshed coffee into the saucer. "My God, you didn't have to say that."

"Well, it's true. With all the trees around Pine Ridge, lights go out every time we have a good blow, or at least they used to."

Sheila's voice strengthened. "Maybe we'd better figure out what we're going to do, you know, if the lights do go out. This house would be awfully dark, out away from town like this, on a cloudy night, if you know what I mean."

Pat made a face. "You're about as much fun to be around as Freddy Kruger. If the lights—"

The sensation was more of a vibration than of a blow, but it was enough to cause some of the timbers of the house to emit a fleeting protest.

Their eyes met, wide, startled.

"Something hitting the house?" Sheila whispered.

Pat, her voice barely audible, said, "I don't think it sounded like that. It was more like something pushed hard against the wall. I couldn't tell if it was inside or outside."

"God, it had better be outside." Sheila whispered, as she glanced toward the phone. "Should I call the sheriff's office?" She hesitated. "I wouldn't want to get them out here on a wild goose chase. It was so brief, it could have been anything."

"Maybe Lud's outside, or one of his deputies," Pat said. "Dain did ask him to check on us. Right?"

"But Lud would come to the door, I'm sure he would," Sheila said.

Pat rose and hurried to the kitchen window. Pressing her face against the glass, cupping her hands to the sides of her eyes, she peered toward the parking area in front of the barn. "Hey, the yard lights are out."

"Yeah, that's how they work. They just stay on for fifteen minutes after they're triggered. Do you see anything?"

"Nope. No head lights or anything. I can just make out the car."

As she backed away, a blast of wind ripping past the house whistled in wild, rising discords. The lights flickered for a second. "Oh, Jesus," Pat said.

Neither moved for several moments. "Thank God!" Sheila said. "I thought the lights were going out for sure. That was exciting stuff when we were kids. Mom would light candles and make sandwiches, we would pretend we were camped out in the woods."

"Yeah, us, too. We would hear all kinds of strange noises outside and run to Dad. He would tell us everything was okay, and we'd go back to bed." Her voice broke. "I remember being over at Bev's once when we were little tykes. The thunder scared us so, her mom came in and slept with us. Now Bev's dead and—"

Sheila gathered Pat in her arms. "Oh, Pattie, don't think about it. We're safe in here, all locked in. Besides, no one knows we're here. And we've got the gun. Dain will be here soon."

Pat, struggled, broke free of her. "I know all that. But we're in a house where the lights are about to go out, a good quarter mile away from any neighbors." Grabbing Sheila's hand, she cried, "Listen, let's head for the car. We'll drive down to Sam's, to hell with the way we look, or maybe just drive up and down the road, anything till Dain gets home."

Sheila, pulling her hand free, shook her head. "No. Don't you see? If we go outside, we'll lose the advantage of being locked in here," she pointed toward the telephone, "and the phone. Listen, I'll call the sheriff's office right now. We'll tell—"

A muffled series of woody protests cut off her words like an aural meat cleaver. Then a slight thump against the closed door to the cellar.

Pat's purse hit the floor with a thud and she shouted, "God damn you!"

Sheila whirled in time to see her charging toward the door, pistol thrust out before her. Too late, Sheila screamed, "No!"

Pat jerked the basement door open to reveal cellar steps descending into a black void. Glaring into the darkness at her feet, Pat yelled, "God damn you! Show yourself and I'll blow your head off, you son of a bitch!"

Glancing back at Sheila, her facial features were so distorted that she looked like a parody of the Pat that Sheila knew. Her voice still loud, she demanded, "Where's the light switch?"

"On your left," Sheila managed to answer.

Pat flipped the switch, but the dark pit remained. She flicked it several times more in quick succession. "God, wouldn't you know it?"

Moving closer to Pat, her voice barely audible, Sheila croaked, "The light was okay yesterday morning. I went down to the foot of the steps, and looked through an old box of clothing."

The house rocked under another surge of wind, and a current of cold air swept up the steps. A sudden shock hit Sheila. *Oh, sweet Jesus, the outside cellar door, it's open. Did Dain forget to lock it?*

Just as Pat grabbed the door, ready to slam it shut, Sheila saw the small cylinder, slightly bent, laying on the top tread of the stairs. Curiosity drove the thought of the errant wind current from her mind. "Wait, Pat. What's that?" she cried, pointing.

Pat leaned over to peer at the strange object, then abruptly straightened. Her voice shrill, she said, "Sheila get a flashlight. I saw one in the top drawer to the left of the cook top."

Sheila started to ask why, and as quickly knew she didn't want to know. Grabbing the small chrome flashlight, she joined Pat by the stairs. They bent forward together as Sheila switched on the torch.

The diamond ring threw back a thousand glitters of brilliance at them. The red painted nail emphasized the whiteness of the small finger.

The next instant, a click, and they were staring at what had been part of Beverly in a circle of light that was the only illumination in the house.

Dropping the torch, Sheila reeled backwards into the dark kitchen, the flashlight catching Pat in its beam as it rolled on the floor. She stood in the doorway, staring into the dark cellar, the gun lowered to her side, frozen with shock. Her voice was unrecognizable. "Oh, dear God, I'm going to die. The bastard's going to get me. Help me. Please help me."

Then Sheila heard the noises below. That and the sight of a defeated Pat ignited her. She clutched at Pat, found her hair, and jerked her backwards. Spinning Pat around, she swung her open palm at her in the dark, trying to slap her. Her hand connected with Pat's temple.

Sheila's voice was harsh. "Snap out of it! Do you hear me? We can hide in our bedroom and shoot him when he comes through the doorway. We can beat this bastard. Now, hurry!"

Behind them, someone started to climb the cellar stairs.

They plunged into the dark rectangle that was the doorway to the parlor. Pat's, "Oh," was followed by a shattering crash.

As scared as she was, Sheila still winced. Dain's mother's precious Chinese vase was no more. Sheila reached for her friend's arm to guide her, found nothing, tried again and seized the sleeve of Pat's blouse.

Behind them, the cellar door slammed back against the wall, and the beam of light from the flashlight on the kitchen floor went out.

"Quick! The stairs are over here," Sheila cried.

The next instant, Sheila could hear Pat's quick intake of breath, and she jerked free, screaming, "I'll kill you, you son of a bitch!"

The flash from the gun's muzzle blinded Sheila for a moment, but the shower of falling glass told her what had happened.

"Oh, God, you shot the cheval mirror," Sheila hissed. "You fired at your reflection."

"No, it was him behind—"

The impact of the blow, like meat hitting meat, and the sound of a heavy object striking the carpeted floor were almost simultaneous.

With outstretched arms, Sheila felt for Pat again, but the shoulder she seized was bulky and muscular.

CHAPTER 27

The Blazer swayed under the violent blows of the wind. Dain slowed to swerve around a branch that lay several feet out onto the highway. *Damn stupid weatherman! The forecast said for the storm to hit sometime tomorrow. And Finestein! The egotistical little prick wasted two hours of my time, trying to convince me of what a clever fellow he is. If it wasn't for that I would have been away from there in time to be home when the girls got to the house. Lucky I stopped for gas and heard them talking.*

The Crescent Valley cops, not knowing Dain, had been reluctant about filling him in on Bev's murder. They had been unable to contact Lud but finally located Ralph. He had spent more than an hour with state and local cops before breaking free to head for Pine Ridge. Any hopes for a fast run vanished once Dain passed Rainbow Lake. The storm was playing hell with the foothill country, and he had been all over the road, avoiding limbs.

Dain picked up speed coming off the last long curve onto the straightaway that topped the last hill before descending into Pine Ridge. He blinked. *What the hell?*

He couldn't see a thing. With lights on the barlow house had stood out like a beacon when he topped that rise. He knew he had left the porch light on. *Oh, Christ. That's all I need, a power outage, and the girls home alone. Why in the hell don't they keep the trees away from the main transmission lines coming into town.*

Suddenly, the windows of Sam's and Brown's Tavern were visible in the soft glow of gas lanterns inside. Dain hesitated for a moment. *Maybe I should go check to see whether Sheila and Pat are at Sam's. No. The girls will be okay if they're there. Being alone in the house could be another matter.*

Braking hard, he swung the Blazer into the driveway. It's headlights lit up the front of the barn. His car was parked in front of the open barn doors. The car's beams turning the interior of the barn into a lacework of dark shadows against highlighted wood walls. *Christ, I closed those doors. The wind! That had to be it.*

His pulse quickened. The house was a pale white in the light of the storm-torn sky, its windows rectangular black eyes. *Oh, God, Sheila and Pat are in the dark house! And there are no candles burning! Sheila knows where the candles are kept in the kitchen.*

He ducked around his car. Opening the driver's door, he seized the big five-cell flashlight from beneath the front seat. Dain turned it on. *Thank God, the batteries are still good.*

Turning, he ran toward the kitchen porch, hoping to see Sheila and Pat charging out the door, raising hell about him being late. He stopped halfway up the steps. Not a sound from inside. *Where are they? Could Lud have driven them down to Sam's to wait until I got back? God, I hope it's something like that.*

Dain tried the back door. Locked. He banged on it, hard. *Christ, they have to be as Sam's. Still, I'd better check the house.*

Racing back down the steps to the Blazer, he detached his dad's spare key from under the dash and ran back to the door. Entering the dark kitchen, he shouted, "Sheila, where are you?"

Something heavy hit the ground somewhere outside, maybe on the other side of the house.

"Jesus, what was that?" he cried aloud.

He flipped on the flashlight. *Why had they opened the cellar door?* Dain started toward the doorway automatically, and then he felt it. Cold air was pouring up those steps. *Oh, Jesus!*

He stormed down the steps, and the flashlight beam found the outside door, some fifteen feet away, standing ajar. Skirting the mounds of boxes, he reached the door and leaned out. The circle of light found the broken padlock, lying at his feet. *Merciful God! The bastard was in the house. Sheila! I have to find her.*

Yanking the door shut, he spun around to face the mounds of boxes and discarded furniture, drawing his gun. Dain retraced his steps to the foot of the stairs, slowly, cautiously. He fought the temptation to charge through the dark house, shouting for Sheila. Mounting the steps one by one, flashlight off, he paused on each tread to listen. Crouching, he stepped into the kitchen.

Dain's nose twitched. With the flow of air from the basement stopped, an acrid odor was filtering into the kitchen. *Cordite. Somebody had fired a gun inside. Pat! She had a weapon with her.*

He sidled through the doorway into the parlor, stepping on what sounded like pebbles crunching under his shoe. Flipping on the torch, he saw what he had stepped on. *Mom's Chinese vase.* Dain swept the circle of light around the parlor, found the ruin of the cheval mirror, let the beam drop, and, *Pat!*

She lay, sprawled on the persian rug among a fan of broken mirror fragments. Her clothes had been cut away, dress, bra, and panties, leaving her naked in a nest of fabrics.

Shrugging off the shock, he lunged across the room to kneel by her side. His fingers probed for her carotid artery. The pulse was there. He shook her, whispering, "Pat...Pat, are you okay?"

She was as yielding as a rag doll. Her arm had been pulled across her breasts at an odd angle, and now he saw why. The smooth flesh was marked with a puncture wound. *God, Amy's arm. She had the same puncture mark. And so had Bev, according to the Crescent Valley cops. My*

God! Had the bastard taken Sheila and saved Pat for Last. Caution lost in his panic, Dain bolted up the stairs, shouting, "You fucking son of a bitch! I'm gonna blow your goddamn head off!"

Upstairs, all the room doors were closed except one, the one to his folks' bedroom.

He pounded down the hall and dived through the open doorway, rolling over and coming back to his knees in one swift motion. The flashlight beam swept the room and found the open sliding door leading onto the small balcony.

And then the light settled on the lovely nude form of Sheila, lying supine atop the bed.

The next moment of time was a near eternity for him. He cried, "No…please, God, no! Not Sheila!" Then, whatever bonds held him dissolved, and he was leaning over her, no blood, his fingers slid to her carotid artery. *Thank God. She was alive.*

His gaze sought her arm. The telltale puncture mark was there. His next thought shattered his relief. *Did I get here in time to prevent her from being raped?*

He rose, the circle of light gliding down her body. *No! No! I can't do that to her. I don't want to know, not until I hear it from her herself.*

Dain remembered the thud he had heard earlier. *The son of a bitch jumped off the balcony. Could the asshole have broken a leg, or maybe his fucking neck?*

Charging out onto the deck, he directed the light at the ground below. The grass was scored by a couple of grooves. The two divots had been uprooted from the lawn. Nothing else remained to mark the bastard's jump, no blood, nothing had fallen from his pockets.

The thought of Sheila, humiliated, exposed that way, sent an uncontrollable rage through him. Dain shouted, his words torn to fragments by the gale. "I'll get you, you bastard! I'll kill you with my bare hands!"

*　　　　　*　　　　　*

Big Ray Logan lay on his cot, his feet sticking over the end by at least a foot, staring at the ceiling of the four-man tent. Pounding against the canvas, the rain seemed like an incessant roar. Ray had the first four buttons of his shirt unfastened, and a thick index finger tapped on his hairy chest.

His jaw tightened. *Goddamn the rain! That's all the fuck it's done since we set up camp. The streams are too damn murky, too high and fast to fish. The logging roads are solid mud. And everything in this goddamn tent has mold growing on it. Hell of a camping trip.*

Sitting up, Ray swung his legs over the edge of his cot. The gas lantern, hanging from the tent's ridge pole, highlighted the misty plume of Ray's breath. *Goddamn, it's cold in here, must have dropped damn near twenty-five degrees since noon.*

Ray's cot and his Harley bike took up most of the space in the tent. leaving room for little else besides a folding table and two big duffle bags lying against the side wall. He eyed the traces of mud clinging to the spokes of the Harley's wheels. *This damn weather, causing me to spend half my time cleaning mud off my bike.*

Turning toward the closed flap of the tent, Ray shouted at the top of his voice. "Skeeter!" Receiving no reply, he yelled again.

A voice, muffled and distant, replied, "Yeah, Ray. Whatcha need?"

"Where the hell are you? Get your ass in here!"

A few moments later, the tent flaps parted, and a short skinny man, clad in jeans and a black leather biker jacket that could have comfortably enveloped him and a twin at the same time, slipped into the canvas enclosure. His voice was unpleasant, high-pitched, with a whining quality to it. Beads of water stood out on his face. "I was next door playing cards. Whatcha need?"

"Jesus Christ! Ain't this goddamn rain ever gonna stop?"

The skinny biker shrugged. "It's slacking off, just a drizzle now."

"Get your ass in gear and bring me a beer."

Skeeter looked worried. "Hey, boss, don't you remember? I told you this afternoon, before we got back to camp. We're out."

Ray came to his feet so fast that the thin biker, jumping backwards, had parted the tent flaps. All but his head, framed by the flaps, was outside the tent again. His irises bounded back and forth like pinballs.

Ignoring him, Ray reached under the cot and pulled out a poncho, slipping it over his head. "You tell them other mother-fuckers I'm going into town. Got that? I don't want any fighting while I'm gone. Hear me?"

Skeeter, obvious relief in his face, held the tent flap back while Ray rolled the Harley outside.

When he brought the big bike to life, heads popped out from a couple of the other tents and as quickly disappeared. Ray glanced up at the shred of night sky showing between the tall spires of the trees and muttered, "Goddamn rain."

With the last glare at the skinny biker, he roared away through the trees, ignoring Skeeter's last apologetic, "Sorry, boss."

*   *   *

Jimmy Brown glanced up at the clock. *Still three hours till closing time, damn night's never gonna end. Everybody thinks I have it so easy with dad owning Brown's Tavern. They should try it, especially on rainy week nights like this. Crowded weekends, now they're not so bad, I can keep busy enough that time don't drag.*

The lights had been back on for fifteen minutes or so but the customers were staying home, not a night they wanted to be out. Looking toward the few pool players in the back, he saw Mike Powers. *Why couldn't that skinny ass little shit head have been one of the ones to stay home.*

Jimmy busied himself, going through his slow night routine of dusting, one by one, the rows of bottles on the shelves below the bar mirror.

"You motherfuckers!"

Christ, why the hell didn't Mike Powers pass out before he started a riot among the only paying customers in the place, the gang around the pool tables in the back room. Out front, there were only the two guys on the stools down at the end of the bar, old-timers who could nurse a bottle of beer for an hour. The small dance floor was vacant, and only one table occupied.

Powers's current bimbo, a broad ten years older than Mike, sat there looking plaintively toward the back room. She was a typical Powers's woman, big-chested, though they were beginning to sag, and with dark rooted blond hair worn too long for her age. The broad wore a red dress so tight he could see the line of her panties.

Jimmy turned at the sudden sound of the motor bike from outside. *A customer.* The two old-timers at the bar had lost interest by the time the outside door swung open to reveal Ray Logan, looking like a drowned rat, his pant legs spattered with dollops of mud.

"Hey, Jimmy!" he boomed. "How about a bucket of water and some old rags. I want to get the shit out of my fender wells before she dries."

Jimmy shot a quick glance toward the back room. Powers had blown off his mouth earlier in the afternoon about the hassle he had had with the bikers. That was all Jimmy needed, a night without enough customers to pay expenses and half the furniture in the place broken up.

He rushed out from behind the bar, heading toward the back, calling over his shoulder, "Sure thing, Ray. I'll bring it out to you. I'm not doing anything anyway."

Logan, looking surprised, said, "Sure, man," and walked back out into the night.

While he waited for the bucket to fill, Jimmy toyed with the idea of calling the sheriff's office. *What the hell could I tell them, that there might be some trouble. They would tell me to call back when there is trouble, especially with Lud being short handed. But, God, I know there's going to be trouble if Ray sees the skinny fucker.*

The bucket filled, he grabbed a handful of rags and hurried through the empty barroom. His raincoat remained on the hook in the store room. Better wet than have an impatient Ray Logan wandering through the tavern, looking for him.

Outside, the rain had stopped, and Jimmy found Logan kneeling beside the Harley. The brilliant red glare from the tavern's neon sign rebounding in a hundred reflections from the bright chrome and flawlessly painted surfaces of the bike.

Scowling in his concentration, Logan was polishing the chrome headlight case with a towel that must have come from the open saddle bag. Without bothering to glance up at Jimmy, he expressed his gratitude with, "What the fuck you waiting for? Bring the water over here."

Relieved at his early dismissal, Jimmy hurried back into the bar to face his other problem, Mike Powers.

The situation in the back room was unchanged. Mike was up to his favorite tricks. Given a bad lie, he would brush the cue ball with his coat sleeve and then spot it two or three inches from its original position. Another of his tricks was to pound the butt of his cue stick against the floor just as his opponent took his shot. The howls of protests from the opponent and bystanders alike would blend with his own shouted obscenities.

When Logan reappeared fifteen minutes later, his jacket off and sleeves rolled up to display mud-streaked arms, Mike Powers was facing the other direction. In the process of showing off, guzzling down a full bottle of beer without taking it from his lips, he was mercifully silent.

Logan, paying no attention to the pool players, motioned with his head toward the door to the restrooms. "I'm gonna wash up, Jimmy. Get me three cases of that Mexican beer. Tie them together so I can strap them on the bike." He vanished into the restroom.

Jimmy looked up, startled by the sound of breaking wood. Mike Powers was poised, knee raised, one half of the broken cue stick in each hand. "Damn cheap-ass cue sticks! I can't play using shit like this."

With his white Stetson on, Mike reeled out of the back room to a chorus of Bronx cheers. Bumping against one of the small tables around the dance floor, he yelled, "Bastard," and, with a hard push, sent it skidding across the floor. Stopping, he looked all around the room, blinking.

Jimmy slowly shook his head. *Christ, the little bastard is so wasted he can't even see the bimbo with whom he came in.*

Apparently she had reached the same conclusion. She called in her whiskey-coarse voice, "Mike, baby, over here."

As he weaved across the room toward her, Powers dug a wad of crumpled bills from his shirt pocket. Raising them to eye level, he fumbled at them with clumsy fingers, trying to count them. A couple of bills escaped his grasp and fluttered to the floor. When the woman bent to retrieve them for him, he slammed his foot down atop one of the bills, almost crushing her fingers. "Leave them alone, Inez. You've gotta do more than that for your money."

Laughter erupted from the pool players. Wheeling, Mike glared at them. They were paying no attention to him.

"Hey!" he shouted, thrusting his middle finger upward. "Rotate on this, you horses' asses."

Jimmy, behind the bar, grabbed a handful of quarters from the cash box. Time to get the jukebox going before Logan figured out who was raising all the hell in the bar.

Mike, swaying as he tried to steady himself, must have decided he wasn't going to get anyone's attention. Glancing at Jimmy, he muttered, "Fuck 'em," and collapsed into the chair across from the bleached blond, his arm landing hard atop the table. The full beer bottle in front of the woman teetered. Mike's leg struck that of the table, and the bottle fell onto its side, sending a flood of golden liquid across the table top.

The woman, crying, "Oh, Christ!" jumped to her feet. Seizing one of the paper cocktail napkins, she dabbed at the lower half of her dress.

The bleary-eyed Mike glared at her. "Sit your ass down! It's just a little goddamn beer."

"But, honey, this is a brand new dress. I bought it just for you. You said I looked good in red." She reached across the table and put a comforting hand on his arm. "You're just upset because you were losing at pool."

He clambered to his feet and shouted, "Just shut the hell up, Inez!"

Powers walked back over to the bar with the careful mincing strides of the very drunk. His last step was too ambitious. He would have fallen had he not clutched the raised rim of the bar.

"Gimme a Bud, Jimmy."

"Don't you think—"

"Don't gimme no shit. You just do what I tell you."

The barman started to protest, then thought, *Christ, one more beer ought to do it. With luck, I can get him out of here before Logan sees him. But Ray's been in the restroom for ten minutes already and will be coming any moment.*

Jimmy slid the beer before Mike.

He was right. Two swallows, and Mike Powers began to disappear from sight. He was like a ship, sinking below the surface of the bar.

Jimmy raced around the end of the bar past the two wide-eyed senior citizens. By this time, Powers was sitting on the floor, legs extended, back against the front of the bar. His white Stetson lay by his side.

"Hey, Inez, or whatever your name is," Jimmy called, "give me a hand here."

This was the tough part, persuading the son of a bitch to leave. Mike was so drunk his arms and legs would no longer work, but he always remembered everything that happened. Ruffle his feathers and his old man would be calling the tavern, raising hell. Jimmy sighed. *The day I inherit this place will be the last day I ever set foot inside it.*

Leaning over Mike, he said, "Hey, buddy, time for you to go home. You've been here six hours."

"So what?" Powers mumbled, his words slurred.

Jimmy forced a smile. "It's not me, ole buddy," he said, picking Mike up like a rag doll. "You know what your dad said, shut you down after six hours. He doesn't want anything to happen to you, friend."

The words seemed to take several seconds to soak in. Then Mike said, "Stupid old bastard! Hey, Jimbo, I ain't been here six hours, have I?"

"You sure have. Almost seven. And we don't want your dad angry with us, now do we?"

A reluctant Inez, reaching the bar, cooed at Mike. "Come on, honey. Let's go home." She glanced at Jimmy, blushed, then added, "I want you all to myself."

The resistance went out of Powers, and he giggled. "Friggin' bitch! Hot for what I got."

As he struggled to stand on his own, the barman nodded at the woman. "Inez, want to hold him up while I get his hat?"

Inez put the drunken Mike's arm over her shoulder as Jimmy retrieved the Stetson from the floor. He jammed it down hard atop Powers's head, with only Mike's ears preventing the hat from covering his eyes. The barman placed the drunken man's other arm over his shoulder, and the trio staggered toward the front entry. But before they could get him out the door, Power's twisted around to where he could see the pool players in the rear of the tavern. The men there had ceased playing and were watching the awkward procession.

At the top of his voice, the drunken man screamed, "Fuck all you ass-holes!" and then allowed himself to be hustled out of the tavern.

Outside, Jimmy paused to let Inez fish the car keys from Mike Powers's pocket. The next moment, Mike broke free of him and sent him reeling with a hard shove. *Oh, Christ, the fresh air is reviving him. Another minute, and he'll be back inside raising more hell.*

But Mike Powers had seen the Harley, its bright chrome flashing a thousand points of light in the neon glow. "Logan!" he shouted. "It's that son of a bitch's bike."

Inez made a futile grab for him. Evading her, he charged the gleaming machine, seized its handlebars and seat, and sent it crashing onto its side. Jimmy would not have believed the falling bike could make that much noise, and Powers was just beginning. He leaped atop one of the wheels, jumping up and down, trying to bend the wire spokes with the heels of his cowboy boots, all the time yelling, so excited he was frothing at the mouth.

"Son of a bitch!" he shouted. "Make me walk to town, will you? You're gonna do some walking when I get through with this pile of junk."

Stumbling around to the other side of the bike, he started dragging it across the pavement, panting. Looking at Jimmy, he yelled, "Don't worry. I'll drag this piece of shit in the ditch where—"

The heavy front door of Brown's Tavern slammed back violently on its hinges. To Jimmy, the Ray Logan charging through the doorway looked ten feet tall.

Ray's loathing for Mike, had been something he had held in check with difficulty. It had festered and smoldered every time he saw the spoiled shithead, but now the little shit had gone too far.

The sound exploding from within Logan's chest was like that of a wounded she-bear trying to save her cub. He covered the distance between him and Mike Powers in a half dozen enormous strides. The sight of the giant man charging out of the bar seemed to have frozen Mike in place. He gaped at the huge man hurtling down on him, his hands still clutching the chrome of the handlebars.

Jimmy's shouted, "Don't!" was as effective as using a fly swatter to stop a battle tank.

The big body exploded with violent coiled tension. Leaping over the fallen Harley, Logan swept Powers off his feet, lifted him into the air, shaking him like a rag doll.

One of the senior citizens leaned out the tavern's door, and Jimmy cried, "Call the sheriff! And for God's sake, hurry!"

"I'll kill you for this, you no good bastard!" Logan screamed.

Powers, apparently too drunk to appreciate his danger, managed to say, "Just wait till my daddy hears about this, you fuck head." He kicked at the biker, trying to smash his testicles, but Logan twisted around, taking the blow on his side.

Jimmy yelled, "Mike, shut up! Are you crazy?" He would get no answer to the question.

Logan released Mike Powers and, in the same motion, hit him with a tremendous right hand that smashed into the side of his face. He followed it with a left to his jaw that sent Powers reeling backwards across the lot to bounce off the side of one of the parked cars.

Mike, spitting a couple of teeth from his bloody lips, mumbled, "Fuck you."

Seizing the gangly powers by the hair, Logan slammed his head down at the same time he brought up a knee into his face. Jimmy heard the sharp snap of his nose breaking. Mike sagged onto his hands and knees, stayed there for several seconds, then, struggling to rise, slid his hand into his pocket and brought out a knife. With a snap, the blade leapt out of the handle. Its glittering length was alive with reflections from the beer signs in the tavern windows.

Logan sprang at him with another crushing blow into the middle of his bloody face. Mike was hurled backwards, his head striking the metal rim of one of the cars' wheels with an odd clunking noise. For a moment, he lay quiet, then convulsed briefly and was quiet again. From where he stood, Jimmy could see the odd angle at which his head rested.

Logan, staring at the recumbent form for a moment, yelled, "Mike?" and then bent over him.

Jimmy backed step by step toward the tavern's door. *What the hell did Logan think, that a man with his neck bent at that angle was okay?*

Inez, who had been rooted to one spot all through the fight, screamed, "You've killed him!" and rushed at Logan. He sent her sprawling to the ground with a hard shove.

The bartender, turning to run for the door, saw Logan leaning over his bike, grasping the Harley's handlebars. He was inside, pushing his way through the sparse milling customers, when the motorcycle came to life outside. By the time the Crescent Valley dispatcher answered his call, the cycle's roar was diminishing in the distance. Jimmy glanced up toward the front door to see the last of the customers rushing out to view the carnage.

CHAPTER 28

Lud jumped, startled. Disoriented, he quickly looked around. *Oh, sweet, Jesus, where the hell was he this time?*

"Unit one. Unit one. Come in unit one."

Lud stared about him wildly. Weeds and trees close by. Parked somewhere back in the woods. Then he realized he was in the patrol car, the door open, his feet on the ground. *My damn feet! They're bare!*

His shoes, socks stuffed in them, sat next to his feet. The shoes were almost unrecognizable, coated with a thick layer of mud.

Sliding out of the car, he glanced down the slope. Far below, the orderly rows of trees that marked an orchard were visible in the night light. The big two story house ablaze with lights. *Hell, I'm parked on the old dump road up above Dain's place. But how?*

He shook his head. *Christ. These black outs.*

Slumping back into the car again, he buried his head in his hands. *Rainbow Lake. I pulled off onto the shoulder there to check whether the waves were eroding the fill. I was about to head to Dain's to check on the women. And, the headache. Just as I got back into the car, it had blasted through my head like a runaway train.*

He lifted his watch, squinting at it in the near darkness. At least three hours had passed. *But what the hell am I doing behind Dain's place? Of course! I came in the back way to see if I could spot anyone lurking around the house. Goddamn shoes are a mess, and clothes muddy, must have taken a spill on this shitty road. Shoes are off because I was trying to clean them up.*

He sighed. *At least these black outs must be just amnesia. I'm still doing my job. No question about it. That's why no one has noticed any strange behavior on my part. God, that's a load off.*

"Unit one. Come in, unit one. I'm receiving no transmissions from your unit. Do you read me?"

Lud frowned. *Jesus, Alice? Why is Alice handling calls?* Lud thumbed the hand mike switch. "Unit one. Alice, what are you doing at the office this time of night?"

"Thank God, Lud. I was about to have Ralph to start looking for you. I've been trying to reach you for thirty minutes. Where have you been?"

Lud's mind raced. *Christ, he had to come up with something good or she would be yapping at me like a toy poodle.* His story came in fits and starts. "The dump road gate was open…figured I'd better check it out, and found some one hiding back in the trees…I gave them a hell of a chase, but I fell into a damn mud hole, and the son of a bitch got away."

When Alice said nothing, Lud figured he needed more story, so he told her he had become worried about why anybody would be back in there and had decided he'd better give Dain's place a look-see.

Alice's voice burst through the speaker with a snort of derision. "You always tell your deputies to call in when they're going to be away from the radio. You sure I didn't catch you sleeping. You sound funny.

"Listen, Lud, there's trouble at Brown's Tavern."

"Oh, Christ, just what we need," Lud said.

"Jimmy Brown called. Ralph picked it up on his extension at home. Said he was so excited it was hard to get any sense out of him. Somebody's hurt bad, maybe dead. He phoned me to come back to the office. Said there might be a lot of radio traffic if it's as bad as Jimmy made it sound. Ralph said he was going to head up that way. I haven't heard anything since. Been on the radio most of the time, trying to get hold of you."

"Yeah, okay, Alice. I'm on my way, over and out," Lud said, putting the hand mike back on its clamp. *This short handed bullshit is for the birds.*

Quickly he slipped the muddy socks and shoes back on, grimacing at the cold wetness against his feet. He paused at the point where the dump road came back on the pavement. Wading into the shallow ditch there, Lud scrubbed at his shoes until he cleared them of mud.

When he reached Brown's Tavern ten minutes later, a knot of people stood near a parked sedan. Two emergency vehicles, an ambulance and Ralph's patrol unit, stood immediately behind the sedan, the blotches of blue, red and white light from their bubble bars chasing one another across the front wall of the tavern.

Ralph, watching Lud climb out of his patrol car, whistled. "What happened to you?" he asked, pointing at Lud's mud-smeared pants and sodden shoes.

"Chased a guy through the woods. Son of a bitch gave me the slip. What's wrong here, Ralph? Who's down?"

Ralph quickly ran through the story. Lud nodded and, raising his voice, ordered, "Customers, back into the bar. Bystanders, go home."

He and Ralph moved aside as the two ambulance men passed them, rolling the gurney on which Mike Powers's body lay. "Christ, there's going to be hell to pay when the old man hears about this," Lud muttered. "Now where's the woman? What did you say her name was? Inez?"

Ralph nodded toward Mike Powers's Jeep. Inez, her face a ruin now with swollen eyes and streaked mascara, was staring straight ahead.

Lud, approaching her, called over his shoulder, "Get Jimmy's statement, and then you can take her's."

He looked down at the woman. "Ma'am?"

She started to cry again as she buried her head in her hands.

"Ma'am, I'm the sheriff. Try to help me here. Did you see which way he went? When—"

Mucus was running from her nose as she lifted her head from her hands. "It was some son of a bitch named Ray Logan. Poor Mike never had a chance. Just took him and killed him." She got a confused look. "He just killed him."

"Ma'am, listen to me. You were the only one out here when he left. Did you see which way he went?"

She nodded. "They said his name was Ray—"

"I know that, lady. Which way did he go when he left here?"

"That way." She pointed west.

"Ralph!" Lud shouted.

The thin deputy came on the run.

"Yeah, Sheriff?"

"Set up a road block here. This is the only road out of those mountains." He grinned as he gazed at the dark forest covered peaks. "And if he heads back into the mountains, just let me say this. He's in my back yard now. Ain't a man alive I can't catch in these woods."

*   *   *

The Harley roared into the campsite and skidded to a halt where the other five bikers sat around the campfire, newly built with the cessation of the rain. Ray Logan, ignoring the shouts of, "Where's the beer?", ran to his tent. Throwing back the tent flap to let the campfire light the interior, he slipped inside, and dragged the two duffle bags over next to the cot. Stooping by it, he pulled out a knapsack and proceeded to stuff it with items form the duffle bags.

Skeeter, who had left the group by the fire, leaned in through the open flap. "Hey, man, what's your hurry? What the hell's goin' on? You act like you seen a fuckin' ghost."

Logan, never stopping his packing, said, "Get your ass out of the light, Skeeter, so I can see what the fuck I'm doin'."

His little buddy slipped inside as Logan continued. "Goddammit, Skeeter, I've fucked myself good this time. "I just killed Mike Powers. Broke the bastard's neck for him. That goddamn Indian will be coming to get me."

Skeeter whistled. "Holy shit! Why'd you hafta do that?"

Logan stopped his packing to glare at him. His eyes flashing in the flickering light. "It was a fuckin' accident, you idiot. A fair fight. Stupid bastard knocked my bike over and I went apeshit." He turned back to the knapsack. "I gotta get out of here fast."

Skeeter, his voice breathless, asked, "Jesus! What are you gonna do? You gonna make a run for it down the highway?"

As Ray stood, he brought the chrome-plated forty-five auto out from under the mattress and stuffed it into the pack. "Hell, no, you damn dummy. That fuckin' Indian'll have that road sealed off so tight a fart couldn't slip through. I'm gonna have to go cross-country."

Ray closed the flap on the knapsack and fastened the straps. Hefting the backpack, he ordered, "Get me some chow, Skeeter, and don't waste no time."

As Skeeter left the tent, Ray pulled the stopped from his air mattress, then put his foot on it to speed up the deflation.

He was strapping the rolled up mattress to the backpack when the rail-thin biker rushed up with a gunny sack full of food. "There's 'nough here for three, four days," Skeeter said. "Which one them trails you gonna take, ole buddy?"

Widowmaker's. It's a hell of a trip, but I can use my bike till I hit that slide area. I'll have to light out on foot from there, but I can still get across the line into Canada tonight."

The skinny biker staring past Logan, down slope toward the road, said, "Good choice, but you better get going, man. That Indian'll be coming before long."

Ray snorted. "You give me a head start, and there ain't no redskin that can catch me."

The little biker's eyes got wide. "Just the same you better get to hell out of these woods as quick as you can. People say ain't nobody ever took off in these mountains that sheriff didn't catch. Say he has that Indian witchcraft shit, and can change hisself into an owl."

Skeeter stared at the top of the tent, mesmerized, as he moved his hand in a circle over his head, relating the story. "They say he circles up high till he sees 'em, then comes down and gets 'em. Gotta get out before he gets in the forest."

As if breaking loose from the spell, Skeeter quickly looked back at Ray. "These woods is his. If'n you hear an owl, better take cover, could be him. I'm tellin' you, ain't nobody ever got away from that goddamn Indian in the wilderness once he gets on their fuckin' trail."

Ray stood with the pack in one big hand and frowned down from his ten inch height advantage. "That's plain bullshit, Skeeter! Ain't no man can turn himself into an owl and fly over the woods and find people. You beat all, you know that? The son of a bitch has got two legs, just like me." He shook his head, exasperated. "Where the hell do you hear these fairy tales anyhow?"

Skeeter quickly shook his head. "Make fun if you want, but it ain't just bullshit, big guy. He has voodoo power. 'Member the time he picked up the Weasel when he was makin' a run to Canada a couple years back? Well, Weasel said he heard an owl. Damn thing followed him for two, three miles, kinda playin' with him like. All of a sudden that sheriff was there, when Weasel looked back, the damn owl was gone. Damn owl turned into the sheriff, he swears it."

Ray moved from the tent to the bike, mumbling, "Owls, voodoo, Jesus Christ." Shaking his head he began strapping the pack to the rear of the bike.

The task finished, he stood, then turned toward the skinny biker who had followed him from the tent. "Don't worry none about that damn sheriff, Skeeter. I been comin' up here for ten years campin' out, two, three weeks at a time. He ain't huntin' no fuckin' tenderfoot."

Straddling the bike, he patted its metal frame, his voice strangely soft. "This baby will get me to that slide area before that redskin can get his thumb out of his ass."

Ray pushed the starter, and the engine thundered to life. He yelled into the scrawny biker's ear. "You know that burned-out gas station seven miles below Crescent Valley? I'll meet you there in exactly forty-eight hours. Contact Elmo early in the morning. You tell Elmo to hike back into the slide and bring my bike out tomorrow. The Indian don't dare try it. He rides, but he ain't that good. And time that redskin gets a chopper up there to lift it out, Elmo can be in and gone."

Ignoring the other bikers, who stood around the fire, uncertain, afraid to ask what was wrong, Ray Logan rode off into the night.

CHAPTER 29

Lud slowed the patrol car as the headlights picked out the wooden sign ahead, reading Black Bear Creek Campground. He pulled in past the sign and doused his headlights. Only one campfire glowed through the weblike tree branches to mar the darkness of the campground. That's the way it usually was when Logan's bunch chose a camping site. Within a few hours, even in nice weather, everyone else up and left, and they had it to themselves.

Shutting down the power plant, he slipped out of the car and stalked silently up the road toward the fire. Freeing his flashlight, Lud played it along the edge of the campground road. Motorcycle tire tracks! Two sets, leading in and out of the campsite. But one going out had been made during a light drizzle, the other after the rain had stopped.

Ahead of him, where the campfire was, he heard voices mixed into the loud chorus of croaking frogs, all partly masked by the thunder of Black Bear Creek, another hundred yards ahead. The stench from the ill-kempt campsite assailed his nostrils. *The damn bikers were more like animals than men.*

He was less than ten feet from them, standing there, when one of the bikers, noticing him, yelped. "Jesus Christ! Where the hell did you come from?"

Heads swiveled, and the five leather jacket clad men scrambled to their feet. The shock of his sudden appearance showed in their faces.

The smallest of them cried, "Dammit, Sheriff, you scared the living shit out of us."

Another of the bikers, a fat one, pointed at Lud's feet. "No wonder we didn't hear him. Look there! He's wearing moccasins. Cops ain't supposed to wear moccasins. That ain't part of the damn dress code."

Ignoring the biker, Lud said, "Evening, boys," smirking at their discomfort. "Nice spot you got here."

The fat biker, made bold by Lud's mild comment, sneered. "Was nice till the storm blew in something that stinks." He looked left and right at his companions, hoping to get a laugh, and added, "Looks like the wind blew in a friggin', slop-eating pig. Ain't you got nothin' better to do than hassle a bunch of law abiding citizens?"

Lud treated them to another toothy smile, switched on the flashlight, and circled them, staring at the ground. Just what he'd thought. The bike must have been there for five or ten minutes. The ground was freshly scuffed in the level area between the fire and the largest of the tents.

His flashlight beam caught the faint impression of a tire track, less noticeable on the thick mat of pine needles. The cycle had headed north out of the clearing.

Just two trails that way: Widowmaker, if a guy's a hell of a rider, or Grizzly Peak, steeper and longer but easier to travel because of the large areas of bare rock. *Thank God, these idiots are so blind they hadn't noticed the tire track, as plain as the noses on their faces.*

When he again faced the bikers, he said, "I don't suppose any of you boys has seen Ray Logan in the last hour or so, have you?"

Five heads shook in unison.

"Ain't seen him since before the rain started, Chief, oops, Sheriff," Skeeter said, showing a lot of brown stained teeth. "Ain't that about when it was, boys?"

"Yep, 'bout then." a burly redhead said. "You know, as I remember, he said he was headin' for Wenatchee."

Skeeter tried for another laugh from the gang. "I think that's right. 'Course he mighta changed his mind. Fact is, he don't always tell us where he's going. Not since he growed up." They all guffawed at the runty man's wit.

Lud waited for the laughter to die before he said, "Never mind, fellas. I just wanted to talk to him about the squabble at Brown's place tonight. But I expect I'll see him before you do."

One moment he was there, and the next there was nothing but trees reflecting the firelight and the faint wind teasing the tree limbs in the darkness overhead.

The bikers glanced at one another. "God, he's spooky," the fat biker said. "Can't even hear the son of a bitch walk."

Back at the patrol car, Lud thumbed the switch on the hand mike. "Unit two? This is unit one."

Ralph's voice came from the speaker with an electronic wheeze. "Unit one, this is unit two. What's up, Lud?"

"Logan's made a break for it through the woods. I'll leave my car pulled off in the trees about a mile below the entrance to Black Bear Creek Campground. I'm going after him on foot. That Harley can't make much better time than me in that country. No point in me carrying the portable radio. I'll be out of range. You're in charge down there, Ralph, till I get back to the car."

"Ten-four, Sheriff."

Sliding out of the car, Lud lifted the PSE Mach 4 compound bow and a quiver of steel-tipped Wasp hunting arrows from the back seat. Slinging his hat onto the front seat, he ducked his head through the loop of the quiver's strap and adjusted it against his back. For a moment Lud toyed with the idea of leaving his gun belt in the car, then decided against it. He hefted the oversized case containing the night vision binoculars from the seat and strapped it around his waist opposite the holster.

As he locked the car door, Lud glanced up at the sky. The clouds were breaking into fragments, and the night was growing brighter. He remembered it was going to be a near full moon tonight, and nodded in satisfaction. Turning, Lud moved up the slope at a trot, and into the woods, the forest floor, with its carpet of disintegrating needles, feeling springy against the moccasins.

Ten minutes later, as he crested a small rise, he saw the glow from the bikers' campfire several hundred yards off to his left. Getting his second wind, he smiled as he settled into a ground devouring gait, Lud glided through the forest, its cool humid air rich with the smell of pine. A musky scent of damp humus from decades of decomposed vegetation pushed up from the wet ground.

In places the trees were so thick and the light so dim, he had to slow to keep his footing. Other times, the trees would thin to where he could make out every detail of the forest floor in the night light. The woods were alive with the sound of running water as tiny rivulets from the day's rains found their way downslope.

The Grizzly Peak Trail came up with a suddenness that surprised him. Lud was making better time through the woods than he had thought. A quick glance assured him that no bike had passed that way. Another fifteen minutes of hard going over a series of small but steep dips and rises, and his course cut the Widowmaker Trail.

At the spot he intercepted the trail, the under footing was bare rock, betraying no sign of the Harley's passage. But fifty yards uphill, the trail turned back onto soft forest soil, and here he discovered what he wanted. The Harley had found rough going at this spot, digging deep grooves into the ground as it struggled across the muddy patch.

Dropping onto his hands and knees, Lud brought his face close to the disturbed ground. The watery sidewalls of the small indentations left by the tire treads were just beginning to collapse. He was no more than fifteen minutes behind Logan.

Standing, he eyed the rising rocky ground ahead. Here, staying on Widowmaker Trail, he could make good time, but so could Logan. Ahead, up on the rocky ridge, the trail changed direction, moving due east along the side of the ridge. It came to an abrupt end where the slides of two years ago had buried the area under a two hundred-foot wall of debris.

Lud paused to think. *Should I keep moving cross-country? The shortcut would shave two miles off the distance to the slide. I could be sitting there, waiting for Logan. But what if I run into one of those jungles of dead-falls that the foothills' violent wind storms leave strewn all over the slopes? That would leave me a half hour or more behind the biker.*

He shook his head, disgusted. *Goddammit, it seems when I have a fifty-fifty choice I get it wrong more than half the time. If I guess wrong, it will put me a half hour or more behind the biker. What the hell, might not be any new dead-falls. I'll take the shortcut.*

Lud shifted the cumbersome binocular case on his hip and turned off the trail into a thick stand of saplings. Later, breathing hard, sweat beading his face, he entered a small clearing and stopped, straining to hear the motorbike. Nothing. The yard-wide brook behind him filled the clearing with a soft, liquid warbling.

Overhead, the pines whispered in the night breeze, always present at this elevation. But he should be able to hear the harsh staccato bark of the Harley's exhaust bounding off the bare rock faces that overhung the shallow valley in which he stood.

He tightened his jaw. *Where the fuck is Logan? Did the Harley quit on him? Surely to hell, the bastard hasn't already reached the slide and discarded the bike.*

Nothing to do but check the place where the avalanche of rocks had erased Widowmaker Trail.

He covered the last mile as quickly as he dared. Coming out into the area where rocks, bounding away from the slide, had shattered the thick stand of trees, he glanced up the canyon wall some hundred feet above him.

Here Widowmaker Trail had been cut into the steep side of the small canyon and simply vanished where the huge rock slide had come roaring downhill. He could see no bike there. *Good, I'll be there when Logan thunders in on his Harley.*

Slipping the bow over his shoulder, Lud started the climb up to the trail. On the precipitous slope, handholds and footholds slippery from the rain, the ascent was treacherous. When, at last, he reached the trail, he dived into the cover of a boulder and hunkered down, gasping for breath.

Once recovered, he came to his feet and drew the night vision binoculars from their case. Resting them atop the boulder, he studied the visible parts of Widowmaker Trail. About a quarter mile of it could be seen, draped along the side of the canyon wall to where it vanished into a thick stand of trees.

The minutes crawled by, and still he heard nothing. *The bastard hasn't made it this far. The Harley would be there on the trail or down at the foot of the slope from where I started my climb. No way a bike could get by that jumble of rocks. Where in the hell is the son of a bitch? Could the bastard be setting up his own ambush? Or has the biker fallen somewhere…broken his goddamn neck?*

Lud's mind whirred with possibilities of what he should do next. *Goddammit, to hell anyway. Should I climb back down the canyon wall and circle back around to where the trail comes out of the woods? Or just pick my way across the damn slide? Either way, I figure I'm fucked if the son of a bitch is watching.*

He would be helpless while he was trying to get down the slope, like a damn bug crawling down a wall. And the night was bright enough that he would be like a moving target in a carnival booth, working his way across the slide in the open.

Lud started a cautious descent across the slide toward the trail without the conscious realization that he had made a decision. He was within a hundred feet of the trees when it happened.

Lud had time to sense motion next to a boulder some fifty feet ahead of him, then the gun muzzle's brilliant flash blinded him.

CHAPTER 30

Ray Logan blinked furiously, as if his lids were windshield wipers that could clear the blackness in the middle of his vision. The forty-five's muzzle flash had left him temporarily helpless. His ears still rang from the gunshot. *Dammit! Did I get him? If that Indian asshole had yelped in pain or had fallen, I couldn't have heard it.*

As Ray, on all fours, leaned forward to peer cautiously around the edge of the large rock that concealed him, he bit down hard on his lip to prevent an outcry. Jesus, the pain in his hip had raced the length of his leg like a bolt of electricity.

He slumped back onto his side, his hand going to his hip. *God, was it broken? If my friggin' hip is smashed, I'll die here sure as hell. Even if I killed that bastard coming across the slide, I'll never get out of here alive. Can't use the Harley to go back, it's dead meat, I don't think there's any question about that. I won't be able to work my way across that jumble of rock, that's for sure.*

"Nothing but bad luck," he fumed. *Son of a bitch, I knew that trail was a bastard, and would take good riding skills. Still, I got careless, got too near the edge as I started to pass this damn rock I'm hidden behind. Just had to get ten more feet before I left the bike. I should have jumped clear, rather than trying to save the it.*

Ray had dropped his leg from the foot rest to the ground, trying to lift the machine back onto the ledge by brute force. The weight of the heavy metal frame with its big engine had crumpled his leg, falling atop him, driving his hip against the trail's bare rock. Something on the bike caught on his jeans, almost taking him with it as it disappeared over the edge, tumbling end over end down the steep grade.

Staring at the slide of big boulders and debris before him, hoping to see some trace of Lud, he cursed himself. *Goddammit! Why the hell did I get impatient and chance a shot with the guy still so damn far from me? A forty-five couldn't hit the damn ground at that distance.*

He risked squirming past the edge of the rock for a better look into the slide area. Nobody there. Suddenly he saw something, it was near a big rock. He strained to see. The thing looked like a leather case of some kind. That must have been what his bullet hit, probably hooked to the guy's belt.

Ray exhaled in frustration. *If I didn't kill him, why the hell doesn't the bastard say something? If it's the sheriff, why doesn't he say some of that shit like, Come out with your hands up? Maybe I did kill the bastard. Maybe the fuckin' redskin,s dead behind that big rock. Why else would it be so damn quiet?*

An owl hoot broke into his thoughts and he automatically turned to see if he could see the bird. The trees were too thick, nothing but shadows. Now only the north wind whispered through the forest. Ray shivered. "Goddamn that Skeeter!" he mumbled. "Just a man like anybody else out there, and probably a dead man now."

He opened his mouth to yell, then thought better of it. *But why the hell not? The guy sure knew where he was. But if it was the sheriff, maybe he had a posse with him. Nah. If there was one close by, they would be on him like blow flies on a horse terd.*

"Hey, you!" Ray yelled. "Come on out. You're stuck on the side of the mountain. Can't go forward or back. If you come out now I won't shoot."

He heard nothing. *Who the hell did the asshole think he was screwing around with?*

"You stupid son of a bitch!" Ray yelled again. "I'm giving you a chance to walk away clean. Ain't you got no brains? Come on out of there."

In his frustration, he forgot. He started to shift his knees under him where he could come up onto his feet. The pain was so great, an involuntary, "Jesus," escaped his lips. The agony caused beads of sweat to pop out on his forehead, despite the coolness of the night.

Ray lay, unmoving, in the silence while the pain subsided. *Damn, it was quiet. The asshole had to be a goner. That forty-five slug must have caught him dead center. Nobody fucks with—Oh, Goddammit, I'm gonna have to be sure. Mrs. Logan's little boy is gonna have to worm his way over toward that rock and take a look see.*

Grabbing the forty-five from where it rested at the base of the rock, Ray pushed himself forward. Just as his line of sight cleared the rock, he saw something come out from behind the boulder. A gun!

A chunk of rock a couple of feet above his head leapt into the air, shattering into a dozen tiny pieces, followed by an echoing report. A second shot slammed into the rock, sending a shower of fragments screaming through the air. And then a third and a fourth.

The pain forgotten for the moment, Ray heaved himself backwards to safety. The slugs slamming into the rock were turning it into a pile of gravel. He could hear the rustle of movement between the well spaced shots. Whoever was out there was getting closer, firing as he came. *Well, fuckin' wise guy, I'm ready for you. This time I'm gonna blow your damn head off.*

Abruptly, the shooting stopped. *Ten, twelve rounds? He'd lost count. Didn't matter, he probably had a couple spare holders to slap six more rounds into what the hell ever he was shooting. It had to be a three-fifty-seven or a forty-four magnum revolver, the way it had knocked those chunks out of the rock.*

Logan frowned. He could hear noise, an odd sort of clattering. *Where the hell is it coming from? It's close. Probably behind that big rock, the one as tall as a man, about thirty or forty feet from me. Damn, I wasn't prepared for him to come charging at me like that, blazing away. Well, you ain't got me yet, you red bastard. Come on in, I'm damn sure ready for you now. Soon as I hear you move again, you're a dead son of a bitch.*

Cursing now with the pain of moving, he wormed forward again to where he could peer around the edge of the rock. Extending his hands before him, he steadied the forty-five, its sight lined up on the side edge of the big boulder. *Has to come out that way, not enough room on the other side.*

Ray saw the blurred movement above the boulder at the same time he heard the odd twang. Several seconds later, something struck the rock behind which he lay. He turned in time to see what looked like a stick, bouncing end over end down the trail. *What the shit was that? Jesus Christ, an arrow! That bastard is shooting goddamn arrows at me! The fuckin' Indian is honest-to-god trying to turn me into a pin cushion.*

"Maybe something good's gonna come out of this." He mumbled. *The sheriff must be out of bullets. Hell, I can crawl over there and blow the son of a bitch away. How the hell can the guy stop me? Ole Tonto will have to step out into view to aim with that bow, and Ray will put a half pound of lead up his red ass before he can notch an arrow. I got the son of a bitch now.*

Ray flinched when he heard the next twang. He twisted his head around to try to follow the arrow's flight and saw it at the last second. Ray grunted with the sudden pain. The arrow, protruding from the fleshy part of his calf, had hit with the sensation of somebody driving a wedge into him with a hammer.

Ray, forgetting, twisted around to get at his calf, crying out aloud as weight came onto his hip. His breathing coming in gasps, he brought his leg, which shook convulsively, up to where he could grip the wood shaft sticking out of his calf.

During his earlier struggles his pant-leg had slipped up to his knee. He slid his hand over the blood-slippery flesh of his leg to its underside to where the arrow's point, stopped by the stony ground beneath his leg, was an inch through that side. God it hurt.

Seizing the shaft, he tugged at it. He stopped, gasping for air. Sweat peppered his face. *Jesus, it feels like I'm shredding my fuckin' leg. What the hell am I gonna do? Break off the feathered end and push it on through? Somebody, something I read, said that.*

He closed his eyes. *God almighty, can I do it? The sheriff. Christ, I forgot about him.*

Rolling back against the rock, Ray seized the forty-five and, blinking furiously, peered at the distant boulder. The next twang seemed as loud as a canon blast. Seconds later, the arrow slammed into the meaty part of his buttocks, slicing down through the one and burying itself in the other. He clutched at himself, moaning at what he felt. The wood shaft bridged the crack of his ass.

The next twang sent a bolt of terror through him. He cringed, awaiting its impact. But the arrow landed a foot beyond him, raising sparks as it rebounded from the rock into the air. It landed, a harmless length of wood, atop his wounded calf. The next arrow seemed to take forever to come down, and when it did, it landed even farther away and flipped on the edge of the trail to clatter down the stony slope.

Ray relaxed. *The rising wind must be fuckin' up the son of a bitch's aim. God, I can't let this go on. When the sheriff tries his next shot, I'll scream as if I'm hit bad and stop suddenly. The guy might try a couple more shots, but with the wind carrying them away from me, I'll be safe. Sooner or later, ole Tonto will have to come out to check on Ray, and then he will find out how forty-five slugs feel. Not a bad trade. A hunk of lead for a frigging arrowhead.*

Ray had no need to fake a scream. The next arrow, on its downward course, barely kissed the side of the rock, losing some of its momentum.

When it penetrated Ray's chest from the back, the rib was enough to change its direction. Sliding along the side of the bone, the uppermost of the arrow's razor-sharp barbs sliced open a gaping wound that ran around to his nipple. The pain had been exquisite as the razor metal sliced him open. The intense pain died almost as quickly, but a warm wetness flooded over his chest.

Taking one hand off the gun, he shoved his fingers inside his leather jacket. The shifting of weight onto his hip brought a scream from him, a wild, alien cry that bounced off the exposed rock faces. His hand, coming out of his jacket, was covered in the night light by a dark fluid.

"I give up!" he yelled. "I'm hurt bad. Help me." Then whispered. "You goddamn son of a bitch." *You're gonna die tonight, I'll make damn sure of that. Just stick your fuckin' red hide out here where ole Ray can see it, be the last damn move you ever make. No son of a bitchen redskin is gonna get the best of me. And if I'm gonna die, I'm gonna make damn sure your sorry red ass is going with me. Come on goddamn you, before I bleed to death!*

"Dammit, I give up," he cried again. "Help me, goddammit!"

All was silent for a moment, then he heard the owl again. Closer this time.

The sheriff stepped into view, holding the bow with the arrow notched but not drawn back.

"I'll kill you, you lousy owl bastard," Ray screamed. He struggled with the forty-five as he tried to lift it with his trembling hands. He was firing, but it had taken him far too long to pull the trigger. The sheriff had no trouble ducking out of sight.

Ray stopped himself just as he was about to squeeze off the last round, sending it out into open space past the rock, where all the rest of his shots had gone. Rolling onto his back, he shouted, "Fuck you, you voodoo, magic, fuckin' owl chief. And fuck the fucking world!"

Ray Logan slid the hot steel of the .45 into his mouth. He tightened his finger on the trigger. And the world, blew apart.

CHAPTER 31

Lud sat behind one of the desks in the outer office of the sheriff's station, his eyes mere slits against the glare of the early morning sunlight reflecting off the desk top.

He stared into the grocery sack that sat, open, between his legs. *What a damn mess. I was kidding myself when I wanted to believe that I still functioned effectively during black outs. I have no idea of how or when I came into possession of the sacks contents.*

His fingers trailed across the stiff, blood-stained fabric of what had been Amy Housley's blouse, sliced in three or four places. *The damn guy didn't even take the time to undress her, he cut the clothes off her body.*

The sack held her clothes and those of Beverly Taylor, as well as the two women's purses. With a groan, Lud buried his face in his hands. *Dammit, I can't remember a thing about these clothes.*

Everything was clear, up to a point. He remembered the exchange of arrows and bullets, hearing that last muffled gunshot, and finally slipping around the rock to find Logan, the top of his head blown off with his own gun.   He had spotted the Harley lying at the bottom of the slope in a fan of spilled food from the gunny sack and had climbed down to it. Lud had removed the knapsack from the bike's rack and, kneeling, was opening it, when a searing bolt of pain ripped through his head. He remembered clawing at his pocket, reaching for the pain pills, and then he remembered nothing.

Lud glanced up at the wall clock. Not till two hours ago. He had found himself sprawled atop his bed in mud-stained clothes and moccasins. Panicked, he had bolted upright, glaring wildly about the room, trying to connect what he saw with where he had been, seemingly only seconds before, crouched by the Harley. His gaze had settled on the stained women's clothing, strewn on the floor around the bed.

Later, having examined the cut up garments together with the two purses he discovered on his desk, their contents strewn across its top, he knew that he had found the clothes Amy Housley and Beverly Taylor had been wearing when they were murdered. But where had he found them?

The knapsack!

Logan's knapsack, rested on the bed at its foot.

Scrambling back to the bed, he had grabbed Logan's pack and freed its flap. But it had been so stuffed with the biker's own clothing, he could never have gotten the dead women's stuff in there as well.

He shook his head in frustration. *Goddammit, why can't I remember? I had to have found the stuff where the biker died. Or did I? Did I go back to Logan's camp site and find the clothing and purses there. Hell, no, that would have been an illegal search. That had been too strongly ingrained. I wouldn't have done that. No way.*

Lud had quickly shed his muddy garments and put on a clean uniform. Stuffing Amy's and Bev's clothing and purses into a paper sack, he had taken the grocery bag and knapsack out to the patrol car. Lud had no time to pull the wet, muddy bedspread off the bed or gather up the ruin of his uniform from the floor. He had to get the evidence into the office and tagged.

Lud sat upright as the key grated in the lock of the station's front door.

Alice charged in, muttering to herself, "Late again." She saw Lud and stopped short, her mouth agape. "Oh, praise God. We thought you might be dead."

Lud glared at her. He had enough on his mind without having to deal with Alice's hysterics.

"Dead?" he asked. "What the hell are you talking about?" Alice came through the gate, her eyes fixed on him. She acted as if he might be a ghost. "Oh, my God!" she cried.

"Quit saying, oh, my God, and tell me what you're talking about, Alice," Lud demanded.

She gulped. Alice was acting as if she were having a hard time getting enough air. "We…we have a search underway for you. When you never radioed in, Ralph went looking for you. That was a couple hours ago, Your car was missing from where you said you'd leave it. After he questioned those bikers at Black Bear Creek Campground, Ralph told me to get a helicopter from Wenatchee up in the air while he deputized a few fellows in Pine Ridge to form a search party."

Lud slapped his hand against his forehead. "Jesus Christ! There goes this year's emergency fund down the damn tubes. What in—"

"Lud, they just spotted Ray Logan's body near the slide on Widowmaker Trail, and Ralph and boys are about to start hiking in. They couldn't see but the one body from the air, but the forest gets thick there, they reported. Ralph thought you might be down near there, too. They were going to bring whatever bodies they found at that location, back down the mountain."

"Goddammit, woman, you cancel that chopper. And tell Ralph to get his butt back here. We'll hire someone to go in there later on today with a pack horse to bring Logan's body out."

The sight of the tall, big-boned woman wringing her hands did little to placate him.

"We're sorry, Sheriff," Alice said. "It's just that we though that maybe you were—"

"Well, I'm not. Goddammit! Get on the radio!"

As Lud sat, listening to Alice's exchange with the helicopter pilot, pain stroked his head with light, quick touches. Whatever the black outs did, they didn't help with his sleep. He was exhausted.

Lud was on the point of dozing off when he became aware that Alice, having carried out his orders, was coming toward him. At the last moment, he remembered the grocery bag with the blood-stained blouse peeping from it. *My God, if Alice saw that—*

But the thought came far too late. Before he could kick the sack into the kneehole of the desk, Alice cried, "Oh, my goodness! What's that?"

He was still trying to direct it into the kneehole with his foot when she snatched the sack from between his legs. Gingerly, with thumb and forefinger, she lifted the blouse into the light.

"Ugh! That's blood." Her eyes widened. "Is that the clothing of the Housley or Taylor woman? Where on earth did you find it?"

Had he not been so tired, he might have thought of an answer that would have satisfied Alice. As it was, he fucked up royally, putting her on the scent like a hound dog.

"Yeah, it's both their stuff," Lud disclosed. "I found it on Logan's bike." He put his foot further into his mouth, explaining that he had brought the garments and Logan's knapsack back to town because he didn't want wild animals to get at them.

Alice had been a sheriff's department employee for twenty years and had learned a few things.

She shook her head. "But, Lud, you ruined the chain of evidence. That slippery old Finestein will have that inadmissible in a minute." Alice blushed.

Any other time, Lud would have been amused at Alice's embarrassment over the advice that had slipped out, unbidden. But her momentary confusion gave Lud his opening. "Goddammit, Alice," he said. "The killer's dead. I won't be taking this to court. Just to the coroner's inquest. I'm the sheriff here. You let me worry about the evidence."

Alice, looking hurt, shoved a cup toward him. "Here."

He nodded. *So that's why she left her desk, to bring me coffee. Christ, what a fuck-up! I better get her out of the office so I can phone Dain and try to cover my ass.*

He shoved the cup of coffee back across the desk top toward her, sloshing a fair share of it out onto a stack of Incident Report Forms. "This stuff is stale. I noticed the can was down to the last grounds. Get some money out of the change dish and go buy a fresh can."

"But, Lud, it tastes alright to me. I just turned the pot on a few minutes ago."

He glared at her. "I don't care how it tastes to you. It's still stale."

"But if I can—"

"Alice, I've been up all night. I was responsible for a man's death last night, and I'm in no mood to argue. Now you get the hell out of here and do what I told you."

They both jumped as the voice exploded from the radio.

"County S.O., Sheriff's Office. This is Flight *HX-four*. I've contacted your deputy. We're returning to base now. Thanks. Over and out."

The interruption failed to distract Alice. "I know you had a hard night, but you don't have to talk to me like I'm dirt. We've all had less sleep since we've been short handed. Okay, I'll go do what you want."

As she charged out the door, she said, perhaps more to herself than Lud, "I was worried about you, damn you."

Lud hurried to the front door and stood, watching, as she got into her car. When her face turned toward the light, he saw the wetness on her cheeks. He'd have to apologize to her when she got back. But god-dammit to hell, it was her fault. She was like a mother hen, she just wouldn't let things be. With a sigh, he turned and, passing through the counter gate, walked into his office.

Lud pulled the phone across the desk. What the hell was Dain going to think of his screw-up. No story he told was going to excuse his sloppy police work. Alice had been on the money about the chain of evidence.

If he hadn't blacked out he would have went right to his car, called Ralph, and the two of them would have hiked back in to the site of Logan's death. At that point, he and Ralph would have checked out everything, got the body out of there, done the damn thing right. But he sure the hell wasn't going to confess about his black outs, not at this late date.

Lud pondered what Dain, what any *DA*, would think if he had to confess he had no idea where the hell he'd found the clothes and purses. The one thing he did remember finding, the knapsack, held nothing but Logan's clothes. Why had he taken it?

The idea hit Lud so hard he wanted to shout. A couple of years back, he had been having coffee with old Judge Enright at Sam's. The old buzzard, who had been retired for at least ten years, loved to talk about unusual cases of law. He had told Lud about a cop in Detroit removing a pile of betting slips from a burning house.

The presiding judge ruled them admissible on the grounds that preserving evidence had precedence over documenting evidence. *Hell, I can say I saw a couple of coyotes near the wrecked bike and knew that the scent of the blood would draw them. If a coyote was hungry enough, he'd eat fabric that had blood on it.*

A warm relief slowly enveloped him. *No doubt that's why I did it. The clothes were probably in the saddle bags on the bike. Alice could raise all the hell she wanted. I'm on rock-solid ground. And, after all, what did it matter? It was probably a moot point anyway, since Ray was dead.*

With a long, drawn-out sigh, he brought the receiver to his ear.

The burst of pain was so great he slammed backwards against the back rest of the swivel chair. The light dimmed, like always, and he wanted to relax, to fall into the blackness that brought relief from the searing agony. But this time he struggled to ward off the darkness. He had to stay alert to tell Dain what he'd found. He shook his head, and the flares of light came and went in slow, measured surges.

Go away. Relax. Go away.

The voice, so close, startled him, even stunned him. He tried to turn his chair to see who it was, who was in the room behind him, but too tired, his legs refused to move. He mumbled, "Who—"

The voice came again. It was as if the speaker were next to his ear, in his head.

Go away. Go away for good. You make peace with the white man like a squaw.

Lud, his head lolling back, the ceiling above him barely visible, managed to say, "Where…who…I can't see you. Oh, my God."

He was being pulled down out of his own head. His eyes were like windows out into the world, and he was drifting away from them, into a darkness filled with a sound like rushing wind. *The voice. It's so strange. Whose voice was it?*

It came again. *I need you no more. Go away for good. I know all you know now. The white men's eyes are clouded now. They see me as you. A warrior takes your place, squaw man. Go away for good. Away!*

Somewhere in the darkness, Lud felt himself spinning round and round, hurtling off into nowhere.

Looking Glass dialed the number for the Barlow place.

CHAPTER 32

The phone rang, jarring Dain from a restless sleep. His hand groped across the bed toward the night stand. He found the portable phone on its stand and pulled it to his ear.

"Hello," he mumbled. His eyes opened and sought the bedside clock. Seven-twenty-five A.M.

"Dain? This is Lud. I got the killer. Thought you would like to know," Looking Glass said.

Throwing off the covers, Dain bolted upright, swinging his legs over the side of the bed. "Who is it? You have him in custody? Did he confess?"

"It was Ray Logan. He had a fight with Mike Powers at Brown's Tavern. Well, you could call it a fight, I suppose. Logan caught him kicking over his motor bike out front and beat him to death. Hell, he could have beat up three Mike Powers at once. Afterwards, Logan took off into the woods on his Harley, which should tell you how stupid he was. I went after him on foot. Caught him up near the slide area on Widowmaker Trail."

"Sorry to hear about Powers," Dain said without much feeling. "You took Logan into Crescent Valley, right? I need to question him as soon as I can." The voice on the other end of the line sounded irritated.

"Goddammit, man, he's in the county morgue, or will be soon. You act like we had a frigging cakewalk back there in the woods. The last time I picked him up he said we'd never put the cuffs on him again, and he meant it. I did my best to bring him in alive, but it just didn't work out. It was him or me.

"But, why in the hell would you want to question him anyway? I told you. We had him dead to rights. The bastard had Amy's and Bev's stuff with him; their clothes, purses, the whole damn works. And I've got an eye witness to his beating Mike Powers to death. What's your problem? Pissed off because I cracked the case?"

"Christ, Lud," Dain protested. "You know me better than that after all these years. It's just that a lot of things don't add up. You think Logan had enough sense to try framing Albert by dumping the typewriter and those boots at his house?

"And where the hell is Albert? Dead? Would Logan go to the trouble of framing him, then kill him? And where is Joe Woods? Then there's those bogus invitations. Logan was almost illiterate. can you see him using a typewriter? Dammit, Lud, we still have a case as full of holes as a loaf of swiss cheese."

"I told you he had their clothes. Now relax. Tell the two, Pat and Sheila, they can relax now. It's all over."

Dain stood, trying to slip into his pants while holding onto the phone. "I hope the hell you're right. Logan was here last night while I was gone…or at least somebody was."

"What happened? Did they see anyone?"

"The son of a bitch came in through the basement door, popped that old padlock off like it was made of paper."

Dain quickly told him what little the women had been able to say and added, "If I hadn't gotten away from Finestein when I did, they would have been dead when I came home. He had them drugged and both women stripped, and Sheila on the bed, ready to rape her before he decapitated her.

"I guess he planned to do the same thing to Pat when he got through with Sheila. But I found nothing here to prove it was Logan. You'd think that big bastard was too damn clumsy, to not leave something behind."

"Well, we do have proof that he was in the vicinity. Just wait till I tell you what happened on the old dump road. The guy I saw in the woods, I didn't get a look at his face, but how many six-seven guys do you know around here? After the son of a bitch gave me the slip, he must have headed for Brown's Tavern. I guess he took his frustrations out on poor Mike Powers."

"But are you sure—"

"Listen, Dain, I'll tell you the whole story when I see you."

After a moment's hesitation, Dain said, "Maybe you're right, Lud. I'm looking for a package without any loose ends.

"At least Sheila and Pat should breathe a lot easier, but I don't know if they're going to stay for the reunion. After the town nurse revived them, it must have been two in the morning, they swore to God, that they wouldn't spend another night in Pine Ridge."

He paused a moment, thinking. "Hey, Lud, what time do you get off duty?"

"I never get off duty these days, not with just one deputy available. Why do you ask?"

"I thought maybe, if you were going to be up here in Pine Ridge this morning, you could come by and have a cup of coffee. Oh, hell! What I'd really like for you to do is to talk to Sheila and Pat and convince them that the danger is past. Tell them about Logan. What do you say?"

"You've got a date. I'll be there about ten. I want those two little ladies to relax, quit looking over their shoulders, and have some fun. And you, too, Dain. We've got the son of a bitch. He's stone cold dead."

Dain put down the phone, his mood ebullient, but by the time he'd finished tying his shoes, he was staring off into space again. *Keeping the clothes. That's the act of a psychopathic personality. Ray Logan was as mean a son of a bitch as ever walked the earth, but psychotic? Was convincing*

Sheila and Pat they were out of danger the right thing to do? But if I don't they're out of here.

He started for the door. *Dammit, Lud has to be right. The killer is in the county morgue.*

✶   ✶   ✶

"Where are we going?" Sheila asked as Dain pulled out of the Barlow driveway and turned east. Although the north wind had a bite to it, in the car, the mid morning sun's rays felt warm.

"I want to check the water level at Rainbow Lake. Then I thought we could run on down to Crescent Valley. I'll buy you cuties ice cream sundaes, and afterwards you can pick up your cars at the motel.

From the back seat, Pat said, "Cuties? Ice cream sundaes? Compliments and calories, the one sounds nice, but that other…oh, what the heck. Let's live dangerously."

Dain, unsure about whether Pat was kidding, glanced anxiously at Sheila, seated next to him.

Sheila laughed. "Why not? I haven't had an ice cream sundae in years."

God, she looked gorgeous. She had on a long sleeve white silk blouse topped off with a light beige slack suit that set off the highlights in her hair.

Pat leaned forward, her breath tickling Dain's neck. "About Rainbow Lake. Do you really think it's going to flood the road? That could put a damper on the reunion."

Sheila and Pat were tougher than he had thought. He had figured he would be spending the morning trying to sweet-talk them into staying around, and here they were discussing the reunion as if nothing had happened.

Earlier, sitting at the breakfast table, nursing horrendous headaches from the drug they had been given, they had listened with little reaction as Lud told them about Ray Logan's death and finding Bev's and Amy's clothing in his possession. Lud had continued to reassure them that the danger had passed, but still, they had seemed indifferent. Finally, they had excused themselves to go back upstairs, leaving Lud looking irritated.

As Dain walked the sheriff out to his car, Lud continued to rail at him about convincing them they were safe. As he stood, watching the sheriff's unit disappear down the drive, he realized how much the success of the reunion meant to Lud. If the reunion was a flop. His old friend must have figured that everybody would blame him, like when they were in school, the dumb Indian had screwed up again.

After Lud had gone, it took the better part of an hour for Dain to coax them into going for a ride. But once they agreed, their mood had changed in a twinkling. They had charged out to the Blazer, all smiles.

Turning, Sheila grinned at Pat. "Not to worry, Pat. Lud sounded so anxious, he'll probably volunteer to row everyone, coming to attend the reunion, across the lake." She glanced back at Dain. "Where are we going to get this sundae that's going to put ten pounds on my hips?"

"Where else? Jake's. Remember the first time the three of us were at Jake's together?"

Sheila laughed. "Do I ever. We were sophomores, and after school one Friday you asked me if I wanted to go down to Crescent Valley Saturday morning and have a soda with you. Pat was spending the night with me, so you said, 'Bring her along.'"

"You do remember. I'm surprised."

She giggled. "I should. It was our first date. I recall it very well."

"When you sounded interested," Dain responded, "I had to ask you to bring Pat. It had taken me two weeks to get up enough nerve to pop the question, I wasn't about to blow it by saying, 'Well, maybe some other time.'"

Smiling, Dain turned to look into the beautiful face beside him. "So what better place to go for a second first date? It worked pretty well the first time. And just maybe, you can find it in your heart to forgive a young boy who got caught in a bad situation that he's regretted to this day."

"Really, Dain?" Sheila's voice was soft. "You mean it?"

"I'd give anything in the world if I could change that Saturday afternoon."

The shower of gravel hitting the bottom of the car and Pat's shout came at the same instant. "For God's sake, man, watch where you're going! If you two are going to reminisce, Dain, at least pay attention to your driving while you talk."

Feeling like a fool, Dain blushed furiously. Sheila her head thrown back, was laughing at him, but when she saw his embarrassment, she stopped abruptly, leaning over to where her fingernails brushed his cheek. "You're a little old for a first date, but you're still kind of cute, Mr. Barlow."

"Christ, Sheila, give me a break, this isn't easy. I've spent several years planning what I would do, what I would say when I saw you. Then, one look at you, and suddenly I'm more tongue-tied than I was when I was fifteen, when it took me two weeks to work up the courage to ask you for the first date."

Her voice was soft, barely audible above the road sounds. "I'm feeling a little bit sophomoric, myself."

Dain gasped. *Christ, I have to get myself under control. She's going to think I'm still wet behind the ears, but, Jesus, every time I look at her, I just melt.*

Dain stared straight ahead through the windshield, knowing he sounded more ridiculous, more like a cop issuing a citation with every word he spoke. "Listen, Sheila, I was worried about what you would think when we met again. I just knew you would remember me as a snotty-nosed punk who had made such a complete jackass of himself back when we were in school.

"Then when you called, suggesting that we meet at Sam's, I was ready to turn cartwheels. I was so happy that even finding Amy's body couldn't kill the excitement. Hell, I walked into Sam's, and seeing you, sitting there, was like getting hit in the solar plexus. I…oh, hell, don't pay attention to me. I don't know what I'm saying."

Her hand came back up to the side of his face, her fingers stroking his hair now. Dain could see the moisture in the corner of her eyes. Her voice was still soft, but huskier now. "I like the way that you don't know what you're saying."

From the back seat, Pat muttered, "Now I know what the expression, being a fifth wheel, means."

Sheila glanced back at her. "Be quiet, Pattie."

Dain felt like stopping to put Pat out beside the road. Instead, he raised his gaze to the rear view mirror, saw her watching him, and gave her a wink. She rolled her eyes, then closed them and slumped back into the corner of the seat. "Don't pay any attention to me, folks."

Sheila didn't. Sliding closer to Dain, she rested her hand on his forearm. "I wasn't even sure you would be up when I phoned, but I couldn't wait. I wanted to hear your voice…to see you. It took me a couple of years of growing up to realize that males and females don't think the same way…you know…that you couldn't help yourself with, that little bitch Candy and her buddy. And then—"

He opened his mouth to protest, but she put her long, tapered fingers against his lips. "Hush, Dain. Let me talk. This isn't easy for any girl. I feel like a real fool. You see, I found out recently that you weren't lying, that, actually they were the one's who raped you."

Dain lifted his arm from the steering wheel, but she caught it and pulled it back down. "No, Dain, not now. Not yet."

His shoulders slumped. "I'm sorry, Sheila. I'm not making a pass—"

"Oh, for God's sake, Dain, don't be silly. Don't you know you can't rush a woman into things like this? I was married. I loved my husband. It…it wasn't the same as you. I know that now, after seeing you again. But I did love him. It will take time to get used to the idea of you again."

He grabbed her hand with his. "Listen, you don't owe me any explanations. I almost married twice while I was in L.A. The first time it was like I was trying to spite you, but thank God, I came to my senses. The second was after I heard about your wedding. I knew you were beyond my reach then and I felt lost. I kept putting off the marriage and finally admitted she could never take your place, and it wasn't fair to her. So here I am, a confirmed bachelor.

"When I heard your husband had been killed, I felt bad for you, and I know I must seem like a jerk to you, but, dammit to hell, I was excited, knowing you were a free woman again."

Sheila turned her eyes up to him, her cheeks, tear-stained. "Shut up. Don't talk that way about Dain Barlow. I think I can understand." Quickly she raised her face and kissed him on the cheek.

The Blazer rounded the curve, and Rainbow Lake came into view. A stiff morning breeze was raising small white caps on the broad blue expanse. Below them, as they came down the grade, waves were splashing against the shore. Dain slowed as he came onto the straightaway that marked the road's lowest point.

"Just what I was afraid of. Look there."

Ahead of them, the water had risen onto the shoulder, and each wave was sending paper-thin fans of water across the asphalt.

Risking a quick glance that included both Pat and Sheila, he said, "Ladies, you've got a decision to make. We will be driving through water on the way home. If you come back up to Pine Ridge with me, you may be stuck there for a week. I'm sure you can reclaim your motel rooms if you want."

"But that means we'd miss the reunion," Pat protested. "I haven't come through all this hell to do that. I'm staying in Pine Ridge…if Dain will have me. I'm going to bring my car up, though, because I want to visit with Gramps before I leave town."

Sheila gave Dain a shy smile. "Staying a week in the Barlow mansion sounds kind of nice to me. I have a good manager at the boutique. All I need to do is call, and the shop will be just fine. How about it, Dain? Do you mind if I stay?"

Pat groaned. "For God's sake, Sheila, be quiet. If you don't stop teasing him, he's going to drive us straight into the lake."

Sheila laughed. "Spoil sport!"

Dain, looking at Sheila, jumped when Pat shouted, "Or get us in an accident! Watch out!"

The car was headed for three leather-clad bikers, coming toward them in the opposite lane. The trio swerved off onto the narrow shoulder to avoid the Blazer. Wide-eyed, they fought the bikes, the rear wheels digging to find traction in the soft material of the shoulder. A second later, the bikers were out of sight behind a low crest in the road while Dain brought the over-corrected Blazer back under control.

Glancing at the white-faced Sheila from the corner of his eye, he mumbled, "Sorry. Hard to keep my eye on the road and you at the same time." *What the hell's wrong with me? I didn't act this silly even back when I was in high school, just learning to drive. Christ, I could have hit those guys and put God only knows how many in the hospital. Goddammit, I have to stop acting like some love starved juvenile.*

He raised his voice, trying to act as if pulling this sort of stupid shit was what cool L.A. guys did every day. "Sorry, Pat. Now you know why cops have to have those sirens and flashing lights when we're behind the wheel. But don't be upset. I'll keep my eye on the road the rest of the way. I promise."

Pat's voice seemed to have a bit of a bite to it. "I'm not upset, but I think those three chaps behind us are."

They were on the long, straight downgrade that led into Crescent Valley. Behind them, maybe a mile back, he could see the three bikers coming after him.

Christ! Deja vu. He didn't need Mike Powers to get on that bunch's shit list. He did the job quite nicely himself.

Once past that last curve near Rainbow Lake where he had encoun-tered the three motorcycle riders, Dain had brought his speed up to sev-enty, taking advantage of the gently undulating road as it came down out of the last of the foothills. Now, nearing the city limits of Crescent Valley, he could see the trio clearly.

The one in front was the redhead who had kept giving Dain the evil eye when he and Mike had had their run-in with the bunch. Built like an out-of-shape line backer, he apparently had taken over as the Alpha dog of the pack with Logan's death. Once they closed the distance, they seemed content to stay fifty yards behind, paying no attention to the Blazer.

Jake's Ice Cream Parlor, located on the edge of Crescent Valley, had kept its quaint name but had evolved into a drive-in, serving as many hamburgers as ice cream. The big parking lot was a concession to mod-ern times.

Just as they reached the entrance to Jake's, Sheila said, "Oh, God, I hope those creeps go on by."

Dain, slowing, turned into the parking lot.

From the back seat, Pat murmured, "No such luck."

By the time Dain parked, released his seat belt, and slid out of the car, the three toughs were waiting for him. He looked across the roof of the Blazer at Sheila and Pat, Coming out of the vehicle on the other side.

"You ladies go on inside and wait for me."

"No way," Sheila said, starting around the rear of the Blazer, followed by Pat.

Dain raised his voice. "Dammit! Get inside!"

They ignored him, joining him where he stood awaiting the bikers.

The redheaded leader grinned. "Now, Mr. Policeman, don't worry your head none about your little cunts. We ain't gonna hurt 'em. Matter of fact, we may take 'em back to camp and give 'em a little thrill. Or should I say big thrill."

The trio snickered in unison. Didn't take the pack long to switch allegiance to the new Alpha dog.

"Listen, I'm sorry as hell about what happened back there on the road," Dain said. "It was my fault. I was distracted and crossed the center line. You guys came over the hill and were on me before I could do anything. I don't blame you for being upset about it. Why don't you accept my apology and let's forget it?"

The new leader of the toughs glanced toward one of his comrades. "You hear that? The cop was distracted. Probably trying to decide which one of his two pussies he was gonna fuck first."

Dain glared at him. "Shut your goddamn filthy mouth, Red. This is between you guys and me. These ladies are not involved. Let me get them inside, and I'll come back."

The redhead laughed. "What are you gonna do if we don't, asshole? Do to us what your buddy the sheriff did to Ray?"

"Logan resisted arrest," Dain said. "He opened fire on the sheriff. Lud had no choice but to defend himself—"

"Defend himself!" the biker yelled. "That bastard tortured Ray, made a pin cushion out of him. That Indian fucker is either sick or crazy. If you didn't have all these people around," he gestured with his head toward several teenagers who had stopped on the sidewalk to kibitz, and watch the show, "you'd have that gun out, shooting the knee-caps off all of us right now, wouldn't you, you miserable bastard?"

"Tortured! Pin cushion! What kind of cock-and-bull story are you giving me, Red?"

The burly redhead had worked himself into such a fury that he was spraying spit as he talked. "Your buddy shot him full of arrows, dammit! Just kept shooting, the way I heard it. Tortured him to where he couldn't stand it. He finally blowed his own head off because the pain was too damn much!"

Dain stared at him. "Where did you hear this?"

"They brought his body into Crescent Valley just before we left. One of the ambulance guys told us. Said it damn near made him sick just to look at the corpse."

One of the other bikers yelled, "Goddammit, Red, quit jawing with the fucker. He tried to kill us just like the sheriff did Ray."

Red shouted at him. "Shut your fucking mouth!" He whirled back to face Dain, his hands balling into fists. "I'm gonna break every bone in your body, shitface. And what I can't break, my buddies will."

"Don't! Leave him alone," Sheila cried. She lunged toward Dain, but Pat, grabbing her, pulled her back.

The third biker yelled, "Finish it, Red! This kid," he was glancing at one of the teenagers on the sidewalk, "says the manager called the cops a few minutes ago."

His other companion leaned over his bike, extracted a baseball bat from the boot, and tossed it toward Red. "Use this on him, man. Break his fuckin' back."

Dain made his move, lunging toward Red's outstretched hand. He managed to knock the bat away as the man's hand closed on the handle. But this left Dain off-balance, his arms wide apart. Before he could recover, Red stepped into him. Dain saw the right hand with two hundred and thirty pounds of flesh and bone behind it coming toward him only at the last split second. The next thing he knew, he was on all fours, staring down at the pavement, his head spinning.

Somewhere, far off, as if it were coming from a tunnel, he heard someone yell, "Kick the bastard's ribs in!"

Dain brought his face up just in time to see Red swinging his foot back, ready to drive it into his ribs. Dain rolled away at the same instant the big man screamed, clutching at his back, as he reeled sideways. He fell forward onto the parking lot's surface and lay, writhing.

Where Red had been, a grim-faced Sheila stood, feet apart, bat in hand, staring speculatively at the fallen figure.

A single word burst in chorus from the teenagers. "Cops!"

A groggy Dain struggled upright to a cacophony of roaring bike engines and a siren's dying wail. The two bikers burst out of the parking lot as Ralph, gun in hand, slid out of the sheriff's unit.

Dain his head spinning, turned back carefully to face Sheila. With only concern for him on her face, she dropped the bat and rushed to him. Her arms going around Dain, she pushed him up against the Blazer. "Oh, darling, are you hurt?"

A bewildered looking Pat, stood staring at Sheila and Dain as Dain heard one young voice on the sidewalk exclaim, "Jesus, did you ever see anything like that? I think she damn near took out a kidney with that baseball bat."

CHAPTER 33

Dain and Sheila left Crescent Valley shortly after two P.M., on their way back to Pine Ridge. Pat followed in her car.

Glancing at Sheila, he asked, "Are you sure Blackwell doesn't mind if you leave your car parked at the motel? This is the beginning of his busiest time of year."

"I don't think he was too happy about it, but after I fluttered my eyelashes at him a bit, he let me park it next to the dumpster in back of the office. Pat needs her car because she wants to drive out to see her grandfather, and she didn't want to borrow yours again. She's the independent type."

Dain glanced toward Sheila. *I can never figure women. When I asked her if she wanted lunch, she had said yes. An hour before that, she had knocked down a huge sundae at Jake's. Then out of the blue she said, Let's have lunch at Kenn's, that I understood. Sheila didn't want food, she wanted to face the ghosts of Candy again, put the past to rest. But her plans had gone astray. It was Candy's day off. We ended up just having coffee.*

Despite the area's gruesome murders, most people in the restaurant had been speculating about just how high the water would rise in Rainbow Lake, not that they gave a damn about Pine Ridge. They were taxpayers wondering about how badly the flood would damage the road. And if it would be as big as the record setter of seventy-nine.

As they neared the lake, Dain glanced upward toward the heavens. The sky was streaked with cirrus clouds, so thick that they gave it the appearance of white ruffles on pale blue cloth. The damp air might bring morning fogs, but the threat of more rain had diminished.

Sheila, still stuffed from the sundae, was content to lie back, her eyes closed, an occasional smile playing across her face. They rode in silence until they rounded the curve where Dain's parents had been killed. He hit the brakes hard, and her eyelids flew open.

Ahead of them, a sheriff's unit was parked on the shoulder of the road, its light bar flashing. Lud stood beside its open door, looking at them. Beyond the car, where the road had been earlier, was a thirty-yard stretch of water.

Dain leaned his head out the window and yelled, "How bad is it, Lud? Can I get through?"

The sheriff said nothing, simply stared at them.

"What's wrong with Lud?" Sheila asked. "He's acting weird."

"Beats me," Dain muttered, then stuck his head out the window again. This seemed to bring the sheriff out of his trance, and he walked toward them at a shambling gait.

Looking up at him, Dain said, "Christ, Lud, you look bad. Didn't you have time to grab a nap today?" Shaking his head, Dain continued, "Up most of the night and day. You better slow down, old buddy."

The sheriff was still acting odd. He turned in a complete circle, gazing about him, as if he had never seen this stretch of road before. Looking at Dain again, his face changed, becoming animated. Reaching the vehicle, he leaned over to where he could peer into the car and said, "Dain? Sheila?"

Pat's car came into view behind them and coasted to a stop. Lud glanced back at her.

"Still acting like the Three Musketeers, eh?" Lud said. "Listen, you guys got back just in time." He nodded toward the submerged road. "About a foot of water's over the road at the deepest spot, and who knows what it's going to be by midnight. I radioed the county road department for barricades."

Leaning across Dain, Sheila said, "Oh, no! I wonder if we should call off the reunion."

The sheriff shook his head. "Little late for that. Besides the flooding report is on TV and radio stations all over the state. Be pretty hard not to know what's going on. I figure anybody wanting to come would have sense enough to know it's today or never."

Dain looked first at Sheila, then at Lud. "That brings up another problem. We might have a few teachers, and all those folks will be bringing their wives or husbands, maybe even some kids. Everybody figured on commuting from the motels in Crescent Valley."

The sheriff rubbed his chin. "Yeah, I thought about that. What I figured was maybe some of the locals would give these people a place to sleep." He hesitated. "You know, I was thinking. You've got several empty bedrooms in your house. I know it would be an imposition, but—"

"Hell, guy, you know me better than that," Dain interrupted. "I'll gladly take in anybody who needs a room."

"Okay, ole buddy. We'll know by mid—"

Suddenly, he came upright and turned away from them, standing without moving for so long that Dain said tentatively, "Lud?" When that brought no response, he asked, "Lud, what's wrong?"

Slowly, the sheriff turned back to look at them, the geniality gone from his face now. His voice harsh, he said, "I can't waste time chatting. You'd better get a move on."

Ignoring the surprised Dain, he charged on up the road, windmilling his arms, yelling at Pat. "Okay, let's move it! You can't park on the highway."

As Dain eased forward into the water, Sheila asked, "What was that all about? Did we say something to make him mad?"

Dain shrugged. "I haven't a clue, other than he's been working himself to death. He's sure been acting strange. I think this thing with Amy and Bev has him shook."

Thirty minutes later, Dain rocked to a stop in front of the Barlow house, with Pat right behind him. She joined Dain and Sheila as they climbed out of the Blazer.

"What on earth did you guys say to Lud to set him off like that?" Pat asked. "He really looked pissed off."

Sheila shrugged. "Nothing. We were as surprised as you are. Maybe the job is getting to be too much for him. You know, with the murders, and the two deputies missing and all. He's sure looking tired."

Pat turned toward the steps. "Well, listen you two, I've got to get going if I'm going to reach Gramps's in time to fix him some dinner." Stopping halfway up the steps, she leered at them. "I do hope you two can purport yourselves in a dignified manner for one night without a chaperon."

Dain, blushed. *Jesus, why did he feel like it was his first time with a woman?*

*   * *   * *

The sound of the front door slamming shut was quickly soaked up by the thick stand of trees surrounding the cabin. Looking Glass halted just inside the cabin, trembling with rage. *The squaw man caught me by surprise. I was standing, looking over the rising expanse of water when the bastard caught me, pulled me into darkness. Only later, standing by the ponyless carriage, talking to Dain and Sheila, had I been able to escape to take over again.*

I must learn the lesson, well. Stay vigilant. I must keep the squaw man in darkness two more suns. Then I will be able to rid myself of the miserable, Lud for all time. The man not worthy enough to have chief's blood running through his veins.

Quickly crossing the room, he shed the detested uniform and slipped into buckskins. Soon he came back out of the cabin and glided along its side, surefooted in his moccasins. The small metal outbuilding stood some twenty-five yards behind the cabin, almost lost from sight.

While he had been waiting for the barricades to arrive at Rainbow Lake, before encountering his blood brother Dain and his white bitch, Looking Glass had made his decision.

The squaw man Lud had found the several blocks of plastique explosive after it had been thrown into a ditch outside Crescent Valley. Some weeks ago, he and a Washington state police unit were pursuing a pickup truck, driven by two drunken men from the reservation. The pursuit had covered some ten miles of ranch roads outside Crescent Valley.

In the roiling clouds of dust, kicked up by the three speeding vehicles, because Lud had been behind the pickup, with the stater behind him, he had seen something the trooper had missed. The suspect vehicle had been forced onto a dead-end road, and a half mile before the end of the line he saw a package sail out the pickup's window.

Later, he had returned, recovered it from the ditch, and discovered the plastique. God knows where the two tribal residents had bought the stuff, but Lud knew them well. The men were all talk and no action. He had no desire to get them into trouble.

Life was hard enough on the reservation. Lud took the plastique out to his cabin to store it in the outbuilding until he decided how to get rid of it.

At about the same time Looking Glass escaped his enslavement for the first brief time, and knew the stupid Lud's completed plan. He intended to waste all that power for revenge by hiking into the back country with the plastique and exploding it at a remote location. The fool, suffering with his headaches, had labored over an FBI manual for hours until he mastered how to detonate the explosives.

Now he, Looking Glass, would take that which the Dark Spirit had given him, the power to avenge Running Fawn. The realization had come clearly to him this afternoon at Rainbow Lake. The Great Spirit wanted the death and humiliation of the four bitches, but he wanted more. The town must pay! All who lived there, all those who had dishonored Running Fawn, must die.

Unlocking the shed, he stepped inside. Reaching under the work bench, he brought the deadly package of explosive material into view. The time had come to rig the blocks of plastique. Stepping out of the small metal structure, clutching a large cardboard box in which he had placed a coil of wire and the bundled explosives, he hurried back through the grove of trees to the cabin.

The north wind had picked up and had a chill to it. Earlier, the sky had been filled with high, thin clouds that promised better weather. Now the sky was a clear blue. Maybe for the next few days they would be able to dry out a little.

Looking Glass was separating the blocks of plastique when he heard the noise outside. *A car door? Who would be coming here this time of night? Dain. No time to hide the stuff, and seeing the light, my blood brother might charge right in.*

Whirling, Looking Glass dashed across the room and tugged the revolver from the gun belt hanging on the wall peg. Racing to the front door, he flung it open and plunged out onto the porch.

Looking Glass saw what had caused the sound instantly. A branch torn away in the rising wind had struck the edge of the porch roof before tumbling to the ground. The parking strip in front of the cabin, still visible in the failing light of day, held no car, no Dain.

Storming back into the house, Looking Glass slammed the door behind him and locked it. The presence of his blood brother was like the heavens on a stormy day, growing darker, more threatening. The two female creatures, the townspeople they were the ones who must die.

Yet it was about Dain that the shadows were growing. The two women had come into the mind of his blood brother and turned him against the noble planning of Looking Glass. Now one course remained. He, Looking Glass, greatest of the Nez Perce, must cleanse the stained spirit of his blood brother. Only through death could this occur.

Dain Barlow must die, and soon.

CHAPTER 34

Dain returned to the table, clutching the champagne bottle by its neck. "Not much bubbly left. Let me top off your glass."

Sheila slid her hand, palm down, over the champagne glass which rested next to the soiled dinner plate. "No more for me. You don't want a drunken woman on your hands."

He leered at her. "Oh? What's that jingle I used to hear? Liquor is quicker." Settling onto the chair across the table from her, he filled his champagne flute with the last of the sparkling wine. Shaking the bottle, he said, "Another dead soldier."

Sheila smiled. "And I don't want a drunk man on my hands, Mr. Barlow. So there!" She stuck out her tongue at him.

"Madame, you wrong me. A toast."

Lifting her glass, Sheila said, "I just have one swallow left."

"More than enough."

"What are we toasting?"

"Gramps," Dain said. "Who else?"

"Gramps! Pat's Gramps? Why on earth are you toasting him?" Then understanding, she blushed. "Dain, you're awful. I wondered why you hustled Pat out to her car like that. I thought you were going to toss her over your shoulder and carry her out."

Dain leered again. "To Gramps."

Laughing, she extended her glass to meet his at the center of the table. The ringing of the crystal somehow called attention to the rising wind, beginning to blow hard now.

Dain watched as Sheila brought the glass toward her lips, then he saw nothing. The room had been plunged into blackness. She cried out, and in the next instant he heard the champagne flute hit the table, bounce, and shatter on the floor.

The silence lasted but a moment. "Oh, God, Dain," Sheila cried. "I broke one of your mom's champagne crystals. I slipped my shoes off when we were eating, and now there's glass all over the floor. Maybe even in my shoes."

"Don't move," he ordered. "You could cut yourself if you try to walk or put your shoes on."

The breaking of the glass had distracted Sheila for a moment from the sudden darkness, but that passed. "God, Dain, the lights! What's wrong with the lights?" Her voice rose. "Somebody must be fooling around with the fuse box."

He felt blindly for her hand across the table but failed to locate it. "It's okay, honey. Remember, the bad guy is dead. Nobody is monkeying with the fuses. It's the damn wind. Probably a limb across the power line. This used to happen all the time when we were kids. It hasn't changed."

Sheila's voice rose still higher. "Dain, I can't sit here. I've got to get up."

"Just a minute, babe. My night vision is kicking in. There's a broom in the utility closet. I'll sweep up the glass."

"Hurry! Please hurry!"

The many years that Dain had spent in the Barlow kitchen held him in good stead. He found his way across the room and removed a broom from the small utility closet. Squeezing behind Sheila's chair, he soon had the glass swept clear of the area under the table. "Okay, feels clean to the touch, nothing in your shoes. Now you can get up."

Sheila pushed back her chair and started to rise, then shrieked. Dain was so startled he let go of the broom handle, and it clattered off the vinyl floor.

"Jesus Christ, Sheila, what's wrong?"

"Outside, Dain. Somebody ran across the yard."

"Ran across the yard!"

Finding him she gripped his shirt sleeve. "It came from behind the big oak. There. Next to the orchard fence."

Shaking free of her hand, Dain sidled around the table to peer out the window. "You saw a man out there? Are you sure?"

"No. It was just…well, I just saw movement, from the corner of my eye, you know. It…it was like a shadow, but it was tall like a man."

The moon was still below the horizon, but the star lit sky provided enough light to see the sodden ground beyond the house. "Well, if there was something, it's gone now. More than likely, it was a deer. I found a hole cut in the fence on the north side of the orchard this morning. The deer have probably found it already." His voice brightened. "Plenty of them around."

Sheila sounded contrite. "I'm sorry. You're right. All I saw was a big shadow. Just nervous, I guess, with everything that's happened."

"Understandable," Dain said with as much cheerfulness as he could muster, for some reason the darkness had him feeling antsy as well.

In the moment of silence that followed, the door leading from the kitchen down to the cellar rattled. Sheila's shrill, "Oh!" startled him. "Did you hear that?" she asked. "The basement door."

Dain couldn't stand Sheila being upset. *What the hell can I say to reassure her? That door has no business rattling. It never rattled, even in the high winds…that is, unless the outside basement door is open. But how could it be open?*

Then he remembered. *Christ, the new padlock! I intended to pick one up in Crescent Valley this afternoon, but then we ran into the bikers, and I forgot all about it.*

Sheila, groping, found him again in the dark and clutched his arm, her fingers digging into his biceps. "It…it wasn't anything, was it, Dain?" When he failed to answer, she said, "Dain?"

"I forgot to get a padlock for that outside door. The wind has blown it open." He pulled her against him. "Calm down, babe. What you need is for me to open that last bottle of champagne. You've got a case of the jitters."

His jaw tightened. *God, listen to me. Mr. cool. That's not what I need to tell her. But dammit, I just want her to be able to enjoy every moment of the evening ahead.*

Drawing her closer, Dain said, "Hey, tell you what. Let's go into the parlor. I'll build a fire, and we can snuggle up on the sofa and talk till the lights come back on. I saw some pressed logs in—"

Slight though it was, the squeak of wood under pressure came through the basement door to their ears like a gunshot. Sheila's arms tightened around him in a death grip. Her voice dropped to a whisper. "God, Dain, did you hear that? I think someone is on the cellar steps. Get your gun out, quick."

Dain could kick himself. *The gun! Shit! It's in my bedroom on the night stand. I put it there just after we got back from town. And the flashlight, Christ! It's in the bedroom, too. When I picked it up from the side of Pat's fallen form last night, I found the bulb broken.*

Rummaging through my chest-of-drawers, I found an ancient four-pack of flashlight bulbs that had lain there since high school days. To my surprise, the bulbs were still good. Restoring the electric torch to working order, I just left it standing upright atop the dresser. I forgot to return it to the kitchen. God, what an idiot.

Dain tried to free himself from Sheila's grasp. Awkward in the dark, they stumbled sideways. "Sheila, let go," he whispered fiercely. "My gun's in the bedroom. So is the flashlight. I've got to go get them. I won't be but a few seconds, honey."

For a moment he thought she was going to obey, but then another noise found its way through the basement door, the sort of shuffling one might do trying to climb unfamiliar steps in the dark.

Sheila Locked her arms onto him again, her mouth near his ear. She was more wailing than speaking. "It's him. The killer. He got Amy and Bev, and now he's coming after me. Lud got the wrong man. Oh, God, he's going to kill me!"

"Honey, I've got to get the gun!" Dain found strength in his desperation and tore free of her. Sprinting, he raced for the parlor. His shoulder smashing against the barely visible door jamb, he careened across the dark room into the hall.

He raced down its length into his room. In his frenzy he hit the night stand, cursed, then grabbed his gun. Atop the chest-of-drawers, the chrome case of the flashlight glittered in the dim light. Seizing it, he dashed back down the hall and into the parlor.

Dain never saw Sheila, who was backing across the room, her eyes fixed on the pale ghostly rectangle of the basement door. Their bodies collided, sending Sheila spinning to the floor and knocking the gun from his hand.

Sprawling onto his knees, he started searching. *His hands sliding quickly around the carpet, in hopes of hitting it. For God's sake, now where did it go? In the corner where the gun lay, the darkness was complete. Damn, why didn't I carry a chrome plated revolver!*

Overturning a chair, he shoved it violently. Even with his hard breathing, he could hear the sounds from behind the cellar door. Whoever was there must have realized that he and Sheila were no longer in the kitchen. He was coming after them as fast as he dared in the dark.

Dain's hand closed over the pistol.

"Now, you son of a bitch," Dain shouted, "just stick your goddamn head out that door!"

Behind him, Sheila, sitting up, cried, "Dain, where are you?"

A split second later, he heard a crash from the basement, first the solid sound of weight striking wood and then a second noise, a shattering of glass. Next came what sounded like a heavy footstep, followed by a resounding thud that jarred the floor beneath his feet. The bastard must have fallen on the staircase.

Dain charged back into the kitchen, snapping on the flashlight. Behind him, Sheila was yelling, "No, Dain, don't! Don't!"

Yanking open the cellar door, he aimed the flashlight's beam down the stairway. Nothing! On the concrete floor, next to the steps, the circle of light found a mass of peaches and syrup, sparkling under a sprinkling of broken glass. *Mom's peaches!*

Dain's father had made a shelf, a single, narrow board, on the side of the stairwell where his mother could store a few jars of homemade jellies and jams that were used daily. In the dark, someone had knocked a quart jar of home-canned peaches off the shelf.

The hard slamming of wood against wood from the back of the cellar sent him sprawling flat on the steps in a reflex action. The outside door. Somebody had slammed it.

Scrambling to his feet, Dain charged toward the rear of the cellar, only to skid to a halt. *Could it be a trick? Is the guy still in here with me, tucked among the piles of boxes, and junk, waiting for me to relax?*

From the top of the stairs Sheila called, "Dain! Dain! Are you okay? Dain, what's happening?"

"Sheila, stay put, please." *Women! They can get a man killed with their theatrics.*

Gingerly he worked his way past the stack of discarded furniture and other mementoes of forty years of Barlow living. The flashlight found no intruder. He was alone in the basement.

Switching off the light, Dain pushed open the outside door and leaned out into the yard. The north wind almost ripped the wooden door from his grasp. He could see nothing on the sodden lawn.

Sheila was right. Lud had caught Ray Logan. The trouble was, he hadn't caught the man who wanted to kill Sheila and Pat.

CHAPTER 35

Looking Glass, coming out of the Barlow cellar, swung around the far side of the house to avoid the kitchen windows. He loped across the side yard and into the open area in back of the barn. Moving cautiously down the side away from the house, he came out in the graveled area where Dain's car and the Blazer were parked. He was almost to his patrol car when he heard the kitchen door open. Abandoning his efforts to be cautious, he sprinted the rest of the way to the vehicle.

Looking Glass knew now that he had been stupid to come in the front way and leave the patrol car parked near the barn. He should have left the patrol unit above the house on the old dump road, like last time. Too damn overconfident. And the muddy condition of the dump road had helped him make the mistake. But he had intended to leave behind him a house of corpses.

Breathing hard, he rammed his cold hands into the pockets of his pants, feeling for the keys. Why had the lights gone out when they did? He had worked around to a position behind the big oak. From there he would have had a perfect shot at Dain, sitting across the table from the bitch. Just five more seconds, and his blood brother would have been dead.

He pulled the key from his pocket, but its serrated edge caught on the cloth. The key fell onto the gravel. Goddammit to hell. Nothing was going right.

Stooping, Looking Glass felt for the keys, found them, and came to his feet. *Goddamn, what a mess. If I crank this metal carriage, Dain will be down here before I can get away.*

Hell, Dain won't need to see the license number. The silhouette of the ponyless carriage, with the light bar, is enough to give it away. With my war pony the color of a dark night, I would have vanished into the night by now.

When Dain had been at the table, Looking Glass saw he had no gun with him. He would be at ease. With the lights out, the odds were still pretty good he could get Dain before he had become too concerned. Lights went out all the time in Pine Ridge. If that one step had not squeaked to give him away. *At least the great spirit has smiled on me, or I might have broken my leg when I slipped on the basement stairs in my haste to get out of there.*

Suddenly another thought struck like a blow. *The great spirit! His guiding hand had caused it all; the lights going out before I got off a shot, the squeaking tread on the cellar steps, Looking Glass blundering around on the stairwell like a nervous buffalo near a cliff. A sign is given, that his blood brother is not to die without a fighting chance.*

Looking Glass was reaching for the door handle when a voice, hard and cold, stopped him.

"Hold it!"

A flashlight illuminated his face. Then he recognized the voice. Dain had caught him.

"Lud! What the hell are you doing here? Christ, I might have shot you."

The sheriff strained to come up with a good answer. This man before him was no fool. "Th...the beams from my headlights flashed across something shinny just behind the first row of trees in the orchard when

I turned in here. I came by to tell you I had no chance to talk with Vern or with Powers about the housing, but wanted you to know I hadn't forgotten you.

But when I saw this object in the orchard, I stopped to check it out. It was a motorcycle. One of Logan's bunch. I pulled on up here with my lights out hoping to catch some son of a bitch prowling around. But I hadn't gone twenty yards when I heard a bike take off down the highway. I was running to the car to give chase when you stopped me."

From a distance, they heard a yell. "Dain! Dain, where are you? Who are you talking to. For God's sake, Dain, answer me! Don't just leave me alone out here."

Turning, Dain shouted, "Over here, Sheila. Other side of the parked cars. I'm with Lud." Approaching the car, he put out a hand and leaned on the hood. "She's shook up. We had trouble with the prowler…one of Logan's buddies, huh? Too bad we didn't catch the son of a bitch. He had us both damn concerned."

The arrival of a breathless Sheila, seeing Lud, cried, "Lud! Why couldn't you have been here fifteen minutes earlier? We would have had him. Somebody tried to kill us!"

Dain reached over and put his arm around her, and pulled her close, to help ward off some of the stiff north breeze. "Now, Sheila, we can't be sure that's what he intended to do. It must have been one of those bikers. Lud saw his bike in the orchard as he pulled in."

With his arm still around Sheila, Dain explained what had happened. When he finished, he said, "You say you just pulled up, just before I saw you? Did you see or hear anyone running in the orchard before you heard the bike start?"

"Not a damn thing, Dain. I might have been able to catch the son of a bitch and ask him what he was doing on posted property if you hadn't stopped me. I damn sure wasn't going anywhere with you telling me to stop, and you with a gun in your hand."

Looking Glass cursed himself. *Dammit! Why wasn't I a little faster getting to the sheriff's unit. If Dain keeps shooting those damn questions at me I'm going to run out of believable answers soon.*

He was spared more questions when he noticed the sudden glow in the sky back in the direction of Pine Ridge. He was about to say the lights had come on in town when Sheila cried, "Oh, look! The lights in the house are back on."

The restoration of power gave Looking Glass an excuse to escape. "Listen, I'd better shake a leg. With the electricity back on, burglar alarms will be going off all over the area. Calls will be pouring into the station."

Dain and the woman stood, holding hands, as he backed around and he could still see them watching him as he pulled out onto the county road.

Had Dain noticed something out of place? *Goddamn! Dain sure had a strange look in his eye there at one time. Maybe he had detected something not quite right. Then came the torrent of ever harder questions.*

Looking Glass had even let his hand creep close to his revolver. But he knew he could use it only if Dain challenged him, the great spirit would not allow it otherwise. It had to be the warrior way. The knowing that the act was done to honor their bonded blood to allow them to cross over into the land beyond was important.

The great spirit wanted him to get the women alone. Then, Looking Glass, the great Nez Perce warrior would be able to give his blood brother a warrior's death, and soon.

*　　　　*　　　　*

Dain, in deep thought, pounded the last of the boards across the outer cellar door. For the last half hour, little things from Lud's visit, had been gnawing at him. *He had just arrived a few minutes before, he said. Yet, the hood and grill of the car were as cold as the devils' heart. Sure the north wind is strong and cold, but that engine had to have been off at least twenty minutes. Lud was there long before the lights had gone out. He had lied. Why would he do that?*

Another thing, he was breathing hard, like he'd been running. Lud was trying to control it, but I could tell. And when I put the flashlight beam on Lud, I thought at the time his uniform was dirty and frayed at the knee…something a fall on the cellar stairs could cause.

The sheriff had been in the alley the night Sheila and Pat had a prowler at the motel, that one motel out the five in Crescent Valley. And he was the last to see Albert before he disappeared. All people who had caused him the most pain when he was in school.

Dain shook his head, as he turned from his handy work. *Christ, I hate to even let thoughts like this clutter my mind, still…*

Dain emerged from the open doorway leading into the cellar, a hammer in his hand. He glanced around the empty kitchen. "Sheila! Where are you?" he shouted, his voice urgent.

She appeared in the doorway from the parlor. "I was sitting in front of the fire. Somehow, lounging in this kitchen in front of an uncovered window isn't very appealing, especially after what happened earlier. We," she flushed, lightly. Knowing the word, *we,* was miss spoken. "You need to install a shade behind that sheer curtain, Dain Barlow."

He glanced toward the window. "I guess you're right. Mom and Dad did without one for years, but times change. There were no crazies on the loose when they lived here. There were times when they would leave, that they would forget to lock the door. Nothing ever happened."

Sheila nodded toward the hammer. "Finished? You sounded like you were rebuilding the house."

"I tore up an old pallet I found in the basement, and put eight one-by-eight boards across that outside door. That should do until I get a padlock. I guarantee nobody is coming through there without a chain saw and a hell of a lot of noise."

Sheila smiled, but he could tell it was still with an effort. "Listen, let me get you another cup of coffee," she said. "You can be company for me while I clean up the dishes."

"I'll do—"

"Never! You just sit there and rest from your labors."

Staring idly at his reflection in the window, Dain's thoughts returned to the sheriff. *Lud knew I'd be gone that evening, I even told him about the old lock on the outside cellar door. Lud said he had to kill Ray, no other choice, but the biker had a different story. And the two dead women, two of the four causing his mother's accident.*

Jesus, I feel like a Judas for thinking this, but there are just too many coincidences. And by pushing these thoughts things begin to fall easily into place.

Dain lost track of time. Sheila must have called his name more than once before he became aware of it.

"Dain," she said, her voice louder than usual, "what's wrong with you? I said you could be company for me. You haven't said a word in ten minutes."

He made a face. "Nothing wrong. I was just thinking. Did you hear a motorcycle start up when we came out of the house?"

Slipping the dish towel over the rack bar, she sat down opposite him with a cup of coffee. "No, but I was so scared I probably wouldn't have heard a crash on the highway."

Dain shook his head. "I didn't hear one either."

"Is that important?"

Dain sighed. *God, I have to be careful. I can't let her find out I think the danger is not over. Maybe just by being so quiet I've aroused her suspicion already. Christ, she'd be more nervous than a sack of Mexican jumping beans, if she had an inkling that I had doubts about Logan's guilt.*

"No not really, I guess." Dain said, as casually as he could. "I was just wondering, how on earth one of those bikes from that bunch, with their ear splitting exhausts, could be started less than two hundred yards away, and neither one of us hear it."

He smiled. "But, like you say, we must have just been too preoccupied with other things."

Dain rose. "Charlie Young was supposed to call me, but I haven't heard from him. I'm going to give him a call, see if he's found out anything about Albert."

He charged out of the kitchen and returned a minute later, clutching the cordless phone. He stood there, trying not to look at Sheila, as it rang time after time. Punching the disconnect button, he lowered the phone.

"Not home?" Sheila asked.

"I'm going to call Albert's place. Maybe he's over there, checking on the house, or maybe Albert's home. Who knows?"

Extracting a small notebook from his pants pocket, he checked the listing Albert had given him and punched in the numbers. As he stood, listening to the insistent bleeps, Sheila, rising, walked past him and disappeared into the parlor.

With a muttered, "Hell!" Dain disconnected and redialed Charlies number. Dain let it ring fifteen times before setting the phone down on the table.

He spoke aloud, too softly to be addressing Sheila. "Dammit! Why didn't he call me? He said he would no matter what he found out."

Hearing Sheila's voice, he walked into the parlor. The room was dark, lit only by the flickering flames of the fire, painting quick orange strokes on the walls and furniture. Sheila, standing by the fire, motioned him close. Slipping her arms around him, she pulled her body against his and raised her face to him. When he did nothing for the moment, she slid her hand behind his neck and drew his face down to hers. Her lips, soft, warm, sought his. The kiss deepened, and her body against his was insistent.

Breathless, she pulled back to where she could see his face again. Her voice had a huskiness he had never heard in Sheila Greene's. "I don't intend to spend the rest of the night talking about Lud, Albert, or Charlie Young. It's windy and cold outside. We're in here, warm and alone, locked away from the world. And I have my man."

Her lips opened again, and this time he didn't have to be prodded. Before the kiss ended, their bodies were in motion, moving sensuously. Her voice, huskier still, said, "Remember what almost happened one day long ago in this room on this carpet? Let's try that again."

She was suddenly very heavy, sinking toward the floor, and all he could do was go with her.

CHAPTER 36

At ten past two in the morning, Looking Glass passed the driveway to the Barlow house. The patrol car made little noise as it passed, going twenty-five miles an hour. He swerved around a big limb in the roadway. The strong north wind had cluttered the highway with limbs and debris.

After leaving Dain's earlier in the evening, he had returned to the cabin to finish wiring the detonation harness for the plastique. He had bought himself a free evening by radioing the dispatcher that he would be at Rainbow Lake, out of the car, checking on damage to cabins, now perilously close to being flooded.

The task would have taken several hours had he really intended to do it. After storing the harnesses, the blocks of explosive, and the clock radio in the car trunk, he had eaten.

Suddenly, fingers of pain stroked his head again, and he was conscious of the squaw man trying to break out of his imprisonment.

The tiny town resembled a ghost town, with it's dark buildings, and cluttered street, as the downtown area of Pine Ridge came into view. The only indication there might be life was the single incandescent street light in front of the church.

As he passed the barely visible bulk of Sam's Diner, he glanced down the road toward the other end of town. Brown's Tavern, unlit, was a mere ghostly outline against the background of conifers, which made a dark, jagged horizon against the night sky.

After a slow pass through town, he headed back. Braking, he swung off Main into the parking lot that fronted the old high school. As he slid out of the car, he glanced across the road and upward toward the house of the watcher, Fred Griffith.

Looking Glass scowled. A faint suggestion of light gave form to one of the distant windows. He wondered, could the old man's unsleeping eyes be open in the dark, watching the street? An hour or so had passed since Brown's closed, and no cars would have come this way after that.

Still, the old man having a bad night for sleep, could be rummaging around and the sheriff's car had caught his attention. The near full moon would give enough light he could probably see him clearly. Could he be sitting in his chair right now, peering through his binoculars?

Looking Glass tried to relax. *Even if the old man is watching, so what? Doesn't the sheriff have the right to run a security check around and through empty buildings?*

Looking Glass eased the car door shut and glided to the back of the vehicle. As he unlocked the trunk lid, he glanced again toward the distant hilltop. *If the old man talks too much, I will bring death to his door.*

Hefting a cardboard box out of the back, Looking Glass hurried to the school's front door. Carefully lowering the box to the ground, he pulled the door key from his blouse pocket and fitted it into the lock. Luckily, he had gotten it back from Dain after their inspection of the school.

Sitting the box just inside the door, he went back to the patrol car for a second box. This contained a plastic tarp, coveralls, and a propane lantern. He was back by the sheriff's unit, locking the trunk when a loud squealing cut through the tumult of the strong north wind. Looking Glass whirled in the act of drawing his gun when he saw what had produced the noise.

The iron gate in the corner of the barlow orchard where it abutted the road and the parking lot had swung back hard on its rusty hinges. As he watched, the gate, its posts off-balance, began to slowly close again. *Damn! Dain must have forgotten to secure it after the ambulance came out of the orchard with Amy's body.*

Leaves and debris scudded across the parking lot at his back, from a stronger gust, causing him to quickly turn. He glanced back at the orchard and felt uncomfortable. The squat trees in orderly rows, beginning to fill out in their spring foliage, were like an army of dark spirits, ready to come at him out of the night.

Looking Glass, ashamed of fanciful thoughts that did not suit a warrior, rushed back into the building. Inside, in the night-shrouded corridor, he picked up the first of the cardboard boxes and moved cautiously away into the building's dim interior. The wind whipping around the school seemed almost as loud as it had the night Amy Housley died there.

*   *   *

Dain glanced at the luminous dial of the small alarm clock on the night stand. Two-ten A.M. After the first wild coupling in front of the fireplace in the parlor, they had retired to Dain's bedroom. Sheila and he had showered separately, still self-conscious at seeing each other move around the room nude, and climbed into bed.

As strong as the urge to possess her again was, he'd been content to lie and talk away the hours with Sheila reliving the events and emotions of their high school days. But now, up on one elbow, studying the lovely body beside him, visible in the faint glow from the bathroom's night light, his breath grew ragged, his pulse quickened.

Sheila must have became aware of him staring at her, because she turned on her back and opened her eyes.

"Have I told you that you're the most beautiful woman I've ever seen, and I love you very much?"

"Ummmm, no, not lately." She giggled. "At least I don't think so. You were always breathing and moaning so loud it was hard to hear what you were saying."

When he didn't answer, Sheila murmured, "You silly, you." Slipping her arms around him, she pulled him down to where his head was on her pillow, his face nestled against her neck.

"Don't you know that no girl ever gets over the first guy she falls in love with? I've played a hundred times in my mind every date we had, remembering what we did, what we said. I don't think you were ever out of my mind completely."

Her words sent a thrill through Dain. It was as if she were saying exactly what he had fantasized she should say once they got back together.

Turning, her ripe lips found his, their touch light and cajoling. Then the kiss deepened, her lips parting. His tongue slipped slowly between them. He gasped, his body tingled, when her tongue found his, its warm wetness insinuating itself around his own. The thrill was electric, surging into his loins. His one hand found the pliant flesh of her rounded thigh. He moved it up into the valley of her tiny waist and still higher, along the sweet mounding side of her full breast.

She pulled her mouth free and, gasping, said, "Oh, God, your hands. I love the feel of your hands on me." Clutching at his hair, she pulled his mouth down to hers again. Now her tongue was insistent, rapacious.

The pounding of blood in his temples matched the throbbing of his male member, hard again against the sweet flesh of her belly. Her cry of, "Oh, God," was muffled against his mouth. Her hand released his hair, flew down his body, and grasped the surging length of him. Having found him, her hand began to slide up and down his member. The only sounds in the room were those of moans, hard breathing, and the faint protest of the bed as weight shifted.

Dain pulled his mouth free of hers and slid his lips down the tender flesh of her neck, which quivered under the hot quick breaths that stroked the soft skin. Then his mouth was on the exquisite white slope of her breast. His tongue flicking, he outlined the areola, his lips aware of the swelling nipple. Then, his control slipping, his mouth closed on the pulsating nipple, drawing it hungrily between his lips.

She cried out, "Oh, Dain, darling!"

His hand was on her other breast, molding it, his fingers teasing its swollen nipple. Dain's mouth slid down the beautiful undercurve of her breast and across her stomach to her navel. His tongue teased it while she squirmed.

Bathing a path across her sensitive skin, his mouth returned to her breasts. He fondled one nipple quickly, gently, as his hand, sliding up her silken thigh, found the downy nest at the center of her being. His finger found her moist, swollen, and ready.

He came up onto his knees and moved between her open thighs. Gripping his member, she guided him into her. Moaning, she shifted her hips to aid his penetration. Her avid arms closed about him and drew him down close atop her.

"Oh, God, it's good," she cried. Her hips undulated sensuously, matching the beat of his own slow thrusts.

Rolling over, he brought her atop him. His mouth sought the breasts, swaying above him, feeding on first one and then the other. Sheila gasped each time he drew one of her hard nipples into his mouth. Atop him, she was moving faster, her thrusts hard, gasping aloud with each. As Sheila neared her climax, her hips widened to receive the hard thrusts.

Dain closed his eyes, shutting out the sight of the beautiful woman crouched atop him, trying to stay his own release. She gripped his shoulders, her nails scoring his skin, as she reached the first shattering wave of pleasure. Her scream of ecstasy filled the dark bedroom.

Dain could hold back no longer. He cried out with the intensity of his climax. Above him, still bucking wildly, Sheila swept from one peak to another. Then, her body still quivering in the afterglow of her pleasure, she slumped down atop him, her passion spent. Their bodies, a faint sheen of sweat visible on them in the dim light, lay unmoving. Later, their breathing quiet again, Sheila rolled over onto her back.

Dain was on the edge of sleep when a sharp elbow nudged his ribs. "Dain, let's not go to sleep, not yet. It's like I don't want the night to end, you know. Let's build up the fire again and sit and watch it. Maybe have a snack. Okay?"

All Dain wanted was to go to sleep. Then staring at his beautiful lady, he smiled. *I could do with the sleep, but I sure the hell am not going to look for trouble, not when I have everything going my way.*

Without a word, he climbed out of bed and slipped on a terry cloth robe. "How about some tea and a sandwich? I noticed some chicken salad in the ice box. I'll call you when it's ready."

"Never mind calling me," Sheila said, stretching. "After I take a quick shower, I'll join you."

Later in the parlor, tea cups empty, sandwich plates holding nothing but crumbs, they sat, watching the fire. Wraiths of firelight danced and cavorted over the walls of the unlit room. Sheila sat on the love seat, her legs curled up under her. Dain sat on the floor below her, arms locked around bent knees, stared at the burning logs. Her hand toyed with the hair on the nape of his neck.

Breaking free of the hypnotic mood cast by the fire, she said, "Penny for your thoughts."

Tilting his head back to where he could see her, he grinned, "Not worth it. I was just thinking about all the lost time, from graduation to now, without you."

"Honey, let's not think of the past. We have a bright future let's concentrate on that.

"Dain, about Lud. You've been awfully quiet since he left. Any reason for that?"

His mellow mood disappeared as quickly as a startled trout heading for deep water. "Well, it's just that I'm concerned for you, after what happened tonight. We know Lud got the killer, but, this prowler thing...I just want to be careful. I don't want you to be alone, anytime. Pat has a gun, so I want you to be with me or her. Okay?"

Sheila, feeling much relaxed now, glanced up at him through the fringe of long lashes. Her voice was small. "Yes, sir. But I'd sleep much better if I had something to tranquilize me." Then her voice became huskier, "Can you think of anything that might help?"

Dain's suddenly interested loins would have known even if he hadn't.

CHAPTER 37

Dain woke early the next morning, restless despite having spent much of the night making love to Sheila. As he pulled back the covers to ease out of bed, he remembered. *Charlie Young! I'd forgotten all about trying his number anymore once Sheila called me to the parlor.*

Pulling on his shirt and pants, he shoved his feet into a pair of beat-up house slippers. At the bedroom door he paused to look back. Sheila, his beautiful Sheila, lay on the other side of the bed where she should have been all these years. Gently, he closed the door behind him and walked down the hall to the kitchen.

Picking up the cordless phone from the table where he had left it the night before, he punched the redial button. After twelve rings, he returned it to the table. Waiting for the coffee maker to finish its job, he glanced out the window where the lawn was taking shape again in the dim light of early dawn.

Dain bit his bottom lip. *I'll just have to drive up to Charlie's. The old boy isn't as young as he once was. Maybe Charlie didn't put the phone back into its cradle right the last time he used it. No, hell, that would show busy. Well goddammit, something's wrong. Hell, could be anything. But he's an old-timer in every sense of the word. If he said he was going to call, he would.*

I guess I could've missed the call, but nothing on the answering machine. Maybe he—Hell, I can, maybe, all day and not get anywhere. Just have to go see.

Then he remembered Sheila. *She'll have to go, too. No way in hell I'm going to leave her here sleeping.*

He figured Sheila would be unhappy about being shaken awake this time of morning. He was right. First, he tried calling her name. That produced no response. Next he pushed her shoulder. This elicited a sort of grumbling but no movement. The movement came when he tried to ease the covers off her.

An arm, moving with the speed of a striking rattlesnake, jerked them from his hand, and wrapped them back around the arm's owner. Only when he pulled the blankets away by brute force, avoiding a couple of well-intentioned kicks, did she give up and come awake.

Thirty minutes passed before a disgruntled Sheila, her face puffy with fatigue, entered the kitchen and collapsed into one of the chairs at the table. She blinked several times as she looked out the window. Her words slurred, she demanded, "Are my eyes out of focus, or is it foggy this morning?"

Dain, struggling to hide his impatience, smiled. "No, princess, your eyes are just as beautiful as ever, and, yes, it's foggy as hell. Now, are you ready for your waffles?"

Sheila groaned. "What I'm ready for is more sleep, but I guess the waffles are a good second choice."

By the time she finished her breakfast and downed a couple of cups of coffee, she seemed reasonably alert. She studied Dain for a moment. "May I ask why we're up at this ungodly hour? I mean, is this what you usually do? Bed a wench, keep her up all night, then rouse her out at dawn? What's next? Am I to be paid a few coppers and then sent on my way?"

Dain had trouble smiling. Time was flying past. "I'm sorry, honey, but I have to go check on Charlie Young. He still doesn't answer his phone."

Sheila sobered. "You think something's…well, happened to the old guy?"

"I really don't know what to think." Dain tried to look away, but she held his gaze. He blurted out his concerns, knowing how dependable Charlie usually was.

"I can appreciate your concern, but why get me up?" Sheila said. "Do you intend for me to go with you? Pat will be back this morning, you know."

He nodded.

"What aren't you telling me?" she demanded.

"Sheila, this business has me so mixed up I don't know whether I'm going or coming. I've uncovered a lot of information, that has led me to think certain things." This was not the time to tell her what those things were. "We know Lud's got the killer. But after last night, I'm not taking any chances with you."

She nodded, but there was no smile. "You'll get no argument from me. Let me get a jacket, and I'll be ready to go."

The strong winds had sudsided during the night, leaving cool, moist air behind to spread a blanket of fog over the foothills. As they climbed into the car, Dain glanced out across the orchard and said, "Jeez, it's dead calm. If we don't get a breeze, this fog could be here all day."

Sheila muttered something unintelligible as she drew her jacket tight around her. Dain sensed that the early hour had taken a bit of sparkle out of last night's romance.

Dain glanced at the high school as they passed. The building was a dark, featureless mass against the fog, somehow lonely and a bit menacing. He shivered and cursed himself for his foolish fantasy.

The swirls of fog grew denser as they rolled into Pine Ridge. Ahead of them, the town's lone street light was a faint blob of luminescence in the dense banks of vapor.

Charlie's small house was two miles west of Pine Ridge and about a quarter mile off the highway. In the fog, the trip took another twelve minutes. Charlie's house was one of three structures in a small clearing. The other buildings were a storage shed and a garage that housed Charlie's forest service Bronco and a truck equipped with a snow-plow blade.

At one time, the ranger station had been located there, but it had been moved up to the national forest boundary further west some five years before. The clearing, a cheerful place in sunlight, had a surreal quality to it this morning with the three structures drifting in and out of the fog.

Dain swung into the loop before the small house and stopped. Switching off the engine, he looked past Sheila out her window at the wood building. The interior of the house looked dark.

Sheila stirred out of her lethargy, peered at the little structure, and said, "Looks like he's not home. Could he be out of town?"

Dain shook his head. "No way. I called the ranger station, and the guy said Charlie was taking three days leave, was trying to find a buddy. Of course, the buddy is Albert."

Dain opened the car door and swung his feet out onto the ground. As he came upright, a flurry of noise shattered the silence, coming from somewhere behind the cabin. Dain whirled, crouching, his hand pulling the pistol free of the belt holster. A deer came from behind the house, running hard. It cleared the wire fence beside the cabin in a graceful leap and disappeared into the grove of trees.

Sheila, eyeing Dain with wide eyes, cried, "My gosh! What's wrong with you, Dain? I thought this was supposed to be a friendly visit."

Shamefaced, he pushed the gun back into is holster. "Sorry, baby, It must be this fog. My nerves are on edge."

Not wanting to try to justify himself, he walked quickly across the yard and mounted the single step onto the porch. He paused there, listening. From here, he could see the yard light, still on. With the heavy fog, the photoelectric sensor had not detected that it was daytime. Coming across the yard, he had glanced up at the chimney. No smoke issued from it. Charlie should have had a fire going, as chilly as the foggy air was, that is if he was inside.

Cupping his hands around his eyes, he peered into one of the front windows.

Sheila called to him through the open vehicle window, "He must still be in bed, Dain."

Dain said nothing.

Sheila tried again. "It's just six-forty." A tinge of maliciousness crept into her voice. "He probably doesn't go to work until midmorning. That's about par for a government worker. Right?"

Dain answered this time, his voice barely audible. "Don't be nasty. Now hush!"

Moving to the front door, he felt its glass pane, The surface was cold to his touch. The interior of the house had had no fire on during the night. He thought of Albert's place. That house, like this one, had been without heat, its wood stove filled with cold, gray ashes.

Dain rapped on the glass pane. After a moment, he tried again. If Charlie was home, he wouldn't or couldn't answer the door. Dain's hand dropped to the knob, expecting to find the door locked. The smooth brass knob turned easily, and he pushed the door open and inch.

"Charlie!" he called. "Charlie Young!"

The house was silent. Dain glanced back at Sheila, then, pushing open the door, stepped inside. He went directly to the wood stove and touched it. Cold as ice water. Stooping, he peered into the fire box. The ashes were old, already caking with moisture.

The stove had held no fire for at least twenty-four, maybe thirty-six hours. Coming upright, he circled through the house, hesitating before he entered the old ranger's bedroom. At his age, Charlie could be there on the bed, dead of natural causes. But the rooms were empty and undisturbed. Only their owner was missing and had been for too long. *Jesus Christ! It's time I faced up to the fact that Charlie might be dead.*

And maybe Albert, too. The ranger might've found out something about Albert and was killed for his trouble. My God, three men missing now and two bodies. Could some son of a bitch have killed five people and still be walking around looking for more?

He shook his head, exhaling. *What a cop I am! The local sheriff is becoming my favorite suspect, and the reunion is starting in less than twelve hours. The reunion! This is scaring the hell out of me. All of this business seems to have something to do with the reunion, be leading up to it.*

Dain shook his head. *If the guy has killed five people this easily, what is he planning to do next? I've been on this case four days, and the most promising suspect is the sheriff. Time, goddammit, it's running out!*

Snapping out of his reverie, Dain rushed from the small house, sensing, at last, that he had very few hours left to unravel this thing. He rounded the corner and trotted across the yard to the garage. An open padlock hung on the smaller door. He swung it open to reveal an empty space. Like Albert's Jeep, the ranger's Bronco was missing!

Dain raced back across the yard to the Blazer, climbed in, and started the engine. He ignored Sheila's questioning look.

As he pulled back out onto the road, Sheila cried, "Dain, what's wrong?"

"I've got to check Albert Martinson's place," he said nothing more. He drove the several miles far faster than he should have, but Sheila said nothing until he turned off onto Albert's driveway and coasted to a stop before the house.

"Would you tell me now what's wrong?" Sheila asked. "Why are we running up and down the roads in fog like a bat out of hell?"

The drive had given Dain a chance to recover his poise. He winked at her. "I forgot about the cat. I promised to take care of it till Albert gets home."

"Are you kidding me?"

This time Sheila joined Dain when he slid out of the Blazer. She pointed toward the house. "This place is an absolute horror in the fog. If you think you're going to leave me alone out here, you're nuts."

The place did look scary as hell, with the steeply pitched roof, the lopsided porch, and the small windows that were opaque black rectangles. Put out of focus by the heavy fog, the house was a witch's cottage.

His hand on Sheila's elbow, they entered Albert's place. The cat's voice came immediately, loud and demanding. Sheila refused to stay in the kitchen as Dain made a circuit of the house's interior, trailing after him.

Somehow he sensed that Albert Martinson would never return to this place. Never again would he sit down opposite Charlie Young for an evening of checkers. He was beginning to wonder if Charlie would ever look down on a checker board again.

After the disgruntled cat had taken a nip out of Sheila's finger, she turned the task of taking the outraged feline out to the car over to Dain. He waited next to the Blazer, holding onto the angry feline, while Sheila careened down the walk, clutching a twenty-five pound unopened bag of cat food.

Back inside the Blazer, Dain glanced into the back where the half-starved cat was clawing at the bag of cat food.

Turning to Sheila, he said, "Why don't I open the bag and get him a little cat food? You can hold him in your lap and feed him from your hand."

Sheila looked first at her tooth-marked finger and then at him. "That's a joke, right? Why don't I drive and let you handle the feeding chores?"

They drove back to town, Dain and Sheila side by side with him driving and Albert's cat in the back industriously enlarging a rip in the sack of cat food.

By the time they reached the Barlow place, the sun was out somewhere above the choking blanket of mist that lay over the foothills. Its coming had, if anything, made driving conditions worse. The fog was brighter but every bit as blinding.

Dain brought the Blazer to a stop before the barn, more cardinal than red in color with the diffused light conditions.

"Wait here a second," he said as he slipped out of the car. He entered the barn and a few moments later reappeared in the doorway, carrying a large plastic bowl. His lips moving, he pointed to the container, and Sheila rolled down the window to hear what he was saying.

"I wanted to check, make sure there was a food dish here. We used it when Mom had the Great Dane. Remember? I'll fill it and set the cat out here in the barn to chow down."

Watching him bemused, Sheila said, "Dain, you've never had a cat before, have you? If you set the ball of fluff down out here, she'll eat, and be on her way back to Albert's in thirty minutes. Besides, what are you going to use for water?"

Dain scratched his head. Well, I've got an old bucket in here. I could use that."

Sheila took charge of the planning and Dain took care of the dirty work, namely carrying the struggling beast into the old enclosed tack room where Sheila had installed bowls of food and water. As they came out of the barn, Sheila grinned at him and said, "How soon you begin to learn the shortcomings of even the most lovable man."

Dain grinned foolishly. She was sounding just like a married woman, and that's what he wanted her to be, a married woman.

Back inside the house, his mood changed abruptly, remembering what the biker, the fat one named Gordy, had said the day he and Mike had the run-in with them. One of them, he couldn't remember who, said something about Peddler's Point after Dain mentioned Albert, and Gordy had said, "Dead men don't climb out of no canyons."

What the hell had he meant by that. The biker must have seen something happen to Albert, but he sure the hell wasn't going to find out by asking. After what had happened to Logan and Red, the rest of the gang wouldn't give him the time of day. Should he drive out to Peddler's Point? He groaned. That would be one hell of a trip in this fog.

From the bedroom, he heard Sheila's distant voice. "Dain, you have a message on your answering machine."

Entering the bedroom, he slapped Sheila on the bottom, and said, "Thanks, baby," and sat down on the edge of the bed. Reaching across the machine's flashing *LED*, he punched its message button.

The voice was reedy and full of wheezes, Fred Griffith's. "I don't give a damn for these answering devices. Usually just hang up when I hear them. But I promised you, son, I'd get in touch if I had anything to report."

For one wild absurd moment, Dain tried to will it into being Charlie Young, but Fred's high-pitched voice would not support the illusion. "Don't know if it's important," the reedy voice continued, "that's for you to say. Well, anyway, that's it. Bye."

"What's that all about?" Sheila asked.

Dain shrugged. "Just like he said. He's seen something. I told him to keep watch on the school. I was just doing it to get away from him, but what the heck. Maybe I'd best drop by and give him a listen."

They both jumped at the sound of the back door opening and closing. Dain was already into the parlor, moving fast, when Pat's voice stopped him.

"Hello? Are you two decent?"

Dain, entering the kitchen, grinned. "What can I say? Decent is in the eye of the beholder. But if you mean are both up, yeah. We had breakfast long ago and have been out having fun driving in the fog."

Pat wrinkled her nose at him. "Smart question, smart ass answer."

Dain waited until Pat had poured herself a cup of coffee and sat down at the table. Then he said, "What are your plans for today?"

She shrugged. "Nothing much. Thought I'd just take it easy, if it's okay with you two. Probably take a nap, then clean up and get ready for the reunion. Be another late night tonight anyway. I'm really bushed. Gramps and I sat up half the night talking about the old days." The memory brought a smile to her face. "It was sure nice seeing him again, but I feel so sorry for him living there alone."

"Great idea," Dain said. He grunted as Sheila, who had come into the room slipped her arms around him from behind in a hug. He continued talking, ignoring the playful Sheila for a moment. "I've got some stuff to do. Fred Griffith wants to see me, and I need to get an allergy shot in Crescent Valley."

He retreated into the bedroom to shave, shower, and change clothes.

When he returned, from force of habit, he stopped before the old cheval mirror to check his appearance one last time. No mirror. One of the casualties of the last couple of days. He was about to turn away, when something Pat said, in her conversation with Sheila, stopped him in his tracks.

"There at the lake," Pat was saying. "Lud looked like two different people. You know I've heard about people who have multiple personalities. They say one personality doesn't even know what another one is doing."

Dain's mouth was agape. All the coincidences, of Lud being around at all the places of trouble, raced through his mind. And he was taking strong pain killers for headaches—a brain tumor, something like that might cause a split personality.

Dain's jaw tightened, and he closed his eyes as a horrible thought struck him. The words came back as clearly as if he had heard them that morning. A nine year old Lud, that summer Dain had accompanied him to the reservation to visit his grandfather, had said, *I wish I'da been Chief Looking Glass. He, alone, killed over a hundred of his enemies.*

And then Lud said. He had killed everyone in Pine Ridge at least five times over those few summers when he was pretending to be Chief Looking Glass. God. was it possible that savage is on the loose in Pine Ridge? And that Lud didn't have a clue? That's why Lud didn't want to talk about his condition. He has periods he can't remember. There had certainly been cases on record similar.

I've got to try and check with the doctor. Maybe if I lay my cards on the table, the doctor will talk to me about it.

He blinked, took a deep breath, and tried to sound normal when he entered the kitchen. "Who the devil are you two raking over the coals now. Was that little giggle brought on by something you said about me? I hope it wasn't a disparaging remark about last night."

Sheila cried, "Honey, how could you say such a thing? Last night was wonderful. We were talking about how weird Lud acted at Rainbow Lake yesterday."

"I forgot about Rainbow Lake." Dain said, hoping to get them off the subject of Lud. "The road may be closed by now."

Pat grinned. "I guess all you can do is go see."

A few minutes later, Dain, on his way out the door, stopped beside the table where Pat and Sheila sat, talking, actually doing more laughing and giggling than talking, "Sheila, remember what I said about sticking together. Don't either one of you go anywhere alone. And I mean anywhere."

Pat's eyes widened. "Why are you saying that, Dain? The danger is over, right?"

"Well, yes, but still, I want you two to stick together."

Rising, Sheila pushed Dain out the door with him still repeating his cautions about sticking together through the long afternoon. His last words were, "I'll be home in plenty of time to take you ladies to the reunion."

CHAPTER 38

Dain left the Blazer in the high school parking lot, as he had last time he visited Fred Griffith. By doing so, he saved the four block drive it took to go around by road. Crossing the highway, he climbed the steep path up the hill to Fred's. With the fog preventing its drying, the trail was slicker than the first time he had negotiated it, and Dain came close to falling into the mud twice. He came out of the brush onto level ground, puffing hard, just in time to see the front door open.

Fred, bone-thin, leaning heavily on his cane, peered down at him. Dain turned to glance back down the path. The walk up was only about fifty yards, but the path was but a faint suggestion in the fog, and the parking lot was invisible.

Raising one frail arm, Fred shouted, "See you got my message, Barlow. Don't have much faith in them damn answering machines. Come on inside before I get a chill."

The cement steps to the porch had been there so long the top had flaked away, showing the bigger gravel under what had once been a smooth surface. Dain followed the old man into the house. He had forgotten how bad it smelled. In the dank morning air, the mixed odors of cat litter, moldy furniture, and some unidentifiable but nauseating cooking smell were overwhelming. Jesus, he hoped he didn't have to put up with this too long.

The only illumination, in the dim house, was from the windows. Looking at Dain, Fred said, "Don't turn on no lights durin' the day, even on a dark day like this. Only turn on the kitchen light at night." Fred shuffled toward the kitchen. "Can't afford to have no lights on, damn 'lectricity's gettin' so a poor man can't use it."

Dain prompted. "You said you had something to tell me that might be important. Right?"

Fred flashed him a toothless smile. "Don't be in such a damn hurry, Barlow. I've got some tea brewing. Come on in the kitchen and set a spell. Let me catch my breath."

Dain, giving up, followed him. Fred gestured toward the table. As Dain settled onto the chair, he saw the source of the cooking odor. A frying pan sat atop the stove, holding what looked like a couple of strips of bacon, covered by a congealed coating of gray grease. He wondered how many days ago Fred had decided not to have bacon for breakfast.

Amidst a clatter of pans and muttered curses from the old man, Dain glanced at his watch: nine-twenty-five A.M. Dammit, he wanted to reach Crescent Valley before the doctor took his noon break.

"Fig'red you'd be back 'fore now." Fred said, as he picked up a mug, and wiped it out with a soiled dish towel. Teetering precariously on his cane, Fred set down the mug of steaming tea in front of Dain. What appeared to be a crust of dried saliva along the rim discouraged any thought he had about drinking it. His stomach churned. "Then it was all over town that the sheriff got the man who did the killin' and you probably wouldn't be back at'll. So I fig'red I'd give you a call."

Fred's knees creaked and popped as he slowly lowered himself with the help of his cane into the well-worn chair opposite Dain's. He took a huge gulp of the steaming hot tea without visible effect, then showed his visitor his gums again. "Almost didn't call, though, 'cause it was the sheriff I seen down there last night."

Dain straightened up. "You saw Lud at the school last night?"

"Yep. You said to let you know if I saw anything odd around that place, so…" The old man took another big swallow and slumped back in his chair. "Good tea, better try some, warm your innards on a mornin' like this."

Dain forced a smile. *Oh, God, I'm going to have to drag every word out of him.* He felt like grabbing him and shaking him. "So? Fred, quit stalling. Tell me about it."

The old man's eyes opened wide, and he nodded, moving his head in quick little jerks, like a small bird feeding. "Don't get so damn excited, Barlow. It was last night, actually about two this morning. I had to get up and take a leak. Damn prostrate's killing me. Anyway," he leaned forward, the steam from the tea veiling his face, "thought I'd sit down in my chair and watch the trees.

"Kinda interesting, the way a high wind moves 'em around. The moon was pretty bright, was wide awake by then, anyway. Saw this car comin' through town, headin' west. Got up at the end of the business district, then she turned around and come back. When she got out in front of the school, its lights went out. That put a stick up my butt. It pulled off into the high school parking lot and stopped about fifty feet from the front door."

Dain tensed, growing excited. "It was the sheriff, you're sure?"

"Dammit, Barlow, don't rush me. I'll get to it."

Dain slumped back.

For some damn reason, Fred felt the need to blow on his tea, now that it had cooled. After a full minute's huffing and puffing, he turned his attention back to Dain. "Got my binoculars right away. Like I said, moon was pretty bright, I could tell it was a sheriff's car. The guy was too big to be that deputy damn near skinny as me. Had to be Lud."

"But you couldn't see what he was doing," Dain said. "Right?"

Fred looked as if he were growing incensed. "Dammit, boy, you don't listen good at times. I said I'd get to it. Stop jumpin' in on me. Anyway I guess he opened the trunk. That had to be where he got them."

"Them?" Dain asked.

"The boxes. He was takin' some kind of boxes into the school. Musta had a key, I guess, 'cause he disappeared inside with them. He made two trips, carrying a box each time."

Fred ran his tongue along his tobacco stained lips, picked up the cup again and took a huge gulp. "Ain't that kinda strange? Why do you think he'd do something like that?"

Dain slowly shook his head. "I don't have a clue, Fred."

"Well, said it might not be important."

"What happened next?"

"Nothin'."

"Nothing?"

"Nothin' I could see. I sat there better part of an hour, and he never came out. I finally got tired and went to bed."

"Thanks, Fred." Dain stood. "I'm still trying to wrap up a few loose ends, so I haven't closed my investigation yet. Keep up the good work. I'll let you know when I don't need your assistance any longer."

Back in his car, he glanced at his watch again. Ten-twenty-four. With Rainbow Lake flooded, he would never make it to Crescent Valley before noon. Sitting there, he recalled the biker's remarks about the canyon. He needed to check the Peddler's Point area, but the canyon would be choked with fog now. Besides, Lud had to be his number one priority. Would Lud's doctor talk to him once he explained the importance of knowing about him? Just one way to find out.

Starting the Blazer, he rolled out of the parking lot and turned in the direction of Crescent Valley. With the fog much thinner at the lower elevation, the Blazer came down the grade onto the stretch of highway that seemed to have some water over it two years out of five when Rainbow Lake was at peak stage.

As he rounded the curve, Dain's heart sank. At least two hundred yards of the roadway was under water, as bad as he had ever seen it.

Ahead of him, an orange highway department truck was parked at an angle across the middle of the road.

Two men wearing hard hats sat side by side on the open tailgate, watching him approach. When he stopped, one of them slid off the tailgate and sauntered up the highway. Leaning over, he said, "Sorry, buddy. You're gonna have to turn around. There's three feet of water over the road. Probably more than that, now," he nodded his head toward the flooded road, "out there in the middle."

"Listen, I've got to get to Crescent Valley," Dain protested.

The highway man snorted. "Well, unless you've got pontoons on that Blazer, you'd better get ready to wade and walk." He guffawed at his own remark.

Dain shook his head. "You don't understand. This is police business. I'm working with the sheriff's department on a murder"

"Yeah? Show me your badge, buddy."

"Look, I haven't got a badge," Dain said. "Leastwise, not a deputy's badge. I'm from *L.A.* I work for the *PD* there." *Why in the hell did I leave my shield case on top of the chest-of-drawers in Pine Ridge? True, it means nothing up here, but a cop is a cop, wherever he is.*

The highway worker stepped back from the Blazer, contempt in his face. "Well, this ain't Los Angeles, in case you hadn't noticed. Now why don't you just turn your rig around and skedaddle back the way you came?"

For the first time, Dain noticed the small aluminum boat and outboard in the lake, tied up just below the parked truck. He poked his head out the window and yelled, "Listen, just let me use your boat."

The tall, wiry man in the hard hat turned around to glare at him. "Use my boat? Shit, man, don't you hear good. Take off like I told you."

Opening the door, Dain stepped out of the Blazer and yelled, "Dammit, call the sheriff's dispatcher. Alice will tell you who I am."

This stopped the road man in mid-stride. "You know Alice? Okay, man, keep your shirt on. That makes a heap of difference. She's my sister-in-law. Don't want her gettin' my wife all worked up."

Ten minutes later, Dain, in the small boat, was nosing into the bank on the other side of the flooded stretch. As another Department of Highways employee helped Dain over the gunwales, the tall man, operating the outboard, yelled, "This guy is some big shot from Los Angeles. I guess we're gonna have to start a ferry service."

By the time Dain clambered up the bank to the road, only a few yards from the sharp curve where his folks had lost their lives, he had heard the bad news. The worker was there alone, blocking the highway, he couldn't leave till his shift was over. He showed no more sympathy than the two on the other side had.

When Dain asked him for a suggestion on how he could get to Crescent Valley, the man shrugged and said, "Well, you can wait till some other fool tries to drive through here and ride back with him, or you can walk. I'm stuck here for another," he glanced at his watch, "five damn hours."

Dain supposed he was lucky, some other fool, showed up twenty-five minutes later and gave him a ride into Crescent Valley. They heard the highway flagman's parting shot as they drove off. "Maybe next time you'll check with the road department before you start, big shot."

Five miles from Crescent Valley, Dain and the car's owner drove out of the fog into a warm spring morning full of sunshine.

Running into Susan at his family's funeral had been one great piece of luck. When the tall blond with the plain but pleasant face walked up to him after the service and introduced herself as Susan, he had panicked. God, not another guessing game, of, remember me? Then, before she got around to asking, he remembered. Susan Renault.

Her folks had lived in Pine Ridge for about a year when Dain and Susan had been juniors. Her parents had hit it off with the Barlows, and the two families became close friends. But after they moved, he saw

Susan no more. She had told him who Lud's doctor was, saying he was the only one of the old gang she ever saw after she moved. Susan was the receptionist in this doctor's office.

With her working there, finding out about Lud's condition should be a piece of cake. At the funeral, she offered to help any way she could. He should have no trouble talking her into letting him take a peek at the records.

When he entered the office, the waiting room was empty except for Susan, perched on a stool behind the receptionist's counter. At last, a bit of luck!

Susan looked up at the sound of the opening door. "Well, well, look what the flood washed out of the hills." She fixed him with a dazzling smile. "Good to see you, Dain, though, if it's not me you want to see, you might as well go have lunch.

"Some kid got his foot smashed by a tractor, and Doc's been called to the hospital emergency. I've spent the last hour canceling appointments. The doctor won't be back before two o'clock at the earliest.

Actually, I don't need to see him," Dain said. "I came in for an allergy shot. I'm sure the nurse can give that. Right?

"It should be okay." Susan stood. "I'll go talk to Marie."

"Hold up a minute, Susan."

Stopping, she eyed him quizzically.

Lowering his voice, he said, "Could you tell me what's wrong with the sheriff? He has headaches all the time, and he won't tell me what's wrong."

Susan glanced toward the closed door to the examination rooms, frowning. "I can't discuss that, Dain. No way. Do you know what would happen if the doctor found out I'd disclosed anyone's medical problem? I'd be through here.

"Not only that, I probably couldn't get another job in a doctor's office, ever. I'd like to help you. I know you're working on these murders, but I just can't. I'm really sorry. But good jobs are too hard to find in a little town.

"Listen, I don't want to get you in trouble, but I really need to know. It's critically important."

The tall blond closed her eyes, refusing to meet his gaze. She took a deep breath and exhaled. Turning, still refusing to look at him, she gazed toward the file cabinets behind her to her left. After staring at them a moment, she shook her head. "I just can't Dain. Please don't ask me about his terminal brain tumor." Her eyes widened. "Oh, God, Dain, please don't tell a soul I let that slip. It'll mean my job, sure."

At the words, terminal brain tumor, a cold knot formed in Dain's stomach. *I've heard that multiple personalities could sometimes be brought on by trauma. The mutilation of those two ladies would be child's play to a savage like, Looking Glass.*

Oh, my God! I have to get to a phone, call Sheila, make sure the two women are never alone with Lud. But no way I can use the phone here in the doctor's office. Always a possibility Marie could over hear something about Lud, and me just talking to Susan, wouldn't be good. I don't want to put Susan through any more stress.

"Don't worry, Susan, I won't breath a word."

CHAPTER 39

Dain, his face drawn with concern, fled up the street to a fast food drive-in, and grabbed a pay phone. *I can still be wrong, but I have to warn the girls, then find Lud. I have to make sure I keep track of him for the rest of the day. If he is guilty, then I can be there to watch him. And if he's not, I can be there to help him.*

As he stood at the pay phone, receiver to his ear, watching a bunch of teenagers, draped over a custom-painted old Mustang, he counted as the phone rang. After ten rings, he put it down, frowning. *From what Pat said about being tired, I thought they would be there. Probably went down to Sam's to see whether any of their classmates have arrived, a little get together, and have lunch. If they're in Pine Ridge, and want to eat lunch, they will have to be at Sam's.*

Hanging up the phone, Dain paused a moment. *Everything that's happened is leading up to tonights first session of the reunion. I don't have any proof of it, but I've got a damn strong feeling, maybe a cop's sixth sense. And what was in those two boxes Lud took into the school? A place where he had encountered a lot of misery. Dynamite? Well, being without wheels, I have a good excuse for sticking with the sheriff. Lot of stuff to do. I've got to get moving.*

The sheriff's office was seven or eight blocks from the restaurant. Hoping he could catch the sheriff there he took off at a trot.

Dain was sweating hard as he crossed the parking strip at the sheriff's office. As he came in, Alice looked up from her typewriter and nodded at him.

"Is Lud around?" Dain asked.

Before she could answer, Ralph, who had risen from his desk across the room, called out, "The sheriff isn't here right now, Barlow. If you want to leave a message, I'll see that he gets it."

Dain's eyes widened in surprise. *Ralph sounded as friendly as a hound that had just seen a strange dog crossing his yard. And Alice was busy at her typewriter, not saying a word, or looking at him. Is something wrong here, or is it just my imagination?*

Dain, reaching the partition that divided the office, pushed at the gate without thought. The barrier was still locked. He turned to look at Alice, who colored faintly. She darted a glance at Ralph, who, after a moment's hesitation, nodded. The lock snapped back with a sound that was loud in the strained atmosphere.

Ralph, reseating himself, tossed the pencil he had in his hand on the desk and glared at Dain. "What's wrong? Did you leave something here?"

Dain bit his lip. *Christ, I wasn't mistaken. This kid is acting as if I just brought in a case of the plague.*

Surprised, Dain stumbled over his words. "I…I wanted to check with Lud about something. When do you expect him?"

Ralph gave him the kind of deadpan look that would have done credit to a more mature cop. "I don't think you understand, Mr. Barlow. When the sheriff called in from Pine Ridge this morning, he said that with the case closed, you were no longer working on it. Lud said we'd better stay clear of you in case some judge got a bug up his butt, what with you not being sworn in, a duly constituted law enforcement officer of the county, we might get our buns in a ringer."

Dain blushed. *Looks like Lud has made me the sheriff department's favorite dumpster. Lud was nobody's fool. He must have sensed the doubts growing in me and gave his loyal deputy an attitude adjustment. And Lud is up in Pine Ridge right now. Well, I came here to get some information. If Ralph knows the answers, I'm damn well going to get it, one way or another.*

Dain decided to ignore Lud's having taken him off the case, and proceed as if he were still the department special investigator. Eyeing Ralph, who was looking everywhere but at Dain, with a strong voice, Dain said, "Deputy, have you people confiscated any explosives during the last few weeks? Have there been any stolen in this area?"

"Explosives! Are you out of your head? This isn't the big city like you're used to. People here don't go around blowing things up. We're just plain country folks,"

Alice's voice, dry, loud, startled them both. "Ralph, how about those Indian fellows, what they were saying about that plastique stuff?"

If looks could kill, Ralph would have had Alice down and bleeding. With a petulant note of outrage in his voice, he said, "You're talking rumors, Alice." Looking back at Dain, he muttered, "A couple of Indian fellows were arrested here after a car chase. They claimed they tossed some plastique out the window of their car before they were stopped. We sure the hell didn't find it.

"Lud even took the two out to show him where they threw the stuff away. spent the better part of a day out there, searching. Didn't come up with a damn thing. If you ask me, they were a couple of small-timers, talking through their hats to get attention."

Alice was undeterred by the looks Ralph had directed at her. She spoke up again. "Ralph, maybe you'd better tell him about those *FBI* manuals. You know, the ones that came a week ago last Monday."

The young deputy sidled over to where he was standing in the direct line of vision between Dain and Alice. "What's that got to do with the price of tea in China?" he muttered. "They aren't the only *FBI* manuals Lud's obtained. He tries to keep us up-to-date, just in case."

"What were these manuals about?" Dain demanded.

Ralph gave an elaborate shrug. "Beats me. I heard Alice say something to Lud the morning they came in the mail, but I didn't pay any attention to them. Lud tells us what we need to know."

Alice could no longer see Dain, but she could still talk to him. "A couple of them were on terrorist tactics, and one was on bombs. Not airplane bombs, but the kind people make."

This was too much for Ralph. The normally low-key deputy showed a vehemence that surprised Dain.

"Goddammit, Alice. You're talking about department business. It's not any outsider's business what the sheriff does. If he wants bomb manuals, he sure as hell has the right to get 'em without you shooting your mouth off. What the hell you bad-mouthing the sheriff for anyway?"

Dain measured his words, speaking slowly. "Ralph, you mistake my intentions. I may not be part of your investigation anymore, but something bizarre is going on, something more than just the murders of two defenseless women. I want to get to the bottom of it, for my own sake and for the sake of a lot of other people. I'm not accusing Lud of anything. God knows, he's the best friend I ever had in these parts."

With Ralph glowering at him but saying nothing, he continued, "We don't know those two fellows were lying. If they weren't, somebody may have found the explosives before Lud and the two Indians went out looking. If that's true someone around here may have several pounds of an explosive that can't be used for construction work. The stuff is used to make bombs, pure and simple. Lud may be thinking the same way I am, about these explosives. Maybe he just doesn't want to raise an undue alarm until he knows what's going on."

The anger in the young deputy's face was replaced by a look of uncertainty. "Then you're not checking on Lud? Right?"

Dain frowned. He wasn't going to lie. "I'm checking on everyone. I'd check on you or Alice if I had reason to. Lud may be ill. He's been having severe headaches. At times he seems bewildered, and at other times he seems like another person. I tried to get some insight into his medical condition but failed."

Ralph had no more than seated himself when he was back on his feet again, his face reddening. "What kind of bullshit are you spouting, now? You said he was your best friend, or at least, he used to be. Now, you talk like you think he's crazy, you bastard. Is that what you're trying to tell me?"

"Take it easy, deput—"

Alice pushed away from her desk, facing them, and interrupted. "I don't know, Ralph," she said hesitantly. "He has been acting strange lately, ever since he went on the morning shift. You only see him when you relieve him and when he breezes in and out during the day. I'm usually around him a lot more than you are."

Ralph spun around to face her. "Hell, yes, he's acting strange. Nothing like this has ever happened in this county. Two women murdered in three days! Hell, we haven't even had one in all the time he's been sheriff, and now Joe Woods' folks are calling here about him being missing.

"All this happening, and I'm the only deputy he has available. Jesus Christ, it's no wonder he's acting strange. Barlow here," he jerked his head toward Dain, "sure as hell hasn't been a lot of help with his insinuations about the sheriff."

Alice shook her head vigorously. "More to it than that. I like Lud as much as you do, but ever since he took over morning watch after we got so short-handed, what's it been, about two weeks ago? However long it's been, he hasn't been the same man. Leastwise, not the same one I worked with since he took office.

"There's another thing. Yesterday morning, you were still up in Pine Ridge, he sent me out for a fresh can of coffee. The other can still had plenty in it for another few days, but he said it was stale. Wasn't stale at all.

"Well, I was so frustrated when I left, I was a block away before I realized I hadn't gotten any money out of the change jar, and my purse was still at the office, so I came back. I hadn't been gone over five minutes.

"At first, I couldn't find Lud, then I noticed the door to the evidence room was unlocked. I peeked inside, and he was in there, had that radio timing device in his hand, the one he put together from those manuals. When he spotted me watching him, he got this wild look. He jumped all over me for sneaking up on him. Actually, it was downright frightening."

"Timing device?" Dain said, suddenly alert.

Ralph answered before Alice could. "The sheriff put together a battery-powered timing thing. Figured it out from the manuals. He just did it to show us how simple it is for people to fix up a bomb with a timer on it. Big deal. That don't make a man crazy just because he made a timer."

"No, that sounds perfectly plausible," Dain said. "If that's all he had in mind when he made it."

"Goddammit, there you go again, trying to make it look like he planned to use it all along. Maybe the boss is having a hard time. But he's not a murderer. My God, he saved my life once. You'll never get me to believe that."

Dain risked squeezing the young deputy's shoulder. "Never said he was, friend. But like you said, things aren't going well with him. You and I need to help him out, need to find out what's going on."

For the first time since Dain came in, the young officer's shoulders sagged. He looked worried. When Ralph limited himself to a quick nod, Dain pushed further. "Why don't you check in the evidence room. You know, just make sure that timer's still there. It should be if Lud was only using it for a teaching device, right?"

Ralph ran a finger under his collar. Initiative could give a man the feeling his shirt was too small for him. Rising, he ambled past the door with its frosted pane into Lud's office. Calling over his shoulder, he said, "Doesn't seem right to be checking on the sheriff, but I don't guess it will hurt to take a peek into the evidence room."

Accompanied by the sound of opening and closing drawers in the sheriff's private office, Dain questioned Alice further about what Lud appeared to be doing with the timer. Ralph's call interrupted them.

They entered the office to find him behind the desk, holding a big ring of keys. "Alice, you don't have the evidence room key, do you?" he demanded. "It's not on the master key ring."

Alice's voice had a trace of indignation in it. "Me? Why would I have the key? I'm not supposed to ever go in there."

"Well, all I know, the damn thing's missing."

"Oh, hell!" Dain muttered and grabbed the phone resting atop the desk, sliding it over in front of himself. He punched in a number and stood, listening, while Alice and Ralph stared at him with disapproving eyes. Dain suspected that the rule was that no one used the sheriff's personal phone but the sheriff.

After six fruitless rings, he said aloud, "Come on Sheila, answer the damn phone!"

Four more rings, and he slammed down the receiver. *Where the hell are they? From what Pat said, I figured they would be home till mid-afternoon at least.* Dain tried to dismiss it from his mind but failed.

Nothing he had found out today made him feel better about Lud. He had to get back up to Pine Ridge as quickly as possible. Dain became aware Ralph was still watching him, disapproval mirrored in his face.

His patience with the sullen deputy ran out. "Goddammit! We've got missing explosives and a timer, designed solely as a triggering device, that's probably missing. If this is Lud's doing, we need to find out and stop him, for his own sake as well as that of others. It means he's sick. Let's eliminate Lud as a suspect, for God's sake. We sure the hell don't need to be chasing false leads."

The deputy still looked defiant.

"Ralph, God knows, I hate to think what I'm thinking. But if Lud is harboring another personality, Chief Looking Glass, as I suspect, that personality could be so savage it would make, Jack the Ripper, look like a choir boy. And if that timer's not in the evidence room, with the missing key, if this is true, and I hope to God I'm wrong, Ralph, believe me, I'd give anything to be wrong. But if Chief Looking Glass is out there, our time to stop him is getting damn short.

"I'm sure if you call him and ask about the key, he'll put you off. And it wouldn't hurt to check with the state lab. I doubt that any of the evidence I gave him has ever shown up there."

"He could be right, you know," Alice muttered.

Ralph capitulated. "Okay, you win. What do you want me to do?"

"Get a locksmith in here, fast, and get that door open. See if the timer's still there."

Wheeling, Dain started for the front door, then remembered he had no transportation. "Ralph, I have no wheels. Could you get somebody to give me a ride back up to Rainbow Lake? I left my Blazer there."

Ralph, his hand already on the phone to call a locksmith, glanced at Alice. "Give him a ride up to Rainbow, will you? I'll cover on the radio. I have to stay here anyway till the locksmith comes."

Alice frowned. "Of all the days for this to happen. I don't have my car. My grandson came by and borrowed it. He went to Wenatchee."

Then her face brightened. "Wait a minute. That car he bought, he left it outside. I've got a key." Apparently realizing her words were proving bewildering to Dain and Ralph, she explained, "He bought a jalopy from a buddy of his. It's an old Pontiac with one of those huge four hundred cube engines, or some such thing. It needs some work, and his mom says she's not paying for a bunch of tickets, so he can't drive it till he gets it fixed up. That's why he went to Wenatchee, to get parts."

Her face exploded into a big grin. Leaning over, she drug her purse out of the kneehole of the desk. Fishing inside, she brought out a small plastic case with a couple of keys attached to it. "Take the Pontiac and leave it a Rainbow. When he gets back, we'll drive up there and pick it up. I'd just as soon walk home as be seen in that thing anyway."

Dain glanced down at his watch and back at Alice. "Well, darn it, I hate to impose on you, but I've got to get back as fast as I can."

Before he could say more, Alice, with a sweeping underhand motion, tossed the keys across the office to him.

Dain, about to push out through the counter gate, remembered Pat's cell phone. Rushing back over to the phone, he punched in her number.

Atop the kitchen table in the empty Barlow kitchen, the cell phone, its battery depleted, emitted a series of barely audible tweets.

CHAPTER 40

Pat's resolution to spend the morning lounging about the Barlow place vanished after a couple of hours of staring out into the translucent mists swirling about the house. Tossing her book onto the love seat in the parlor, she walked to the foot of the stairs and called up to Sheila.

"Hey, what's say we run out to Gramps's and fix him a good lunch? We could take one of those casseroles out of the freezer. Beat him having an old cold sandwich."

When Sheila appeared at the head of the stairs, Pat added, "He wants to see you, anyway. Wondered if you were still as pretty as you were when we were in school. Besides, I'll have two pots of coffee drank, if we let this fog keep us shut up in here all day. Be nothing but a bundle of nerves by the time Dain gets back."

Coming down the stairs, Sheila glanced out the front window. "I guess it would be all right, if you don't mind driving in this soup. I'll leave a note for Dain, in case he comes home and we're not back yet. You'd better grab a jacket while I'm writing it. That fog will be chilly."

When Pat returned to the kitchen, Sheila was at the table with a note pad before her, a pen beside it, staring out the window.

"Hey, what's wrong?" Pat asked.

Sheila shrugged. "I don't know. Just thinking about the reunion tonight. It's finally here, after all the trouble, and maybe no one can even make it because of the flooded lake. It just seems a shame."

Pat, hands on hips, said, "Yeah, you know, it's kinda funny. At the last reunion, Dain and Lud never showed up, now at this one they may be the only ones who can make it."

"Yeah, the two guys in our class who have lost the most. If the others don't show up we may as well forget it and just have dinner at Sam's tonight. It sure won't be a very festive occasion."

"Maybe if it were anyone but Lud," Pat said, "we could still have a reasonably good time of it. But I still get the feeling he hates our guts."

Sheila nodded. "Well, you know, when he sees us, it's got to remind him of what happened to his, mom. I don't feel real comfortable around him either. And that's not his fault, I just feel so guilty."

"We should have told him, or at least, you should have," Pat said. "You didn't even know that we'd been guzzling Amy's dad's brandy and wine when you climbed in the car with us." She grabbed Sheila's hand. "What a bunch of little shits we were, talking you into saying you were driving because you were the only one of us who had a driver's license. We didn't even think about the insurance, that you would be stuck with that. It's time I told Lud what really happened."

Sheila nodded. "Maybe both of us should talk to him."

Seizing the pen, Sheila scribbled a short note to Dain and, rising, said, "We'd better get started for Gramps's."

Ten minutes later they were on their way. The road was still choked with drifting banks of vapor, and Pat was driving so slowly Sheila was afraid someone might rear-end them.

Pat risked a glance at her friend. "Why was Dain so insistent that we stick together? Lud cleared things up a couple of nights ago."

Sheila smiled. "I think now, that we have gotten back together, he's being a little overly protective. But I don't mind. As a matter of fact, it feels pretty good to have him looking after me again."

"Well, don't worry princess, with my two friends, I'll keep you safe for him."

"Two friends? What are you talking about?"

Grinning, Pat reached under her legs and pulled her purse into view. Glancing down at it, she felt for the catch. "Smith and Wesson, my gun, silly. I have—"

"Look out!"

The wheels of the car bounced hard on the corrugations of the road's shoulder. "Jesus," Pat cried as she pulled it back onto the pavement.

Sheila grinned weakly, and shook her head. "With this fog, you'd better just drive, and I'll quit talking."

Twenty minutes after they pulled into the driveway at Gramps, having traversed four miles of rutted gravel road, the trouble started. Sheila had the plastic wrap off the casserole and was sliding it into the oven when she heard Pat say, "Gramps, what's wrong with you? You haven't said a word in five minutes. Last night you never stopped talking. Cat got your tongue with Sheila here?"

The old man's voice was strained. "The pain's back again."

"Pain? What pain?" Pat demanded.

"In my chest. It's in my left arm, too, now. It woke me up about four, but then it quieted down, and I figured it was just something I ate. You know, I don't get a good meal like we had last night very often any more." He groaned. "Pat, honey, I don't feel good at all."

"Does Pine Ridge have a doctor now?" Pat asked.

Sheila and Gramps said, "No," at the same time. Then he added, "There's a registered nurse, though. She's part of some rural medical program. The doctor from Crescent Valley comes up one day a week."

Pat glanced at Sheila, who had returned the casserole to the table and was watching them. "Call the nurse and tell her we're bringing Gramps in. Explain what his symptoms are."

"Can't," Gramps said, his voice more breathy now. "That wind last night must have knocked down the telephone line. The phone's dead."

Pat jumped up. "No problem, Gramps. We can get you into town faster than an ambulance could make the round trip anyway. Sheila, would you back the car up next to the door? I'll get a blanket and pillow for him."

Between them, they supported the old man out to the car and settled him in the back seat. Knowing how upset she must be about her grand-father, Sheila felt guilty about letting Pat drive. But Pat had always been much better in emergencies than she was.

Most days in the foothills the fog lightened as time went on, but this day proved the exception. Visibility had grown worse.

Driving faster than she should in the dense fog, Pat, studying the odometer, muttered, "Couldn't be over five more miles."

Sheila turned to look at Gramps. He seemed so tiny huddled in the seat, the pillow behind his head.

"Won't be much longer," Sheila said. "How are you—"

The bang was not loud, but it came from somewhere around the car. She managed to say, "doing," before the vehicle swerved across the road onto the shoulder and then back onto the pavement again, swaying from side to side, the back end fish-tailing. She heard the flapping from beneath the car a split second before Pat shouted, "Blowout!"

They stopped with the right side tires mere inches from a ditch filled with running water.

"Merciful God," Pat said, and then, releasing her seat belt, twisted around to look into the back seat. "Gramps, are you okay?"

Staring steadily at her, his eyes clear, he nodded.

Turning to face Sheila, she asked, "Have you ever changed a tire?"

"Yeah, once, but I'm not very good at it."

Grabbing the door handle, Pat said, "Stay put. I'll check which tire it is. No point in both of us getting cold till we have to."

Once outside, she pointed toward the left front tire and then walked back to the trunk. The banging at the rear of the car went on for close to a minute, then Pat was back at the driver's door, pulling it open. She climbed back in, looking unhappy. "Guess what? The darn spare's flat."

Sheila glanced toward the car's rear and lifted her eyebrows.

"I know," Pat muttered. Keeping her voice low, she said, "Jesus, Sheila, not over fifteen families live between here and road's end, and how many of them do you think would be out on a day like this? Do you know how close to town we are?"

Sheila frowned in concentration as she looked around, trying to pick out a land mark in the white shroud of fog. After the blowout all was ghostly quiet. Suddenly she remembered the small clearing to the right. "That side road we just passed, can't be over a hundred feet or so back, it's the road to Lud's, I'm pretty sure. That would mean it's about a four-mile walk to town."

Pat chewed her lip. "I don't know about you, but that's an hour and a half hike for me." Lowering her voice, she added, "I don't think Gramps can wait that long."

Sheila glanced out the window into the cocoon of whiteness that covered the car. When she spoke her voice was unsteady. "That's a really dark stretch of forest, kinda spooky even on a sunny day. Not but a half mile or so to Lud's, but I hate to have to go in there, he's probably home though. At least he should be. Dain said he was going to take tonight off for the reunion."

She shifted around to where she could look into Pat's eyes. "We could get him to take Gramps into town. Really, if we had to have a blowout, this was a good place for it."

Fitting the two parts of her jacket zipper together, Pat drew it up under her chin with a quick motion. "Well, good place or not, I don't have a choice. Lud's it is. I'd better get started. I don't like the way Gramps is breathing."

"Wait! We'll both go. Remember what Dain said about staying together. Besides, I know the way in to his place."

Pat shook her head. "Nope. I'm elected. One of us has to stay with Gramps. I'm wearing the shoes for it, and I do a lot more hiking than you do."

Sheila grabbed Pat's wrist. "Wait! Gramps will be all right here for no longer than we'll be gone. And there's a couple places, if you're not careful, you could take the wrong fork in the road. It's no place for anyone who doesn't know where they're going."

Pat jerked her arm free, her voice rising. "You can tell me about those places. I'm going in alone. My granddad needs you here. Just shut up about it."

Sheila made no further protest. Quickly she gave Pat directions for finding the isolated cabin.

Pat nodded. Turning toward the elderly man in the rear, she said, "Gramps, I'm going to get help. I should be back within forty-five minutes. Sheila will stay with you." She hesitated, then said, "You gotta hold on granddad, okay?"

The old man looked as if he wanted to say something, then closed his mouth and moved his head in a barely perceptible nod.

"Great. I'll be back as soon as I can."

Pat opened the car door and climbed out, slipping the strap of her purse over her shoulder. Opening the handbag, she lifted out the revolver.

"No, you take it," Sheila protested.

Pat shook her head. "Better for you to have it. Those bikers might come by. It's loaded. All you have to do is aim it and pull the trigger. Will you be all right?"

Sheila nodded, and Pat added, "If Lud's not home, for some reason, I'll break a window to get to the phone. If his line's down too, I'll use the darn police radio. We have an emergency here, he'll understand that."

Straightening, she closed the door. Within eight strides, she had vanished into the fog.

How like Pat, Sheila thought. No goodbyes.

CHAPTER 41

By the time Pat reached the gravel road that marked the way to Lud's cabin, she was alone in a silent world without form. She turned to look back at the car. Her eyes found nothing but a featureless curtain of pale mist. She fought against the urge to flee back to the sanctuary of her car. *There's no way I can go back, I have to go on. Gramps is in really bad shape, looked awful when I left the car. I only hope I can make it in time, I have, too.*

She tried to see through the cloak of white mist into the edge of the forest. The quiet was eerie, like all the forest creatures had holed up, waiting for the fog to lift. *God, this is a desolate place, if I just had Sheila along, but there's no way I could leave Gramps in the car, maybe dying, with no one around. Why is it always me who has the hard things to do?*

Taking a deep breath, she started down the gravel road.

Fifteen minutes later, she had edged over to the right side of the lane, afraid she might miss the twin tire tracks that Sheila had described as leading off through the densest part of the woods to Lud's place.

The thing that had been worse about her hike had been the utter disorientation. Here the ground bordering the lane was clear enough that she had seen nothing, not one dim shape looming out of the translucent vapor around her. Twice, as she stared blindly about her, she had stepped into shallow potholes full of water.

When, at last, the tracks branching away from the lane appeared, she felt a surging sense of relief. Soon she was walking between the tracks on a thick mat of disintegrating forest debris. When the first dim shape loomed out of the mist, fear coursed through her and her heart skipped a beat. Then, realizing what it was, a sapling whose branches must have brushed the side of every car that passed, she relaxed.

On the gravel road it had been tomb quiet, but back in here, with trees all around her, the air was alive with the sound of the thousands of drops of water falling from tree branches. Now the dark pillars of huge tree trunks were close around her, and the fog had become a deepening shade of gray.

Could I have taken the wrong path? Missed the one I was supposed to take, then taken the next one? It seems like I've come a lot farther than a half mile. Sheila said that's about what it was to Lud's. Stopping, uncertainty building, she sniffed the damp air, hoping to pick up the scent of wood smoke. Sheila had told her the cabin was heated by a wood stove.

Something crashed to the ground off to her right, and she jumped. Her heart skipped a beat as her head snapped around in that direction. Staring into the murky haze, she was ready to flee back up the trail.

A limb! She started to breath again. *Nothing but a limb falling.* From one of the closely packed trees about her, barely visible in the white vapor, its wet feathery fingers of green still swaying from the fall.

Automatically, Pat felt of her purse, then remembered she had left the gun with Sheila. Licking her lips, she peered into that quiet, yielding curtain of fog, trying to divine what lay ahead.

Pat shivered. The dripping from the tree branches was beginning to effect her like a Chinese water torture, grating on her nerves. Almost to the point, of screaming out. *God, if I don't find something familiar, and soon, I'm going to be a basket case.*

The slightest hint of breeze touched her cheek, and the mist ahead of her parted for a moment. The tire tracks curved around a tight little grove of saplings. *Sheila had described something like that being within a few yards of Lud's.*

Her heart beat pounded in her ears, and she begin walking as fast as she dared, she rounded the small trees and saw a white blob in the fog ahead of her. Another step, and Pat knew she was looking at a county sheriff's unit.

A flood of relief surged through her as she let out a ragged breath. *Thank God, I found the cabin. And Lud's home, what a relief it's going to be to see him.*

As she rounded the front of the vehicle, the cabin seemed to rush out of the fog into view. The windows were dark, but a whiff of wood smoke reached her nostrils.

Pat rushed across the last few yards of open ground and mounted the porch steps. Her hand was raised, ready to rap on the door, when she realized the house was silent. She thought of the windows again. The blinds were up, and the interior was dark. Lud was asleep. It didn't matter she had to wake him. She tapped on the door. When that got no results, she called softly, "Lud, are you home?"

What's wrong with me? If he was awake in the next room he couldn't hear a tentative voice like that. Darn it, why is it I feel like a robber checking to see if a potential victim is home? Lud will understand, God, he would want me to wake him.

Pat knocked again, much louder this time. "Lud?" she called. "Are you home?" And her voice, this time, at least to her, sounded terribly loud.

Still no response. *Well, I've got to wake him.* She seized the door knob, and it turned in her hand, unlocked. Pat eased her head through the opening, aware of the warm air flowing past her, trying to fathom what she saw in the near darkness. Stepping inside, she eased the door shut behind her.

Here in the cabin, the faint sputter of burning wood within the stove was overridden by a rhythmic snoring. Her eyes growing more accustomed to the dimness, Pat could see the corner of a bed through the open door on the left hand side of the room. The snoring came from there.

Her gaze turned back to what she had come all this way to find, a telephone. It rested atop a telephone book on Lud's desk next to the police radio.

Pat's eyes widened. The police receiver's dials were dark, and its speaker was without the usual static. *Why wasn't it on? Cops, especially the sheriff, were supposed to keep their radios on all the time, weren't they? Didn't they have to know what was happening in the county?*

Oh, I forgot. Sheila said he was off tonight, probably wanted to get a good nights rest before the reunion started. After all, if something came up, the sheriff's office could call him by phone. Probably left instructions to that effect.

Standing as still as a statue, still apprehensive at standing in Lud's house in the dark, uninvited, she nibbled at her bottom lip? *Should I wake Lud from a sound sleep? Maybe I could just make the call without waking him. But what if he hears me? Lud might figure he had a burglar and come charging out of the bedroom, gun blazing.*

Standing there, uncertain of what to do, Pat's gaze wandered. She saw the other door, ajar. *I bet that's his mother's old room. Sheila mentioned something about it when we drove down to Crescent Valley. Said Lud had boarded up the window, didn't use the room anymore.*

And then told me how spooky Lud had acted when she asked if she could look inside. The look never changed, she said, when Dain asked him why he hadn't cleaned it out and used the room.

Lud continued to snore, dead to the world. *He'll never know if I take a quick peek inside. Taking the uninvited liberty isn't right, but what a hoot it will be, teasing Sheila and Dain about it. I'll be the only one who knows the secret of the sheriff's locked room.*

The compelling urge to see inside the room, to see how Lud had kept it in her memory, was strong and getting stronger.

Pat thought about Gramps. *Darn it! Getting him the help he needs is the highest priority right now.* She started to turn away, then hesitated. *It'll take just a moment, then I will retreat to the front door, open it, and start yelling for Lud, as if I just got here. After all, I don't need to use the phone, I'll just get Lud to rush Gramps into town.*

Pat's curiosity moved her, like a moth drawn to a flame, and she crossed the space in half a dozen quick light steps to the forbidden room and pushed open the door. Disappointment flooded through her. The room was dark, and what little light came into the room from the dim living room revealed nothing.

She made a face. *The odor is odd, but a closed room can get pretty stale. The matches. I have some matches in my jacket pocket that I picked up at the motel. The smell of a burning match will not even be noticed in this musty room. No way it'll wake Lud.*

As she felt her way cautiously into the darkness, sliding one foot ahead of the other, she extracted the matches from her pocket. Pat almost tripped, close to losing the matches, when her foot encountered something heavy but yielding. Recovering her balance, she struck the match.

Pat gasped aloud and almost dropped the match. Her sudden shock had made her reaction too loud, she knew. Before her, the flickering light revealed a large painting on a dresser, less than three feet in front of her face. Two unlit candles sat on the bureau top, one on each side of the picture.

Then she saw the painting more clearly. *Lud's mother! God, he had the room fixed up like a shrine.*

The long tapered candles framing the beautiful face. Pat's mouth went dry. *Oh, my God! I've got to get out or here. Lud may have heard me, and I can't be found in this room.*

As she turned to go, her foot encountered the bulky bundle on the floor again. Without thinking, she struck another match and glanced at what her foot rested against. Charlie Young, the forest ranger, lay on his back, his khaki shirt blotched with blood, his mouth gaping open. His face seemed twisted in a silent scream that would last forever.

For a second, her throat was frozen, and she was unable to breath, unable to swallow. But then the sickly smell of putrid flesh reached her, and reeling backward, she began to scream. Then somehow, she was out of the den of horrors and running toward the front door.

The form seemed to materialize out of nowhere. An Indian, clad in buckskins.

As he closed on the screaming Pat, she had time for the thought that the face, with its streaks of paint, looked like Lud's. The next moment, Pat felt the hands on her throat.

*   *   *

Pulling back the sleeve of her jacket, Sheila glanced at her watch. Pat had been gone for over an hour, far more than enough time for her to have reached Lud's and returned with him.

Twisting around, Sheila studied Gramps. His skin had a terrible gray cast to it, and his breath was coming in quick, short gasps. His eyes behind the slitted lids seemed unfocused. She wondered whether he was sinking into a coma.

"Gramps?" she called, her voice soft. When he failed to respond, she tried again, louder. "Gramps, are you okay?"

The lids came open, and his eyes, unfocused, shifted. Then they found her, and his gaze sharpened. His, "What, Sheila?" was almost inaudible. At least he knew her.

"Gramps, are you doing okay?"

He tried to smile, but failed. "Hurt a lot…it's not getting any better this time," he said in the almost indiscernible voice.

Sheila picked at her lip. *Oh, God, what's keeping Pattie? Gramps is getting worse. What could have happened to her? Did she get off onto the wrong road? There's no other explanation. God knows it'd be easy enough to do in that dark forest, and in this fog. But even if Lud wasn't home, she should have been back long before now.*

Darn it, I can't think about Pat. Even lost in the woods, nothing will happen to her in the next hour or so. Gramps is the one who desperately needs help. I've got no choice. I'll have to go down that dreadful road to Lud's.

Hesitating, Sheila glanced out the window in the absurd hope that Lud's vehicle would materialize out of the fog as she watched. She glanced back at Gramps again. His eyes were closed. Her mind was made up.

"Gramps, listen to me."

His eyes fluttered open.

"I've got to hike in to the sheriff's and get help for you. Pat must not have been able to find the house. I'll be back as soon as I can." *If only Pat had left the keys. I'd drive into town on this flat piece of rubber, or at least until I found help. I don't care about the darn rim, or the tire.*

Unable to get out of the car on her side without stepping into the ditch, she prepared to scramble across the console and out the other door. Pat's chrome-plated revolver lay on the driver's seat.

Staring at the pistol, she wondered what to do with it. *Should I leave it with Gramps? No, he was in no condition to use it, and he had no need for a gun. Anyone who came along would know Gramps? They would probably see he was in trouble and take him to town themselves.*

Seizing the gun, she shoved it into her jacket pocket. With a great deal of grunting, Sheila managed to scramble over the console and out the door.

Leaning back in, she said, "Gramps, I've got to go. I'll be back as quickly as I can."

The old man in the back seat gave no acknowledgement of her words.

The initial rush of adrenalin carried Sheila down the short stretch of highway and onto the gravel lane. But long before she reached the twin tracks, she was chilled and growing more frightened with each step. She knew she should be calling out for Pat, in case she had wandered off the road and was blundering about somewhere close. But the quietness around her and the ominous white vapor, held her mute.

Sheila thought back to that faint suggestion of a cry she had heard, the one that had prompted her to stir out of her torpor and check her watch in the car. It couldn't have been Pat. The sound had been too faint, too far off. And now Sheila was unsure that she had heard anything.

The sight of the twin tracks swerving off the gravel lane brought a surge of relief, then apprehension as she remembered she'd have to pass the spot her nightmares had always taken place. *Stop it,* she admonished, *Dain's right, it's just a dream. Another fifteen minutes and I'll be at Lud's, safe and sound. If Pat isn't there, Lud can radio for a search party while we rush Gramps to town.*

Walking between the tracks on a veneer of tree needles and tiny disintegrating shreds of bark, her feet made no noise. She felt like a ghost in a world without form. The woods were alive with the patter of falling drops of moisture, but they seemed more a part of the silence than a counterpoint to it.

Here, in the thickest part of the grove, the trees were close about her, the dark columns of their trunks looming in and out of the mist as she passed. Despite the thick banks of vapor, she had a good idea where she was. She slowed, then shivered. Just ahead was that ancient stump that had been the focus of her nightmares.

With Sheila's next step, disaster struck. Her right foot came down on a large rock in the road, turning her ankle, and it gave way under her weight, pitching her head-first toward the ground.

She threw out her arms in an effort to break her fall, but among the soaked litter of the woods, they skidded as if on ice, and she struck the ground hard, her face smacking against the dank veneer of needles. The pain from her ankle, and in her breasts hitting the ground caused her to cry out.

For a moment, Sheila lay, stunned, trying to make certain nothing was broken. Her ankle hurt badly and her lip stung. Hopefully the ankle was just a sprain, but her mouth had a salty taste.

Only when she felt the dampness of her clothes against her skin did she gather her wits about her. Sheila rolled over onto her back. She brought her hand up to wipe her stinging lip, and when she drew it away, she saw the red smear against the back of it. Her lip was split.

Wiping her hands against her jacket, she pawed at her face, trying to clear the clinging needles from it. Pushing herself into an upright position elicited a throb of pain from her ankle. *God, what if I'm not able to walk? What am I going to do? Lud's place is still a hundred yards away. I have to make it some way, Gramps needs help badly. I'm his only hope. I need something to provide support. A stout branch. That's what I need, It'll at least get me the last hundred yards to the cabin.*

Sheila turned her head to scan the ground around her. Her heart pounded. For a moment fear so tightened her throat that she could make no sound. Then an odd trilling escaped her lips, but she couldn't scream. Her nightmare was taking place before her eyes.

The dim figure, barely visible in the fog, was no tree, no shrub. What was there was human, and moving toward her.

CHAPTER 42

She lowered her eyes, unwilling to confront whatever it was, and so what she saw first were the moccasined feet. Then she saw the pants. Not pants, really, some sort of leggings made of leather with fringes running up the sides. *Some mountain creature, camped in the woods? Maybe that's what happened to Pat!*

Sheila remembered the gun and jammed her hand into her jacket pocket. *Thank God, it was still there.*

For one long, agonizing moment, with the flannel lining on the pocket clinging to her wet hand, the gun refused to come free. Then she had it in her outthrust hand, trying to remember what Pat had said about a safety. It's sight wavered back and forth across the slowly advancing figure.

She bit her lip. *God, I can't pull the trigger.*

Far too loud, Sheila cried, "Who's there? Lud? Is that you, Lud?"

Another step and he was out of the fog. Looking Glass stared down at her, unsmiling.

In her relief, she wanted to giggle. He looked so ridiculous in the garish costume he wore, like a chief in a Western movie. The outfit was too new, too clean to be something a real Indian would wear.

"Thank God, it's you," she said. "I was scared to death."

"Let me have that gun before it goes off," he said. "You wouldn't want to face the charge of shooting the sheriff."

Before she could either offer it to him or put it down, he plucked it from her hand.

The voice. Lud had a sore throat, flashed to mind, but left just as quickly, at least it was Lud. Narrowing her eyes, Sheila asked, "Why are you dressed like that? You look like you're going to a costume party."

He scowled. "Always dress in this manner when I go into the forest to hunt. Is that what you think Indian clothes are, costumes for children?"

Sheila blushed. She had committed a gaffe. "Oh, no, Lud, I didn't mean it that way. What I meant was, what you're wearing looks new. Like it's the first time you've had it on, not like something you've been wearing in the forest every time you go hunting."

A trace of a smile touched his face. "You're quite right. These skins have never seen the outdoors before, but it is time now. Believe me, it is time." The smile broadened, as if his answer had amused him.

Extending his hand, he said, "Come. Let me help you up. Have you hurt yourself?"

In her relief, Sheila began to talk, her words pouring out. "I think I've sprained my ankle. I came looking for Pat. We need to use your telephone to get help. Pat left about an hour and a half ago to hike in to your place, and she never came back.

"We had a blowout on the road just past your turnoff. Gramps, you know, her grandfather, is with us. I think he's had a heart attack. He's in bad shape and getting worse by the minute. We were going to ask you to take him into town, or, if you weren't here, we planned to break in to use the phone. It's an emergency, after all.

"But, are you out looking for me? Did Pat find you? We have to hurry. I…oh, God, I think he's going to die unless we get him medical assistance soon. Please, Lud." She gasped for breath. "On the way into town with Gramps, you can radio for volunteers to search for Pat. She must be lost in the fog."

The scowl, which had never left his face, deepened. "Enough! I know all about it. Your friend is at the cabin."

Sheila stared at him. "But why isn't she with you? And why aren't both of you in your car on the way to pick up Gramps?"

Blinking, he stared at the ground, saying nothing for a long moment. "Lud," she said, "are you all right?"

His face cleared. "We called the nurse. She is coming out in her van. I was on my way out to the road to flag her down when I saw you on the ground. Your friend is trying to reach the garage to have them come out and fix the car, but they do not answer."

"But why aren't you in your car?" Sheila persisted. "You could take us all to meet her."

His voice was harsher, more unfriendly than she had ever known Lud to be. "Hush, woman! Don't you understand my words? I said I am going out to flag down the nurse. I will guide you to the cabin first. Your friend thought you might come after her when she didn't return right away. Now, come, let me help you up." Without waiting for a response, he seized her hand.

Wincing, she cried, "Ouch!" Pulling her hand free of his grasp, she sank back to the ground, growing apprehensive. This was not the Lud she knew. "I don't know whether I can walk or not." She slid her hand down onto her ankle. "It's really swollen. Maybe I'd——-"

His arm shot out, seized her wrist, and yanked her to her feet. In one fluid motion he pulled her arm across his shoulder. His other arm went around her waist and drew her against him, hip to hip. "Lean on me, little lady," he said. "It's but a short distance to the cabin."

A cold shiver went up Sheila's spine. For the first time, she was truly frightened of him. The man who had her in his grasp was a stranger. Staring straight ahead, he was almost dragging her toward the house. Sheila knew she had to get his hands off of her.

"Lud, please, wait! Let me try to walk by myself." Sheila attempted to shrug free of his embrace, but the arm around her waist tightened, holding her pinioned against his side. She pawed at his arm with her hand, trying to loosen the vise like grip he had on her waist. Her hand closed on his wrist, feeling his watch, her fingers touching its band.

She froze. *Oh, God! That band! The two gemstones set just below and above the watch. Big ones.* Hot fear enveloped her like a fever. *That night, in Dain's dark house, when the intruder caught me on the upstairs stairway, during the struggle with him, I felt a watchband just like the one Lud wore now, the two stones, in the odd places.*

Dear, God! It had been Lud in the house. He was the one who killed Amy and Bev. That's why Dain told me and Pat not to separate. He suspected. We told him we would stay at the house. A shiver shook her body. *Oh my, God.*

Her knees went weak, she stumbled, on the point of collapse. All her weight was against him.

Looking Glass looked at her sharply. "Why aren't you walking?" he demanded. "I keep weight from sore foot."

"My ankle. I think it may be broken. I feel faint. I think I may pass out."

He shook his head. "No! You must remain conscious till we get to the cabin! You rest here, little woman feel better soon." He lowered her to the ground.

Sheila was in a state of agitation. *God, what's that all about, I must remain conscious? And the way he talks, skipping words, in a monotone, except when I do something he doesn't like. This is a stranger who occupies Lud's body, nothing close to the guy with whom I grew up.*

Sheila strained to slow her breath, knowing she was perilously close to hyperventilating. Fighting the revulsion, she seized his hand. "Please, Lud, don't you understand? It's not going to get better. I think my ankle's broken. I need pain killers, and I need somebody to set it."

He shook his head. "No. We must get to the house. I will carry you. Soon, will be no more pain. I will fix it. Now I will lift you."

She squirmed back from him. "No, Lud. I can't stand getting jostled around with you carrying me. Get the car. Please. Come back with Pat, and you two can take Gramps and me to town."

Looking Glass studied her without expression. "I said your ankle would hurt no more once we reach the house. I take care." Tears ran down her cheeks. "Listen to me. The pain is getting so bad I'll scream if you try to move me. I know I won't be able to stand it. Just get the car, Lud. Please."

He backed away from her. "Stop your chatter. I'll come back for you myself while your friend fixes hot coffee."

Sheila felt foolish the moment she asked the question. "Could...could I have my gun back? I'd feel a lot better if I had it." She saw in his eyes that she had kindled his suspicions.

He took a step toward her, frowning. "Gun! Why do you think you need a gun?"

"You know, in case a bear comes around. My lips been bleeding, maybe they can smell the blood."

"Bear! There are no bear in these woods. You stay here until I return."

Turning, he disappeared into the mist. His moccasined feet did nothing to betray his movements.

Sheila's mind raced. *What can I do? Where's Pat? Could Lud be holding her prisoner in the cabin? Must be, he said she was at the cabin. I don't have much time. He'll be back in a few minutes.*

Sheila climbed to her feet, testing the ankle. The pain was there, but for now it was little more than a ache, nothing like a real sprain would have produced. She had to move.

Sheila wanted to head for the highway. Somebody would come by, sooner or later. Turning, she hesitated. *No, I can't go there, that's where Lud would expect me to go. He knows I'm no woods woman. When he doesn't find me, he'll head for the road. And in the fog I will never know he's there until I run into him.*

From someway off, she heard the sound of the engine, muffled by the fog. *My God, so soon?* Reflexively, she whirled and plunged in among the trees. Within ten yards, she was lost, disoriented. But she did know one thing. She was moving toward Lud's cabin, not the highway. Moving in the confusing world of a fog-filled landscape, the car seemed to be etching a circle around her, but then it stopped, and the engine shut down.

She sniffed back a tear. *I dare not go no farther, not the way I'm thrashing around, churning through low brush. Dain said he could track a cougar across rock.*

Diving into the shelter of a triangle of head-high saplings, she got as comfortable as she could. Wanting no cramped muscle to force her to move. If he heard her and got his hands on her again. She closed her eyes. No way she could let that happen. The only noise in her world was the slight sound of her breathing.

Time seemed to stretch on forever, but she knew it could not have been more than a few minutes.

When the voice came, it was so close she almost cried out. Lud, seemingly within a few yards of her, called out, "Sheila, where are you? Don't be a fool! I can help you and the old man. And Pat wants to see you."

Another minute dragged by. This time his voice came from only a few feet behind her, thundering, "You murderous bitch! Your friend Barlow cannot help you, now. He is trapped down in Crescent Valley."

Turning her head slowly, her aching eyes strained to see through the mist, but the only forms she saw were of two dark pines. She stared, she was right, two trees. She dared not turn further, afraid that the slightest rustle would reach his ears.

And then she saw the moving darkness, stalking across the interval between the two tree trunks. From beyond the second tree, his voice came, raspy, more insistent. "I'm going to take you, slut! I will seed your loins, and then I will take your head, as you bitches took the head of Running Fawn."

Sheila closed her eyes, tightly, as if the effort might stop the horrible words. Pat was his prisoner, for sure. She prayed the depraved man would soon leave. Maybe she could make it to the cabin before he killed Pat.

Sheila jumped at the sound of the patrol car's engine starting again. *My God, how did Lud get back to his car so quickly? Only moments ago he was just a few feet away. He made no sound, no branches brushing against clothes, no needles crunching underfoot.*

Sheila fought to stave off the panic. Fear was like a long cold worm inching up her spine. *Please, hang in there Pat. If I don't make some stupid blunder, I'll be at the cabin as soon as I can to try and set you free from your hell.*

The car idled for what seemed like an eternity, then moved away along the track toward the road. Sheila released her pent-up breath. Soaked up by the cloying fog, the rumble of the car's motor diminished into silence, and Sheila was alone, surrounded by the dimly perceived shadows that was the forest. *Lud has to figure I would run for the road. He will be lurking there, near the disabled car, waiting for me.*

She struggled with the realization that Lud intended to kill her! And kill Pat, too! And she was at the cabin. *Oh, God in heaven please help us.* Sheila began a toneless whimpering. *I can't just wait here, like a rat in a trap. I have to make some effort to save Pat, if she's still alive, and save myself. I have to figure out what on earth to do. There's got to be a way out of this.*

Lud will stay near our car for a while to catch me when I come out of the woods. If he stays long enough, I might be able to make the cabin. He's got a telephone. If I can find the place in the fog, I can dash in, use the phone, and then if Pat is drugged like before, I can drag her into the woods and hide until help arrives.

She nodded. *It's a chance I've got to take.* Sheila moved cautiously through the grove, her only clue as to direction the vaguely remembered sense of where she had first heard the car motor. The need to move slowly to avoid running into brush and low-hanging tree limbs was taking too long. She was running out of time. Panic closed in on her.

Sheila was on the edge of slumping to the ground and bawling when she realized she had come out of the trees, and the cabin, dark and forbidding, stood immediately ahead of her.

Although she had been desperate to find it, she was no longer sure that it was what she wanted. Her rational mind told her that Lud was gone. He had driven off in the direction of the highway, and she had not heard him return.

But Lud and his home seemed of one piece, mysterious, brooding, menacing. *Pat! Surely Lud had only had time to drug her, and she was somewhere in the cabin waiting his return. Locked in a room, or tied up.* Suddenly she knew where she would be. *Lud's mother's room!*

The minutes were flying by while she just stood here. She could wait no longer.

Her heart beating so hard she felt nauseous, Sheila ran across the open ground and up the porch steps. She dared not stop now or she would turn and run off into the woods to be tracked down by him at his leisure.

In the moment before she seized the door handle, Sheila had the sickening thought that Lud may have locked it. The cold round metal knob turned easily under the pressure of her hand.

The door swung open to an interior so dim that she could discern nothing but small feathers of flame behind the glass door of the wood stove. The inside of the cabin, quiet, except for the muffled sounds of burning wood within the steel box.

Once inside, she slumped back against the closed door, waiting for her eyes to adjust. The room's only light, apparently the only light in the house, was the fog filtered daylight spilling in through the windows. Once her eyes adjusted to where she could make out the furniture in the room, she crossed it to the doorway into Lud's bedroom. Although the bedspread was rumpled and the pillow bore an indentation, the bed was empty. Bending over, she peered under the bed. No Pat.

Not a very logical place to find her, but who knew where a demented mind would place her. She couldn't miss any possibility. A swift glance showed her the room had no other place, not even a closet, that could have concealed her.

Ever more conscious of how little time she had, Sheila rushed back into the living room. There, with her eyes better adjusted to the dimness, she saw what she had missed before.

A thin knife edge of light, faint, flickering, and yellowish, seeped from under the closed door to Lud's mother's room. Probably the most logical place. The sight of that thread of light drove all other thoughts from her mind. Dear God, what was that? Lud's dead mother sitting there facing the door, hideously scarred, waiting for her? Like in the movie, Psycho?

She quickly shook her head. Trying desperately to shake the macabre thoughts away. *No, that can't be, and please not Pat.* The memory of the motel room in Crescent Valley came to mind. Sheila could see that ceiling fan moving, the horror that was Bev's head hanging from it. *Lud? Could he be in there, waiting for me? No, he was out by the highway in his car. I haven't heard a sound, he can't be there.*

Tearing her gaze from the thin edge of light, she saw what she had come for. The telephone.

Sheila took a quick step toward it, paused, and turned back to stare at the closed door, a door that might be the entrance to hell, for all she knew, but might also have only an unconscious Pat. "God!" she cried aloud as she lunged across the room.

She flung the door open and stepped inside. She had entered hell.

A dresser stood in the middle of the floor. A huge painting of an Indian woman sat atop it leaning against the high mirror, flanked by two burning candles. Lud's mother. He had a painting of her. Sheila, not wanting to look at her face, dropped her gaze and saw three bulky objects centered on the top of the broad dresser between the two tapers.

Well, not really centered, there was one, a space, then the other two. The long candles so tall that at first she could see only the tops of them. All three seemed to be covered with mats of long fine strands of material reflecting light. Then an errant breeze sent the flames dancing, chasing the shadows away.

The heads of Amy, Bev, and Pat stared back at her, open-eyed.

She gasped, and started to back away, feeling for the door behind her, and then she saw Pat's body, lying farther back in the room, headless, nude, the legs spread obscenely, lying in an ocean of drying blood.

Sheila crammed her knuckles into her mouth, chewing on them so hard she drew blood, trying not to scream. The bile surging into her throat burned like acid. Her nose caught the odor of decay, and she saw the source in the next instance.

Lying partially obscured behind the far side of the bed was Charlie Young. His open eyes were staring at her, and he seemed to be smiling, the lips drawn back in the death rictus to reveal his teeth. Even in the pale light of the burning candles, the face was turning dark with putrefaction. Suddenly, the empty place among the severed heads took on meaning. Lud had saved that spot for her head!

Sheila, her mouth opening and closing in a series of soft shrills, reeled backwards into the living room. Tears streaking her cheeks as she tumbled against the sofa. She had to find fresh air. She made two retching noises.

Taking in great gulps of air, she fought the churning in her stomach. Lud could be coming, vomit on the floor would say, I'm here, come and find me. Slowly she begin to gain control.

Now, she wanted to slump down onto the floor, to open her mouth and scream forever. *God, the phone! I've got to call somebody.* Fifteen feet from it, she reached out with her arm as though she could clutch it.

Holding herself that way, she staggered across the room, knees so weak, her legs threatened to fold under her.

She shrieked when the police radio came to life.

"Unit One, this is Unit Two. Do you read me?"

Her hand closed on the phone's receiver, but she was too weak to bring it up to her ear.

"Unit One, this is Unit Two. Come in Unit One. Do you read me? Over."

CHAPTER 43

The Pontiac was pretty much what Dain had thought it would be, a well-nurtured and huge power plant, surrounded by rusty, sun-bleached sheet metal and worn, discolored upholstery. The car's frame protested with creaks and rattles every mile of abuse the big engine forced on it.

The front wheels were badly out of line, the steering loosey-goosey, and the rusted-out muffler pumped exhaust fumes into the interior. The power windows had long since quit working, so the missing right rear window provided the only ventilation in the car.

Speeding toward Rainbow Lake, Dain's mind was on the girls. *I don't think Looking Glass would come by the house, but God, who knows what he was liable to do? He had been there once before when I thought the women were safe. But after last night I don't think he will come back unless he knows for sure the ladies are alone.*

Dain's heart sank. *Jesus H. Christ, I mentioned to the deputy the women were supposed to be at the house but they didn't answer the phone. If the sheriff called in to the office, and the deputy let it slip. Oh, God!*

Knowing better than to do it, Dain let the big power plant take over. The tires screamed at every curve. Nearing Rainbow Lake, he was doing nearly seventy with the engine still purring contentedly. Topping a rise, he saw the second, slightly higher, hillock two hundred yards ahead. Just

over its crest, he knew the road made the dangerous ninety-degree
curve to run directly along the shore of the lake.

Dain tapped the brakes twice hard. His speed down to forty, he
topped the second crest and braked hard to dive through the curve and
on to a stop before the barricades blocking the road at the water's edge.
One second his foot was on the brake pedal, feeling its resistance, and
the next it was flat against the floorboard. Dain opted to try to complete
the turn, rather than riding the old Pontiac straight out over the bank
and into the lake.

He never had a chance. The car was barely into the sharp curve when
the left side wheels lifted off the pavement. Dain could feel the tires on
the other side slipping sideways toward the embankment while his side
of the car lifted higher and higher. Halfway through the curve, there was
no more road left, and the Pontiac dropped over the side, beginning to
tumble as it did, onto the rock embankment. The vehicle had completed three-fourths of a full roll when it hit the water surface with a jar
that jolted every bone in his body.

The impact was hard enough that the Pontiac had no chance to float.
Dain had barely enough time to take a deep gulp of air before the vehicle's interior filled with water. He could sense that it was still, rolling,
tumbling down the underwater slope. Fumbling at his waist, he tried to
find the buckle for the seat belt.

The damn kid had installed some cheap mail-order belt. The water
around the car was darkening as it descended. Then abruptly, the car
came to a halt, and the seat belt latch popped free. He felt for the window handle, then remembered the electric controls that didn't work.

Grabbing the door handle, he pulled, then slammed his body against
the door. It didn't budge. The water around him had robbed the blow of
any force. *Christ, I have to get out.*

Twisting around, he brought up his feet, putting his legs against his
chest and kicked with all his strength against the door. Its metal
squealed, but the door refused to open. The tumble down the rocky

slope must have bent it, and his efforts were merely burning oxygen fast. *Think, dammit! I can't let this damn lake take the whole Barlow family.*

Then, through the desperation and myriad of thoughts, he remembered the open rear window. *I got to hurry. My lungs are growing tight, beginning to burn, but I have to use my head, can't let panic take over.*

He clambered over the front seat into the back. The metal groaned and the car shivered. The pressure on his ears told him he was twenty-five, no deeper than thirty-five feet below the surface. If the car started rolling again, it could go all the way to the bottom, a hundred and seventy feet down. Have to get out now!

Dain's hands found the open window, and his heart sank. The Pontiac's open window rested against the rocky slope. But there was space, maybe enough for him to squirm out. Starting to squeeze through the window, his hands found the projection on the rock outcrop bulging into the car, holding it where it was.

Clutching at the car's sides, he wormed his way through the opening, feeling his jacket catch for a moment against something, and then coming free. Dain was almost clear of the car when it shifted again. The vehicle's movements moved the car forward, and the rock pinned his ankle against the car's top.

In the first flush of panic, he stroked furiously at the water with his arms but went nowhere. *God, I gotta have air. Lungs burning so, got to hold on.*

His lungs felt as if they were about to explode out of his chest. Bending down, Dain seized his trapped leg. His hands told him what his senses already had. It and the outcrop were supporting part of the weight of the car now. The pain in his ankle was increasing. Pushing against the side of the Pontiac with his arm and his other leg, he struggled to free himself. It was no use. The weight holding his ankle was too great.

In the midst of the welter of increasing panic, he had a rational thought. *If I can move my leg to the side of the rock a bit, the rock was rounding, possibly, just possibly the pressure of the car and the rock together will cause it to pop free. The car might cut me to the bone but if I don't get out of here it won't matter.*

Bending forward once more, his vision beginning to darken, he pressed down against his shin. Nothing happened. *Don't panic, Dammit! Fight this damn thing to the bitter end.*

His strength was ebbing away, when suddenly, the ankle came free sending a stupendous jolt of pain up his leg. He heard the sound of rending metal and knew that the car had come free again to resume its dive to the bottom of the lake.

As Dain clawed his way upward toward the faint luminescence far overhead, he felt a big rock slam into his other leg. Apparently the rock had worked its way free because of the vehicle's tumble down the sharp incline and the churning of the lake water.

Dain broke the surface a bare moment before his mouth would have opened involuntarily, filling his lungs with water. His only thought for the moment was to stay afloat and draw in long, sweet breaths of air. Then he begin to feel the numbness of his extremities. *Jesus, I'm cold!* The thought reminding him, the water was much too frigid to be in it for any length of time without the proper equipment. *I got to get out, and soon.*

Looking around him, he saw that he was about fifty feet offshore and almost even with where the road dipped under the lake surface. *A hundred yard swim, goddammit, I have to make it.*

Turning, he sought the far side of the water gap. *Jesus Christ! Isn't anything going to go right?*

The Blazer, stood at least thirty yards out into the water. The lake surrounding it was so high the waves were lapping against the headlights. *Why the hell didn't those bastards from the road department, before they left, push it back up the road to where it would be out of danger?*

They and their truck were gone, leaving a line of barricades across the road some fifty yards beyond the water's edge. His jaw tightened in anger. *Son of a bitches made sure the barricades would be out of the water but not my Blazer. They had even taken the boat with them when they left. Assholes!*

Dain, starting to swim toward the Pine Ridge side of the water gap, became instantly aware that his ankle was in bad shape. He propelled himself through the water with his arms, letting his legs trail without motion.

Dain knew the word had to be out by now that the road was closed, so no one would be coming down it this far. *Everything's just swell. My screwed-up ankle, the other leg sore, several miles to hike, and two women who, hell, maybe a lot more than that, were going to die unless I make it to the reunion on time.*

*   *   *

Glaring at the police radio, Sheila shouted, "Shut up! Damn you, shut up!"

Her anger steadied her, and she was able to grip the phone. She had it against her ear, hearing the dial tone, wondering why no one had answered, when she realized she had not punched in a number. *Who Should I call? Try Dain? Oh, God yes.*

She tapped the keypad numbers and listened to the throaty warble of the phone's ringing. Hearing Dain's voice, she cried out in relief, but the next instant realized what it was…the answering machine. She slammed down the phone as a burst of static came from the radio next to her.

Oh, God, what did that mean? Was Lud back? She had to think.

She had to get in touch with somebody. Sam? What good would that do? The only people hanging around the cafe this time of day were a bunch of decrepit retirees. Call Vern? She didn't even know where he worked.

Sheila pulled her ear away from the receiver, listening, dreading to hear the patrol car returning.

Call the sheriff's department? She shook her head. *The deputy would never believe her, she could hardly believe it. The nurse. She'd call the nurse. She—*

"Unit two? Lud here. What's your problem?"

Sheila stepped back from the radio, staring at it in horror, as if Lud himself were going to come spilling out of the speaker.

"Sheriff, where are you? Still in Pine Ridge?"

"Yeah. Coming up on my place right now."

Sheila reeled. *Coming up on his place? What did he mean by that? Oh, my God! He's left Pat's car already.*

Wheeling, she took a step toward the front window, forgetting she still had the phone's receiver in her hand. Behind her, the deputy's voice issued from the radio again.

"Looks like you're stuck there then. The road department reports the road's under four feet of water at Rainbow. I guess there's lots of fishing boats on the Pine Ridge side though. By the way Sheriff, I can't find the key to the evidence room. Have you got it?"

"Yeah, I got it. Why the hell do you need in the evidence room?"

A moment of dead air followed before Ralph answered. "Dain Barlow was in here nosing around. With what he was saying, well, I just thought I would check the evidence room. Maybe it'd shut him up."

Even on the radio, Lud's voice sounded harsh. "I told you he was out of the loop, goddammit! Whatever that bastard says don't mean shit. Get me? Over and out."

Sheila managed to catch the phone just as it started to slide off the desk. In the moment of silence that followed, the muffled sound of tires crunching gravel came through the closed door. Dropping the telephone receiver into its cradle, she lunged toward the window.

The sheriff's car stopped abruptly, the front end dipping as it braked. Lud came out of the car fast.

Sheila was beside herself. *Oh, God, I have to get out. The back door! Where is it?* She raced across the floor into Lud's bedroom. The line of the walls was unbroken. Then she remembered what Dain had said about the cabin having only a front door. *Who would build a house without a back door? It would be dangerous in case of fire.*

Spinning on her heels, she raced back into the living room, faltering at the sound of Lud's heavy steps climbing onto the porch. Sheila's gaze darted about the room, seeking a place to hide. None! *God, help me. Wait! Maybe I could open the window in Lud's room and climb out that way.*

From the corner of her eye, she saw him pass the window, the front door two strides away. Sheila had no idea how she got back into the candlelit room full of bodies and decapitated heads. Her next conscious thought was of pushing the door shut behind her. The sounds of its latch catching and the front door opening were simultaneous. The tapers' flames danced crazily in the wind of the closing door.

The front door was open but a few seconds and then it closed again. Sheila could hear nothing! *Had he merely leaned in and then gone back out?*

She remained motionless for thirty seconds, aware of the vibrations in the flooring beneath her feet, and then she understood what she was hearing. What she had first thought were wind-driven noises from outside were the scuffing of moccasins against the wood floor. He was inside, moving around, but strangely quiet.

Sheila was shivering. *God, what if he decides to come into the room! I have to hide! But where? The bed! Under the bed, that's the only place I can go.*

The spread covering the mattress hung down till it was no more than six or seven inches above the floor. Sheila took a step, wincing as she put all her weight on the ankle she had turned earlier. She had not noticed it until now. With the hurt and trying to be quiet made her feel clumsy. *I sure can't stumble over anything in this dim candlelit room. And dear God,*

*let there be no creaking boards. My head will be on top of that dresser with
my classmate's!*

Trying to still her breathing, trying to hear what he was doing outside
the room, she lowered herself onto her hands and knees. She made her
way toward the foot of the bed. By going under that way she could avoid
going near the bodies. Metal struck against metal out in the living
room, and she jumped, almost crying out at the sudden sound.

Going flat onto her stomach, Sheila squirmed in under the low cross
member of the bed's frame and inched her way forward. Reaching out
with her arms to help herself, she felt her right arm contact a thick,
sticky substance on the floor. Startled, she jerked back her arm, turning
her head as she did.

In her revulsion, her stomach turned. The huge pool of blood that
had flowed from the stump of Pat's neck had spread so far under the
bed that she was unable to avoid it. She would have to crawl through it
to get her legs out of sight.

Her feet were barely out of view when the door opened. From where
she lay, Sheila could see the lower part of Lud's legs, up to his knees. He
still wore the buckskins and moccasins. Lud stopped in front of the portrait of his mother atop the dresser. Something heavy, maybe metallic,
hit the top of the bureau supporting the three gruesome sacrifices. She
could see the flickering light as the candles' flames wavered with the
impact.

The seconds dragged by. Lud stood absolutely still, making no sound.
Seconds became minutes and then, grunting, he dropped onto his
knees.

Sheila, afraid he was going to bend over to the side of the dresser and
peer under the bed, edged backwards but was stopped by something
with weight, something that seemed oddly fragmented. Forgetting herself, she jerked her head around.

For a moment, Sheila bordered on the edge of a mental collapse. She was lying on the cold, dead hand of Charlie Young, her elbow resting against the still colder grip of the pistol protruding from his holster.

Lud's sudden outburst may have saved her sanity. He began to chant. The words, if they were words, she did not recognize. The sounds from his throat were guttural with an odd cadence, quiet at first, but then building in volume until they were a near shout before fading to the barely audible again.

She thought it would never end. But then the chant changed and was no longer rhythmic. The unfamiliar words were loud, harsh, and came in short bursts. Without warning, a long hunting knife flashed downward into the flooring and buried its point deep in the wood. Quivering, its blade gave off satiny reflections of the candles' flames.

Abruptly, Lud bent forward to where his forehead touched the floor, and was visible under the short legs of the dresser, his eyes closed. If he rolled his head to the side and opened his eyes he would be looking right at Sheila. Sheila silently prayed. *Please don't let him look, please.*

With his arms extended, a sort of wailing came from his throat, rising and falling. Saliva was coming from his open mouth in driblets onto the floor, his eyes still closed. Then abruptly he stopped, and his eyes opened.

Sheila, cowering under the bed, repeated her silent prayer. *Please, don't let him turn his head.*

Lud stirred.

CHAPTER 44

Lowering the radio mike, Ralph glanced at Alice. "Well, you heard him as well as me. What do you think?"

Alice shook her head. "God, Ralph, don't ask me. I'm just a dispatcher and general flunky. It's not my place to get mixed up in this."

Ralph flushed. "Dammit, Alice, you've had your opinion on everything that's happened up till now, so don't give me that poor working girl crap. You know him as well as I do."

His words seemed to have hit home. Alice turned to stare out the front window a few moments before answering. "It's what Barlow told us would happen, isn't it? I can't remember Lud ever taking the evidence room key out of the safe before and going off with it. What do you have to say about that?"

Ralph wanted no part of her staring into his face. He turned to look into the open door to the sheriff's private office where he could see the small floor safe, its door ajar, that should have held the key. "Dammit, I'm just a deputy. I'm not supposed to be talking about my boss, much less accusing him of God knows what."

Going into the sheriff's office he slammed the safe's door shut, then retraced his steps to his desk. His gaze back on Alice, he said, "Dammit, Alice, you're right. Lud's not acting like himself. And there's these times the last few weeks when we haven't been able to raise him on the radio."

He slammed his fist into the palm of his other hand. "Hell, I couldn't find him the night the Housley woman was murdered. He was off that night, but I tried to raise him two or three times before midnight. Sam called, thought someone should cruise through Pine Ridge a few times while all the lights were out up there. No trouble here so when I couldn't get him I went up myself. Just said he was asleep and didn't hear the radio.

"First damn time I can think of when he was off, he didn't hear ever damn thing that went on. And you said you tried to raise him a half dozen times the night Mike Powers died. The guy who broke into the Barlow house and drugged those women was there about the time you were trying to get in touch with him."

"What do you want me to do now, Ralph?" Alice asked quietly.

"Call the damn locksmith and see what the hell's keeping him. Remind him this is an emergency and we need him to get his ass down here."

She started to reach for the phone, then stopped. "How about the call from that hiker who claims he saw a body along the creek below Peddler's Point?" Shouldn't you check on that?"

Ralph glared at her. "What the hell can I do about it now, Alice? I'm stuck here unless I want to swim across Rainbow Lake. I phoned the airport in Wenatchee. They won't have a helicopter free until seven tomorrow morning, unless it's an emergency, and I didn't figure a corpse was going anywhere. And even then it depends upon the fog conditions up there. Now, just get off my back!"

Seeing the instant hurt in Alice's face, he said. "Christ, don't mind me, Alice. Jesus, I have the responsibility for most of the county now, and I'm taking it out on you."

Alice smiled at him, a weak smile, but a smile never the less. "I'll get that locksmith, Ralph."

He remained next to her until she had made the call before wandering back over to his desk. He was shuffling through a stack of shift reports, not remembering a word of what he was reading, when the phone rang. Ralph glanced up when Alice, her palm cupped over the phone, said, "It's the state lab, returning your call."

Picking up his own phone, he identified himself. The male voice, cool and impersonal, quickly told him what he dreaded hearing. "Technician Westerfield here. Deputy, we double-checked everything we've received in the last four days. We have no forensic specimens from your office. We have material from the Crescent Valley P.D. for the Beverly Taylor murder but nothing from you. Better check to see what kind of mixup you have. We'll do our best to rush it through when it arrives."

Ralph unwilling to hear any more, cut him off, and the state lab technician sounded offended. What the hell. He could apologize later. Ralph fought the temptation, the need, to tell Alice what he'd found out. But, like she said, it was not her business. Instead, he muttered something about how slow the state boys were and poured himself a cup of coffee.

Ralph was standing by the front door, the cup of coffee in his hand, when a white van with a picture of a padlock and blue lettering on the side pulled into the lot.

The locksmith, a plump man of medium height in his mid-fifties, charged through the front door. His round face was wreathed in smiles.

"Thought you cops could keep track of your keys better than this. Hope you don't get as bad as me. I've had to get a new key for the house twice in the last year."

Ralph forced a smile. "Just don't you go telling tales about us or we'll have to do some police harassment on you."

He led the still chuckling locksmith past Lud's office and into the short hallway leading to the evidence room. The minutes seemed to drag by while the plump man fussed first with the lock and then his key blanks.

Ralph was on the verge of telling him to his face that he was the slowest individual he had ever seen when the fat little man finally fitted the key into the lock and the door swung open.

Once the job was finished, the locksmith seemed ready to entertain Ralph with a series of rib-splitting missing key stories. Alice finally rescued him with a lie about an important call. Ralph watched as the locksmith, still talking, disappeared out the front door.

With the man gone, Ralph scurried into the evidence room. The room was small, and the search took but a couple of minutes. He came back into the big room to find Alice pushed back from her desk, watching him. He was sure she could see the answer in his face, but still, she said, "Well?"

Ralph shook his head. "Not there. The timer, box he kept it in, both gone. Dain sure the hell has called every turn so far. You know, Alice, I don't know what it is, but every time I get around Dain, I feel a little bit like a school boy in the principal's office."

Ralph wandered over and stood looking out the front window, then continued, "I think maybe part of it's because he seems so damn sure of himself. Makes me feel like he's looking at me in a condescending manner. Dammit to hell, I'da give a months pay if he had been wrong."

"Don't be too hard on yourself, Ralph," the dispatcher said speaking to his back as he continued to stare out the window. "Dain's been looking into this case since Amy's death, you haven't been in on it at all. Been busy just holding down the fort. It's just been him and the sheriff. And I'm not at all sure Dain has anything more than a suspicion. What's that you got in your hand?"

He raised his arm, which held a three-foot long tightly rolled cylinder of paper. Gesturing with it, he said, "Not sure. Found them in the room, I've never noticed them before. Thought I'd see if I could figure out why they're in there."

Striding over to the long flat table next to the
railing, Ralph slid off the rubber bands and tried to spread them out flat. "Looks like some kind of blueprints." The blue and yellowish white sheets of paper refused to stay uncurled.

"Wait a minute," Alice called. "I'll get something to hold them open."

Using the office's supply of coffee cups, she weighted down the four corners.

"They're blueprints, all right," Ralph said.

Alice peering past his shoulder, said, "Yeah. But of what? They look like house plans, but there's so much to them. And the paper's about to tear."

Bending forward, squinting, Ralph said, "Building plans, all right, but this is a big building." He fingered the edge of the uppermost sheet. "This paper is damn old. I just wonder what the hell they're the plans of, and why Lud had them in there? Had to be him who put them there. Weren't there the last time I looked. And Bob and Josh were gone the last time I was in there. Strange."

He stepped back, rubbing his chin and watching Alice. She was carefully folding over each sheet as she examined them, one by one. When she finished examining the last sheet, she turned slowly to look at him. "Ralph, I think we've got trouble. Bad trouble."

Her voice seemed so calm, so commonplace, that for a moment the meaning of her words did not strike him. She was tapping a rectangle in the lower right corner of the bottom sheet.

Still uncertain whether he had heard her right, Ralph stepped forward to read what was printed in the rectangle. *Pine Ridge high school, February 1926.* Beside the printed rectangle, a single word, written in Lud's hand and circled. Boiler room.

When he glanced up, he found Alice staring at him. "Does this mean what I think it means?"

His voice was little more than a whisper. "Could be. We've got possible missing plastique, and a timer to trigger explosives."

Alice's voice was as low as his, so low that she might be afraid Lud was there, listening. "God help us."

He glanced at his watch. "Dain should be home by now. Phone him, Alice. And keep at it till he answers."

As it had done earlier that day, the cordless phone in the Barlow house rang again and again. Each call ended by the metallic sound of Dain's voice on the answering machine.

*   *   *

Dain wallowed through the waist-deep water, sensing the road's surface beneath his feet. Ahead of him, some fifty feet away, stood the Blazer. With the water becoming more shallow, the pain in his ankle was intensifying. And the knee where the rock had hit the other leg was a little swollen, but he could work that out.

The problem with the ankle was not a sprain. The pain was concentrated around the prominent bone that protruded from the side of his ankle. *What the hell was it called, the malleolus? Something like that.*

The rock and the frame of the roof, sliding together, must have fractured the side of it. The pain had lessened since that first agonizing moment, but walking on it was only going to make it worse. And he had to keep his mouth shut to keep his teeth from chattering.

Reaching the hood of the Blazer, he leaned over it, shivering, taking the weight off his foot. Dain became conscious of his stinging wrist and clasped it with his other hand. His watch. It was gone. Pulling up his sleeve revealed two angry welts on his wrist. The metal band of his watch must have caught on something as he struggled to get out of the car.

From where Dain stood, he could see down the road to where it turned to climb the slope above the lake. The visible quarter mile of highway was deserted. Wading around the side of the vehicle, he glanced into the interior. The absurd hope that he could start the engine vanished at the sight of water so high only the top of the dash was visible.

With a muttered, "Shit!" he rested his head against the Blazer's roof, closing his eyes. *What the hell am I going to do? Everyone in Pine Ridge must Know by now the road's closed. And the only vehicles that use this section of the highway is through traffic between Pine Ridge and Crescent Valley.*

He sighed, then muttered. "Oh, man, why me?"

The clusters of vacation homes along the big lake were serviced by a road that turned off the highway some five miles away. This was the most desolate stretch between the two towns.

"Goddammit!" Dain muttered. *The nearest house belongs to the old coot who hangs out at Sam's all the time, Ned Parker. And his place is at least four miles from where I'm standing, four miles all uphill.*

Automatically, he glanced up, seeking the sun, forgetting the fog. *Jesus, what else can go wrong, losing my watch like that? How long has it been since I went off into the water? Half hour? As bright as the fog is, the sun must still be high overhead. The time can't be past two, two-thirty, at the latest. I've got to hurry.*

His laugh aloud was without mirth. *Hurry, hell! God, a one-legged man hiking along a deserted road is going to hurry? Yeah, right, like a turtle with three legs.*

As he sloshed out of the water onto the dry pavement, Dain had his one bit of luck. An oddly shaped piece of wood, twice the thickness of a broomstick and about five feet long, lay awash at the water's edge some ten feet beyond where the road dipped into the lake.

Gingerly Dain worked his way down over the rocks and pulled it from the water. The length of wood looked like a leg from a surveyor's tripod. Whatever it was, it was just what he needed.

Time was only one of Dain's problems. He had been walking maybe an hour and a half when he realized he had no idea how far he had come. Flashes of water, through the forest trees, were still visible far below him on the lake side of the road, but he had long since lost sight of the half-submerged Blazer.

As often as he had driven this damn road, he would have sworn he knew every inch of it. But here, on foot, tired, with a cold sweat over the goose bumps, nothing looked the way it did peering out of a car window.

What the hell! As the old saying goes, just keep putting one foot in front of the other.

On the inside of a sharp curve, Dain limped off the road and sagged onto the exposed root of a giant fir. His knee reminding him, that it was not without its troubles. He was unsure if the fog was thickening or if the banks of mist looked grayer because the sun was sinking.

Dain had left the lake with the idea he would hike all the way into Pine Ridge, if he had to. But now he knew that was nothing but stupid bravado. A wave of nausea and depression struck him. *How in God's name can I make it another ten miles to the house, when this short walk has damn near done me in?*

Leaning over, he felt his damaged ankle. The injured area was swollen but concentrated around the area where the pain was centered. He pushed down his sock to look at it. There was a cut. The cold water had probably helped to stop the bleeding, just seeping a little now, and the flesh showed a collection of colors—purple, green, and maroon that was flat-out ugly.

But as bad as his ankle hurt, that was far from his worst problem. Besides the knee on the other leg, his hand ached so much he could barely grip the wood shaft; his shoulder and back felt as if somebody were working a knitting needle in and out of it, and the chill felt like it was bringing on a fever. And his goddamn arm! Tremors ran up and down the damn thing.

Dain sucked in a labored breath. *Christ, if I sit here another minute, I'll never get up.*

Dain struggled to his feet and staggered back out onto the pavement.

He almost walked past Ned Parker's house, a small, weathered structure tucked back into a thick grove of young pines, without seeing it. For at least the last hour he had been walking head down, eyes mere slits, forcing himself into every step he took.

Dain was so damn tired that even the realization that he'd reached Ned's stirred no joy in him. He stood there for several seconds, eyes blinking, unsure whether he should believe what he saw.

Finding himself on the porch, he couldn't remember getting there. But there he was, pounding on the door. "Ned! Dammit, Ned, let me in!"

Tears were welling in his eyes. *Goddammit, is the whole world against me?*

The next moment, he was at the window, driving his walking stick through it. Still bleary-eyed, he pounded at the jagged triangles of glass, still protruding from the edges of the frame.

Leaning through the opening, he shouted, "Ned, are you home?"

He realized how stupid the question was and swung one leg through the gap. With the finesse of a crippled elephant he worked his way through the window.

Inside, the glass crunching under his feet, in the dim light, Dain stared wildly about the room. This was the living room. *Where the hell is the phone?*

The place was a mess, like something out of a bag woman's fondest dream. Stacks of papers stood waist-high around the walls, and two TV tables held untidy piles of plastic microwave containers, crusty with dried food.

Dain shook his head. *Never knew he ever had a meal at home.* The dining table, coated with dust, looked as if it hadn't been used since his wife, Verda, died when Dain was still in high school.

Dodging trays and newsprint, Dain entered the kitchen. Its interior made the living room seem neat. On a low table in one dim corner, he thought he saw a phone and lunged toward it. When his hand closed on the disemboweled shell of a small portable radio, he flung it against the opposite wall.

Loudly cursing Ned, Lud, the Pontiac, and the world, Dain careened through the rest of the house, through the heaps of dirty, acrid smelling clothing littering the bedroom floor, and a fourth room, stuffed with junk retrieved from the town dump. "Goddamn Ned Parker." He grumbled. *He rents out five lakeside cabins and is too damn cheap to have a telephone.*

Dain's hand was on the knob of the front door, ready to plunge out onto the road again, when he remembered the car. The fabulous Parker Cadillac. *Ned's Caddie was one of the legends of Pine Ridge. The only times he drove it was to funerals, to check on his renters, and to business at the bank in Crescent Valley. Ned's everyday vehicle was a twenty-year-old pickup.*

Dain charged back through the house to the room full of junk, which had an exit door to the garage. There beside the door was a nail holding the Caddy key. He almost shouted for joy. *Now if the old bastard didn't have the door into the garage locked.* Dain sighed when the doorknob turned under his hand.

He stepped into the garage, and there it was, long and low under its canvas wrap, the fabulous Caddie. Seizing the protective cover, he slid it off the car.

Ned's pride and joy was a 1974 Cadillac with a gleaming black surface that one could use as a shaving mirror. The big Caddie was such a tight fit that Dain had to inch his way around the front bumper, conscious that he was leaving handprints on the pristine hood. He punched the door handle's release. *My God, it's open! He didn't even keep it locked.*

Dain lumbered past the rear of the Caddie, seized the handle of the overhead door and rolled it up. He cried out at the pain of raising his right arm above his head, but it didn't matter. He would be in Pine Ridge within twenty minutes.

Five minutes later, Dain, seated in the driver's seat of the Caddie, was staring at the rear wall of Ned's garage. *Dead. The sonofabitching battery was dead. Not one lousy volt of juice in it.*

The starting motor had given two or three clicks, and now it refused to even do that. He hit the steering wheel with the heel of his hand.

Dammit! Why the hell didn't the old son of a bitch at least drive it enough to keep the battery up.

He glanced back over his shoulder at the driveway beyond the garage. The outside light was fading, and it wasn't from the thickening fog. The sun was going down. The time must be at least seven.

All he could do now was to hike to the next house, which was another mile. *Sheila! I'm so sorry, honey, I sure let you down. What a laugh! I'm a cop from L.A. and I can't even protect my girl in this jerkwater place. All she's got is Pat and that pea shooter of hers. Oh, God, I've got to walk. Got to stop thinking about her.*

As Dain was climbing out of the car, he saw the battery charger, one of the big commercial types on wheels. A dirty tarp was draped over it. He would never have noticed it except for a trick of the late afternoon light.

Working furiously, he rolled it across to the Caddie. He had the hood up, the clamps on the battery terminals, and the cord plugged in when he realized he didn't know what the hell he was doing. The small chargers he and most people had, they would never start a car until several hours had passed.

This monster didn't work the same way. What the hell would happen when he tried to start the car, if the fluid was low? Would the damn battery explode, set Ned's pride and joy on fire, maybe the whole damn house? What the hell, he was guilty of breaking and entering and auto theft. He might as well add arson to it.

Dain scrambled into the Caddie, took a deep breath, and turned the key.

Five minutes later he was racing up the highway. Ned's car did better than he thought it would on the winding road. The heavy vehicle took curves a lot faster than Dain's car. As he roared down the highway and the turn off to the orchard came into view, Dain gritted his teeth. What would he find when he got there?

The Cadillac swerved into the Barlow driveway with that regal dip and lift that marked the suspension of nineteen-seventy-four Cads. Dain hoped he would see lights as the house came into view, but the tall white structure was unlit.

The Caddie's headlights picked up his car in front of the barn, but Pat's was gone. He relaxed. *With me running this late, Sheila and Pat had decided not to wait. They've gone on to the reunion.*

Then he remembered the plastique, and he felt as if someone had hit him in the stomach. *My God! That bomb might go off any second!*

CHAPTER 45

Dain stood before his chest-of-drawers, nude, searching through it for clean underwear and a shirt. The hot shower had warmed his chilled body, maybe got back a degree or two, but had done nothing for his aching shoulder and hand.

His ankle had paid the price for the long hike. The swelling had moved down into his foot, and he was unsure whether it would fit into any of his shoes. He had bandaged the cut, but the area around the broken bone was an angry deep purple. He couldn't go much longer without seeing a doctor.

Dain looked bemused. *If Sheila and Pat went on to the reunion, why didn't they tear up the note on the back door. The fact that it said they were taking lunch to Gramps tells me the message was written before noon. Maybe they got back later than they intended. Driving in the fog, after all, could lengthen time on the road.*

Maybe they ran into someone over at Sam's and was in such a hurry, and the excitement of getting ready for the reunion, that they just forgot about the note on their way out. Goddammit, too many damn maybes.

The shrill electronic bleep so startled him that he dropped the shirt he was pulling from the drawer. Still naked, Dain hopped across the room, favoring his injured ankle, and seized the portable phone from the night stand.

"Sheila?" he cried.

"Dain Barlow? Is that you? Thank God, you're alive."

Dain recognized the voice. Lud's deputy Ralph was on the other end of the line. "Alive? What do you mean?" Dain asked. He knew the answer as soon as he asked the question.

Ralph's explanation came in a furious torrent of words, relating how the oil slick on the lake had been discovered about three o'clock and how there was no search and rescue unit closer than Wenatchee and how it would be morning before they could be on the scene to search for his body. By process of elimination, they had figured that it must be the old Pontiac that had gone into the drink, he told Dain.

Dain tried to slow the excited deputy's flood of words, but it was hopeless. Taking a deep breath, Ralph continued. "I've been calling your house every thirty minutes since then, hoping against hope you made it out of the car and swam to the Pine Ridge side. I told the boys that—"

"Hold it, Ralph. Have you heard from Lud?"

This question brought a long silence. Then Ralph, his voice subdued, said, "I was wrong about the sheriff. Everything you thought about him is true. I called the state forensic lab. They hadn't received one damn thing from us. And there's that timer."

His voice growing sharp, Dain said, "Spill it, Ralph. We don't have time for anymore delays. Personal feelings have no place this late in the game."

"Well, the timer's missing from the evidence room. And, I got in touch with those fellows out on the reservation who claimed they had the plastique. They swear to God it's true. And, well, goddammit, they say the sheriff's car wasn't fifty yards behind them when they threw the stuff out the window. Lud had to have seen where it landed."

"Oh, shit! I have to get over to the high school. He's planning to blow it up, sure as hell. Thanks—"

"Wait a minute! That ain't all. I…well, dammit to hell, I found the plans of the old Pine Ridge High School tucked away in the evidence room, and on one of the sheets, Lud had written what looked like one word and circled it. Boiler room.

Dain had trouble finding the breath to speak. "Oh, Jesus Christ. He's going to kill everyone in there, including Sheila and Pat."

He was in the act of lowering the phone, not bothering to say good-bye, when he heard Ralph's, "Sheila? Wait a minute."

Dain, the receiver back at his ear, shouted, "What? What about Sheila?"

"Lud has phoned four times this afternoon, wanting to know what you said. And then about two he called and asked if we'd heard from anyone called Sheila?"

Dain, his voice growing louder, cried, "What did he say? Tell me exactly."

"He said he had a missing person's report from the parents of this Sheila. Said they called saying their daughter was hysterical, babbling something about being lost in the fog, somewhere in the forest, that she had stumbled into a deserted cabin to make the call. She was so shook up that their number was the only one she could remember.

He said, Sheila was so scared and paranoid, she might say anything, could even claim someone was after her. God knows what a rattled female might claim. Lud said that if she called to tell her to stay where she was and that I'd personally come up to get her.

"I asked him why her parents didn't call the sheriff's office instead of him personally. Man, he about bit my head off. Said, he grew up with her, and knew her folks really well, they had his home phone number and wanted to get hold of him. Then he shouted, 'Now do what you're told, goddammit!' Hell, Mr. Barlow, I wasn't—"

"Was that all? Did he say anything else?"

"Well, let's see. He said earlier not to bother him with the radio, that he was going to get some rest. He said to wake him, though, if she called. He was real clear about that."

His words sent Dain's mind into a turmoil. He tried to sort it out, to ask exactly the right questions. "You said he called you several times. Did he mention her again?"

"No, I don't…just a minute." He heard muffled talking in the background that lasted about thirty seconds, then Ralph was back on the line. "Alice said he called twice more, asking if we'd heard from her. That makes six calls altogether. He doesn't sound like he's in good shape, does he?"

With a muttered, "No, he doesn't," Dain punched the off button on the portable phone. *So much for my worries about Pat and Sheila. Lud hasn't found them. They're safe at the reunion.*

He glanced at the clock radio. Eight-ten. *Safe! My God, have I lost my mind? Sheila is in a building that is going to blow all to hell, and damn soon.*

At the closet, Dain seized the sport coat he had planned to wear, ripping away the cleaner's plastic. From their hanger he yanked the first pants his hand encountered and hurled them atop the coat on the bed. A pair of shoes followed, bouncing off the mattress onto the floor. Dain stepped into his undershorts, crying out when he put his weight on his damaged ankle.

Slumping onto the bed, he wiggled into his pants and slipped on the shirt, never noticing that he had buttoned it wrong. He grabbed the shoes, remembered that he had not gotten out socks, and pulled them onto his bare feet with a loud, "Fuck it."

Rising, he saw himself in the closet door mirror, a wild-eyed man wearing a beige cashmere jacket, blue jeans, a shirt gaping where it was miss buttoned, and white athletic shoes.

Dain was halfway across the kitchen, grunting each time his damaged foot touched the floor, when he reached back to slap his hand against his holster. The gesture was an automatic one, done a thousand times before. His Biretta. It must be lying at the bottom of Rainbow Lake.

He mumbled. "Oh shit." *Dad's gun! He told me about buying a three-fifty-seven a couple years back. But where the hell would he keep it? The drawer to their* bedside table!

Dain climbed the stairway, cursing with every step he had to take on his ankle. Charging into his parents' room, he yanked open the drawer. A couple of packs of cigarettes, four dog-eared paperbacks, and not another goddamned thing. *Where? The gun cabinet in dad's office!*

Sliding down the steps on his backside, holding the one leg out stiffly in front of him, he headed for his dad's office. The gun cabinet held the two rifles and two shotguns that had been his father's, but the shelf behind the glass door was bare.

A sudden thought struck him. *Oh, Christ, maybe he sold it.* Then he thought of the two drawers for ammunition at the bottom of the cabinet. *That's where he might keep it!* Bending over, he seized the left drawer's knob and pulled. Locked! He tried the other one with the same result.

Before Dain completed his snarled, "You son of a bitchin' cabinet! Why should you be easy, when every other goddamn thing has turned to shit on me today." he was out of the office and hurrying down the hall.

Two minutes later, he was back with the biggest screwdriver his dad owned. Looking at the beautifully kept walnut front of the gun cabinet with regret, he slammed the screwdriver in behind the drawer's front and broke it away with a splintering of wood to reveal the big Smith and Wesson revolver.

Dain sighed. *Now if I can just get to the school before the whole town lights up with the damnedest explosion this county has ever seen.*

As Dain approached the parking lot fronting the high school, his headlights, shining along the fence, revealed a gap. The gate at the lower end of the orchard was open. Slowing to turn into the lot, he glanced into the orchard. The side glow of the headlights was just enough to reflect off a chrome bumper, betraying the presence of a car, parked back among the apple trees.

To provide enough people, each year's class always invited all the past graduates of the school for the dance that followed the class's dinner and the picnic at the Bear Creek Camp Ground on Saturday. Sam had said the usual attendance was between fifty and sixty.

Probably less this year because of the flood, but still there could be quite a few. Dain's first thought was that the car's driver had not found a space in the school parking area and had backed in among the orchard trees. But that conclusion proved erroneous when he found what would amount to about a half dozen parking spaces on the inside row.

Picking up a flashlight from under the front seat, he slid out of the car. Toying with the idea of checking out the vehicle on his property, he glanced at the dashboard clock, then changed his mind. Eight-forty-two.

Pine Ridge people went home early, maybe not tonight, however, Lud wouldn't want to take the chance. The damn bomb would probably be set to go off before 9:00. Chief Looking Glass would want to make sure he got as many of his white enemy as he could.

Everything else forgotten, he limped toward the school's front door on his bum ankle. As he stepped inside, he heard the distinct clunk of a car door being shut in the dark behind him.

The hall reverberated to the sound of loud music coming from the gym. The corridor was empty, without the usual furtive smoker or two, outside for a quick fix.

He was counting on two things. Lud knew little about plastique. And the circled words, boiler room, on the blueprints. Those two things being so, he would probably place it in the foundation wall behind the boiler where he used to secrete his lunch to keep the other kids from stealing it. With Lud having no reason to think anyone would be wise to his plan, the timer would be straight forward, with no fail safe gimmick that would set it off if anyone tried to disarm it.

God, he hoped he was guessing right. That the notation was not something written long ago and meant nothing. He would only have enough time for one cursory search—if he even had that. The old building didn't have a fire alarm…if he turned up nothing on the quick search, he'd just have to evacuate the building.

Panic building in him again, he started for the boiler room, as much skipping as walking, trying to stay up on the toes of his injured foot. Just outside the gym, the double-door entry was flanked by rest rooms, the men's on the right. At the back, beyond the row of urinals, a door opened onto concrete stairs that descended into the boiler room.

Dain remembered the place as a stark concrete pit, poorly illuminated by naked light bulbs. The boilers filled most of the space, and the heat was barely tolerable, even on the coldest of days, when they were in use.

Nearing the gym, he saw several guests, surprise in their faces, watching him from inside the open double doors. He must look a sight with what he was wearing, a flashlight in his hand, and moving like a broken-legged flamingo. He swerved off toward the rest room just as they fixed smiles of greeting onto their faces.

Inside the rest room, Bob Turner, one of his old classmates, looked up from where he was taking a leak. Grinning, he stepped away from the urinal and zipped his pants. "Dain Barlow! Jesus Christ, I haven't seen you in years, buddy. How the hell's the world been treating you?"

Dain brushed by the unwashed hand stretched toward him for a shake without breaking stride. "Talk with you in a minute, Bob. There's a problem I need to check on in the boiler room." Yanking open the door, he flipped on the light and started down the steep steps.

Behind him, Bob Turner called, "Jesus, what could be so important you couldn't stop and say hello? Guess the damn big city's made you forget all your old country friends. Was gonna ask why you were limping, but who the hell gives a shit."

Turning his head, Dain was ready to try to appease an old friend, then remembered the time. He'd explain later.

As he inched his way around the boiler, his back brushing the concrete wall behind him, he heard the outer door of the restroom swing closed, then all was quiet. *Alone at last, thank, God.*

Reaching the niche in the wall, a dark void interrupting the long stretch of dull gray concrete, he flipped on the flashlight. Aiming the beam into the gap, his spirits soared. Not long ago, someone had disturbed the fine dust that had settled in the crawl space over the years.

He would have to worm his way into the crawl space, a vast area with only eighteen inches of clearance between the dirt and the long transverse beams beneath the floor. Even though it was a large area, Lud probably wouldn't have gone too far from the small opening. It would be slow—*Wait, the plywood covering!*

Dain retraced his careful path around the boiler to where a line of plywood panels just above the concrete barred the way under the building. Seizing a crowbar from atop a junk laden table, Dain pried one of the panels loose, then another. Slipping off the treasured cashmere coat, he tossed it onto the junk table, then hoisted himself up onto the cold, dry soil that lay under the school.

The opening from the missing panels let the dim light into the narrow space under the flooring. It took but a glance to see the line of heavy wood beams running to the back wall of the school. He heard the door from the hall to the rest room open, the sound muffled by the closed door at the top of the steps. Someone was walking across the rest room, his footsteps sharp on the tile floor.

Dain ran the narrow circle of light from the electric torch along the ground. He saw where the disturbed ground from the crawl hole stopped. Swinging the light up to the nearest support, he found what he was looking for immediately. The plastique would have looked like an odd mud-dauber's nest had it not been for the two wires buried in it.

God, he had hoped against hope that he had been wrong about Lud and the plastique. But now there was no question.

The voice was so loud in the confined space of the boiler room that it made him jump. "Dain, baby! Jimmy Haig here. Bob says you've got trouble down there. What the hell's wrong?"

Why didn't they just leave him alone? He didn't have time for all these interruptions. Christ, the stuff could go off any minute!

The crawl space under this part of the school was so low that he had to slither on his belly to move forward. The disturbed ground went two more supports to his left but there were three to his right. He could see all of them in the beam of his flashlight, but only on three could he see the plastique. On two others he saw wires that curved out of sight.

But the timer was what he needed to find. Could he just jerk the wires out of one of the blobs of plastique and not disturb the others? *God, what would that do? Would Lud have some sort of safeguard, something to cause the bomb to blow if someone screwed around with the wires?*

Probably not. But Lud had learned it from a manual. I damn sure don't want to bet my life on it. Goddammit, why in hell didn't I take that refresher course the LAPD offered last winter on explosives?

Jimmy's voice filled the small room again. "Bob said you wouldn't even stop long enough to say hello. If you think you're too damn good for any of us, why didn't you just stay away like you did last time?" There was a brief pause, then, "Okay, fine, screw you, too, Dain, you stuck-up bastard."

Dain checked the one post to his right that he was unable to see. Wrong choice. *I might have known. Dear God, the plastique has to be nearing zero hour. Lud wouldn't risk waiting much past nine. I don't have time now to get the people out of the building, I have to keep up the search and hope to God I can find it soon.*

He squirmed across the dry dirt toward the post to his left. His shoulder, sore from using the cane, sent jolts of exquisite pain into his neck. His arm hurt so badly that twice his hand straightened involuntarily, letting the flashlight roll free. Dain, at the next post, unsure that he could go any farther, got lucky.

His face, easing past the post, was a bare two inches from the timer. In the flashlight's beam, he saw everything he needed to know. The clock showed nine-oh-three and the timer was set for nine-oh-five.

As he watched, the minute numerals flipped over to nine-oh-four. Sweat pouring off his face, he eased the clock out to where he could see behind it. The wires ran through the ventilation slot in the cardboard backing. The backing was attached to the plastic frame by four tiny screws. But he had no way to work them loose. *I have to do something!*

Dain forced two fingers into the ventilation slot, one to each side of the wires. *Sweet Jesus Christ, will it set the bombs off if I yank away the backing? Maybe. If so I'm dead either way. Unless I disarm it, the thing will go off before I can even scoot five feet away.*

Beads of sweat dripped from Dain's nose and chin as much from his nerves as from the warm spot behind the stove. He took a deep breath, squinted his eyes and pulled. The cardboard ripped away, exposing the wires attached to the battery terminals.

He grabbed the wires, "So long, Dain," he muttered aloud and jerked them free.

Dain released an explosion of air as the wires came loose. *Life is sweet, and I'm still alive.* Sweeping his forearm across his sweat covered brow, he sank back against a concrete pillar.

From the rest room, Jimmy, his voice liquor-loud, shouted, "Lud! What the hell's going on? First Dain hauls ass down into the boiler room, and now you come storming in here," the laughter was a raucous, grating sound, "looking like you're going to some heathen Indian pow-wow. Are you going to a masquerade party? Oh, I get it. You're dressed up like a fuckin' Indian Chief. Is that 'cause everyone used to call you, Tonto?"

The silence lasted no more than a couple of seconds, and then Jimmy, one of the big guys who used to pound on Lud when he was in the lower grades, mistakenly thinking he could still bully the Indian, his voice louder still, shouted, "Goddammit, you stupid squaw fucker, I asked you a question. What the hell's goin' on?"

Sweat bathing his face again, Dain scrambled toward the gap in the plywood. *Oh, Christ! Lud's coming after me. The crazy bastard means to kill me right here.*

Something heavy hit the rest room wall with a resounding thud. Up there at the top of the steps, he could hear loud grunting and feet shuffling. Jimmy and Lud were fighting. Unless Jimmy had done a hell of a lot of conditioning over the years, he was dog meat.

Jimmy, no longer sounding drunk, shouted, "Jesus, man, put the knife away! I don't want—Goddamn, you've cut me, you crazy fucker!"

Dain heard running feet, and the rest room door slammed open once and then a second time. The muffled shout, "That goddamn Lud's gone cr—", reached Dain, then nothing.

Dain scowled. *My God, Lud has gone over the edge!*

CHAPTER 46

Quickly Dain lowered himself back to the boiler room floor, with desperate haste, he grabbed his coat and charged up the steps.

He saw the blood on the rest room floor, a startling crimson against the white tiles, and heard the screams at the same time.

Hobbling toward the door, grunting each time the damaged foot contacted the floor, Dain burst out into a hall crowded with people, all staring down the corridor toward the front entry. Some sixty feet away, Jimmy Haig lay on the floor of the corridor, an arrow protruding from the upper part of his back. Bob Turner lay just beyond him, curled in a fetal position, facing Dain, an arrow shaft buried in his sternum.

Dain careened up the hall to stoop beside them, knowing, even as he did so, they were beyond anyone's help. Then he remembered Lud. *Where the hell was he?*

Rising, he pulled the big .357 free of its holster.

This proved to be the catalyst that relieved his audience from their stunned silence. Two women pushed their way out of the mass and raced toward the fallen men, screaming.

Fifty voices began to tell him what had happened, none louder than that of Tim Blaylock, who had been a gym teacher when Dain was a Freshman, a short, rotund man of about fifty.

Dain raised his arm to quiet them. "Hold it! No need to panic. Are any of you guys packing?"

When nobody responded, he shouted, "Goddammit, you're not going to get into trouble. I need your help."

Two men, both tall, rangy, and bearded, raised their hands.

"You two go over to Sam's," Dain said. "Call the local nurse. Then call the sheriff's office in Crescent Valley. Tell them what happened and that we need help."

The two men shuffled forward, but Blaylock stopped them with a booming voice that belied his size. "Sheriff's office, hell! The sheriff is the son of a bitch who killed them!"

Dain shouted back at him. "Shut up, Tim, we're wasting time."

Tim recoiled like he had been slapped, but only stared at Dain.

"You two do what I told you," Dain continued. "Tell them we need help up here right away. Better let them know they need a boat to get around the flooding at Rainbow Lake. Either that or they'll need a chopper. Anybody here willing to drive down and pick them up if they have to use a boat?"

Four or five hands went up.

"Fine. You fellows take your wives back to where you're staying, then come back to Sam's."

Blaylock's voice boomed out again. "Just hold up a damn minute. What the hell are you going to do, Barlow, besides giving damn orders?"

Dain fought down the urge to coldcock the loudmouth. He tried to ignore him instead.

He had been searching the tightly packed mass of faces ever since he had risen from beside the bodies, looking for Sheila. "Anyone seen Sheila Greene or Pat Cromwell?"

A chorus of voices informed him that they had not seen them at all that night.

Blaylock refused to be put off. "We're still waiting for you to tell us what the hell you're gonna do, Barlow," he yelled. As if to assure Dain that he spoke for the whole group, he turned both left and right to look at the crowd behind him.

Dain, his voice still raised to be heard above the two women huddled by their fallen husbands, said, "I'm going after him. I need to go alone. He's holding Pat Cromwell and Sheila Greene as hostages, or at least, I think he is. If we all show up there together, he'll kill them, sure as hell."

"Bullshit!" Blaylock said. "We know you. That redskin kissed your ass all through high school, and you intend to return the favor by letting him escape. Well, I've got news for you. We're gonna string that bastard up! We're not taking a chance on some sob-sister jury letting him go because he's a goddamn downtrodden minority fucker."

Blaylock was losing a lot of his support. Several women and a couple of the men had slipped past Dain to comfort the two grieving women. Others, obviously uncomfortable with Blaylock's antics, had drifted back into the gymnasium. A tight group of near a dozen supporters remained clustered around the rotund little man.

When Dain eyed him silently, Blaylock seemed encouraged, "So you just get your ass out of the way, pretty boy, and let a real bunch of men settle this the right damn way."

Dain had had enough. "Blaylock, shut your fat mouth. You're not going to do anything." His angry green eyes were locked with Tim's stare. "I'm the nearest thing to law there is here until the deputies arrive. Until then, we play it my way. If you don't like what I tell you and you want to kick my butt after this is over, I'll be happy to accommodate you! But right now, if you want to apprehend Lud, keep your mouth shut and do what you're told!"

A woman standing next to Tim Blaylock, her face with its sharp beak of a nose pasty under the corridor lights, her voice artificially high, called, "That's right. Threaten someone twenty years older than you and half your size."

A rail-thin man clad in blue jeans and a faded pink tee-shirt yelled from the back of the pack, "You better find that Sheila Greene first, so's she can help you. Way I understand it, she's the one what kept Red Fryhover from whipping your ass."

Dain, his face flaming red, turned his back on them and limped down the hall, unaware that he had stepped into the spreading pool of blood around Bob Turner's body. A trail of gory footprints marked his course toward the door.

The drive to Lud's had almost ended in disaster several times. The fog had lifted, and with the coming of night, a full moon bathed everything in bright moonlight, leaving perfect visibility. He had pushed the car's speed far beyond what he should have, as thoughts of doom bombarded his mind. *How would Lud react toward the women now that he knew I found the explosives? God, I hope to hell I haven't made it worse for them.*

Looking Glass would want to make sure he got rid of the one's who had caused his mother so much misery, even if the mass destruction he had planned, failed. His rage would turn to them, more determined than ever to kill them! His sick mind might tell him he couldn't face his mom in the spirit world if he didn't at least get Pat and Sheila. God, who knows how a crazy mind works?

With the distraction of the thoughts of horror, twice, the tires screaming, he had come close to sliding off the road. Now, coming around the final curve some hundred yards from the turn-off to Lud's, his headlights found the automobile parked on the side of the road.

His heart skipped a beat, then pounded in his ears. Pat's car! And it was headed away from Pat's grandfather's place. They had been on their way back. His last hope disappeared. *Lud has them!*

Skidding, he swerved off the road just beyond the parked vehicle. Coming out of the car, he drew the gun from its holster and hobbled toward the abandoned auto. *Thank God, the shadows from the tall trees has the car hidden from the moons bright light. Lud would know that I would stop when I see Pat's car. With Looking Glass's plan at the school shot all to hell, he might be ready to blow me away from ambush.*

Reaching the back of the auto, he crouched low and started to work his way forward to the driver's side door. Lifting his head, he risked a peek into the car's interior. Someone was in the back seat! A pillow was pushed up against the glass of the back side window with the top of someone's head resting against it.

A breeze rustling through the trees, and a chorus of frogs in the tall weeds beside the road were the only sounds he heard in the night. Nobody moved inside the car. Dain would have been able to detect the slightest stirring with his hand against the car's side.

With dread, Dain, swallowed hard and caught his breath, *Something's wrong. The noise of my car swerving off the road and the slamming of the car door had to be enough to bring commotion from the car. If they were able to move! God, whoever is in there hasn't even stirred.*

He bit his bottom lip. *Pat or Sheila? Maybe both, with the other one lying on the floorboards. Oh, my God, am I too late? Is this part of a savage's death game? Well, hell, I'm not going to solve the mystery huddled outside the car this way.*

Inching forward, Dain seized the handle and jerked the front door open, Slamming his hand against the button that turned on the dome light. Rising as far as he could without losing contact with the light button, he said, "Hey, wake up," knowing he was probably wasting his breath.

As he suspected, the person in the back failed to stir.

"Oh, shit, which one is it?" Dain muttered and dived into the car, pulling the door behind him quietly. Cautiously raising his head to peer over the front seat back, he flipped on the flashlight. Its beam spotlighted an elderly face, faded blue eyes staring into the light, unblinking.

Fourteen years had passed since Dain had last seen the man, but he recognized Gramps, Pat's grandfather. Even before he reached over and closed his fingers on the cold, stiff arm, Dain knew that Gramps was long dead. *What was he doing here? What the hell had happened?*

Dain was back in his own car and starting the engine without clearly remembering how he had gotten out of Pat's vehicle. He pulled out onto the road, tires spinning, then jerked his foot off the accelerator the next second. *Christ, I can't just go charging into Lud's place like a cowboy on his wonder horse.*

I'll have to ease the car along with its lights off as far as I dare and try to sneak up to the house on foot. And then hope to hell Lud isn't waiting outside.

The moon was high enough now, that its rays falling down through the tall conifers clearly illuminated the gravel lane. Only fear that the noise of the engine would reach the cabin kept him from driving faster. Once he turned off onto the twin tracks, he slowed to a crawl. The overhead growth was so thick here that little moonlight reached the ground.

In the near darkness, Dain almost collided with the stump that had been a backdrop to Sheila's nightmare. He had come far enough in the car. His injured ankle begged him to drive still closer, but it was too risky. The cabin was less than a hundred yards away.

Reaching up, he flipped off the dome light switch and struggled out of the car, easing the door shut behind him. Dain came close to yelling at the first contact of his injured limb with the ground. *Christ, I hope I can make it.*

Breathing hard, from frayed nerves and excitement, he considered easing the car on up to the cabin. *Hell, no! I might be signing Sheila's and Pat's death warrants if I drive up there.*

Carrying the unlit flashlight in his left hand, he limped down the road. The woods were eerily quiet, not any sound from up ahead. Just when he thought he would have to surrender to the pain and sink onto the forest floor, he saw the dense growth of saplings that masked the cabin's front.

Dain pushed his way through the stand of young trees, then froze at the edge of the forest. A light was burning in the front room, but he saw no one through the window. The patrol car was pulled up close to the porch. The bright moonlight bathed everything is silvery light, and nothing stirred outside the cabin. He scanned the outside a second time. Nothing. *Goddammit, where is he?*

He had to move to his left if he wanted to get a better look into the place's interior. With the thought that he must be inside, he forgot about being cautious. Dain slipped out from behind the concealing branches of the last sapling, moving toward the shelter of a huge pine ten feet away.

His awkward movement on his ankle had him making too much noise, he knew, as he pushed to get to the tree. Just as he became aware that he was in the open, much too long, under the moon's bright light, a blow to his left shoulder spun him halfway around, bringing his weight onto his injured foot. His ankle gave way, and he sprawled onto the ground, his head scraping the gravel, the flashlight bouncing free of his hand and rolling out onto the exposed parking area.

The realization that he had been hit came instantly, and his mind reeled. His shoulder felt as if a white-hot knife were pressed against it. Pawing at his shoulder with his right hand, Dain felt the hot stickiness oozing through a rent in his jacket sleeve.

Then he understood. One of Lud's razor-sharp hunting arrows had sliced a deep cut into his flesh as it grazed his arm. *Where the hell had it come from? The shadowy side of the house?*

His body was still exposed to that side. Twisting sideways, he pulled the heavy revolver free of its holster with his right hand. Then, flat on his stomach again, he squirmed toward the sheltered darkness behind the huge pine. He crawled with the expectation of another arrow tearing through his flesh.

Once behind the tree, he pulled himself up to where he was sitting with his back against its trunk. Straining to hear, he took in slow deep breaths, trying to stave off any shock from the sharp arrow. He had to keep his wits about him.

He stifled a groan. *Christ, my shoulder hurts. The pain has a sharp edge to it, like the knife wound I got in that alley one time in L.A.*

Resting the revolver on the ground, he gripped his injured shoulder with his free hand. Blood still flowed freely from the deep cut. Pulling a soiled handkerchief from his jeans pocket, he shoved it down into his shirt against the wound.

Dain frowned, remembering Lud's accuracy with the bow. *Lud could strike the head of a match at thirty paces, with an arrow. I've seen him do it many times when we were in high school. Had he intentionally missed? Well, not missed exactly. Was he playing with me, or had something caused a killing shot to go astray?*

Dain was pinned down in the shadow of the pine tree. The light from the front room window and the moon illuminated the ground on both sides of the trunk. Maybe he could speak to his old friend. *Maybe I can find some spark of the old Lud inside the crazed man who confronts me. Talking isn't going to betray my position. Lud sure as hell knows where I am.*

Again he strained to hear. Only the rustle of the light breeze could be heard over his labored breathing. *If I can just get him to talk, let his voice tell me where he is.*

A drop fell from his nose. He felt his forehead, it was bleeding. A moment of panic gripped him. *Jesus Christ, I'm not even doing a good job of taking care of myself, much more and I'll be unable to help the women.*

Turning his head, he shouted, "I thought we were blood brothers." Dain's voice boomed into the still forest. "Do blood brothers ambush each other? Is that all our vow means to you?"

Following his outburst, all was quiet. Even the wind that prompted the treetops to a restless stirring had ceased. The seconds became a minute, and that became another one. *Where is Lud? What the hell is he doing?*

Dain risked another shout. "Don't I deserve an answer, brother? Am I not your equal? I know you are unwell. That explains the things you have done. Lud, I'm your friend. Talk to me, goddammit!"

The voice came out of the impenetrable shadows on the porch or next to it. Lud's words were slurred and seemed to come out one by one, disconnected, like those of a robot. "Lud? There is no Lud. He has gone someplace from which he will not return. It is I, Chief Looking Glass, who is your brother. But if you claim that right, why do you cower behind the tree like a squaw? Show yourself, and we will parley."

Despite his fear, his hatred of the man for what he had done to Amy and Bev, Dain felt pity. Lud was insane; he didn't know what he was doing.

His voice much louder, Looking Glass shouted, "Well? Are you my brother? If so, show your face."

Dain lowered the gun, holding it against his thigh. He still couldn't tell where Lud was exactly. *Goddammit! I can't just come out wildly shooting. I've just got six shots. This gun's the only hope I, and the women have of walking out of here tonight. I'll be damned if I'm going to holster it. I'm not going to commit suicide. I just have to get Lud's trust, get him to show himself, or I'll never be able rescue Sheila and Pat.*

Taking a deep breath, Dain stepped into view from behind the tree. "I am here, brother," he said.

This time the arrow scored a solid hit on his right arm. Its force drove his two hundred twenty pounds back a couple of steps, but he stayed on his feet. Dain knew he had been hit by an arrow, but he could hardly accept what he saw when he looked down at the long shaft protruding from his biceps.

The sharp pointed arrow head was only a few inches out the other side of his arm. The arrow must have hit the bone or it probably would have passed clear through the arm. The pain lasted only a few seconds. The arm was quickly numbing from shoulder to fingertips, but he could tell he no longer held the gun. *Where is it?*

He looked down at his hand. God, he could hardly move a finger. The back of the palm and his fingers were red, and blood dripped steadily from them to the ground. His gaze returned to the arrow shaft. The cloth of the cashmere jacket was dark and sodden. A wave of nausea hit Dain, and an on set of dizziness threatened to buckle his knees. Dain's stomach churned, and he thought he was going to be sick.

Dain raised his eyes, seeking the source of the arrows. He more sensed than saw motion, and then Lud came into view, standing on the porch, the light from the front room window illuminating his face—the face of a savage.

Dain shook his head, not sure he was seeing clearly. Before him stood a savage over a hundred years removed from his era. The black piercing eyes looking out from a painted face, the streaks of bright reds, yellows and greens startling in the golden light from the window. Two eagle feathers, and a sea shell were braided into his hair and hung down from his head.

A knife and gun held in their leather sheaths, hung from a rawhide tie at his waste. A quiver full of arrows fit snugly to his back, and the compound bow was in his hand. The consummate, savage, Nez Perce warrior, ready for all out war, was the last vestige of the person who had once been the sheriff, his good friend.

He wavered, on the edge of passing out. He fought back, he was the only chance the women had. No way he could loose consciousness, he just couldn't…he wavered again.

CHAPTER 47

Dain sucked in big gulps of air, fighting the dizziness. From the porch a voice boomed. "You approach me with a gun and call yourself my brother," Lud shouted. "You are corrupted, but I will purify you, cleanse you of what the whites have done to you. And then, dear brother, we together will go this night to the Spirit World and live forever among the people." He stopped talking as if waiting for an answer.

Dain, in his confusion, wondered what he was supposed to say. *Sheila! I have to know about Sheila.* A dizziness swept over him, making him stagger. *My God, if I don't get a pressure bandage on my arm I'm going to bleed to death. How? Both my arms are near useless.*

Come, my brother, we waste time." Lud's voice had a curious ringing quality to it, and the light from the window seemed to come in waves, flaring and then growing dim.

Dain knew he was near to fainting. He saw Lud move. *Christ, he's fitting another arrow into the bow!*

The harsh voice broke the silence again. "If you won't come to your blood brother, and only stand there, your legs are of no use to you any longer in this world, and I shall take both of them from you."

Jesus, he was going to die and never know what had happened to his Sheila.

A sudden wave of nausea hit him, and he slowly bent over, dry-heaving. Then as he straightened back up, he saw the three-fifty-seven lying on the parking strip, almost concealed by the shadow of a big rock, about six feet from him, where it had been flung by the reflexive action of his arm when the arrow struck. He was exhausted, both physically and emotionally. He couldn't hold out much longer.

He steadied himself. *Can I reach the gun before Lud puts an arrow through my heart? My right hand's too numb, useless. Can I handle the gun well enough with my wounded left arm to get off a shot? No way with the bow ready and Lud's hand on the string. but if I can talk Lud into lowering the bow and arrow for a moment, I might have a chance. A slim one, but still a chance. I've got to try.*

Dain peered at Lud. "You'll…you'll have to help me, my brother. I'm hurt, bad. I'm losing a lot of blood. And I think my ankle's broken. Give me a hand…please." Dain's vision blurred, and he shook his head.

A resounding, "No!" came from Lud. "You are of my blood, a warrior. I haven't taken your legs, walk through your pain. You are one of the people. Come to me, white brother, and we will go quickly together into the land beyond.

"Come, blood of my blood, and we shall start the long journey past time into the great beyond. The sun will shine upon us always. There will be game for our bellies, and the water will be as sweet as nectar. Let us leave this place. Come, I say."

Lud made his mistake. In saying come, he had removed his hand from the bow string, lowering the bow, he reached out as if to draw the wounded Dain to his side.

In that instant, Dain dived toward the gun, knowing in the act of doing it that he lacked the strength in one leg to reach the revolver. But he also knew this was his only chance. His skin crawled in anticipation of a deadly shaft.

The first gunshot shattered the stillness of the forest clearing. Lud's cry rose through the sound of a shower of glass crashing onto the boards of the porch.

Dain had a moment to gather his wits before the next shot came, four gunshots at regular intervals, followed by the pinging of a firing pin striking empty cartridge casings, three, four, five times before the shooter seemed to realize the gun was empty.

Dain raised his head from where he was sprawled on the gravel to see Lud on his hands and knees, head down. Gasping, his body jerked with each gunshot, until he collapsed on the porch.

Dain's mind began to function again. *Who the hell had shot Lud?* Pushing himself, laboriously, to a sitting position, he glanced toward the cabin's lighted window and saw the answer.

Sheila, just inside the cabin, was trying to see out into the darkness, a small revolver clutched in her right hand. Her gaze found Dain on the ground. "Oh, my God! Dain! He shot you!" she cried.

A moment later, the front door flew open, and Sheila raced across the porch and down the steps to him. Seeing the blood on the ground, her hand flew to her mouth, and she cried, "Oh, my God, please say you're not going to die!"

Sheila swayed, and he thought she was going to faint. The next moment she was on her knees next to him, grabbing the arrow with one hand.

Dain slapped her hand away. "It's okay, Honey. I'll be fine."

Jumping up, she raised a bloody hand to her mouth and said, "Dear God, I'm sorry Dain. I should have shot him sooner. But I was afraid. He was too far from the window." Her words rushed out none stop. "I had to make sure he was so close I couldn't miss. I never shot a gun before. Had to wait till he stood still. I didn't dare miss."

"Shhhh, shhhh," Dain said. "It's okay. You did just fine."

When the grunt came, Sheila whirled to stare at the porch, just in time to see Lud get a leg under him and rise.

She pointed a trembling hand toward the porch. "Look! Dain! Lud's not dead!"

Dain watched, stunned, as Lud, bent double, moaning, staggered the length of the porch and disappeared over the edge. He hit the ground hard and thrashed about for several seconds. Dain could no longer see him, but he could tell when Lud regained his feet. He was moving across the cleared area beside the cabin, dark in shadows, grunting again with each step he took. Lud was dragging his feet, not gliding across the open ground as he always did. The noise of his passage fading.

Dropping to her knees again, she cried, "Oh, my God! Lud's still alive! He's escaped! I thought I killed him, but he's not dead. Oh, Dain, what are we going to do? He's crazy!" She grabbed his arm.

Dain yelped at the abuse of his wounded flesh.

Sheila stared, wide-eyed, at the dark stains around the rip in his coat's sleeve. "This arm's bleeding, too! Quick, we've got to get help for you. We'll take the patrol car. I'll radio for help and—"

"Stop it!" Dain shouted. Then, dropping his voice to where it was barely audible, he ordered, "Get me the gun. Quick!" he pointed toward the three-fifty-seven. "That one you keep waving around is empty. Lud's bad hurt, I think, but as crazy as he is, he may not feel the pain like somebody else would. We've got to finish it, here and now."

Sheila crawled over to get the gun. Dain wasn't sure, through his dizziness, he was seeing right. *Crawling? Is Sheila crawling? Why? She looks as much a mess as I do. Blood around her mouth, on her hands, on her jeans.*

"Help me up, Sheila," he said. "I think my ankle's broken and my right arm is useless."

By the time they reached the patrol car, Sheila's blouse was blood-soaked, and she was gasping from the effort of supporting a man who outweighed her by a hundred pounds.

Dain slid into the front seat of the patrol car and slumped down across it to where he could operate the radio with his left hand. Sheila crouched behind the open door in case Lud came back.

Dain switched on the radio and thumbed the hand mike. "Dain Barlow to any available sheriff's units."

He tried a second time before the radio came to life. "Dain, this is Ralph. I got the call about the homicides. We'll be on our way in thirty minutes. There's me and Josh and four state troopers. We couldn't get a chopper. There are no landing sites up there cleared for a night flight. We're taking a boat trailer up to Rainbow and some of your boys are going to meet us on the other side." He paused a moment, then asked, "Are you using Lud's radio? Does that mean, Lud's dead?"

Dain keyed the mike. "I'm in his car out at his cabin. Lud's wounded. Bad hurt, I think, but he made it out into the woods. We'll have to dig him—"

Sheila tugged at his pants leg.

"What?" he yelled.

"Tell him about Pat and Charlie, you know, Charlie Young."

Dain stared at her, bewildered. While Ralph bombarded Dain's ear with shouts of, "Dain, come in. Dain, come in," Sheila, in a rush of words, told him what was in the chamber of horrors that had been Running Fawn's bedroom.

When Dain repeated the story to Ralph, the deputy mumbled, "Oh, Jesus, this is awful. Goddammit, why didn't I pick up on Lud's erratic behavior?" Then, louder, he said, "Barlow, we'll probably be there in little over an hour. You be careful. 'Course, I probably don't need to tell you, but the poor son of a bitch could still kill you."

Dain pushed himself back upright with a moan and not wanting to take the effort to reach the radio, just dropped the mike. He seized the long five-cell flashlight lying in the front passenger seat and painfully eased himself out of the car, trying to avoid striking the arrow shaft against the steering wheel.

Pointing to the Smith and Wesson in Sheila's hand, he said, "Put it back in my holster."

She stared at him. "But how can you get to it, Dain?"

He ignored her question. *Oh, Christ, I'm feeling light-headed again, stomach churning.* Slumping back onto the car seat, he directed Sheila to cut off strips of his shirt and use them to bandage his arms.

The arrow would have to stay where it was. Very little blood was oozing from where the puckered flesh was gripping the shaft. *God knows what will happen if I try to pull it out or push it on through. Besides more bleeding, I'd pass out from the excruciating pain, sure as hell.*

Dain was dancing on the edge of shock again, light-headed, wanting to sprawl back and go to sleep. He pulled himself upright out of the car, the pain in his left arm so intense he felt as if someone were shoving a red-hot ice pick into it.

His head reeled, and black spots danced in his vision. He blinked his eyes. The ground seemed to move. Dain shook his head. *Goddammit, I have to stay conscious, have to protect Sheila.*

Dain wavered by the car door as he clinched his jaw. *I have to know if Lud is near the house. If he is and even in half way decent shape, I've got to kill him quickly. If I don't get it done soon, I'll be too damn weak to move. Even in another fifteen minutes, I'll be out on my feet, if I'm able stand. Sheila will be left, alone, helpless.*

He eyed Sheila. She was in as bad a shape as he was because of everything she had endured today and what she had had to do to Lud. Grabbing her shoulder, he shook her gently and saw her eyes come back into focus.

"Honey, listen. Lud has some ski poles in the front room, leaning against the wall by the stove. Get me one of them. And hurry."

He saw understanding come into her face. Agitated, she cried, "Dain, darling, you can't—"

"Honey, do what I tell you!" He shouted, then his voice softened. "Please, I have to do this. There's no one else."

Apparently realizing his desperation, she raced up the porch steps and disappeared inside. When she returned a minute later with a pole, Dain ordered her into the patrol car, telling her to lock the doors.

He had no time to say more. The minutes were running out on him.

Limping badly, he rounded the corner of the porch and stopped. Flicking on the flashlight, he directed it across the porch floor. A sizable pool of blood glistened where Lud had fallen, its surface marred only by Sheila's footprints. Next to it lay Lud's bow. The blood trail across the porch was a gory pathway. Lud could not go far.

He turned off the flashlight. In the open, enough moonlight filtered through the trees that he could see without it.

Dain had to walk only a short distance.

Lud, on his side, was about fifty feet beyond the house, lying in a small, bright patch of moonlight, unmoving, at the edge of a thick stand of trees.

Dain stopped, uncertain what to do.

*   *   *

Lud stirred, then coughed, a sudden burning pain gripped his chest. Feeling the cool breeze on his face, he thought, *the air is coming in through the bedroom window.*

His woozy mind told him he needed to close the window, then start a fire. Trying to get up, he moaned as pain racked his body.

He grimaced and moaned again. *Jesus, what in the hell is wrong? I can't move. Hurt like hell.* His eyes fluttered open, and he became more confused as the treetops wavered into view. "Where...oww." *God, I can hardly talk and the slightest effort to move brings sever pain...the brain tumor? Could it have me hurting this bad? Must be about the end.*

Glancing down at his burning chest, he saw blood. *Goddamn, someone shot me, must've ambushed me, only way they could get me.* Closing his eyes again, he fought the nausea and pain. *Christ! I'm in a bad way, can't breath worth a shit.*

Lud found he could only take shallow breaths without bringing on the searing pain. *Another goddamn black out, someone got to me while I was blacked out. But where the hell am I? On the ground…it's night…somewhere in the forest.*

Closeing his eyes, he took a few painful shallow breaths.

Lud opened his eyes again. The treetops wavered in and out of his vision, then all was black. *The goddamn brain tumor has taken my sight!*

*   *   *

Dain had no idea how long he stood there, watching Lud struggle to breath, with the woods silent around him and with shafts of moonlight falling down through the trees in long, misty spills of luminescence. The form in the pool of silvery light lay still, only an occasional moan and ragged breathing to show the prone man had life. But maybe it was enough life to allow Lud to bring up the gun.

Dain cautiously started forward again. *I'm too damn tired. It has to end here, even if Lud has the strength to kill me.*

He was about ten feet away when Lud grunted, then slowly rolled over onto his back. "Who, is it?" Lud asked, the voice was little more than a whisper. His hands were empty.

Dain knelt beside him. "It's me, Dain."

Lud blinked several times, and, his voice soft, dreamy, said, "Dain? Can't…see worth a shit. What…what happened out here? Someone shot me. Who…who the hell was it?"

Ignoring the agony coursing through his body, Dain placed his hand on his old classmate's shoulder. "Lud, is that you?"

Lud blinked again. "Is it me! Have you gone loco, buddy? Or can't you see, either? Christ…man, 'course it's me! His attempt at a smile made the painted face even more grotesque. "Same old Dain. Always kidding…even in the worst situation."

Dain forced a smile onto his face. "Never could kid you, though, could I, buddy?"

Lud slowly moved his hand across his chest toward Dain's arm but had trouble finding it, then gripped his wrist. He had no more strength than a small child. "Who shot me? Where…am I?" A note of panic crept into his soft voice, causing it to rise in pitch. "Where am I, old buddy?"

Dain squeezed his shoulder. "You're at home, old friend, out in the yard behind the house." He hated to lie, but there was no way he could tell his dying, old high school chum the truth. "It was one of Logan's buddies. He bushwhacked you."

Lud's unfocused eyes closed, and for a moment Dain thought he was gone. Then the lids come open again slowly, as if his eyes were desperately tired. Staring past Dain into the starry sky, he coughed, then, his voice raspy, he said, "Did you get the bastard?"

Dain nodded. "He'll never bother anybody else again."

Lud made an attempt at a smile. "Still looking after your blood brother…just like high school days…eh, old buddy?"

"Apparently not well enough, Lud."

Lud released his wrist and plucked at the beaded front of the deerskin shirt he wore. Still staring into the night, he coughed again, his face distorted suddenly, and he gasped. Lud took several deep breaths, and then said, "Ain't I wearing the ceremonial outfit I keep on display? How…I mean what—"

Dain patted his shoulder. "Don't you remember? You wanted me to come by and take a picture of you in it before we went to the reunion. You wanted to have it blown up and put on the wall beside your mother's. The Nez Perce princess and her son. That's why I'm here, why I came by."

"Listen, Dain," his voice growing weaker. "Need to tell you. I've been forgetting a lot…having black outs." He coughed, and a gout of blood burst from his mouth to stain the lower part of his face. His voice turned shrill again, sounding frightened. "How bad is it? How bad am I hurt? You think I'm gonna make it?"

Dain shot a glance up toward the pure beauty of the moon, high overhead. *Why did it have to be on a night like this?* "You're going to be okay, old friend," he lied again. "You're not going to die."

Lud closed his eyes, and shook his head. The gesture, slow and weak, was as if he had suddenly given up, then he moaned. The voice was a mere whisper when he spoke. "Oh, God...it's best I die now. Don't waste no ambulance on me, Dain. Even if I could get over the gun shot, I've...got a terminal brain tumor. My head's been hurting so bad I've wanted to kill myself a lot of times over the last two weeks.

"And the black outs. I swear, sometimes it seemed like somebody else was in my head with me. The doctor said I should place myself on sick leave, give up the job of sheriff, but I couldn't do that...not till the reunion was over."

He coughed again, a horrible, racking cough, and this time a trickle of blood coursed down his cheek from the corner of his mouth. When he spoke again, he had so little voice that Dain had to lean forward so that his ear was only a few inches from Lud's mouth. "You tell them, at the reunion, I was shot, Dain. Tell them I'm in the hospital. That's why I'm not there to help them celebrate."

He took in a gurgling labored breath, then continued. "I wanted to attend at least once while I was sheriff, wanted everybody to see that I made something of my life. Was that so bad, Dain? All of them but you thought I was just a lazy, good-for-nothing Indian boy who," he stopped to breath, "would wind up just another drunk back on the reservation."

From behind him, Dain heard cars pulling up in front of the cabin. Among the babble of male voices, he heard the clear voice of the town nurse ordering someone to get the stretchers out of the back of the van.

Lud didn't seem to notice. He gasped again. "God, it hurts. Remember...tell the gang I'm sorry I can't be there. Tell them I done a good job as sheriff…never let anybody down…was a good sheriff. Will you do that one last favor for me, old buddy?"

Dain sniffed back a tear. "Sure, Lud, you know you can count on me."

In the moonlight Dain saw his lips move, and he more read his lips, "Thanks, buddy," than heard it. He pushed his ear against Lud's bloody lips. The voice was so weak, it was a mere breathy whisper. "Awfully tired. Think I'll sleep awhile, blood brother." Lud's eyes closed.

In the silvery light under the full moon and a star filled sky, Luther Light-Under-Deer left the world and took his first steps along the trail to the land of the spirits.

Dain put his head on Lud's chest, tears filling his eyes. "Goodbye old friend," he whispered. "Maybe there will be forgiveness in the next world. Gotta be. You had no idea what you had done."

Two flashlight beams found Dain at the same time. They locked on the arrow protruding from his shoulder. A male voice cried, "Jesus Christ, the son of a bitch put an arrow through him."

The nurse's voice, somewhere in the advancing cluster of bobbing flashlights, cried, "Get the stretchers back here! Quick! This man's lost a lot of blood."

A burly man, nearing where Dain waited, said, "Never mind a stretcher for this piece of shit. We'll drag him to the damn road."

Dain clambered to his feet. "You! You treat him with respect or I'll beat your stupid head off. The sheriff was sick, didn't know what he was doing. He was twice the man you are."

Another male voice called out. "Yeah, Roscoe, shut your damn mouth," Dain's attention was drawn to the speaker, a stranger, "or I'll beat the hell out of what's left of you when Barlow gets through. When Lud was well, he was a damn good man, good sheriff, too. Hiked twenty miles to my place, on snow shoes one winter, a blizzard so bad no machinery could move, just to bring medicine for my Kate. Saved her life. Walked all night and most of the next day. That Indian did more for the people of this county than any sheriff we've ever had. So I don't want to hear any more of your goddamned bullshit."

As they carried Dain across the yard on the stretcher, he glanced up at the moon, in his weak dreamy state he wondered whether Lud's spirit had heard the praise from the man whose Kate he had saved. And knew his old friend must have touched so many people in a good way, sometime, somewhere, while he was the sheriff.